A CALL TO
ARMS

For a complete listing of Baen titles by David Weber and
by Timothy Zahn, please go to www.baen.com

A CALL TO ARMS

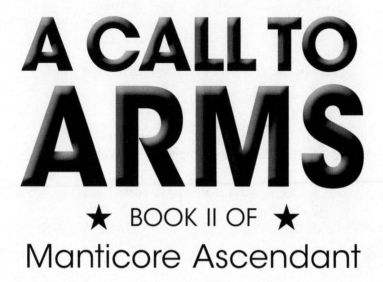

★ BOOK II OF ★
Manticore Ascendant

DAVID WEBER &
TIMOTHY ZAHN
with **THOMAS POPE**

A Novel of the Honorverse

A CALL TO ARMS: BOOK II OF MANTICORE ASCENDANT

This is a work of fiction. All the characters and events portrayed in this book are fictional, and any resemblance to real people or incidents is purely coincidental.

Copyright © 2015 by Words of Weber, Inc., Timothy Zahn, and Thomas Pope

A Baen Books Original

Baen Publishing Enterprises
P.O. Box 1403
Riverdale, NY 10471
www.baen.com

ISBN: 978-1-4767-8085-6

Cover art by David Mattingly

First printing, October 2015

Distributed by Simon & Schuster
1230 Avenue of the Americas
New York, NY 10020

10 9 8 7 6 5 4 3 2 1

Pages by Joy Freeman (www.pagesbyjoy.com)
Printed in the United States of America

To Susan Shiflett, from me and Harry.
You married him forty-six years ago,
and I can still see the love in his eyes.
David

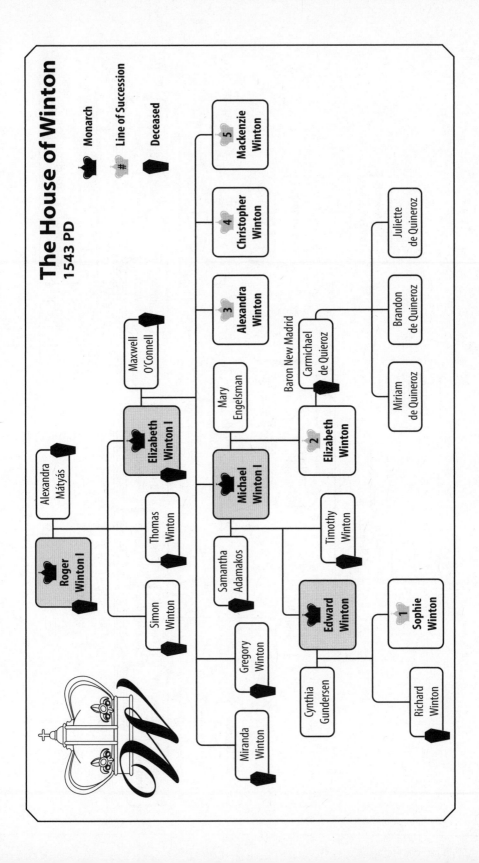

The House of Winton
1543 PD

Monarch

Line of Succession

Deceased

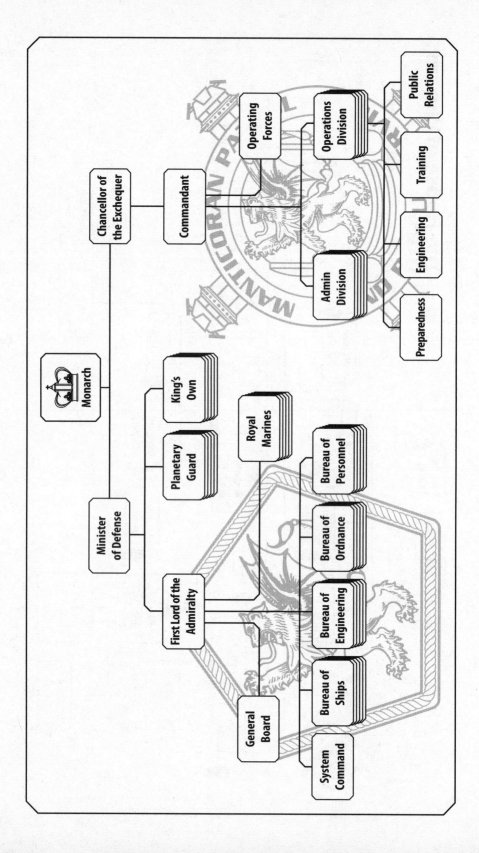

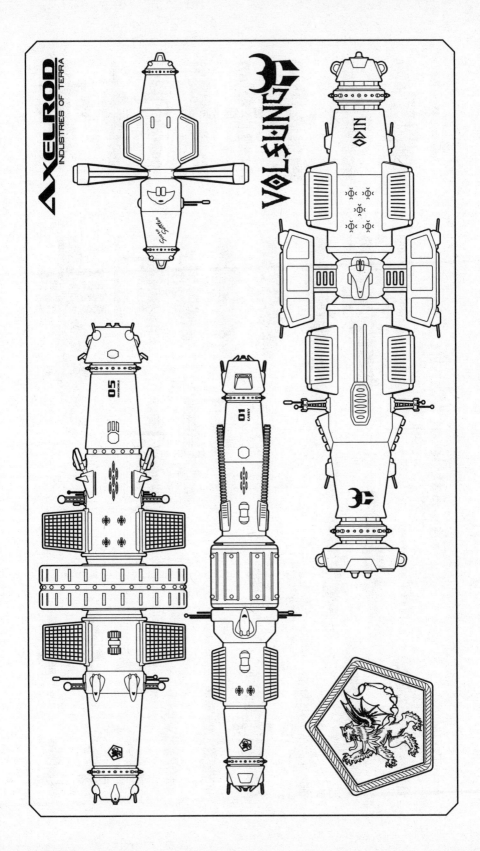

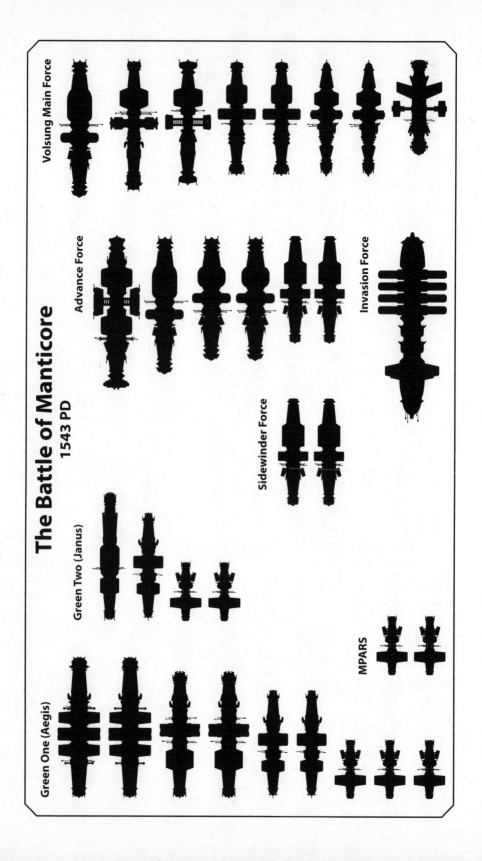

The Battle of Manticore
1543 PD

Volsung Main Force

Advance Force

Invasion Force

Sidewinder Force

Green Two (Janus)

Green One (Aegis)

MPARS

BOOK ONE

1539 PD

CHAPTER ONE

"YEAH, THANKS," THE TEENAGER SAID, swiping his tangled mop of hair out of his eyes. "I'll let you know."

"Very good," Lieutenant (Junior Grade) Travis Uriah Long said, giving the kid his best professional smile as they shook hands. "Feel free to come by if you have any questions."

"Yeah, sure," the kid said. "S'long."

Travis held the smile until the recruiting office door swung closed behind the teen. Then, with a sigh, he sat back down at his desk. *That* was half an hour of his life he wouldn't get back.

Because the kid wasn't interested in joining the Royal Manticoran Navy. Not even close.

Oh, there were parts he'd liked. He had enough fashion sense to appreciate how snappy the black and gold RMN uniform looked. And the idea of heading out into space had definitely intrigued him.

But like a lot of kids his age, he had no idea what he wanted to do with his life. And it was for sure that he wouldn't like the discipline and order that life in the Navy required of its people. The hair alone showed that much.

Still, the boy had sparked memories. Except for the hair and the probable lack of interest in order, that could have been Travis himself standing there ten T-years ago.

Ten years.

Absently, Travis pulled over his tablet and began updating the log of this latest interview, his fingers running on autopilot as his

3

mind drifted back. Ten years. Jumping more or less on impulse into the Navy, going through boot camp and his first training, then assignments to *Vanguard* and *Guardian,* the completely unexpected but exciting offer of an officer track, a degree in astrophysics, Officer Candidate School, HMS *Thorson* and shore duty, and now post-grad work and recruitment-station duty.

Ten years.

Sometimes it seemed like the time had gone by in the blink of an eye. Other times it felt like those years had been a sizeable slice of eternity.

Across the room, the door opened. Travis looked up, automatically smiling his professional recruiter's smile, wondering if this next visitor would be a little more serious.

And felt the smile collapse into open-mouthed astonishment.

"Hello, Lieutenant Long," Lieutenant Commander Lisa Donnelly said, smiling an amazingly radiant smile as she walked toward him. "Lisa Donnelly, in case you'd forgotten."

With an effort, Travis found his voice. "Not a chance, Ma'am," he assured her, belatedly bounding to his feet as more memories flooded back. She'd served with him on both *Vanguard* and *Guardian*, and in the aftermath of the crisis in the Secour system he'd harbored vague and very secret thoughts that she might actually like him.

But then *Guardian* had returned to Manticore, and Travis had been dropped into the madness of college and OCS, and somehow in the past five years their paths had never crossed again.

And now, suddenly, here she was. In *his* recruitment office.

"I gather you've been busy," she said as she finished her walk and stopped at the far side of his desk. "And an officer, too, obviously. Congratulations."

"Thank you, Ma'am," Travis managed. On impulse, he stuck out his hand. "How have you been?"

"Busy," she said, taking the proffered hand easily and giving it a properly formal shake. "Not as busy as you, but I've managed to stave off boredom. What about you? How was *Thorson*, for starters? I hear Captain Billingsgate is something of a martinet."

"Really?" Travis said, thinking back. *Thorson* had certainly been run by the book, but as far as he was concerned that was a plus, not a minus. "I didn't have any problems with him myself, Ma'am."

"No, I guess you wouldn't," she said. "Sorry—I forgot how well you and regulations get along."

"Yes, Ma'am," Travis said, feeling his face warming.

"That's not a criticism," she said hastily. "I just meant that while some people find procedure burdensome, you actually thrive on it. That's not bad, just different."

"I suppose, Ma'am," he said. "Though a lot of people think it's...more than just different."

"People think a lot of things," she said. "Don't worry about them. A strong dedication to duty is nothing to be concerned about. Certainly not to be ashamed of."

"Thank you, Ma'am," Travis said, feeling a little relieved.

And with the easing of tension came the sudden recognition of neglected manners. "Won't you sit down?" he invited, gesturing to the chair the teenager had just vacated.

"Thank you," she said, seating herself with the same grace he'd noticed aboard ship. "By the way, given that we're both officers, I think you can drop the *Ma'am* in informal settings like this." She cocked her head, as if studying his face. "In fact, given all we've been through together, I'm fine with making it *Lisa* and *Travis*. In private, of course. If *you're* all right with that."

"I—" Travis worked furiously to find his tongue, which had somehow gotten lost again. "That would be...very nice, Ma—Lisa," he amended hastily. "So...uh...how have you been? I mean, what have *you* been doing?"

"The usual Navy round-robin stuff," Lisa said. "After Secour I spent some time dirtside, picked up some more schooling so I'd be qualified for beam weapons as well as missiles, transferred to *Damocles*, and got promoted to lieutenant commander. Oh, and between school and *Damocles* I got married."

"Oh," Travis said, his heart plunging straight to his shoes.

"And then got divorced," Lisa continued. "Big mistake. One I'm never making again."

"Getting married was a mistake?" Travis asked timidly.

"Getting married to the wrong guy was the mistake," she corrected. "But that's a whole different story for a whole different day. For this particular day—" she hesitated "—aside from catching up with you, of course, I also came by to ask a favor."

"Sure," Travis said, most of his brain still back on the marriage, divorce, and marriage to the wrong guy thing. "What is it?"

"It's a big one," she warned. "I don't know if you were aware of it, but *Damocles* is leaving next week for Casca."

"Yes, I'd heard that," Travis said. Though if he remembered correctly she was supposed to have left *last* week, not next. Still, such scheduling changes weren't exactly trumpeted from the parapets.

Nor were the patrols themselves, for that matter. Five years ago, in the wake of the attack at Secour, First Lord of the Admiralty Cazenestro had made an art form of playing up the various out-system trips, citing them as the Royal Manticoran Navy's commitment to protecting the people of the Star Kingdom.

Now, though, with every pirate-hunt having come up dry, and with the anti-Navy forces in Parliament starting to crawl back out from under their rocks, Cazenestro was keeping such missions a bit quieter. "Is this another pirate hunt?" he asked.

"More a show-the-flag trip," Lisa said. "A good-will visit to Casca to show the Star Kingdom's commitment to stand by our neighbors." She frowned. "Speaking of hunts, didn't *Thorson* go on one a year or so ago?"

"Closer to two," Travis said. "I'd just been transferred to post-grad school and I missed it."

"Just as well she didn't find anything, then," Lisa said. "With you not there, they'd have been in big trouble."

"Uh...I guess," Travis said uncertainly, trying to figure out whether she was being serious or mocking. "Well..."

"Actually, *Damocles* will be doing triple duty on this one," she continued, saving him from the problem of trying to figure out how to respond. "We're showing the flag, but we're also picking up Casca's latest batch of data for pirate footprint analysis and handing off ours. There's supposed to be a freighter from Haven coming in about the same time we are, and if we can make contact we can also get their data instead of having to wait for the Cascans to sift it and send it on. And if *that* wasn't enough to justify our existence, we're also providing freighter escort."

"One of Haven's?" Travis asked. The entire Star Kingdom had exactly three commercial cargo ships in service at the moment, and the last he'd heard all three of them were out doing their great-circle trade routes.

"One of ours, actually," Lisa said. "One of Countess Acton's anyway. *Goldenrod*'s ready for her maiden voyage."

"Already?" Travis asked, frowning. "Has she even had her builder's trials yet?"

"Last month," Lisa said. "Manticore to Gryphon and back again. Had a couple of small glitches, but Acton's apparently decided she's ready to go out and play with the big boys."

"And Cazenestro tweaked your departure so you could escort her?" Travis asked, hearing his voice drop a couple of tones with reflexive disapproval. Escort duty was important, of course, despite the fact that in five years none of the escorts had ever actually run into a pirate. But the thought of the Admiralty doing scheduling somersaults for a mere civilian bothered him.

"You disapprove?" Lisa asked mildly.

This was hardly the time or place for such a discussion, and for a fraction of a second he was tempted to deny it. But as he looked into Lisa's eyes— "A little," he conceded. "From what I've heard, the routes and schedules Haven freighters run these days are pretty fixed. If you push your departure too much, you won't be able to pick up the Havenite data you mentioned."

"Which wouldn't be the end of the Kingdom," Lisa pointed out. "I also assume Cazenestro has taken that into account." She paused. "And there are other factors involved than just simple efficiency. I take it you don't follow Parliamentary politics?"

Travis felt his lip twitch. "Not really."

Lisa winced. "Oh, right—your brother. I'd forgotten."

"*Half*-brother," Travis corrected automatically. "Not that that makes much difference, I suppose."

"What makes the difference is that he's a separate, individual person, not you," Lisa said, a hint of severity creeping into her voice. "*He's* responsible for what he says or does, not you."

"I know," Travis said. He'd heard that tone from her before, and it usually meant he'd said something stupid. "Sorry."

"That's all right," she said. "That being said, there *is* a tendency on the part of some people to link people by blood instead of by personality, values, and goals."

"I've noticed," Travis murmured, thinking about the citation he hadn't been awarded after Secour.

"It's a laziness thing, really," Lisa said. "Saves on having to actually think and evaluate. It also manifests as people rating other people solely by their money or position." She waved a hand. "Countess Acton, for example. You seemed to think she was the one who'd shifted the Navy's schedule. In fact, from what Captain Marcello said, it's as much her doing *us* a favor as the other way around. Possibly even skewed a bit to her side. She ravaged her rear making sure *Goldenrod* was ready to fly so that Cazenestro could argue to Parliament that *Damocles* would be running triple duty."

"And she probably has sympathetic friends there," Travis murmured.

"Quite a few," Lisa confirmed. "She and that new managing director of hers, Heinrich Hauptman, are quite well connected, especially after all of Hauptman's work on the *Casey* refit. No, it's going to be hard for even Breakwater to squawk on this one."

"I'm sure he'll find a way."

"More likely he'll just ignore it," Lisa said. "He has enough axes to grind with the rest of the Navy without opening himself to unnecessary criticism."

"I suppose," Travis said, scowling to himself. Chancellor of the Exchequer Anderson L'Estrange, Earl Breakwater, had been sniping at the RMN for at least the past ten years. Probably longer.

Part of his motivation was obvious. The Star Kingdom's home guard, the Manticore Patrol and Rescue Service, was under Breakwater's authority. With a shortage of money and an even more critical shortage of trained personnel, the Chancellor had apparently decided that anything that decreased the RMN would increase MPARS, thereby adding to his own power and influence.

Why Travis's half-brother, Gavin Vellacott, Baron Winterfall, had allied himself with the man in that crusade was less clear. What was even more of a mystery was why Breakwater and Winterfall thought that leaving the Star Kingdom open to external threats was a good idea.

Because there *were* threats out there, despite the denials that peppered Breakwater's speeches. There were mercenaries, pirates, and other star nations, any of whom could suddenly decide that Manticore was a nice plum ripe for the plucking.

Never mind that there was nothing on any of the Star Kingdom's three worlds worth the trouble of conquering. The distant planet Kuan Yin wasn't worth a full-fledged damn, but that hadn't stopped Gustav Anderman from moving in, taking over the whole planet, and renaming it Potsdam. And then, for good measure, taking over five more worlds for his newly named Andermani Empire.

Granted, some of those conquests had been in self-defense. And, granted again, Anderman had gained a *lot* of points with the original Kuan Yin colonists by rescuing them from starvation. But that didn't mean he might not suddenly make a hard right-hand turn into full-bore despotism.

Certainly some of his other neighbors had concerns about possible future expansion. Travis had heard rumors that Haven had sent a team to the New Berlin system to open diplomatic talks, and probably to also assess the situation. Other, closer systems were reportedly scrambling to hammer out defense alliances, though the fact that the last such alliance had wound up being absorbed by the Empire was probably giving them pause.

Current wardroom opinion was that Potsdam was too far away for Anderman's mercenaries to be a direct threat to Manticore. But that didn't mean someone else wouldn't take a page from his strategy and take a shot at the Star Kingdom.

If enemy warships settled into orbit over Landing, it was unlikely that any of Breakwater's high-minded speeches would deter them.

"But that's politics," Lisa said into his thoughts, "and I try to avoid discussing politics with friends. To bring this conversation back to its launch point: my dog."

"Your dog?" Travis said, consciously disengaging his mind from his frustrations with Parliamentary politics. "Oh, right—the favor. What about him?"

"Her," Lisa corrected. "She's a Scottish Terrier—tiny little thing. Anyway, with his usual exquisite timing, my ex asked me to take her while he goes off to Sphinx for some long-term research project."

"Sounds kind of presumptive," Travis commented disapprovingly.

"Not really," Lisa said. "She was originally *our* dog, but he got her in the settlement, and I usually like taking her when I can. The problem is that the girl we used to hire to take care of Crumpets when we were both out has inconveniently decided to graduate high school and go to college—" she took a deep breath, huffed it out "—and I'm kind of up the creek. So. I know your mother has a business breeding dogs. Does she also board them?"

"That's a good question," Travis said. "I don't know, but I can certainly ask."

"Thanks—I'd appreciate it," Lisa said. "There are a couple of other dog boarders in Landing, but I'd feel better if I had a connection with the people taking care of her. Even if it's a second-hand connection."

"I understand," Travis said. "Don't worry, I'll make sure she—what was her name again?"

"Crumpets," Lisa said. "As in tea and." She shook her head. "Don't ask."

"I wasn't going to," Travis said. Actually, he *had* been planning to ask that very question. Now, of course, he couldn't. "Don't worry, I'll handle it."

"Thank you," she said. "You don't know what this means to me." She stood up. "And I'm sorry to chat and run, but I really have to be going."

"No problem," Travis said, scrambling awkwardly to his feet. "Let me know when and where I need to pick her up. You have my number?"

"I can get it," Lisa said. "It'll probably be the end of the week." This time, she was the one who offered her hand. "Thanks, Travis. You're a life-saver."

"You're welcome," Travis said, taking her hand. "I'll have everything arranged by the time you call."

"Good. Thanks again." With a final smile, she turned and left.

The door closed behind her. Slowly, Travis sat down again, his brain spinning. Lisa Donnelly, back in his life. Even if it was over something as small and temporary as boarding her dog.

He had no idea if his mother boarded dogs. In fact, he hadn't spoken to her for months.

But he would find out. And if she didn't, he would take the dog himself. The *Damocles*'s mission had a five-month timetable—two months each there and back, plus one at Casca—and Travis still had a short stint at BuShips once he finished his post-grad work. He would be in Landing and Casey-Rosewood for at least the next five months, and could easily handle a pet.

Meanwhile, there were a host of other matters to ponder.

Matters such as what had happened to Lisa's marriage, whether he'd been a fellow officer, and what exactly constituted being the wrong guy. Matters such as whether Travis and Lisa were now truly friends, or if she'd just been saying that, or even whether they both meant the same thing by that word.

He had no idea what the answers were to those questions.

In five minutes Lisa had completely upended whatever their

relationship had been before, and it was all just a little bit scary. Uncharted territory always was.

But he would get through it. He'd been walking uncharted territory for the past ten years, and he would get through this patch, too. Once he had, it wouldn't be uncharted anymore.

And when all of that was finally settled, he would make it his business to find out why a sane and normal person would name a dog *Crumpets*.

CHAPTER TWO

"IN THE HISTORY OF EVERY SO-CALLED CRISIS," Breakwater intoned, his voice permeating every cubic centimeter of air space in the House of Lords assembly chamber, "there comes a point where one doesn't quite know whether to laugh or to cry. Sadly, this is the point where I find myself regarding the Star Kingdom's massive hunt for roving bands of elusive pirates."

Seated four chairs to Breakwater's left, Winterfall eased his gaze unobtrusively around the chamber, his eyes automatically measuring faces, his brain automatically gauging the moods and attitudes behind those faces. He would never be as good at this kind of analysis as Baroness Castle Rock, say, or Breakwater himself. But ten T-years of practice had made him far better than he'd once been.

Ten years.

It had been an extraordinary decade. Toiling away at the bottom of the Parliamentary power pyramid, his presence in the House of Lords due solely to the serendipity of his grandparents being one of the first fifty investors in Manticore, Limited, Winterfall had been destined to be forgotten by history, just one more nameless peer whose only contribution to society and the Star Kingdom was to vote however the more powerful and influential of the Lords ordered.

And then, out of nowhere, Breakwater had invited him into his inner circle. Had chosen Winterfall to be part of the group of Lords and Ladies standing at the Chancellor's side against the resource pit that the Royal Manticoran Navy had become.

Breakwater's selection hadn't been random, of course. Winterfall knew that. There'd been subtle but good political reasons for the Chancellor and his Committee for Military Sanity to pluck the young baron out of the mass, not the least of which was that Winterfall's half-brother Travis Long had just joined that same Navy. If one had close family in an organization, after all, it must certainly follow that one would do only that which one believed to be best for that organization.

Still, at the time of Breakwater's offer, it had been clear that the Chancellor had assumed Winterfall would remain just another face and warm body to stand behind him in silent support of his policies and his convoluted bids for additional power and prestige. Breakwater and his circle had explicitly said as much.

It was a role Winterfall would have been perfectly willing to play. Reflected glory and recognition were still better than no glory and recognition at all.

But to everyone's surprise, it hadn't worked out that way. Winterfall had been asked a question at a high-level meeting, he'd answered the question and offered a suggestion, and suddenly he was being seen as a voice of reason and compromise by everyone from King Michael on down.

Winterfall had expected the limelight to fade away quickly. To his surprise, it hadn't.

He'd weathered the *Phobos* debacle. He'd survived the fallout from Dapplelake's investigation of the incident, which had implicated not only two high-level RMN officers but also three members of the Lords who'd had information they'd failed to pass on to higher authorities. He'd even made it through HMS *Guardian*'s return from Secour, and the subsequent surge in Navy prestige that had followed Captain Eigen's report of pirate activity in the region.

In fact, he'd made it through that surge better than Breakwater himself. The Chancellor and MPARS had both taken a political double-punch, and while the loss of status had largely been kept out of the public eye Breakwater had taken the Navy's new popularity very, very personally.

But like the crafty politician he was, the Chancellor had bided his time, staying low and quiet and watching for signs that his opponents' position was weakening. And once that erosion started, he'd been more than willing to grab a shovel and help the process along.

And the shovel he was about to wield was a very hefty tool indeed. One that he'd been preparing for just such a moment as this.

"Because the fact of the matter is," Breakwater continued, "that while I say *elusive*, I might just as well say *nonexistent*. Because, really, that's what they are. That's what they've always been."

No murmur of interest or excitement ran through the assembled Lords. Nor had Winterfall expected one. Breakwater railing against the Navy and Defense Ministry was so commonplace that anyone who'd been here for the past ten years—which, with a very few exceptions, was pretty much everyone—knew what to expect whenever the Chancellor got onto this topic.

But as Winterfall continued to look around the room he noticed that a few heads which had been bowed over their tablets were starting to come back up. Breakwater had a simmering fire in his voice, a passion that had been largely absent since *Guardian*'s return from Secour. The change in tone was striking, and the more astute among the peers were taking note, wondering where the Chancellor was going with this.

"This isn't just my opinion," Breakwater continued. "In fact, it isn't opinion at all. Ask First Lord of the Admiralty Cazenestro. Ask Defense Minister Calvingdell. Ask any of the hundreds of men and women who've gone on months-long patrols to neighboring star systems hunting in vain for signs of these alleged marauders. All of them will tell you there's not a single scrap of evidence that any pirates were ever working this region, let alone that there are pirates working here now."

Winterfall smiled to himself. As always, it was all in the wording. There were certainly *hints* that someone was preying on merchant ships out there. There were vanished freighters, unexplained gravitic footprints that suggested someone might be coming or going at the edges of various systems, and even a couple of possible sightings by freighters whose sensors weren't adequate to the task of distinguishing between real images and hyper ghosts.

But *evidence*? As Breakwater said, not a scrap. No actual pirates or pirate ships had been caught in the act. No one had spotted or boarded the gutted, blood-spattered remains of captured freighters. No identifiable cargo from any of the vanished ships had turned up in local markets or, as far as anyone had heard, the more distant Haven or Solarian League ports.

Though there was always Silesia. The Confederacy had started off as idealistically as Manticore, but there were signs things weren't going to stay that way. They appeared to be settling into a client-patron arrangement that favored special interests over broader based policy decisions. While Winterfall was well aware of which side of his bread was buttered, he was also aware—more aware than certain other Peers he could have mentioned—of the downsides of that sort of system. More to the point at the moment, however, the Silesian government's insularity, and disinclination to cooperate with its neighbors, even when known problems reared their heads, offered little reason to believe it would have any interest in dealing with piracy. At least, not so long as that piracy was afflicting someone *else's* shipping. If Winterfall was a pirate, he'd mused on occasion, that was where he would go to peddle his stolen merchandise.

It was even possible that someone in Silesia had set up a black-market system to buy and sell the pirated ships themselves. Certainly the ships were the most valuable part of the loot, assuming that the pirates managed to take them even partially intact.

But of course, any such thoughts would undermine Breakwater's argument, which was why he would never bring them up. What Winterfall found interesting was that no one on the other side ever brought up the Confederacy as a counter-argument. Probably they just realized that lack of proof was of no value in political arguments.

"But the true, even frightening irony is that while the First Lord claims that all this is making the Star Kingdom safer, it is exactly the opposite," Breakwater went on, his voice deepening in pitch even as it rose in volume. "Each needless voyage translates into many additional hours' worth of maintenance, refitting, and replacement. Each useless trip into the void takes with it hundreds of men and women whose talents and skills could be used right here at home instead of locked away inside a metal tube for weeks or months on end. Each wild-goose hunt eats up resources that could be far better spent upgrading or maintaining miners, freighters, and other civilian spacecraft."

More heads were starting to come up now as Breakwater's passion began to prick the notice of even the most oblivious or cynical Lords. The Chancellor was coming out of the shadows where he'd been nursing his wounds, rising again to challenge the Navy and its supporters.

Some of the Lords would be pleased by that. Others would be dismayed. Still others wouldn't much care either way, but would merely enjoy the break in the general air of legislative boredom that seemed to have settled around Parliament these past few months.

"And the final paradox of all: if someday an actual pirate *should* by some miracle stumble upon the Star Kingdom, where will the very ships be that we would need to defend us?" Breakwater intoned, lifting his hand as if in supplication to an invisible protector. "Exactly. They'll be scattered across the cosmos, completely and utterly useless."

He brought the hand down to slam the edge of his fist firmly against the top of the podium. "No, My Lords. For all these reasons, and more, this situation is unacceptable.

"But that's about to change. This very afternoon, I intend to meet with King Michael and First Lord Cazenestro to discuss the situation. And I'm confident that we'll come to an understanding that will set the Star Kingdom of Manticore along a new and more sensible road."

With that, and with the entire body of the Lords finally giving him their full attention, he gave a little bow to Prime Minister Davis Harper, Duke Burgundy, and resumed his seat.

Again, Winterfall hid a smile. It was one hundred percent pure Breakwater: a strong, eloquent teasing of the audience, culminating in a smooth halt just as they were starting to hunger for more. It was a flair for the dramatic that Winterfall unfortunately didn't have, and knew he would never be able to pull off.

Breakwater had it in double handfuls. More than that, he knew when and where to bring that flair to the forefront. The entire House of Lords was now aware that something significant was in the works, and within minutes of the session's close the media would know it, too. An hour after that, all of Manticore would know. By the time Breakwater emerged from the palace this afternoon, the entire planet would be primed and ready for whatever he had to say.

And no matter what happened in that meeting, they wouldn't be disappointed. Breakwater would make sure of that.

Winterfall almost felt sorry for First Lord Cazenestro. Almost.

☆　　☆　　☆

By all rights, Captain Edward Winton would reflect later, he shouldn't have been at the meeting. For that matter, he shouldn't have been on Manticore at all.

As usual with such things, it was all in the timing. He and his ship, the heavy cruiser *Sphinx*, should have been on patrol with the rest of Green One, the nine-ship task force assigned to protect the space around Manticore and Sphinx.

But like every other ship in the Navy, *Sphinx* was dripping with maintenance problems, spare-parts issues, and short crews. This time it was the tuning on the Beta nodes of the aft impeller ring that had gone gunnybags, and the necessary repair work had been deemed serious enough for Admiral Carlton Locatelli to order it to be handled in space dock. Edward had brought his ship in, gotten the repair work up and running, and assigned his executive officer to ride herd on the operation. After that, invoking commander's prerogative, he'd engineered a three-day leave for his son Richard from the Academy, then slipped off groundside to spend a couple of precious days with his wife, son, and daughter.

It was an escape he very much needed. Captaining a heavy cruiser was challenging and time-consuming enough, but Edward had the extra burden of being crown prince. That meant keeping tabs on everything that was happening in the Palace, the government, and—for that matter—the entire Star Kingdom.

At least, that was what it theoretically meant. In actual practice, Edward had been more than a little lax on that latter set of duties. His ship's travel schedule often kept him away from Manticore—or even out of the system entirely, given the Navy's aggressive anti-piracy stance since Secour—when there were meetings and Parliamentary events that he should be keeping an eye on. At the same time, his lack of anything approaching free time had forced him to mostly ignore the Palace's daily reports.

It had been a nagging sore spot between him and his father for a long time. Eventually, the King had given up trying to press Edward on the point, but Edward knew that his father's frustration and disappointment were still there.

Every time the guilt bug bit—and it bit on a fairly regular basis—he promised himself he would do better. Accordingly, as he headed home for his impromptu escape he promised himself that after a few hours with his family he would head to the Palace and check in with his father.

He was exactly four and a half hours into that escape when his father called one of the King's Own security men assigned to Edward and requested the Crown Prince's presence at the Palace.

Edward's first concern, that the King was having some serious medical problem that his haphazard skimming of the daily reports had missed, lasted until he reached the Royal Sanctum where his father was waiting. King Michael seemed a bit more frail than the last time Edward had seen him, but was clearly and thankfully not anywhere near death's door.

The resulting sense of relief lasted until Edward found out that he'd been summoned for a meeting with Chancellor Breakwater.

The final souring of a previously wonderful day came when he learned the precise topic of the meeting.

He couldn't let his annoyance show, of course. He was the Crown Prince, he was at the side of the King, and the need to maintain absolute solidarity in public was one of the first lessons he'd been taught by his grandmother as a young child.

But years in the Navy had taught him how to seethe invisibly. He did so now, passionately, all the way to the conference room.

He'd given up an afternoon of board games with his wife, son, and daughter for *this*?

They reached the conference room to discover no surprises at all awaiting them. Chancellor Breakwater was there, of course, as were First Lord of the Admiralty Cazenestro, Admiral Locatelli, and Defense Minister Clara Sumner, Countess Calvingdell. Flanking Breakwater in support of his side of the issue were his two strongest allies in his ongoing anti-Navy crusade: Earl Chillon and Baron Winterfall.

Edward eyed the latter as he rounded the table toward the chair that had been reserved for him at the far end. Several years ago, in the aftermath of the *Phobos* debacle, King Michael had warned Edward that Winterfall was someone who needed to be watched. At the time, Edward hadn't been convinced.

But seeing Winterfall here brought back those memories. Especially since the typical service life of one of Breakwater's political sock puppets was only a couple of years. The fact that Winterfall was still around was strong indication that the young man hadn't yet outlived his usefulness to the Chancellor.

Maybe that was the real reason Edward had been so resistant to keeping up with Manticoran politics, he mused as he found his seat at the table. Not the inconvenience of distance or even the chronic lack of time, but the fact that he hated the genteel infighting and backbiting that seemed to have become a permanent part of the Star Kingdom's operational machinery.

That was one reason he'd gone into the Navy, in fact. Not just to protect his home and his people—though those were certainly important—but because the whole naval structure was different. There were politics, certainly—far more than he liked. But in the end, when push came to shove, there was always a clear line of command, and a clear set of regs and standing orders that everyone followed.

And as King Michael grew steadily more frail, Edward was also increasingly aware that the day was coming when he would never again hold a space-going command. When he would be embroiled in these dirtside politics for the rest of his life.

Across the table, Breakwater was watching him, though clearly pretending to be studying his tablet, and Edward wondered yet again why the Chancellor hadn't used the Crown Prince's neglect of his political duties as yet another stick with which to beat the Navy. Certainly it was an easy enough target.

The answer, unfortunately, was probably that Breakwater had decided that Edward's disengagement from the political fray suited his own purposes.

He felt his lip twist. Yet another reason for him to feel guilty.

"We appreciate your time, Your Majesty," Breakwater said after the formalities and greetings had been dispensed with and everyone was once again seated. "Your Highness," he added with a respectful nod to Edward.

Respectful, but with an odd half-frown to it, as if he was wondering why exactly the Crown Prince had even been invited to this get-together.

Edward wasn't offended. Breakwater liked to be in control of his environment, and adding an extra person to the group weakened that control.

Besides, Edward was wondering about that himself. With luck, maybe he and the Chancellor would find out together.

"As you all know—as most of you know," Breakwater corrected himself with another nod toward Edward's end of the table, "MPARS is once again in the midst of a logistics crisis. We have far too few ships to patrol the regions we've been assigned to protect, particularly the Unicorn Belt. The ships we do have are undercrewed and are forever struggling to obtain spare parts and orbital dock space."

Which wasn't exactly true, Edward knew. In fact, Breakwater's whole diatribe was edging close to outright falsehood. MPARS might not have any sizeable ships, but they had a half dozen converted ore and mining craft that had been refitted as patrol-and-repair ships. As for personnel, they'd stolen over three hundred officers and enlisted from the RMN five years ago for their ill-fated *Phobos* project, and as far as Edward knew they'd never given them back.

He looked over at Cazenestro, waiting for the First Lord to call him on that one. To his surprise, though, the rebuke didn't come.

"It's not any better in the Navy," Cazenestro said instead. "In case you hadn't noticed. If you'll look to the bills you and your colleagues have passed over the past few years, you'll see that the various planetary infrastructure rebuilding and expansion programs are still getting first priority in terms of resources and personnel."

"Yes, thank you, I understand that," Breakwater said, just as coolly. "And I would be the last person to take food from the mouths of babes."

There was, Edward knew, an opportunity there for a *very* sarcastic comment regarding Breakwater's policies. Fortunately, everyone present had too much class to take the easy shot.

"But that same rebuilding has led to more miners than ever plying the asteroid belts, and their lives and safety are also important to the Star Kingdom," Breakwater continued. "And it cannot be overemphasized how important the raw materials so obtained are to our current rebuilding—"

"If you please, My Lord," Calvingdell interrupted in her clear soprano. "I believe we're all well acquainted with your views and thoughts on this matter. Can we please move to the bottom line?"

"If you insist, My Lady," Breakwater said, inclining his head to her even as his eyes gave a small flash of annoyance. Clearly, he still had some drawing-room oratory he'd wanted to trot out. "The bottom line is that the Navy has a group of ships that it really has no use for, and which MPARS desperately needs. Namely, the seven *Pegasus*-class corvettes."

"You must be joking," Locatelli said, his voice a sort of dis-believing outrage. "If you'd ever bothered to study naval tactics you'd have learned that corvettes are *the* ship of choice for flank protection and long-range triangulation."

"I *have* studied tactics, thank you Admiral," Breakwater said, his own voice the smooth confidence of a man who's anticipated the objection and has already formulated a counter-argument. "The only reason you use corvettes that way is that there's not much else you can do with them. Your *Salamander*-class destroyers are equally effective for that kind of duty: almost as fast, and better armed."

"Except that we only have six destroyers," Cazenestro pointed out. "Losing the corvettes would cut our useful flanking force in half."

"That assumes you actually have need of a flanking force," Breakwater said. "But that leads us to the real core of our pro-posal. At the moment the Navy's forces are split into, I believe, three groups: Green Task Forces One and Two in the Manticore-A system, and Red Force out at Manticore-B. Distributing your forces that way means that, at any given time, only three spots in the entire Star Kingdom are truly safe." He lifted a finger. "Whereas if the seven corvettes were with MPARS and patrolling other regions of our space—"

"Just a moment," Locatelli interrupted. "Are you suggesting that the corvettes would still be *armed*?"

"Of course," Breakwater said, frowning as if that was obvious. "They wouldn't be much use against your roving pirates if they weren't."

"I thought you didn't believe in pirates," Calvingdell said mildly.

Edward focused on her. Calvingdell had taken over the Ministry four T-years ago, after the *Phobos* investigation came to an end and the former Defense Minister, Earl Dapplelake, had handed in the final report and his resignation. Completely unnecessarily, in Edward's opinion, especially given that the report hadn't laid even a hint of the blame at the Defense Minister's own door. But Dapplelake had considered the debacle ultimately his responsi-bility, and neither the Prime Minster nor the King himself had been able to talk him out of stepping down.

Calvingdell wasn't a bad choice to fill his shoes, really. She understood people and numbers, and could deal with both.

The problem was that she didn't understand the Navy. Not the way Dapplelake had understood it. Certainly not the way Cazenestro or Locatelli or Edward himself understood it.

And like a miscalibrated impeller wedge, that blind spot might end up costing them. Badly.

"There are a lot of things I don't believe in," Breakwater said, his eyes focused directly on hers now. Like a Kodiak Max targeting the weak one of the herd, the irreverent thought flickered through Edward's mind. "But I'm willing to concede that my knowledge is imperfect, my opinions not always correct, and the future may throw some surprises our direction. Even if there are no genuine threats out there right now, diversifying the Star Kingdom's defensive capability still makes sense."

"Hardly," Cazenestro said, throwing a sideways look at Calvingdell that probably wanted to be a glare but couldn't quite bring itself to cross the line of propriety. "If a threat *does* present itself we need to be able to counter with a strong and focused response. I doubt an attacker would sportingly hold off his operation while we gathered our ships together from every corner of the Kingdom."

"On top of which, MPARS has no training in the use or maintenance of such weapons," Locatelli added. "It would take years to bring your people up to speed."

"Which is why we're not asking that all seven corvettes be transferred at once," Winterfall spoke up. "Nor is there need for them to be armed. At least, not yet."

All eyes turned to him.

"Explain, please," Cazenestro said, his voice cautious.

"Chancellor Breakwater is looking to the future," Winterfall said. "But if the past has taught us anything, it's that small steps are often the prudent course." He tapped a key on his tablet, the command popping a set of diagrams and data pages onto the tablet lying on the table in front of Edward. "I've therefore taken the liberty of working up a compromise suggestion."

Edward picked up his tablet, mentally shaking his head as he skimmed through the report. Just as he had back in the early *Phobos* debate, Winterfall had picked the precise psychological moment to undercut the whole basis of both Breakwater's suggestion and Cazenestro's objections.

"So you're saying you don't want the missiles at all?" Cazenestro asked warily.

"As I said, perhaps in the future," Winterfall said. "If and when we get solid proof that there's a threat to the Star Kingdom, we'll want as many armed ships as possible. Until then—" he gestured to the tablet "—I think a pair of hull-mounted rescue pods would be more useful to MPARS's primary mission of search and rescue. It would also make sense to take the opportunity to also do a complete overhaul and upgrade. If we needed to rearm them in the future, we'd want to make sure *all* of their systems were fully serviceable and up to date. We should probably also fit them to tow other ships in an emergency."

"Interesting," Calvingdell said as she scrolled down the pages. "So the rescue pods would simply replace the missile box launchers?"

"Exactly, My Lady," Winterfall said. "And the launchers could always be restored. The necessary connection points are already there, and I understand box launchers are designed for relatively easy removal and replacement."

"*Relatively* being the key word," Locatelli rumbled. "Have you run the design by anyone else?"

"Not the full design," Winterfall said. "But everything in it is off-the-shelf technology, so I don't anticipate any major surprises."

"It would certainly be a welcome sight to a distressed mining ship," Calvingdell commented.

That point, at least, was unarguable. Edward ran his eye down the list of emergency equipment, spare parts, tools, and survival gear that would make up the bulk of one of Winterfall's proposed rescue pods, all arranged so that individual sections could be split off and dropped alongside a ship in distress. The second pod, in contrast, was a last-ditch solution for when all the repair gear failed: a compact life pod where survivors of a wrecked ship could huddle together, cramped but safe, while the corvette ferried them back to port.

"I'm sure it would be," Cazenestro said. "But it doesn't change the fact that this would pull seven vital warships out of service." He looked at the King, who had been watching the verbal duel in silence. "I presume, Your Majesty, that you recognize the potentially dire situation this would leave us in."

"I do," the King said. "But I also recognize that Chancellor Breakwater is correct. MPARS's resources have been stretched beyond the limit, and that situation needs to be addressed."

Edward stared down the length of the table. Was his father

actually *agreeing* with Breakwater's transparent grab for ships and power? Especially after Secour?

"We would, of course, take another page from Baron Winterfall's list of small steps," the King continued. "We should begin by transferring just two of the corvettes to MPARS instead of all seven." He gestured to Cazenestro. "Do you have a suggestion as to which two, My Lord?"

Cazenestro looked like he'd just eaten something sour. But he knew an order when he heard one. "Probably *Aries* and *Taurus*," he said reluctantly. "They're currently attached to Red Force at Manticore-B, which is where the bulk of the MPARS patrols are anyway. They should feel right at home there. Though it seems to me, Your Majesty, that there's no reason to remove their box launchers *or* approve their transfer until it's been confirmed that Baron Winterfall's modules are actually practical."

"Agreed," Michael said. "And of course, the transfer can't take place until MPARS has men and women capable of crewing them. Chancellor Breakwater's first task will be to have those crews chosen, after which you'll arrange for them to be run through the Academy and Casey-Rosewood."

Cazenestro sat up a bit straighter. "They'll be coming to *us*, Your Majesty?"

"I doubt standard MPARS training includes corvettes, My Lord," Michael pointed out dryly.

"Yes, Your Majesty, I understand that," Cazenestro said, floundering a bit. "But there's no significant difference in the basic systems between those ships and the ones MPARS already has in service. In fact, the *primary* differences are all combat systems."

"And the tactical training to use them, of course," Calvingdell murmured.

"Of course," Cazenestro agreed. "Neither of which are MPARS priorities. My thought was that I could simply detach some of my instructors on a temporary basis to handle the degree of familiarization they'd need where the core systems are required."

"As Baron Winterfall said, those ships might someday be pressed into combat," Breakwater put in smoothly. "In such an event, the fact that the crews had undergone military training might prove crucial to their success and survival. In fact," he went on, as if the thought had just occurred to him, "it might be a good idea if *all* MPARS personnel underwent such training."

"An interesting proposal," Michael said, turning to Cazenestro. "My Lord?"

"Under current conditions, I'm afraid that would be impossible, Your Majesty," Cazenestro said stiffly. "We simply don't have the facilities to accommodate such an influx of new people." He glowered at Breakwater. "Unless the Chancellor would be willing to fund an expansion for those facilities."

"Unfortunately, Parliament's budget has little room for such extras at the moment," Breakwater said. "But again, we can leave that for the future. We'll just focus on training the corvettes' future crews and leave the full regimen for another day."

"I think we have a plan of action, then," the King said. "We'll meet again when the final details of these rescue pods have been settled and some cost estimates worked out. I presume that will be agreeable to everyone?"

"Yes, Your Majesty," Calvingdell said.

"Very much so, Your Majesty," Breakwater confirmed.

Michael nodded and gestured to them. "Then we are dismissed," he said. "Thank you all for coming."

The exit formalities were shorter than the entrance ones. Edward remained standing beside his chair until all but the King had left the room. The door closed behind the last of them, and Michael turned to his son.

"I trust you found that amusing?" he suggested, rising from his chair and gesturing toward the more intimate circle of lounge chairs off to the side of the room.

"*Amusing* is hardly the word I would use," Edward said, heading for the conversation circle. "Are you really going to just give Breakwater those corvettes?"

"I assume you have an objection?"

"More than just one," Edward assured him, waiting for his father to sit down and then taking the chair across from him. "With your permission?"

Michael inclined his head. "Please."

"Let's start with logistics," Edward said. "If we give MPARS even a single missile, we'll have set the precedent for two services competing for the same small stockpile of *very* expensive ordnance."

"Seems to me I remember the exact opposite argument being made when Breakwater wanted to break up the battlecruisers," Michael pointed out mildly.

"It wasn't me making that argument," Edward pointed out in return. "The fact remains that we have only a limited number of missiles to go around."

"We can always get more."

"Not with Breakwater's death grip on the purse strings we can't," Edward countered. "Remember that old Defense Ministry policy forbidding the use of missiles in non-combat situations unless it's specifically authorized practice?"

"Which has since been rescinded," his father pointed out.

"No thanks to Breakwater," Edward said. "Point two: training. Breakwater's right about his people needing a full military run-through. Cazenestro is also right about the facilities for such an influx of new people not existing. Bottom line: every slot that MPARS takes is one less slot we'll have for a future RMN officer or spacer. We're already behind on our personnel expansion, and that would slow it down even more. As Breakwater and Winterfall no doubt had in mind the whole time."

"Ah—so you *did* note the collusion," Michael said approvingly. "Despite the surface conflict in their two proposals."

"Please, Dad—I wasn't born yesterday," Edward said with all the scorn he felt he could deliver to a sitting monarch, trying to ignore the fresh flicker of guilt over all those missed briefings. "Winterfall's last fully independent act was back at the first *Phobos* discussion when he undercut Breakwater's original demands. Breakwater saw how well that worked and adopted the gambit, and Winterfall's been playing dagger to Breakwater's rapier ever since."

"Nicely put," Michael said with a small smile. "Dagger to rapier. I may steal that one. Anything else?"

"The biggest one of all," Edward assured him. "Command and control. You may have noticed that the Navy and MPARS don't exactly get along, at least not at the top. If the Star Kingdom ever *was* attacked, trying to get coordinated action from two services who've been competing for everything for years would be difficult at best and impossible at worst. And *impossible* in a combat situation usually means *catastrophic.*"

"Good points, all." Michael leaned forward slightly, his expression more intent. "My turn now. We'll skip the dramatic buildup and go straight to the big one. Namely, Countess Calvingdell and First Lord Cazenestro *want* to give those corvettes away."

Edward felt his jaw drop. "They *what*?"

"No, you heard correctly," Michael said. "We discussed this in detail some time back. A conversation you'd have been included in had you been available." His eyes held Edward's for a moment, and the Crown Prince felt his cheekbones heat as his father's expression mirrored his own earlier thoughts. He wondered for a moment if Michael was going to make the message more explicit, but then the King shrugged and settled back. "They've decided they don't want them anymore."

"But—" Edward broke off, sensing a babble coming and determined to cut it off before he sounded as stupid as he currently felt. *Yes*, he should have kept up with the reports, especially those that dealt with the Navy. But even so, what in the name of heaven were they all *thinking*?

"They want to just give them to Breakwater?"

"So they've told me," Michael said. "And before you start wondering about their sanity, understand that no one's making a spur-of-the-moment decision here. Breakwater may have thought he was blindsiding us with this proposal, but there've been hints coming out of the Exchequer's office for a couple of weeks now. Calvingdell and Cazenestro have had plenty of time to think this through."

"But why?" Edward persisted. "MPARS doesn't need warships."

"Perhaps not," Michael said. "The more salient point is that the Navy doesn't want to keep pumping resources into non-hyper-capable, under-armed, hundred-year-old ships. At the same time, it would be a shame to simply scrap them—they're still useful, at least for certain duties. The obvious solution is to give them to Breakwater, where they'll be eating at the MPARS lunch counter instead of the Navy's. As an added bonus, the transfer will free up—what is it, forty-five?—forty-five spacers per ship for reassignment elsewhere."

Edward suppressed a glower. Maybe on paper a corvette's compliment was forty-five officers and spacers. In reality, each of them was having to make do with thirty. The whole Navy was undermanned, and that wasn't going to change any time soon. Especially if Breakwater won out with his idea to poach spots in the rosters of the Navy's training facilities.

"Furthermore, you have to admit that having a few small armed ships wandering around the asteroid belts isn't a bad idea," Michael continued. "An in-system raider looking for easy prey could do worse than a fat miner who's loaded to the gills with high-grade ore and is hours away from any military assistance. There are also the extraction facilities outside the hyper limit, which usually have modules full of refined materials ripe for the picking. A harmless-looking rescue ship that suddenly shows herself capable of sending a missile down the pirates' throats would be a highly unpleasant surprise."

"I thought Winterfall agreed we weren't going to arm them."

"Not at the start," Michael said. "But we all know that's the direction Breakwater will eventually carry the discussion."

"All right," Edward said slowly. "But if everyone's agreed, why are we fighting about it? If Calvingdell and Cazenestro want to give him the corvettes, why did we even have this meeting?"

"Because it's never a bad idea to let Breakwater think he's won a battle," Michael said, a grim twinkle in his eye. "It's an even better idea to make him think he owes the Navy a favor that can be called in somewhere down the line."

"I'm not convinced Breakwater thinks that way."

"Possibly not," Michael conceded. "But I think Winterfall could be persuaded that direction. And even if Breakwater doesn't give a damn about debts, there are times a politician—even our Sabrepike of a Lord Chancellor—has no choice but to pay up when the debt gets called publicly and under the right circumstances." He smiled tiredly. "Besides, he likes to think of himself as a visionary whose name will resonate throughout Manticoran history. People like that sometimes have to act like statesmen, whether they want to or not."

Edward wasn't convinced of that, either. But it was clear that the decision had already been made, and made far above his own position. All he could do was accept it and deal with whatever consequences arose from it.

And he could also ask one final question. "So why exactly am I here?"

The twinkle faded from his father's eye. "Because when it comes time to make that deal and call in that favor," he said quietly, "you'll probably be the one making it. Because *you* will be the king."

Edward stared at his father, his earlier concerns about the older man's health roaring back. "What are you saying?" he asked carefully.

"I'm saying it's time for you to start looking to the future," Michael said. "For years now you've been merely a naval officer." He lifted a hand. "I know; that's what you wanted, and there's nothing *mere* about serving your kingdom. But that time is coming to an end. The Navy can no longer be allowed to completely fill your life. You're the Crown Prince, and you need to live and act accordingly."

"I understand that," Edward said through stiff lips. "Can we back up a minute to the whole I'll-be-making-the-deal bit? Is there something going on I should know about?"

"It's all right, Edward," Michael soothed. "Come, now—don't look so serious."

"Don't give me that," Edward countered. "Anyway, you started it. What's going on?"

"Nothing you need concern yourself with right now," Michael said. "If that changes you'll be the first to know."

"No, no, you don't get off that easy," Edward insisted. "I'm the Crown Prince, remember? *Everything* is my concern. You just said so."

"Easy there, hexapuma," the King chided, a hint of the earlier twinkle coming back into his eye. "Even a crown prince isn't allowed to badger his king. I'm pretty sure that's in the rules someplace."

"I'm not a prince badgering his king," Edward said quietly. "I'm a son worried about his father."

"And I appreciate your concern," Michael said. "But for now I need to keep this quiet. And I need you to keep what *you* know quiet, as well."

"That won't be hard," Edward growled. "Given I don't actually *know* anything."

"See?" Michael said with a smile. "You're already learning how this politics thing works."

"Hooray for our side," Edward said, trying hard to read his father's expression. Was he ill? Tired? Depressed?

Was he somehow being pushed out of office?

The thought chilled Edward right down to the bone. Could Breakwater have amassed so much power in Parliament that he could actually force the king himself from the throne? Was that what this whole corvette transfer was about, that Cazenestro and Calvingdell were acceding to the Chancellor's demands because they literally had no choice?

It seemed absurd on the face of it. But maybe it wasn't. The Constitution provided for the removal of a monarch by a three-quarters vote of both houses of Parliament, but that was normally only for "high crimes or misdemeanors," which would be a ludicrous allegation in King Michael's case.

But he could also be removed for incapacitation. And *that* one was not nearly as unthinkable.

Could the King's health be much worse than he was admitting? Could Breakwater have learned something about Michael's medical condition which he'd so far managed to keep secret?

Even from his own son? If so, Edward wasn't just a crown prince. He was one half of a constitutional crisis, the like of which the Star Kingdom of Manticore hadn't seen since its formation. And he might also be a son with a father he was likely to lose far sooner than he'd dreamed.

But his father clearly didn't want to talk about it. And Edward knew from long experience that a King Michael who didn't want to be moved, wasn't. At all.

"Good," Michael said, some of the darkness fading from his tone. "And really, don't look so worried. We have very good briefing officers, even if you haven't had the time to spend with them." The King's smile might have held just a bit of a bite, Edward thought. "You'll have time to get up to speed before it becomes necessary."

He stood up. "And now, I believe that matters of state have taken enough of your planned family time. Get yourself home, and be sure to hug Cynthia and Sophie for me. How's Richard doing at the Academy?"

"Very well," Edward assured him as he also stood up. "But he's still not too old to hug."

"I should hope not," Michael said with a smile. "Give him a hug from me, as well. Oh, and if you get a chance, you might try to touch base with your sister before she leaves."

Half-sister, Edward's brain made the automatic edit. Elizabeth was eleven years his junior, the offspring of his father and his father's second wife, and Edward had been wrangling with the little upstart ever since she was old enough to understand what wrangling was. He'd occasionally thought that one of the minor perks of being in the Navy was the fact that it put him out of reach of her honed and entirely too opinionated tongue.

Still, in the five years since she'd married Carmichael de Quieroz, Baron New Madrid, and set up housekeeping with the widower and his three children, Edward had heard that some of her rougher edges had smoothed a bit. It would probably be worth the time and effort to check that out for himself. "Where is she off to this time?"

"Sphinx," Michael told him. "They're joining a peak bear hunting party."

"I hope they're not bringing the children."

"Your sister may be headstrong, but she's not stupid," Michael said with a fond smile. "Mary and I will be watching them."

"So trading off a potential mauling versus guaranteed and unabashed spoiling?"

"Something like that," Michael said. "Enjoy your time with your family."

"I will," Edward promised.

And he did.

But before that, before even leaving the room, he made sure to first hug his father.

CHAPTER THREE

GROWING UP, JEREMIAH LLYN had hated being short.

Not that he was *that* short. Not really. No more than nine or ten centimeters shorter than the planetary average. But ten centimeters had been more than enough to set off the jokesters in primary school, the brawlers in middle grade, and the more elaborate hazing during his teen years. Young adulthood had been marginally better, with at least a veneer of politeness and civilization covering up the derision. But even there, he could see the mental evaluation going on behind employers' eyes as he was passed over for promotions and the truly lucrative jobs.

Now, with the perspective and maturity that fifty T-years of life afforded a man, he found his lack of towering stature not only comfortable but valuable. People, even supposedly intelligent people, tended to underestimate shorter men.

In Llyn's current position, it was often very useful to be underestimated.

Llyn wasn't sure why Haven's maximum-security Deuxième Prison relied on human cleaning staff instead of remotes. Possibly it was because they still needed people for maintenance and had simply combined the departments; possibly it was because remotes were more easily reprogrammed or electronically hijacked than people. Either way, it had made the job of infiltrating the prison much easier than he'd expected.

He'd started by crafting himself a cleaning outfit, with the proper coveralls and a faked ID. Once inside, he'd found an opportunity to trade up to a guard's uniform, the guard in question no longer requiring it. Another tweaking of ID, the activation of the worm his cohort on Haven had slipped into the prison's computer two days earlier, a hijacked uni-link call and soothing noises made to a concerned woman on the nighttime security monitor staff, and within an hour of entering the grounds he was standing in the cell of the prisoner he'd traveled all the way from the Solarian League to see.

The man's name was Mota, and he was a pirate.

Rather, had been a pirate. His gang had been all but wiped out five T-years earlier at a botched raid on Havenite warships in the Secour system. Mota had been one of the gang's chief system hackers, tasked with chopping through the ship's layers of security, which was why he'd managed to stay alive while the Havenite Marines were slaughtering his fellow pirates. He'd been briefly questioned at Secour, then brought back to Haven for a more thorough interrogation.

According to the documents Llyn had dug up, Mota's interrogators had learned a lot about the gang itself, some of their previous crimes, and how the Secour scheme had been developed and laid out. They had, unfortunately, learned exactly zero about who had hired Guzarwan and his men to steal the ships in the first place.

Haven wanted to know that. Wanted it very badly.

Because while most mercenary groups were more or less aboveboard, there were some who weren't. The former were unapologetic guns for hire, available to prosecute brush wars between small star nations or to provide defense for systems or private companies who couldn't afford to build and maintain navies of their own. In some places those groups were officially licensed, and for the most part were careful to maintain a good, even honorable reputation.

The latter type weren't straightforward, weren't licensed, and the only reputation they had or wanted was the kind that was whispered in back rooms between people as unsavory as themselves.

They were also those who had learned to keep a very low profile over the past half T-century or so, as the galaxy at large got around to dealing with them. In more than one case, some of the more honorable mercenaries had been hired to eliminate the significantly less honorable ones, the result of which had been that the first group rose to the slightly more respectable status of paramilitary force, while the second group went completely underground. That kind of low profile made them difficult to find, even for someone with Llyn's extensive list of dubious contacts.

In many cases, such mercenaries were barely more than extremely well-equipped pirate gangs. The Havenites, having had their share of run-ins with local pirates, and having seen what armed mercenaries like Gustav Anderman's group could do to an underdeveloped system, were naturally anxious to learn who might have such ambitions in their part of the galaxy.

But according to Mota, who was the single bridge-crew survivor of the battle, all of the men who'd actually met their employers had died at Secour. Now, five years after the debacle, the interrogators still occasionally pulled Mota out of his cell for a chat, but they'd given up any real hope that their prisoner knew anything.

Fortunately for Llyn, Haven's failure was his own golden opportunity.

No one hired pirates to steal a couple of heavy warships, not unless he had some pressing need for that kind of firepower. The Secour debacle wouldn't have alleviated that need, and it had occurred to Llyn that the would-be warlord's logical next step would be to look for a piratelike mercenary gang whose own ships could be used for whatever task he'd planned for his missing prizes.

Which, by a happy coincidence, was exactly the kind of mercenary gang Llyn wanted to hire.

And not just Llyn. Other agents were spread all across the civilized galaxy, trying their own approaches to the problem. Some were poking around dark corners of the Solarian League. Others were backtracking through the aftermath of unexplained military action. Still others were sifting through the records of the more legit merc groups, looking for defectors who might have gone into business for themselves.

Lying back on his bunk, closing his eyes, Llyn replayed the scene over again in his mind. Mota waking up abruptly to find an unknown person in his cell. Mota attempting to call for help, but already fading from the drug Llyn had administered in the man's sleep. Mota falling into the hypnotic state where his memory would be more open to discovery.

The Havenites had already used drugs like this, of course. Their problem was that they hadn't asked the right questions.

So Llyn had passed up all the obvious ones: name, age, home planet. He'd skipped the standard logistical stuff, too: the pirates' home base, suppliers, previous jobs. The Havenites had asked all of those, and had gotten mostly useless answers for their trouble. Llyn's hacker contact in Nouveau Paris had snagged him a copy of the official report, which he'd read thoroughly and tucked away for possible future reference.

Mota knew something important. Llyn was convinced of that. The trick was that the man didn't know he knew it.

And so, he'd asked all the questions the Havenites hadn't.

Who was with Guzarwan when he went to make the original deal?

What planets, systems, or cities did any of these men reference during the months of training and preparation for the job?

What odd or offhanded comment did any of these men make during prep?

What jokes did any of these men make during prep?

What vids did any of these men watch or comment on during prep?

What music did any of these men listen to during prep?

It was on that last one that Llyn finally hit the clue he'd been looking for. It seemed that Dhotrumi, Mota's fellow system hacker, had taken to humming a particular tune, but only when Guzarwan barged into their work room to check on their progress. The tune seemed to annoy Guzarwan, and after a few repeats of that particular interplay Mota had asked Dhotrumi about it.

But Dhotrumi had merely given a wink and a knowing smile and assured Mota that it would become clear after they finished the job. Mota had accepted that explanation, and they'd gotten back to work.

A few months later, the job had gone sideways, Dhotrumi and Guzarwan and most of the rest of the pirates had been killed, and Mota himself suddenly had more pressing matters on his mind than a private joke between two dead men. The Havenites had grabbed him, hauled him back to his new four-by-four-meter home, and the tiny musical mystery had disappeared into the far reaches of his brain.

Until Llyn had arrived and dug it out.

The freighter *Soleil Azur*, with Llyn as one of its eight paying passengers, had left Haven on its great circle route around the various regional ports only a few hours after he slipped back out of the prison. The close timing was deliberate, of course—there was no way for Llyn to keep his nighttime prison incursion from eventually being discovered, and he needed to make sure he was off-world before the authorities could organize an investigation and search.

But those few hours had been enough. With the aid of a melody search engine and Haven's vast cultural database, he'd been able to identify the tune as part of an old ballad called *Bound for the Promised Land*.

The title wasn't especially helpful. But the first two lines were:

> *On Jordan's stormy banks I stand and cast a wishful eye*
> *To Canaan's fair and happy land, where my possessions lie.*

Canaan.

It was an obscure world, in a group of equally obscure systems loosely clustered between the Solarian League and the Haven Sector. But as with many out-of-the-way nations on pre-Diaspora Earth, and other star nations since that time, anonymity hadn't translated to peace and quiet. Instead, living in the shadows had led to despotism and subjugation.

Canaan's experience had been a particularly brutal one. The world had been taken over thirty T-years ago by a military junta, which had been itself overthrown by a popular movement secretly organized by one of its own generals, a man named Khetha. Once firmly in power, Khetha had proclaimed himself to be the Supreme Chosen One and settled into absolute rule.

Four years ago, that rule had come to a sudden and violent end. The people of Canaan had overthrown his government, and Khetha and a small group of his inner circle had beaten a hasty retreat off-planet.

For a couple of years afterward Khetha had tried playing the role of legitimate and wrongly-ousted government leader, first with a couple of League planets and then with Haven, hoping they would force the new Canaanite government to reinstate him.

But no one had been interested in assisting with his counter-coup. Eventually, Khetha and his entourage had given up the effort and settled down into an unobtrusive and sulking role as government-in-exile.

In Quechua City. Right in the middle of the Cascan capital.

The very next stop on *Soleil Azur*'s route.

Llyn hadn't expected things to work out nearly so neatly. His plan had been to ride *Soleil Azur* to its first major port, get off, and wait for the next freighter heading in whatever direction his interrogation of Mota had indicated. It would have meant months of idleness waiting for freighters or perhaps an occasional passenger liner, plus more months of travel. But after the five T-years that had already been spent moving this operation forward, a few more months wouldn't have made much of a difference.

Now, thanks to good luck and perhaps the only local government with the kind of "live and let live" cultural ethos that would let Khetha settle on its soil without also putting him under full-press official observation, Llyn was suddenly ahead of the game. Unexpectedly but gratifyingly ahead. The odds against his getaway ship just happening to be bound for his ultimate destination were so astronomical that they wouldn't even have been worth the trouble to calculate.

Sometimes, he mused, the universe went out of its way to be helpful.

He smiled at the ceiling of his tiny cabin. Bound for Casca. Bound for the Promised Land.

I'm bound for the Promised Land...

The Promised Land wasn't Casca, of course. From a born-and-bred Solarian's point of view, Casca was little more than a fly speck on the back end of nowhere.

But it was on the road to that Promised Land. To a land of milk and honey.

To the Star Kingdom of Manticore.

Three worlds. A triple fly speck, from the League's point of view.

Only the League was wrong. Five T-years ago, researchers from the megacorporation Axelrod of Terra had stumbled on the groundshattering possibility that there was a wormhole junction somewhere in the Manticore system. Axelrod had immediately launched a twin-pronged Black-Dagger-classified operation, with the researchers continuing to dig into the data while Llyn and his associates laid the groundwork for a move on the Star Kingdom should the junction prove to be real.

The last report, which had arrived on Haven just prior to Llyn's infiltration of Mota's prison cell, had included new modeling that had raised the likelihood of the junction's existence to nearly eighty percent.

Unless that tentative conclusion somehow went off the rails in the next couple of years, the men and women at the uppermost pinnacle of Axelrod's power would make the decision to take over Manticore's three worlds.

It wouldn't be easy. The Star Kingdom boasted a far more powerful navy than a colony system that size had any business having. It would take an equally powerful force to win out over it; and, moreover, a force that couldn't be traced back to Axelrod.

Such backtracking would come later, of course, after the junction's existence had been announced. Fortunately, the machinery for muddying that particular puddle of water was already in motion. While Llyn hunted for a merc group to do the initial heavy lifting, other agents were quietly assessing various star nations with an eye toward bringing in one of them as Manticore's "official" conquerors. Once the Manticoran military forces had been defeated, that nation would assume control of the Star Kingdom, more or less legitimately as far as the rest of the galaxy was concerned. When the wormhole junction was subsequently "discovered," the figurehead government would call in Axelrod as "consultants," and the future would be in Axelrod's hands.

But the first crucial step along that path was Llyn's.

Hiring a mercenary group was relatively easy. Hiring one that was willing to play fast and loose with established rules of warfare was tricky. Finding one he could hire without leaving any tracks behind was trickier still.

But that was fine. Tricky was Llyn's specialty.

The intercom in his cabin gave a soft chime, signaling to the passengers and crew alike that the evening meal was ready in the ship's mess room.

Llyn wrinkled his nose. The food aboard *Soleil Azur* was bland and uninspired, as was only to be expected from a no-nonsense working freighter. The passengers, mostly industrialists, low-level government officials, and high-level sales agents, were for the most part equally bland and uninteresting.

Nevertheless, Llyn had looked forward to their times together over the past few months of travel. He would eat with them, talk with them, and laugh with them.

But mostly, he would listen to them. Very, very closely.

Because knowledge was power. And one could never predict where and when those nuggets of power would be found.

Getting to his feet, snaring his dinner jacket from its hanger, Llyn headed out into the corridor.

CHAPTER FOUR

DAMOCLES WAS SETTLING INTO ORBIT over Casca when the roster of those who would be joining Captain Marcello in the first shuttle came through.

Tactical Officer Lisa Donnelly's name was third on the list, right behind the captain himself and Executive Officer Susan Shiflett.

Lisa smiled, hoping the smile wasn't big enough or gloating enough for the rest of the bridge crew to notice and resent. It wasn't like anyone was getting cabin fever, after all—sixty-three days in hyper hadn't exactly been a burden on the crew's collective psyche. Certainly not when compared to the three and a half months it had taken *Guardian* to reach Secour on Lisa's first trip outside Manticoran space.

But this trip was different. At Secour, Lisa and the rest of the crew had spent the entire time in orbit, never making it down to Marienbad proper. She'd never heard an official reason why none of the Manticoran contingent had been allowed ashore, but rumor had it that the local government had been so thoroughly outraged with the events that had taken place above their world that they'd issued a flat no-landing policy.

But here, things were going to be different. Here, she was going to actually walk in a foreign city under an alien sun.

And she was going to be one of the very first of those aboard *Damocles* to do so.

She could hardly wait.

It was a feeling that was probably shared all through the ship.

Certainly it was being felt beside her. "Congratulations, Ma'am," Chief Petty Officer MacNiven murmured from the helm station to her left.

"Thank you," Lisa murmured back, noting with a mild twinge of guilt that MacNiven himself wasn't on the list.

But that had been how Marcello had set this whole thing up. Commander Pappadakis, *Damocles*'s engineering officer, wanted to tear down Life Support Two, which had developed a minor scrubber glitch en route to Casca, and he was the sort who objected to the very notion of grass growing under his feet. He would be staying aboard to oversee the operation, which neatly covered the Regs requirement that a senior officer remain aboard at all times. With the legalities—along with plain simple common sense—satisfied, the captain had thrown the rest of the crew into a lottery, giving each of them an equal chance to be aboard the first shuttle to land on Cascan soil.

Lisa had always liked and respected Marcello as commanding officer. This kind of foresight and sense of fair play just made her like him a bit more.

"TO?"

Lisa straightened to attention and swiveled around. "Yes, Sir?"

Marcello was eyeing her, his lips curving with that faint smile that always made her feel like he was reading her mind and liking what he saw in there. "Don't just sit there," he admonished mildly. "You saw the list. Go get yourself ready to feel real gravity again."

"Yes, Sir," she said. "I was just waiting until *Goldenrod* made it to her final orbital attitude."

"*Goldenrod* is perfectly capable of handling that herself," Marcello said. "Go, Commander. That's an order."

"Yes, Sir," she said, returning his smile. Unstrapping from her station, she grabbed the handhold on the back of her seat and launched herself through the bridge's zero-gee toward the aft hatch.

"That's full dress uniform," Marcello called a reminder after her. "Let's show the Cascans how it's done."

Twenty minutes later, the shuttle dropped away from *Damocles* and headed toward the blue-green planet below.

Packed to the gills with the best-dressed group of officers and ratings Lisa had ever seen outside of a parade ground. Dress uniforms, with buttons gleaming and impressive rows of "fruit salad" medal ribbons, as far as the eye could see.

Having served with most of these men and women for the past T-year or more, she'd had no idea that some of them cleaned up this good.

"I just hope they know how to behave themselves," Captain Marcello murmured from the seat beside her.

Lisa smiled. For some officers she'd served with, appearance was everything, with style at the top of the list and results a distant second. Other officers barely cared that they even *had* formal wear. Marcello fell somewhere in the middle: perfectly able to cut a respectable profile if he needed to, but more focused on making sure his ship and crew functioned to their fullest abilities. "They will," she assured him. "The XO and bosun beat it pretty bone-deep over the past few days."

"Good," Marcello said. "I have to say, I was a little concerned that the delay in our departure from Manticore would cause us to miss *Soleil Azur*. Glad we didn't."

Lisa felt her forehead crease. She knew perfectly well that *Soleil Azur* was still here. She'd been on *Damocles*'s bridge when CIC made contact with the Havenite freighter, confirmed it was indeed the ship that had brought Haven's current pirate data to Casca, and relayed that information to the captain. For Marcello to bring that up now, barely ten hours later, seemed a bit odd.

Was the captain actually trying to make small talk? With *her*?

"Were we planning to meet with anyone aboard?" she asked, aware that the question wasn't really small talk but not sure how she was supposed to continue her end of the conversation.

"I'm assuming not," Marcello said. "Haven's usual pattern has been to send just the data, without any analysts or couriers riding herd." He cleared his throat. "Speaking of analysts, is there a reason why Townsend has brought a personal with him?"

Lisa blinked. Personal computers were midway between the ubiquitous tablets that everyone aboard used and *Damocles*'s heavy-duty central net, with its slightly less ubiquitous collection of terminals scattered across the ship. Why Townsend would bother lugging something like that around on shore leave she couldn't imagine. "No reason that I know of," she told the captain. "In fact, no reason I can even think of."

"There's at least *one*," he said, his voice going a little darker.

"A couple of years ago, when *Pegasus* made its show-the-flag trip to Suchien, one of the ratings slipped a personal out of the ship and tried to sell it to one of the local computer companies."

Lisa stared at him. "I never heard anything about that."

"That's because Cazenestro made sure the whole thing was hushed up," Marcello told her. "The company was smart enough—or paranoid enough—to pass on the deal, even though it would have given them a nice leg up on their local competition. They also blew the whistle on him, and the CO and XO were waiting when he got back to his shuttle."

"I assume he was charged with theft?"

"And a couple of other things," Marcello said. "My point is we don't want to see any Naval equipment try to grow legs here and now."

"Yes, of course," Lisa murmured, mentally pulling up everything she knew about Townsend.

There wasn't a lot in there, she realized. Charles Townsend was a petty officer first class, who'd transferred aboard *Damocles* barely three months ago, right before they shipped out for Casca. By all accounts he worked well with superiors and subordinates alike. He had a somewhat raucous sense of humor, but he seemed to have it mostly under control and knew where the invisible lines were drawn.

The only exception to that rule—and the only black spot on Townsend's record aboard *Damocles*—had come from a newly minted ensign who had written up Townsend six days into the voyage up for insulting him to his face. Unfortunately for the outraged junior officer, the XO's subsequent investigation had concluded that what Townsend *said* and what the ensign *heard* were two entirely different things.

Townsend had kept a low profile since then. But Lisa doubted the ensign had forgotten. Ensigns never forgot things like that. If Townsend put even one of his oversized Sphinxian feet over the line, she had no doubt the ensign would be there to nail it to the floor.

Townsend wasn't stupid. Under the circumstances—especially under *these* circumstances—the man would have to be crazy to attempt to sell one of His Majesty's personal computers to a foreign government or company.

So why was he lugging the thing all the way down to Casca?

Marcello was sitting silently, his unasked question hanging

in the air between them. "I have no idea, Sir," she conceded. "I could call Lieutenant Nikkelsen and see if he knows anything."

"No, that's all right," Marcello said. "If you see Nikkelsen later, ask him to keep an eye on him." He snorted under his breath. "And let's make damn sure that the personal is still in its carrybag when Townsend returns to the ship."

☆   ☆   ☆

There was a small delegation waiting on the Quechua City landing platform when the shuttle touched down: a dozen men and women, wearing a mixture of high-class civilian outfits and Cascan Defense Force uniforms.

And smack in the center of the group, wearing the most impressive of the CDF uniforms, was a man Lisa recognized.

More astonishing to her was the fact that he recognized her, too.

"Commander Donnelly," Commodore Gordon Henderson greeted her after all the formal introductions had been made and *Damocles*'s captain and XO officially greeted. "It's good to see you again."

"And you, Commodore," Lisa said, smiling at him through the flood of memories. Henderson had been the senior CDF officer during the unpleasantness at Secour, and despite having been thrown into the deep end of the pool by the attack—which, admittedly, all the rest of them had been, too—he'd held up his end admirably. The last time they'd seen each other had been as *Guardian* prepared to return to Manticore and Henderson prepared to take Casca's newly purchased heavy cruiser home.

Clearly, the Cascan Defense Force's assessment of Henderson's conduct during that time had matched Lisa's own. A navy the size of the Cascans' couldn't have very many commodore slots to hand out, and they'd given one to Henderson. "Congratulations on your promotion, Sir," she added.

"Thank you." Henderson turned back to Marcello. "The reason I asked specifically for you to bring Commander Donnelly, Captain, is that I have some disturbing news, and I wanted to get the commander's input as soon as possible." He gestured behind him at the Customs Clearing Center. "If you'll come with me, I have a conference room waiting."

☆   ☆   ☆

Lunch had been served and eaten, and with two glasses of wine inside him Torrell Baker was even more cheerful and effusive than he'd been aboard *Soleil Azur*.

Which was fine with Llyn. After five wearying days of crimi-nal gang activity—hunting for them, meeting with them, paying them off, and finally convincing them that he wasn't a police plant—Baker's out-of-the-sky lunch invitation had actually been a welcome relief.

Llyn enjoyed the games he played for Axelrod. But sometimes it was nice to just spend a little time with someone who wasn't looking for an opportunity to knife him in the back. Or vice versa.

"Well, have a great stay in Quechua City," Baker said, giving Llyn's hand and arm an final enthusiastic farewell handshake across the table. "I'm off to continue my quest to bring the glories of molecular crafting to the citizens of Casca."

"I hope it goes well," Llyn said. "You'll be here four months, I believe you said?"

"If I'm lucky," Baker said. "A cottage factory like this typically takes three just to get uncrated, assembled, checked, calibrated, and running. If there are any bugs—and there are *always* bugs with something this complicated—it could take me another three or four just to chase them down."

"Well, good luck with that," Llyn said. "And good luck finding a freighter going the right direction when you're ready to go back."

"Hey, the company's paying for it," Baker said philosophically. "If I get stuck here, there are supposed to be some nice vacation spots on the other side of Casca. How are your sales meetings going?"

"Reasonably well," Llyn said. In fact, that part of the mission was pretty well settled, with the gang now sitting back and waiting for the message that would bring them onto the scene.

But Phase Two would require a bit more prep work, and it wouldn't do to have Baker spot him wandering the streets alone when he should be ensconced in meetings or at least surrounded by eager potential buyers.

"I've had some preliminary get-togethers, but two of the main participants are elsewhere on the planet and can't get here for three more days. Guess that means I'm going to have to play tourist a little longer."

Baker harrumphed. "Between you and me, friend, if you think touristing is something you *have* to do, you really need to relax more."

"I had plenty of relaxation time aboard ship," Llyn reminded him.

"Not exactly touristing per se," Baker said. "But to each his own, I guess. Maybe you'll be able to make your deals before the *Soleil Azur*'s ready to leave and you'll be able to skip the tourist thing entirely."

"That's my hope," Llyn confirmed. "If not, I'll just have to wait for the next ship through."

"Well, good luck," Baker said. "If you miss the connection, be sure to look me up. I'll teach you how to tourist properly."

"It's a deal," Llyn said. "And if the deal goes through, first dinner is on me."

"Right." With one final pump of Llyn's arm, Baker turned and headed out of the restaurant into the bright Cascan sunlight.

Llyn followed more slowly, pretending he was looking up something on his tablet. Baker was decent enough company, but the interlude had sufficiently refreshed him and he was ready to get back to work.

Besides, much more interesting at the moment than Baker's prattle was the large group of men and women in Royal Manticoran Navy uniforms passing the restaurant.

His first reflexive reaction upon seeing a swarm of foreign military personnel had been the normal wariness of a man on a covert mission. But it had been quickly clear from their casual behavior and lack of sidearms that they weren't on the hunt for anyone, let alone him. Apparently, his arrival at Casca had simply overlapped with that of a visiting Manticoran warship.

Six years. The number ran through his mind as he let the line of chatting spacers pass and then fell into step behind them. There were a fair number of older faces in the crowd, most of them officers and senior petty officers. Still, most of the men and women were young. Some possibly on their first voyage, many of them probably planning to make a career out of this.

Six years. If the operation kept to Llyn's tentative timetable, in six years the Star Kingdom of Manticore would suddenly find itself under attack by forces beyond their wildest expectations. Certainly forces beyond any hope of their successfully resisting.

If King Michael and the RMN leaders were smart, they would quickly surrender. If they were stupid or stubborn, they would fight.

Many of the young men and women Llyn was passing would be aboard the warships Michael would throw against the invaders. How many of them, he wondered, would be dead hours later?

Six years.

Some of these people had just that much longer to live.

But that wasn't Llyn's problem. Ultimately, their fate was in the hands of their leaders.

He hoped those leaders would make the smart decision.

☆   ☆   ☆

"I apologize for the quality of this recording," Commodore Henderson said as he slipped a data chip into the slot on the display. "They were barely able to get it aboard *Soleil Azur* before she left Haven. In fact, I believe she'd already left orbit and they had to transmit it to her via com laser instead of packing it in with the rest of the pirate data. We've had a couple of days to run it through the scrubbers, but unfortunately this is probably about the best we're going to get."

Lisa felt a flicker of anticipation. Had they actually found evidence of pirate activity in the region?

She hoped so. It would certainly shut up doubters like Chancellor Breakwater.

A second later, her brain caught up with that first reflexive thought. She was *hoping* some helpless merchant ship had been hit and robbed?

The display lit up.

But it wasn't the list of data or fuzzy sensor readings that she'd expected. It was, instead, an overhead view of a small room.

No, not a room. A prison cell.

She caught her breath. The image was a bit fuzzy, but it was clear enough for her to easily recognize the man lying on the bed against the far wall. It was one of the handful of pirates that the Marines had captured at Secour.

She shot a look at Henderson, who nodded. "That's Mota," she identified the figure for Captain Marcello. "One of the survivors of the Secour pirate attack."

"Exactly," Henderson said. "And the only one of their bridge personnel we took alive."

"Yes, I recognize him from the reports," Marcello said. "Who's that with him?"

Lisa frowned. With her full attention on Mota, she hadn't even noticed the hint of another figure at the very edge of the field.

Not that there was much to see. The camera was nearly on top of him, and his back was to it, leaving his face hidden. His hair was a medium-length and somewhat tousled blond, with one ear and the right side of his neck the only other body parts in view. The corner of a mustache was visible, and at the base of the neck she could see was what seemed to be the top of some sort of uniform collar.

"The Havenites have no idea," Henderson said. "That's a prison guard's uniform he's wearing, taken from one of the men who was on duty that night."

"Without the guard's permission, I assume?"

"Without permission or even a memory," Henderson said grimly. "Whatever the intruder used to knock him out, it also erased the section of memory leading up to the attack."

"The prison doesn't have security cameras?"

"Lots of them," Henderson said. "All the recordings were erased. Apparently, he loaded a worm program into the system that first allowed him entry into this restricted area and then erased the recordings of the whole period when he was there."

On the display, Mota gasped, his whole body stiffening. The figure by the camera moved forward, pulling a light plastic chair with him. Positioning it by Mota's head, he sat down.

And as he turned, Lisa finally saw his face.

Her first reaction was a twinge of disappointment. Somehow, she'd expected that a man who'd broken into—*and* apparently then out of—a maximum security prison would look the part: steely-eyed, square-jawed, ruggedly handsome, perhaps with a scar he'd decided to keep as a memento of some former job.

Her second reaction was embarrassment that she'd even thought along such lines. The best master criminals, after all, should look as bland and completely commonplace as possible.

In which case, the man leaning over Mota was about as good a master criminal as she was ever likely to see. Aside from the mustache and blond hair his profile was as unremarkable as she could imagine: dark eyes, average nose, smooth skin, and no scars at all. He might be a little shorter than average—it was hard to tell with him sitting down.

"Hello, Mota," the man said softly. His voice was as nondescript as the rest of him. "I'm going to ask you a few questions. You're going to answer them. All right?"

"All right," Mota said, his voice vague and distant.

"Drugged?" Marcello murmured.

"To the eyeballs," Henderson confirmed.

"Your chief, Guzarwan, contracted with someone to steal a

pair of Havenite ships at Secour," the intruder said. "Who was with him when he made that deal?"

"Vachali," Mota said. "Shora. Dhotrumi."

"No one else?"

"No."

The image abruptly jumped, wavered violently, then settled down. "—refer to during your preparations for the job?"

"They talked about Secour," Mota said. "Ueshiba. Haven. Casca."

"Were all of those conversations and references related to the job?"

"Yes."

The interrogator nodded. "What odd or off-handed comments did any of these men—"

Abruptly, the image dissolved into snow. "Is there anything else?" Marcello prompted after a few seconds of the static.

"There's one more piece," Henderson said. "I'm leaving it running just so you'll see how little time is actually spent in his interrogation before—"

As abruptly as it had arrived, the snow vanished. Mota was now lying back on the bed, his eyes closed. The visitor turned toward the camera, an eerie, self-satisfied smile on his face, and disappeared from view as he left the cell. The cell door closed behind him, and for several seconds they watched Mota sleep. Then, suddenly, his eyes popped open once more, his entire body convulsed, arching sharply before it went abruptly and totally limp. This time, his eyes stayed open, staring sightlessly into infinity, and Lisa swallowed hard. The imagery lasted perhaps another thirty seconds, then vanished again into snow.

"And that's all we've got," Henderson said somberly as he ran the record back to the last view of the murderer. "The techs were able to salvage this much—the cover note Haven attached said they used a back-scrub something or other—but couldn't get anything more before *Soleil Azur* left."

"Of course, that was nearly a year ago," another voice came from the back of the room. "They may have more of it by now."

Lisa shifted in her chair to look behind her. The man who'd spoken was middle-aged, wearing civilian clothing. He wasn't part of the group that had been with Henderson's welcoming committee a few minutes ago.

"And you are?" Marcello prompted.

"Sorry," Henderson apologized. "I meant to introduce you

when he came in. This is Professor Cushing, head of our Military Intelligence and Decryption department."

"Really," Marcello said, sounding interested. "You have a full department? I'm impressed."

"Don't be," Cushing assured him. "It's all of four people, and most of us work there part time. Our main job is to analyze the pirate data that comes in via freighter from you and Haven." He nodded toward the display. "Since this came in along with the Haven data, we caught it along with the regular stuff. I'm hoping more of the recording will be forthcoming."

"I doubt it'll show anything more," Lisa said.

Cushing smiled. "You must have a low opinion of Havenite technical cleverness."

"Not at all," Lisa assured him. "It's just that if it had been vital that we have it, they could have dispatched a fast courier that would have arrived months ago."

"She has a point," Henderson said. "It also follows that they haven't been able to identify the intruder, either." He looked at Lisa. "Which brings us to you, Commander. Of everyone currently on Casca, you were the one who had the most contact with the pirates, both the ones who died there and the handful who were taken alive." He tapped the edge of the display, and the image of the mystery man he'd frozen there. "Is there anything about him that strikes you as familiar? His face, his voice, his mannerisms?"

"You're thinking he might be a brother or relative of one of the other pirates?" Marcello asked.

"Exactly," Henderson said. "Commander?"

Reluctantly, Lisa shook her head. "I'm sorry, Sir, but I don't see anything at all. Of course, my only real contact with Mota was when our TO asked me to sit in while he questioned him about the missile the pirates had had aboard *Wanderer*." A missile the pirates had nearly had an opportunity to use, she remembered with a shiver.

"I know," Henderson said. "That's all right. We knew it was a long shot, but as long as you were here anyway, I thought it was worth trying."

"Nothing from facial recognition, I assume?" Marcello asked.

"Not that the Havenites had found by the time *Soleil Azur* left," Cushing said. "We're running a similar search through our own records, but I'm not expecting us to find anything." He smiled humorlessly. "Our people don't get out very much."

"He must have found what he was looking for, though," Marcello said. "Otherwise, he should reasonably have started working his way down the rest of the prisoner list, and Haven would have a whole string of bodies to deal with instead of just one."

"Point," Henderson said. "Well. Nasty business, but not really our concern, I suppose. If Haven comes up with anything they think we should know they'll presumably pass it on with the next freighter." He tapped another key, and the image disappeared. "To a more pleasant topic. I assume, Captain, that you've been briefed on the arrangements we've made for your people?"

"Yes, Sir," Marcello said. "We appreciate your generosity."

"No problem," Henderson said, waving a hand in casual dismissal. "There's no reason for everyone to have to go back to *Damocles* every night when the Hamilton Hotel's just two blocks from here." He smiled faintly. "I trust they won't make me regret Casca's hospitality?"

"They had better not, Sir," Marcello said ominously.

"I'm sure they'll do the Star Kingdom proud," Henderson said. "Well, then, I think that's all for now. We'll be meeting tomorrow morning at oh-nine-hundred for Professor Cushing's preliminary report on the Havenite data, with a meet-and-greet buffet breakfast starting at oh-seven-hundred. Until then, I hope you'll take the opportunity to enjoy everything Quechua City has to offer."

"Until tomorrow, Sir," Marcello said, standing up.

A minute later the two Manticorans were walking down the street. "And with that," Marcello commented, "I guess it's back to more standard Navy business. As soon as everyone from Shuttle One clears the entry procedure, Commander, I'd like you to escort them to the hotel, just to make sure they know where they're going and what they're doing. I'll do the same for Shuttle Two."

"I can do both shuttles, Sir, if you'd like," Lisa offered.

"I appreciate the offer, Commander," Marcello said. "But you heard Commodore Henderson. We're to enjoy the delights of Quechua City, and I wouldn't dream of asking you to disregard a superior officer's order. Not any longer than necessary, anyway."

"Aye aye, Sir," Lisa said, putting a formal snap into her tone.

"Good," Marcello said. "If it makes you feel better, you'll be in charge of the first drunk the Cascans throw out of one of their bars."

"Thank you, Sir," Lisa said, wrinkling her nose. "I can hardly wait."

CHAPTER FIVE

FOR SOMEONE WHO CLAIMED to be a wrongly ousted head of state, and who supposedly was seeking foreign allies and champions to restore him to power, Llyn mused, General Khetha was proving to be damned hard to find.

The uni-link number listed for the Canaanite Government-in-Exile led to a vague recorded message. The physical address, a modest space on the third floor of a large office building in downtown Quechua City, was closed and had the look of a place that hadn't been visited in weeks or months.

A backtrack on the address led to another uni-link number. That one didn't even have a canned message attached, but simply continued to trill without any answer at all.

A gentle probe into the official Cascan governmental information system proved equally useless. Apparently the Cascans' cultural *live and let live* philosophy extended to political refugees, even the less than savory ones.

Which, in retrospect, should have been a clue to Llyn as to where to start his search for Mota's employer in the first place. The kind of person who was willing to hire pirates would likely find an air of official acceptance mixed with a lack of official surveillance irresistible.

Llyn tried going by the Canaanite office twice more, just before noon and again two hours later. Still locked, still apparently empty. He thought about breaking in, but by this time it was clear that there was unlikely to be anything of real interest behind the door.

In fact, it was starting to look like any contact with Khetha would have to come from the Supreme Chosen One himself.

Which was the main point of visiting the office so often. It was as Llyn left the Canaanite office that final time that he'd finally caught their interest enough for them to put a tail on him.

Patience is a virtue. Llyn's mother had been fond of quoting that one when he was growing up. *The squeaky wheel gets the grease.* That one had come from his uncle.

Personally, Llyn preferred the advice that had been offered by his controller when he'd first been hired by Axelrod of Terra fifteen T-years ago: *Never start something you're not ready to finish.*

Today, it seemed, all three aphorisms were going to come together.

He gave it an hour, mostly for the amusement factor, roaming around the city on foot like a simple visitor to the big city and letting his tails do their job. They were reasonably competent, he saw, swapping out with each other on a regular basis and occasionally switching hats or shirts between shifts to obscure their identities even more. They also knew the city well, utilizing short-cuts and alleys to get ahead of him and even anticipating which shops he might stop to browse at.

For a while Llyn toyed with the idea of intercepting one of them in one of those alleys, which would show his own competence as well as providing the venue for a private chat. But with a man like General Khetha running the show, such a confrontation might quickly turn violent, and that wasn't the kind of competence Llyn was trying to demonstrate today.

Clearly, a more civilized approach was called for. And so, after leading his tails around for an hour without them making an approach, he found a comfortable bench in one of the city's expansive parks and used his uni-link to record a message onto a data chip. When he'd finished, he set the chip down on the bench and walked leisurely out of the park and into a restaurant-intensive street.

He was studying one of the window-display menus, trying to decide what sounded good, when his uni-link trilled. He pulled it out and keyed it on. "Yes?"

"What do you want with the Supreme Chosen One?" a harsh voice demanded.

"Oh, hello," Llyn said calmly. "Good; you got my message. Tell me, is this Tan Shirt or Floppy Hat?"

There was a slight pause. "What?"

"Tan Shirt or Floppy Hat," Llyn repeated. "Those were your most obvious tags when you first started tailing me. If you'd prefer, I can call you Blue Shirt and Pinstripe. Never mind—I see Blue Shirt behind me, and he's not on a uni-link, so you must be Pinstripe."

"You haven't answered my question," Pinstripe growled. He was back on balance and sounding more annoyed and suspicious than ever. "Who are you?"

"I thought my message already answered that," Llyn said. "My name is Noman. I have a deal to offer General Khetha that will—"

"There is no such person," Pinstripe snapped.

Llyn frowned. "I assure you, I'm very real."

"I mean this General person," Pinstripe bit out. "He is the Supreme Chosen One. You will address him as such."

Llyn sighed. "I have a deal to offer the Supreme Chosen One," he corrected, "that will return him to Canaan and once again make that title official."

There was a moment of silence. Probably, Llyn thought, Pinstripe was trying to decide whether or not he should point out that the title was eternal and didn't need anyone to make it official. "Describe this deal," he said at last.

"I'll be happy to," Llyn said. "But to the Supreme Chosen One. No one else."

Pinstripe snorted. "You think him a fool?"

"I think him tired of being trapped on a third-rate world in a fourth-rate region of space," Llyn countered. "And of course I'm not suggesting that he should meet me alone. That *would* be foolish, for both of us. No, he's welcome to bring all the guards he wants. But as I said in my message, they need to be people he absolutely trusts."

"He trusts all those who stand loyally at his side."

"That's nice," Llyn said. "But there's loyalty, and there's loyalty. And when finances are involved...well, I don't expect you to understand. You're a soldier, and soldiers obey orders without question. But the Supreme Chosen One has dealt with politicians. He'll understand what I mean."

There was another pause. "I will pass on your message," Pinstripe said. "The Supreme Chosen One will then decide."

"That's all I ask," Llyn said. "One other thing. On that data chip you picked up is a hidden file that can be unlocked with the name *Khetha*. In that file is the combination to a lock box in Quechua City Bank containing blue diamonds worth approximately fifty thousand Cascan sols."

There was a derisive snort. "You expect his price to be so low?"

"Not at all," Llyn assured him. "It's a gift, free and clear, for him to have whether he chooses to meet with me or not. Think of it as earnest money, a down payment on a venture which will yield a vastly more valuable reward for both of us."

"I will tell him," Pinstripe said. "If he wishes to continue with this conversation, you will be contacted."

"Thank you," Llyn said. "Now, if I may beg one small indulgence?"

Another snort. "Let me guess. You wish us to stop following you?"

"Not at all," Llyn said. "It's your day—if you want to spend it walking behind me, knock yourselves out. I just wanted some advice." He pointed to the window display he was still facing. "The Kung Pao chicken here. Is it any good?"

☆   ☆   ☆

"Okay," Electronic Warfare Tech Second Gregor Redko said as he tapped a couple of final keys on the personal Charles Townsend—"Chomps" to his friends and fellow petty officers— had brought down from *Damocles.* "Should be up in a second. I assume you want to start with the pirate data?"

"Let's see if we can find a summary first," Chomps said, glancing reflexively around the room. The two other spacers who'd been assigned to their hotel suite were long gone, headed out into the fleshpots of Quechua City in search of local color, local drinks, and probably local women.

But the sheer audacity of what he and Redko were doing had slathered a thick layer of paranoia onto Chomps's gut, and he found himself increasingly checking to make sure no one was watching them.

He looked back at the personal just as the scramble of nonsense characters on the display reformed themselves into orderly columns of clear English.

"There you go," Redko said with satisfaction. "Okay, you wanted a summary. Let's see..."

"Wait a second," Chomps said as an item marked with a pair of red stars caught his eye. "That one looks interesting. Can you open it?"

"Probably," Redko said. "It's the same encryption the Havenites are using with their other official stuff. Well, mostly the same, anyway. Looks like a video, though. Unless they found some pirates carousing in port, I doubt it's any of our interest."

"Probably not," Chomps agreed. Still, something in his paranoia-infused gut was rumbling at him. "Play it anyway."

It was indeed a video. But it wasn't pirates, carousing or otherwise. It was a spotty, glitchy, seriously scrubbed recording from some kind of prison cell.

They watched it all the way through in silence. An increasingly dark, grim silence.

And when it finally ended...

For a long moment the two men just sat in silence, staring at the blank display. Then, Redko stirred in his seat. "Was that what I think it was?" he asked uncertainly. "Did we just see a man *die*?"

Chomps took a careful breath. "I do believe we did," he agreed, feeling a deep chill in his stomach.

Which on some level was strange. He'd been in the Royal Manticoran Navy for ten years, during which time he'd lost at least five of his close colleagues to accidents or disease. Not even counting the whole *Phobos* tragedy and debacle. Death was supposed to be something military men and women were trained to handle.

But seeing someone die when a crane slipped was a horrible, tragic accident. Watching someone slowly slip away on a recording was somehow different.

Especially when the odds were good the man had been murdered. That took things to an entirely different level of horrible.

Worst of all was the killer's smile. That hollow, hard-edged smile on his face just before he left the field of view.

And *that*, Chomps realized suddenly, was what was really driving the chill into his gut. The sense of genuine, casual evil coming off that smile.

"So what do we do?" Redko asked.

Chomps rubbed his cheek. When he'd first agreed to do his uncle this favor, it had been a simple data hack-and-grab. Nothing confidential or groundshattering, and certainly nothing the Star Kingdom wouldn't have anyway in a couple of months when *Damocles* returned to Manticore.

And this wasn't their business anyway. This was Havenite governmental and legal business. Nothing to do with Manticore.

On the other hand...

Information on the whole Secour incident had been spotty, at least the stuff that had been released to the general public. But Chomps knew *Guardian* had been involved, and his old friend Travis Uriah Long had been aboard her at the time. His part had undoubtedly been minimal, of course, given he was only a petty officer third class at the time.

Or maybe it hadn't. While his name hadn't shown up anywhere in the official report, it was shortly after Secour that Long was suddenly plucked from the ranks of petty officers and dropped into OCS. *Someone* must have been impressed enough with him to have engineered that.

And now, one of the pirates from that incident had been murdered. Travis might like to know what had happened.

With luck, he'd be interested enough to trade what Chomps knew for a few details of his own about the Secour thing. "Let's start with the spaceport records," he told Redko. "We can get into those, right?"

"Probably," Redko said cautiously. "Uh..."

"And we'll want to see if there's more information in the Havenite mail packet," Chomps continued before Redko could assemble the words for a proper objection. "We can download everything, right?"

"I—we can get most of it, probably," Redko said, and Chomps could hear the rising level of discomfort in his voice. "But we were only supposed to get the pirate data. This is... not that."

"I know," Chomps assured him. "Oh, come on, Reddy. Where's your spirit of adventure?"

"Walking three steps behind my spirit of not wanting to get court-martialed," Redko countered.

"Fine," Chomps said. "You can go. Just leave me the personal."

Redko hissed out a frustrated sigh. "Like you have the first idea how to really do this," he said in a resigned tone. "Fine. Just remember, you owe me."

"Don't worry," Chomps said grimly. "I doubt either of us is ever going to forget anything that happens today." Especially, he added silently, the killer's smile as he walked away from his crime. "Come on—let's pull that data before someone spots the hack."

☆   ☆   ☆

Llyn had finished his Kung Pao chicken and was looking over his city map when his uni-link again trilled.

It was Pinstripe. "The Supreme Chosen One has agreed to see you," he said without preamble. "Be at the corner of Fourteenth and Castillon at seven o'clock tomorrow morning. You'll be transported from there to the place of meeting."

"Excellent," Llyn said, impressed in spite of himself. That was quick work for a measly fifty thousand in bribe money. The Canaanite Government-in-Exile was possibly draining its funds faster than he'd realized. That could be a good sign, or a *very* good sign. "Please thank the Supreme Chosen One for his generosity. I trust you made it clear that he needed to bring only his most trusted people?"

"The Supreme Chosen One neither needs nor appreciates the unnecessary repetition of words," Pinstripe growled. "Fourteenth and Castillon, seven o'clock."

"I'll be there," Llyn said, resisting the urge to point out that that, too, was an unnecessary repetition of words.

The uni-link went dead.

With a sigh, Llyn put the uni-link away. Khetha wouldn't be at that corner, of course. Nor would he be in the vehicle they sent. No, they would put Llyn in a car or van and drive him to some secret, undisclosed location where the Supreme Chosen One would be waiting. They would have their talk, and then Llyn would be bundled back into the vehicle for the ride back. Depending on how eager Khetha was, or how clever he thought he was, the trip could be short or could be unnecessarily long.

Because despite having the entirety of the planet to lose himself in, Khetha wasn't hundreds of kilometers away from Quechua City. In fact, he probably wasn't even skulking on the outskirts or in the suburbs. He would want to be close to the communication, business, and political center of Casca. More importantly, he'd want quick access to a shuttle that could get him off-planet and to whatever ship he surely had stashed out there.

No, he was right here in the center of town. Possibly within sight of the restaurant where Llyn was currently sitting.

Paranoid people were so predictable.

Not that paranoia would do Khetha any good. By this time tomorrow, no matter how cautiously he played the game, Llyn would have the information he'd come all the way out to the Haven Sector to obtain.

And the Supreme Chosen One would be dead.

According to the city map, there was a shop two blocks away that sold handmade formal-wear scarves. Collecting his things, making sure to leave a good tip with his payment, he headed back out into the sunshine.

☆ ☆ ☆

The evening was still young, and so far the men and women of HMS *Damocles* seemed to be behaving themselves.

So far.

Letting her gaze drift across the crowded Hamilton Hotel ballroom, listening to the buzz of conversation and jumping a bit with every slightly raucous laugh, Lisa sent a silent prayer skyward that they would continue to do so. The party, which was theoretically supposed to be more or less confined to the hotel, had already spilled out into the streets, a development which the Cascans' live-and-let-live philosophy seemed perfectly fine with.

Still, spacers were spacers, they'd been in space a long time, and the last thing Lisa wanted was for the Navy to earn a bad reputation with their Cascan hosts on their very first night off the ship.

Tomorrow things would be different. Tomorrow it would be back to business, with the start of an intensive regimen of meetings and cultural events. The Manticoran and Cascan officers and spacers would be visiting each others' ships, with plenty of time allotted for talking shop and the exchange of procedural and operational suggestions. Later in the month there would be some tourist trips planned, with the locals no doubt hoping the Manticorans would boost their individual slices of the economy along the way.

But tonight was the first night of shore leave, and their CDF hosts had insisted on throwing a party.

There was a movement from her side, and Lisa looked up as Commander Shiflett sat down in the next seat. "TO," the *Damocles*'s XO greeted her. "Aren't you supposed to be down the street at Commodore Henderson's little get-together?"

"I was there half an hour ago, Ma'am," Lisa said. "I was given to understand it was a casual drop-in, drop-out affair."

"Theoretically, yes," Shiflett said in a tone that suggested she didn't entirely agree with that assessment. "I think the captain would appreciate it if you spent a little more time there." She nodded toward the mass of spacers and petty officers filling the room. "Not, shall we say, slumming."

Lisa winced. Shiflett was a cousin to one of the Peers—Lisa forgot which one, exactly—and she had a definite Peerage slant to her ideas of how Navy officers should behave. As well as who she thought they should behave with. "I wanted to make sure things were going smoothly, Ma'am," she said in explanation.

"Very commendable," Shiflett said. "But that's what petty officers are for."

"I understand, Ma'am," Lisa said. "But the captain gave me responsibility—"

She broke off as one of the faces across the room suddenly seemed to jump out at her. Plain, average, topped by a neat flow of short blond hair...

An instant later, the face registered: Coxswain Second Class Plover. Definitely not the murderer from the Havenite recording.

"TO?"

"Sorry, Ma'am," Lisa apologized. "I thought I saw something."

And instantly felt like an idiot. Because there was no way the murderer could have gotten from Haven to Casca this quickly. Not unless he'd had a fast courier standing by at his beck and call.

Or had been aboard *Soleil Azur* herself.

Lisa frowned. He *hadn't* been aboard *Soleil Azur*, had he? Surely someone had checked on that.

Hadn't they?

"Sorry, Ma'am," Lisa said again. "You're right. I should go back."

"Good," Shiflett said. "Let's go."

The lounge that Commodore Henderson had set up for the senior officers' get-together was more elegant, more refined, and far quieter than the bash going on down the street. Lisa found Captain Marcello near one of the buffet tables, chatting with Commodore Henderson, each man holding a glass of some fragrant wine. "There you are," Marcello greeted Lisa as she came up. "We were just wondering where you'd gotten to."

"I was checking on the spacers' party going on down the street," Lisa said. "Commodore, this is probably a silly question, but someone *did* check *Soleil Azur*'s crew and passenger lists to make sure Mota's murderer wasn't aboard, right?"

"I'm sure they did," Henderson assured her. His smile seemed to go a little more brittle. "On the other hand, empires have risen and fallen because someone was *sure* something crucial had been done." He craned his neck, looking around the room. "Come on—I see Commissioner Peirola over there. He's head of the Department of Ports and Customs."

Commissioner Peirola was a short, plump man, the sort who clearly loved the good life and didn't care who knew it. He was standing in the middle of a small circle of officers, some from *Damocles*, others wearing Cascan Defense Force uniforms, his arms waving expansively yet without spilling so much as a drop from his glass. As Lisa and the others approached she discovered he was discoursing on the joys of imported wines. A stray and probably unfair thought flicked across Lisa's mind: that Peirola had taken the post of customs chief mainly so that he would have first crack at any delicacies that might arrive at the Quechua City spaceport.

"Of *course* they were all checked," he huffed after Henderson finally found an opening in the monologue to ask his question. "Standard procedure, my dear sir. Not to mention plain common sense."

"Of course," Henderson said. "You wouldn't mind checking again, would you? Just to set our minds at ease."

Peirola gave a theatrical sigh. "This *is* supposed to be a party, you know. But I suppose our brave men and women in uniform never rest. Come—my tablet's over with my coat."

Still holding his glass, he led them to the cloak room and pulled a compact tablet from one of the coat pockets. He dithered a moment, then carefully set the glass on top of the hat ledge and turned on the tablet. A quick punching in of password and access codes—

"All right," he said, turning the tablet around for the others to see. "Here are the crew photos . . . here are the passengers. Whose file do you want me to pull up?"

"Commander?" Henderson invited.

Lisa scowled, again feeling like an idiot. None of the faces on Peirola's tablet looked like the killer on the prison recording. "None of them, Sir," she said. "Sorry. It was an odd thought."

"That's all right." Henderson gestured to Peirola. "Thank you, Commissioner."

"No problem," Peirola said. He turned the tablet back toward him, reached for the power switch.

And paused, a sudden frown creasing his forehead. "Commissioner?" Henderson asked.

"A moment, Commodore," Peirola said, still frowning. "It looks like someone's been into the packet the *Soleil Azur* brought in last week."

"Someone who?" Henderson asked.

"Someone whose call mark I don't recognize," Peirola said. "Someone... no. Someone who hasn't *got* a legitimate call mark."

"You saying you've been *hacked*?" Marcello asked.

"Unless someone's changed their call mark," Peirola said, still studying the tablet.

Lisa and Marcello exchanged glances. "And this doesn't worry you?" Marcello persisted.

Peirola shrugged. "Not really. A fair amount of the data in the packet is public record—news from Haven, the League, and elsewhere. We don't charge for most of that, you know. Or maybe you didn't. As for personal notes and business transactions, well, it's up to the parties involved to encrypt that properly, and most of them have done so."

"What about the pirate data?" Lisa asked.

"That's in with the government data, which are the most heavily encrypted files in the lot," Peirola said. "I shouldn't have to tell *you* that—I presume you have the same key as we do."

"I don't think that's what Commander Donnelly was asking," Marcello said. "I believe she was wondering if those files had also been hacked."

"Oh." Peirola peered at Lisa a moment, then returned his attention to his tablet. "Let me see... yes, I believe they were. In fact, it looks like those were the first group of files that were tapped into."

"Including the video?" Lisa asked.

"There's a video?" Peirola asked, looking up again. "They caught some pirates on a *video*?"

"Not exactly," Marcello said. "Can you see what else they got?"

"I don't *know* that they got *anything*," Peirola said, a little testily. "All I can tell is that they got in. I can't tell from here whether anything in there was copied."

"Then you'd best go someplace where you can, hadn't you?" Henderson said.

"Really, Commodore, I don't think it's that serious," Peirola protested. "Just because someone got past the firewalls and copied some files doesn't mean they'll be able to access them. The encryptions are unbreakable—trust me. They're not going to be able to get anything critical."

"How do you know?" Henderson countered. "I hardly think our hacker is just someone who's impatient to get their mail. This needs to be looked into. As in, *now*."

Peirola sighed. But he clearly knew the discussion was over. "Very well, Commodore." He threw a last, longing look at his wine glass, then tucked his coat under his arm and hurried through the sea of uniforms toward the exit.

"Anything we can do?" Marcello asked.

"I don't think so," Henderson said, his eyes following Peirola across the room. "Peirola's right about the encryption—aside from the public information like news bulletins most everything in a mail packet is going to be unreadable."

"Unless the hacker already has the decryption code."

"True," Henderson conceded. "Either way, it looks like there's some critical timing involved here. Otherwise, why not wait until the particular message file of interest was delivered and grab it then?"

"Hasn't everything been delivered already?" Marcello asked, frowning. "It's been a week since it arrived, hasn't it?"

"Your question implies a much more efficient mail system than we have here," Henderson said. "Most of the files are delivered within a couple of hours, but there have been cases where something got hung up in the system for a couple of days. Bureaucratic or computer problem—I don't know which. We get so few mail deliveries in a typical year that apparently no one's had enough incentive to fix it. There's also a *will-call* option for people who want a message left in the central clearinghouse until they use their passcode to retrieve it."

"Odd arrangement," Marcello rumbled. "Why not just collect it and just read it later?"

"There are a few reasons," Henderson said. "The legitimate ones usually involve business transactions where both parties want to see the message or data at the same time, and in each other's presence. The less-than-legitimate ones are criminal groups who don't want a fixed address that can be tracked."

"A question, Sir?" Lisa spoke up. "Is it possible that the hacker didn't go in to *find* something, but to *delete* something?"

Henderson huffed out a breath. "Wouldn't *that* be cute?"

"You still wondering about the passengers or crew?" Marcello asked.

"Or else something in the pirate data," Lisa said.

"Well, that one, at least, we can check," Henderson said. "We copied those files over as soon as *Soleil Azur* arrived in the system. A simple check will show whether there's any difference between our copy and the original."

He squared his shoulders. "In fact, I think I'll go over to my office and do that right now. Captain Marcello, Commander Donnelly; please enjoy the rest of the evening."

He headed off in Peirola's wake. "I think, TO," Marcello commented, "that our mail-pickup duty just got interesting."

"Yes, Sir," Lisa said. "Orders, Sir?"

Marcello pursed his lips. "Just a suggestion that you follow Henderson's suggestion and enjoy the evening," he said. "I'm guessing that starting tomorrow we're going to be joining the Cascans on a snipe hunt."

CHAPTER SIX

THE BUILDINGS AT THE INTERSECTION of Fourteenth and Castillon were, in clockwise order, a café, a small-appliance repair center, a breakfast/coffee shop, and a specialty food mart. All were still closed at seven in the morning, though the breakfast shop was getting ready to open. The lack of traffic was probably why Khetha's people had chosen this particular place and time.

There were good reasons, as well as ominous ones, why the Supreme Chosen One might not want witnesses to the rendezvous. Fortunately, Llyn had reasons of his own for going along with that strategy.

He'd had a private bet with himself that, despite Pinstripe's statement that he would be picked up, that he might instead be hustled into one of the buildings on or near the corner. Zinc-plate dictators like Khetha liked to think they were being clever.

But in this case, security concerns apparently outweighed the urge to impress the visitor with the Supreme Chosen One's cunning. The ground car that pulled up to Llyn's side as he reached the corner was large, heavy-looking, and had the traditional darkened windows of such errands. The door opened as it rolled to a halt, and a large figure in the shadows beckoned to him.

Llyn climbed in. The inviting hand changed position, turning palm-upwards in silent command. In equally silent compliance, Llyn handed over his uni-link, stood still for the quick weapons wanding, then reached behind him and pulled the door closed.

They were rolling again almost before the door was completely shut. "Nice vehicle," Llyn commented, peering across the darkened interior. Aside from the large man sitting beside him, there was only one other person in the rear part of the car, a thin man occupying a drop-down jump seat across from the two of them. An opaque barrier blocked the view of the driver and whoever else might be in the front. "I appreciate not having to go with the bag-over-the-head routine."

One of Khetha's mid-level associates would probably have made some polite but neutral comment. A higher-level associate might have tried a gentle probe, a casual question as to whether Llyn did this sort of thing often. Simple, low-level guards would say nothing.

Llyn's companions said nothing.

Which was as Llyn had expected. A clever despot, as opposed to one who merely thought himself clever, might have sent someone to sound out the mysterious visitor during the drive. That could have been inconvenient, on a number of different levels. Not only might a competent intermediary have smelled the proverbial rat before Llyn ever got to Khetha himself, but it might also have left a potentially embarrassing witness out of easy reach. But Llyn's warning about Khetha letting only the most trusted people in on this had apparently trumped the dictator's good sense. It appeared he *had* alerted only his most trusted henchmen to the meeting.

The probable bonus was that there was now a good chance he'd alerted *all* of his trusted subordinates. That would put them all in one handy spot when the time came. It was so convenient to deal with someone predictable.

Of course, if Khetha brought his closest cronies he would also have a of number of armed and dangerous men in attendance. But that, too, was perfectly fine with Llyn. He'd had a week to read everything the Cascan archives had on Canaanites in general and Khetha in particular, and he had a pretty fair feel for how this meeting would be staged and formatted.

The first tick on that mental checklist was Khetha's eagerness overcoming caution and cleverness, embodied in the fact that the drive turned out to be short. Barely fifteen minutes after leaving the rendezvous the car pulled to a stop. The man across from Llyn opened the door and stepped out, glanced around, then motioned the passenger to join him. Surreptitiously crunching the outer coating on the pill he'd tucked into his cheek before leaving his hotel, Llyn did so.

He found himself in a tunnel running from the street to what was probably an underground parking garage. He was still looking around when the other man from the back seat exited and closed the door, and the car took a sharp left into a curved connecting tunnel, presumably heading back to the street.

The thin man got a grip on Llyn's arm and headed down the tunnel, walking briskly toward an unmarked door halfway down to the left. Llyn followed in silence, the third man bringing up the rear. As they approached the door it opened, and Pinstripe and Blue Shirt, Llyn's tails from the previous day, stepped out into the tunnel. Pinstripe gave the area a quick scan as the new-comers approached, then gestured them inside. Beyond the door was a short hallway leading to another door, this one clearly heavily armored.

The outer door behind Llyn closed with a solid-sounding click. Pinstripe brushed past them to the big door, with Blue Shirt now playing rearguard, and pulled it open.

Beyond the door was a small room, metal-walled and probably soundproof, with a long table in the center. At the far end of the table sat a man in a muted military tunic with rows of medals plastered across his chest: General Amador Khetha, the Supreme Chosen One himself. Just around the corner of the table to the general's right was a second man, considerably more plump, dressed in casual civilian garb. Both were watching Llyn closely as he and his escort stepped into the room. Standing behind Khetha was a pair of large men, one on either side, their hands folded loosely in front of them in standard bodyguard stance. They were watching Llyn even more closely and suspiciously than the general. A third chair waited at the near end of the table, clearly intended for Llyn.

On the far left side of the room was a short table holding a steaming samovar and a row of mugs.

Llyn suppressed a smile. Tick number two on his list. The Canaanites had a whole spectrum of hospitality rituals, which varied according to the social and economic status of the two sides of a meeting. The samovar-and-tea setup was reserved for first meetings between strangers who might be expected to become associates in business or politics. The subtle nuances would be lost on someone who wasn't intimately familiar with Canaanite etiquette, but all indications were that Khetha had clung to the customs of home with the deathgrip of an involuntary expatriate. Llyn had guessed that Khetha would follow that pattern, even though the dictator would have no way of knowing whether or not his guest understood all of the implications.

Or perhaps this was a test, something Khetha had deliberately set up to see just how thoroughly Llyn had researched his hoped-for associate and Canaanite culture.

Ultimately, though, it didn't matter. There were other approaches Khetha could have taken, and Llyn had plans to cover each of them. But the samovar gambit would certainly be the easiest to play off of.

It was always so gratifying when the fish baited his own hook.

Up to now, Khetha and his men had had most of the initiative. Time to even things up a bit. "Good morning, General Khetha," Llyn said briskly as he stepped to the table and sat down. The pill had started to kick in, and he could feel his heart pounding almost painfully in his chest. "I appreciate you seeing me on such short notice." He cocked his head. "I'm sorry. Should I be addressing you as 'Your Worship'?"

The plump man bristled. But Khetha merely smiled. "'General' will do," he said. There was movement to Llyn's right and left as his two companions from the car took up guard positions to his sides. From behind him came more sound of movement, and reflected from the wall behind Khetha he caught a fuzzy glimpse of Pinstripe shoving the door closed, leaving him and Blue Shirt outside in the corridor. "Please don't assume my presence here means I necessarily have any interest in doing business with you," Khetha continued. "You're here simply because you intrigue me." A faint, unpleasant smile touched the corners of his lips. "You had best hope you continue to do so. Let's start with your name."

"I'm afraid that would mean nothing to you," Llyn said. "More well-known, at least in the upper-level circles where the true decisions of the galaxy are made, is the name Pointer."

The man at Khetha's side snorted. "I believe that's a breed of dog."

"Correct," Llyn said, inclining his head to the other. "And be assured that I'll be as doggedly persistent in my service to you as my four-legged namesake." He shifted his attention back to Khetha. "But first things first." He reached into his jacket.

And froze, warned by the sudden movement at the corner of his eye. Carefully, leaving his hand where it was, he looked at the guard to his left.

The man had brushed back the right-hand flap of his jacket and was gripping the butt of a side-holstered pistol. A Paxlane 405 10mm caseless, Llyn's brain automatically identified it.

"My apologies, General," he said. Slowly, he eased his hand out of the jacket to show the data chip between his first two fingers. "As your time is valuable, I thought it only fair that I compensate you for your generosity in allowing me some of it." With a careful flick of his wrist, he sent the chip sailing across the table to land in front of Khetha.

The general made no move toward it. "Ulobo?" he said.

With a brief wrinkling of his nose, the plump man carefully picked it up. He pulled a tablet from his jacket and plugged the chip into the slot. "Another lock box combination," he said, peering at the display. "Purportedly containing another fifty thousand in diamonds."

"A very generous gift," Khetha said, eyeing Llyn thoughtfully.

"Merely gratitude for your own generosity," Llyn assured him. Especially since that gift had also shown him exactly where one of his guards' weapons was located. Fifty thousand was a very fair price to pay for that kind of information. "May I take it that means you're granting me a hearing?"

Khetha smiled. "Certainly. You have ten minutes."

"Then I'll be brief." Llyn nodded toward the samovar. "I wonder if I could also prevail on your hospitality to the extent of a cup of tea?"

Khetha smiled again, this one with a hint of triumph flavoring it. By asking for tea instead of waiting for it to be offered, Llyn had lowered his status vis-à-vis his host's, which had now put Khetha into a stronger bargaining position. If the visitor knew the custom, Khetha had just won a point.

If he didn't, well, it wouldn't affect the upcoming negotiations at all. But it would still mean a great deal to Khetha.

And maybe that was all the Supreme Chosen One really cared about. People who'd lost almost everything gripped what little they still had even more tightly.

The nuances and motivations of this particular bit didn't matter a frog's damn to Llyn. All he cared about was getting some tea.

And now, having won the round, Khetha could afford to be a thoroughly gracious host.

"Of course," he said, gesturing to Ulobo. Scowling some more, clearly still wary of the visitor, the plump man pushed back his chair and headed for the sideboard. "Your minutes are running," the general added.

"The situation is simple," Llyn said. "Four T-years ago you were deposed and exiled from Canaan. Ever since then you've been looking for a way to return and reestablish your rule. Over the course of that time, you must certainly have made the acquaintance of some large pirate or mercenary groups whom you hope to interest in supporting that effort."

"We've had contact with one or two," Khetha said. "Most of them are too constrained by legalities or outmoded ethics for my needs. All of the others are quite expensive." He gestured to the data chip. "I appreciate your contribution to that fund."

"And therein lies the crux of your problem," Llyn said. "As you say—" he broke off, nodding Ulobo his thanks as the other set a steaming mug of tea in front of him "—the most effective mercenary groups don't come cheap." He paused again, picking up the mug by its top and pretending to take a sip.

Not that he had any intention of actually drinking any of it, of course. Not only was it too hot to touch without burning his tongue, but he had no idea what secret ingredients Khetha or Ulobo might have put into it. Lowering the mug, he set it back onto the table.

And as he did so he dropped the two small capsules he'd been palming into the steaming liquid.

"*My* problem, on the other hand, is just the opposite," he continued, casually pushing the mug a few centimeters farther from him. "My client finds himself in need of one of these, shall we say, below-the-radar groups. And while he has plenty of money—as you've no doubt already noted—he has no idea where and how to contact one." He pursed his lips. "Nor do I."

"A dilemma, indeed," Khetha said. "How do you intend to resolve it?"

"My hope is that you and I can build our respective problems into a pair of solutions," Llyn said. Was the pounding of his heart starting to ease up a little? "You have contact information. I have access to money. I propose that you offer me an introduction to the most promising of these groups. In return—" He smiled. "My client will provide the funding for your return to power."

Ulobo sat a little taller in his chair. "The *entire* funding?" he asked disbelievingly.

"The entire funding," Llyn confirmed. Yes; his heart was definitely slowing from its earlier frenetic pace.

"You're very generous with your client's money," Khetha said, his expression giving nothing away. "One has to wonder if he would approve."

"No worries," Llyn said. "I have his complete confidence, along with financial carte blanche. He also knows that the timing at our end is critical—the longer we delay in making a deal with your mercenaries, the less profit he'll realize. Assuming the operation is launched within the next, say, five years, his profit will be high enough that paying the extra fee for the mercenaries to reestablish you on Canaan would be hardly noticeable."

"It must be a high-profit venture, indeed," Khetha said thoughtfully.

"It is."

"And you could easily spend those five years you mention simply exchanging messages with mercenary groups in hopes of finding one which will meet your needs."

"As you said, my dilemma," Llyn said. "You, in contrast, have nothing to lose and everything to gain by agreeing to this joint venture." He smiled. "And the gain won't *just* be your return to power."

"What do you mean?" Ulobo asked.

"He means," Khetha said, "that if his client pays all costs, then the fund we've been building will no longer have to go to the Volsungs." He cocked an eyebrow. "And no one outside this room would ever need to know that."

Ulobo's face cleared. "Ah."

"Which fund, I'm guessing, already runs into the hundreds of thousands of sols, Solarian credits, or whatever," Llyn said, suppressing a smile. So now he had a name: Volsungs. One step closer to making his move.

"You're still asking a great deal," Khetha said, "on what basically amounts to your word."

"Not really," Llyn said. "The worst possible case is that I take the name and contact information and you never hear from me again. In that event, all you've lost is a little time before your return. Time, I might point out, which your enemies are using to rebuild Canaan's economy. Actually, now that I think about it, the longer you wait, the more you'll have to return to." He nodded toward the chip still in Ulobo's tablet. "And you'll still be a hundred thousand sols ahead."

Khetha looked at Ulobo. The plump man still didn't look exactly happy, but he gave a reluctant nod.

"But all this presumes that your merc group has the resources my client needs," Llyn continued before either of the others could speak. "I've laid out my cards. Time to lay out one or two of yours."

Khetha inclined his head. "What do you wish to know?"

"Let's start with their location," Llyn said. "Planet, city—all of that."

Khetha pursed his lips, then gave a small shrug. "They're headquartered in Rochelle on the planet Telmach. That's in the Silesian Confederacy—"

"I know where it is," Llyn said. Interrupting a despot's ego was risky, but he had no choice. His heartbeat was nearly back to normal, and he needed to close this off quickly. Any minute now Ulobo or one of the guards would notice that his hands were starting to feel a little numb. "What kind of resources do they have? Specifically, how many warships and what types?"

"They have what you need," Khetha assured him.

"How many?" Llyn repeated.

Khetha's eyes narrowed. But he merely nodded to Ulobo, who tapped a fresh access code into his tablet. "They have four battle-cruisers," the plump man reported, peering at the page that came up. "Cruisers—let me count—eight of them, light and heavy, plus ten destroyers and frigates. They also have three troop transports and a handful of other auxiliaries."

"Excellent," Llyn said. Yes; Ulobo's hands were definitely moving slower than they had earlier. Fortunately, his brain was slowing down in the same proportion, which meant that his recognition of his puzzling clumsiness should take another few seconds. "That should do nicely. And you have contact names and recognition codes for someone in the group?"

"Not just *someone*." Ulobo tapped his tablet. "Our contact is the head of the group, Admiral Cutler Gensonne himself."

"I'm impressed," Llyn said. There was no harm in soothing Khetha's ego a bit, after his impolite interruption a moment ago. "I presume you also have a ship standing by that can take us to him?"

Ulobo frowned. "Excuse me?"

"A ship," Llyn repeated. He was pretty sure the answer was yes, given the Supreme Chosen One's hasty departure from Canaan four years ago. But he needed to be absolutely sure. "One that's sufficiently fueled and stocked to travel to Telmach."

"Of course we have a ship," Ulobo said uncertainly, sending a frown toward his boss. "You're not suggesting we leave *now*, are you?"

"Not at all," Llyn said. "At least, not the *we* part."

And as Ulobo's frown deepened, Llyn reached up to his left, brushed aside the flap of his guard's jacket, and yanked the Paxlane 405 from its holster.

The guard tried to stop him. He really did. He tried to step out of Llyn's reach, tried to swing his hand down to grab Llyn's wrist.

But he had no chance. The soporific that Llyn had released into the air through his steaming mug of tea had turned the man's muscles into mush, his judgment and self-awareness into colorless fog, and his reflexes and entire nervous system into slow-flowing mud. Llyn evaded his fumbling hand with ease before firing off a point-blank shot into the man's chest that ended any hope of resistance. With the report from the shot still echoing across the room, Llyn tracked the gun in a one-eighty-degree arc, taking out the guard to Khetha's right, then the guard to his left, and finally the guard to Llyn's right. All three men collapsed to the floor still fumbling uselessly at their holstered weapons.

Khetha was clawing his own tunic open, his expression that of an angry and desperate thundercloud, and Ulobo was cringing in helpless horror, when Llyn's final two shots sent them to join their bodyguards in hell.

An instant later Llyn was out of his chair, leveling his gun at the door behind him. If the room wasn't as soundproof as he'd assumed, Pinstripe and Blue Shirt could be charging in at any second to find out what all the shooting was about.

But the door remained closed. Either the room *was* soundproof, or else it wasn't abnormal to hear the sounds of violence coming from inside. Keeping his eyes and gun on the door, Llyn backed around the table to Ulobo's glassy-eyed corpse. He picked up the tablet, wiped the few stray drops of blood off onto the back of Ulobo's jacket, and took a close look.

The ever-present danger with this kind of operation was that the soporific's timetable might have made him jump the gun, that Ulobo might have been rattling off the warship stats from memory. But no. The Volsung Mercenaries file was still sitting there, wide open to the universe, with all the necessary contact names, uni-link numbers, addresses, passcodes, and even copies of the correspondence Khetha and Admiral Gensonne had exchanged across the void over the past couple of years.

And with that, Llyn had everything he needed to open his own negotiations with the Volsungs for Axelrod's covert operation against Manticore. Best of all, by using Khetha's contact information, any backtrack anyone might attempt in the future would dead-end here in this room on Casca. There would be no data track that could ever point to Axelrod.

Not that there was likely to ever be such an investigation. The winners wrote the history, after all, and Axelrod had made it a point to always be among the winners. In fact, Llyn had explicitly been informed by his controller that if he had to leave Khetha and his group alive, that would be acceptable. But Llyn's policy was to always, *always* cover his tracks.

Speaking of which...

Crossing back to the bodies on his side of the table, he retrieved his uni-link. He'd set up the message template inside the *Soleil Azur*'s mail packet during the long voyage from Haven, tucked away in the will-call folder. But the final details couldn't be entered until he knew where Khetha would set up their meeting. He checked his uni-link's GPS reading—as he'd predicted, they were right in the center of Quechua City—then added the location to his message. After that, it was simply a matter of sending a quick and innocuous code word to the criminal gang he'd hired, which would send them to the message drop and set their part of the job in motion.

And even if they screwed up, it wouldn't matter. None of them knew Llyn's name or employer, or who it was they were going to be disposing of. They'd certainly never seen his real face. A few more hours, and there would be literally nothing that could ever be backtracked to Llyn, the Volsung Mercenaries, or Axelrod.

Making a copy of the Volsung file was the work of a minute. Finding the data on Khetha's private ship, including its parking orbit, access codes, and start-up procedures, took another five. Next on the list was locating Khetha's private shuttle, which turned out to be stashed away in a private hangar at the Quechua City spaceport on the southwest side of the city.

A shuttle that size typically required a minimum of two people at the controls. A spacecraft was more complex, with anywhere from a ten- to twenty-man crew necessary for safe operation. Llyn had only himself.

But he was confident he'd be able to handle both vessels without serious difficulty. A man like the Supreme Chosen One wouldn't assume that a crew would be ready when he needed to make a quick exit. For that matter, he probably wouldn't assume that even his closest advisors and guards would be ready.

And a man living on the edge—a man, more importantly, who would never allow his own skin to be dependent on anyone else—would make damn sure his escape vessels were sufficiently automated and preprogrammed that he could get out completely on his own.

Which led directly to the next tick on Llyn's checklist: both the shuttle and courier ship were heavily automated, with both the engine and impeller systems as foolproof and failproof as it was possible to build them. In addition, the ship's helm systems included a menu of preplotted courses to a dozen different systems.

Llyn had a fair amount of training in ship operations, including piloting, astrogation, and engineering. He had no doubt that he could handle this one.

And if he reached the courier and found it not quite as much of a one-man operation as he was expecting, that would be all right, too. Over the past week he'd also spent a few hours laying the groundwork for hiring a small crew who could get him to a system where he could touch base with another Axelrod operative and obtain alternative transport.

He spent another two minutes sifting through Ulobo's tablet at random, letting luck and serendipity guide his search. Khetha had someone keeping tabs on events back on Canaan, he noted with interest, no doubt making a mental list of who he would execute first when the Volsungs returned him to power. An expensive hobby, given the cost of data transference across interstellar distance, but one he wasn't at all surprised that the Supreme Chosen One had taken up.

Those men and women would be able to sleep better from now on. Not that they would ever know it.

And with that, his mental count-down reached zero. He probably had another ten or fifteen minutes before the criminals he'd summoned showed up, but he had no intention of cutting things that close. Especially not when the instructions were to *deal with and eliminate* all evidence at this location. The clean-up crew probably wouldn't include any of the higher-ups he'd dealt with, and he would hate to try to convince a simple grunt squad that he was their employer.

At best, it would cost valuable time. At worst, it would mean more bodies for the survivors to dispose of. Turning off the tablet, he set it back on the table in front of its former owner. Then, crossing the room, he pushed open the door, shot Pinstripe and Blue Shirt before either could begin to register that they were being attacked, dropped his gun beside the bodies, and headed back up the tunnel.

It was still reasonably early, but Quechua City was finally starting to come alive. Llyn took a moment to orient himself— the customs complex over *there*, the downtown market over *there*, the Hamilton Hotel over *there*—and headed off down the street. He could grab a cab later, but it was always best to leave the scene of a crime on foot. Eyewitnesses were unreliable; cab records weren't.

Besides, he had a little time still to kill. Most of the city's air traffic hadn't yet started, and there were few things more obvious and notable than a single vehicle flying through an otherwise empty sky. Another hour, and he could make his way to the airport and fire up Khetha's shuttle.

Meanwhile, his early-morning activities had caused him to miss breakfast. Smiling to himself, he turned in the direction of Fourteenth and Castillon and headed off at a brisk walk. The preopening aromas from the coffee shop on that corner had been most promising.

CHAPTER SEVEN

COMMANDER SHIFLETT, IN HER INFINITE WISDOM, had decreed that the men and women of HMS *Damocles* should start the day after their first-night bash on Casca with some exercise on the streets of Quechua City.

The Royal Manticoran Navy, in its infinite wisdom, had decreed that such workouts should be administered by the ship's petty officers.

Chomps didn't mind. He'd learned long ago to moderate his partying, especially when under the shadow of an early-morning order like this. Besides, after being cooped up aboard ship for two months, the chance to get out and stretch his legs was an appealing one.

Sadly, not all of *Damocles*'s crew had his foresight or self-control. Of the five men and three women he'd been assigned to flog a few times around the block, fully half of them were sagging like wet noodles. The other half were vertical enough, but clearly less than thrilled at the prospect of sampling any world beyond their own eyelids.

But the XO had ordered sweat, and she was going to get it. Lining them up, making sure to point out that EW Tech Redko's squad was already half a block ahead of them, Chomps verbally kicked them off the curb.

And off they went on a glorious two-klick run together in the early-morning cool.

They'd gone three blocks when Chomps heard the sound.

The sounds, rather. There were two of them, a sort of *thump-thump*. Not very loud. Certainly not very clear.

But there was something about them that sent a sudden shiver up his back.

"Hold it," he ordered his squad, looking around. Peripherally, he noted that Redko had also brought his squad to a halt and was also looking around. "Hey—Redko. You hear that?" he called, jogging up to his friend.

"Yeah, I heard it," Redko said as Chomps stopped beside him. "Don't know what it was, but I heard it."

"Sounded like shots," Chomps said.

"I don't know," Redko said, his forehead creasing in a frown. "They sounded to me like...I don't know. Just out of place. What do you think we should do?"

"Call it in," Chomps said, raising his arm and punching the uni-link on his wrist out of standby mode. The prelanding info packet had included the local three-digit emergency code. He punched it in, trying to organize his thoughts—

"Emergency," a brisk voice came back.

"I think I just heard a pair of gunshots," Chomps said. "I'm at the corner of—"

"Identify yourself."

Chomps took a deep breath. In the Star Kingdom, the identity of the uni-link's owner came up automatically when Emergency Services was called. Apparently, whoever had set up the connections for the Manticorans' visit hadn't gotten around to that part yet. "This is Missile Tech Charles Townsend of the Royal Manticoran Navy," he said, trying to keep his voice calm. For all he knew, someone could be bleeding out right now. "I'm at the corner of Barclay Street and Marsala Avenue. You need me to repeat that?"

"No, I got it," the dispatcher said. Some of the snap, Chomps noticed, seemed to have gone out of his voice. "Gunshots, you say?"

"That's what it sounded like, yes," Chomps confirmed. "Probably inside one of the buildings or parking garages—they weren't very loud. There was a sort of echo to them, too, like they were coming out an open door or—"

"Yeah, got it," the dispatcher cut him off. "Okay, thanks. We'll get someone over there as soon as we can."

There was a click, and the connection went dead.

"Well, *hell*," Chomps growled, punching out of the connection and glaring at the uni-link for a moment before dropping his arm back to his side. "*That* was a whole lot of nothing."

"What did he say?" Redko asked.

"That he'll send someone," Chomps said. "But he won't. Or at least they won't break any speed records." He nodded at the handful of citizens in view, none of whom was showing the slightest reaction to the sounds he and Redko had heard. "Not surprising, I suppose, given that no one else seems to have heard anything. He probably figures it was a figment of the crazy foreigner's imagination."

"Do you want to call it in to the lieutenant?" Redko asked, his tone strongly suggesting that Chomps shouldn't.

Chomps couldn't blame him. Redko clearly wasn't as bothered by the sounds as Chomps was, and he wasn't interested in collecting the fallout of waking up an officer to tell him they'd heard some bouncing garbage cans or something.

And given the lack of alarm anywhere on the street, Chomps had to admit the odds were against his interpretation of events.

But the odds didn't matter. He knew what he'd heard.

"Let's take a quick look around first," he told Redko, glancing over their two squads. Nine in his group, eight in Redko's. "You and your squad head around that way. Split into pairs and look for anything suspicious. My squad will take those streets and buildings over there."

"Okay," Redko said, a little doubtfully. "How long do we give it?"

"Ten minutes," Chomps said, making a quick command decision. He glanced at the two groups' trim running outfits, noting with annoyance that no one except the two petty officers had bothered to bring their uni-links along. Normally, that wouldn't have been a problem. Today, it might. "Pick a spot for your squad to rendezvous, compare notes, then call me."

"Okay," Redko said. "You heard the man, Spacers. We meet back here in ten."

Chomps gestured to his squad. "We'll meet at that corner," he said, pointing to an intersection a block farther toward their designated search area. "Spread out and keep your eyes open. And watch each other's backs."

Ninety seconds later, with the rest of his squad having peeled off, Chomps was alone, jogging down the street and wondering distantly what the bosun was going to say about this. Not to mention what Lieutenant Nikkelsen, Commander Shiflett, and possibly Captain Marcello himself would say.

At least he'd put the others in pairs, which was shipboard SOP in any kind of potentially dangerous situation. Still, the fact that he himself was now alone was probably not the smartest thing he'd ever done. Sphinxian strength and Navy combat training were a great combination, especially in Casca's .93 G field, but they didn't confer any special bullet-dodging powers. He would have to make an extra effort to watch his rear.

Around him, the city was starting to wake up, and a few more pedestrians and vehicles were making their appearance. A block ahead on the other side of the street was a line of three apartment buildings, each with a vehicle-sized opening that probably led to an underground parking garage. If he'd been right about hearing an echo in the gunshots, those would be good candidates for a quick look. Ahead was a crosswalk; turning into it, Chomps crossed the street.

A dark-haired man just passing on the opposite sidewalk looked over as Chomps neared him, his eyes flicking up and down the big Sphinxian's body. It was a common reaction among the Cascans, Chomps had already noted, and he gave the man a reassuring smile as he approached. The man smiled back and continued on his way. Chomps reached the sidewalk and turned the opposite direction toward the apartment buildings.

He'd gone four steps when a sudden thunderflash seemed to light up his brain. The man's smile...

He jerked to a halt, spinning around and staring at the man's back. Right height, right build, wrong hair, wrong face—

"Sir?" he called.

The man took another step, then paused and turned. "You talking to me?" he called back.

"Yes, sir," Chomps said. "I'm looking for the Manderlay Arms Apartments, and I can't find it in any directory. Can you point me the right direction?"

"Sorry," the man said. "I don't think I know the place."

"No problem," Chomps said, smiling. "Thanks anyway."

The man smiled back, and turned around and continued on his way.

Chomps turned back, too, a mass of ice settling around his heart. No mistake. The smile that he would never forget he'd now seen again. Twice.

The dark-haired man was the murderer from the Havenite recording.

He kept going, knowing better than to try to engage the man a second time, certainly not without a better excuse, definitely not alone. Lifting his arm, he punched Redko's number into his uni-link.

"Find something?" the other's voice came back.

"Maybe," Chomps said. "Can you see me? No—never mind me. Can you see the man heading west on Barclay Street? Short, dark-haired, wearing a gray suit?"

"Uh...yes, I see him."

"I need you to take a picture of him," Chomps said. "Do you think you can do that without being spotted?"

"Sure," Redko said. "Who is he?"

"I think he's the murderer from the Havenite recording," Chomps said, eyeing the parking ramps ahead. An enclosed van had pulled up beside the first of the openings and a group of men in workman coveralls were filing out. "And *don't* get too close."

"Okay," Redko said. "You want me to try calling the cops again?"

"Not yet." He could just picture what the dispatcher would say about a criminal identification made purely on the basis of a smile. Especially a smile he and Redko had had to hack into official government records to see in the first place. "Get the picture first. Then send it to them and tell them he's a person of interest or something—say whatever you need to say to get them to pick him up."

"Got it," Redko said. "What about you?"

"I'm going to check out some parking ramps," Chomps said. "And watch yourself, okay?"

"Bet on it," Redko said. "You, too."

The six workmen had collected some large, heavy-looking bags from the rear of the van, and as Chomps continued down the street five of the men strode off into the nearest of the three parking tunnels, leaving the sixth leaning against the vehicle's side. At least Chomps wouldn't have to bother with that one—if there was a freshly killed body in there he'd probably hear the workmen's screams all the way out here when they spotted it. If Cascans were too manly for screams, he'd know when they beckoned silently but frantically to their loitering coworker.

Chomps frowned. Only the man leaning against the van wasn't looking into the tunnel where he could be beckoned to. In fact, he was looking everywhere *but* the tunnel: at the street, on the walkways, up at the windows of the surrounding buildings, and at Chomps. Maybe even especially at Chomps.

And there was something about his stance and expression that was kicking off quiet alarms in the back of Chomps's brain.

The man wasn't just watching the van, or loafing off.

He was on guard duty.

And Chomps was headed straight toward him. Toward him, and whatever the others had gone into the tunnel to do.

Too late to turn back. The guard had him locked, and any sudden changes in direction would instantly brand him as suspicious. If the workmen were the source of the gunshots earlier, suspicion was the last thing Chomps could afford. There was no cover anywhere nearby, either, even if going to ground while unarmed wasn't a totally useless waste of effort. Calling the cops was out, too—he was already too close to the guard for that.

Which left him really only one option. *In for a centicred*, the old saying whispered through his mind, *in for a credit*.

The workman and van were four steps away. Bracing himself, Chomps walked right up to him.

"Hi, there," he said, putting on his best embarrassed smile. "Can you help me? I met a girl last night, and she asked me to pick up her car this morning. Is that the garage down there?"

"Yes," the man said. His eyes flicked to the RMN logo on Chomps's sweatshirt. "What was her name?"

"Sylvia, I think," Chomps said. "Or Linda, or Katie. Something like that. I'm still working through the fog. Thanks."

He headed down the tunnel, feeling the man's eyes on his back. Whatever they were up to down here, they would hopefully shy away from the straight-up murder of a foreign national. That was the sort of thing that would likely kick them to the top of the Cascans' find-and-nail list, and no one wanted that kind of trouble.

He just hoped they were smart enough to follow that same impeccable logic.

There was an open door off the tunnel to his left. Three steps away from it, Chomps lowered his eyes to his waist, fumbling in his side pocket as if looking for something. He passed the door, shot a quick look up from beneath his eyebrows, and continued on without slowing.

The glance hadn't shown him much. But it had shown him enough.

Two of the workmen, kneeling beside a pair of long black sacks lying on the floor.

One of those workmen scrambling to his feet, as if belatedly trying to block the view.

Another door behind them opening into a small room, with three more workmen crouching beside something on the floor.

Something Chomps was pretty damn sure was a body.

He worked his pocket another two steps, finally retrieving the key to his locker aboard *Damocles*. Letting it dangle ostentatiously from his fingers, he continued down the tunnel, which he could see now made a hard right fifty meters ahead, presumably into the garage proper. Once out of sight of the men behind him, he would call the police, try again to convince them to get their butts over here, then find some place to go to ground until they showed up.

He turned the corner into the parking garage proper without anyone shooting him in the back. Puffing out a sigh of relief, he started to key his uni-link as he looked for an empty parking slot where he could go to ground. The closest was about halfway down the first line—

"You!" a voice growled from behind him. "Hold up."

Chomps clenched his teeth. He'd hoped they would be slower on the uptake. Unfortunately, with nothing but deserted echoing parking garage in front of him, there was nothing to do but continue playing stupid. He turned his head to look over his shoulder, coming to a casual halt as he did so.

"Yes?"

Two of the workmen were striding toward him, their faces cool and suspicious. Neither was holding a weapon, but both had significant bulges in their right-hand side pockets and another inside the chest fastening strip. "You look lost," one of them said, his gaze dropping briefly to the uni-link blinking its ready signal on Chomps' wrist. "You looking for someone?"

"Not some*one*; some*thing*," Chomps corrected. "A car. I met a girl at a party last night, and she asked me to come over here this morning and get her car for her." He held up his key.

"She did, huh?" the second man said, eyeing the key. "Bad news, buddy—you've been chumped. That thing's not a car key."

"Well, sure it is," Chomps insisted, peering at the key. "It's the same size as my car key back on Manticore. What else could it be?"

"What kind of car did she say it was?" the second man asked.

Chomps thought quickly. One of the cars parked near the hotel had had the word *Picassorey* on the rear. "A light-green Picassoree," he said, mentally crossing his fingers.

The second man guffawed. "You mean a Picasso *Rey*?"

"Oh," Chomps said, wincing. Sometimes playing it stupid was easier than expected. "Sorry. It was noisy in the bar."

"Yeah, well, that's still not a car key," the man said. "Not on Casca."

"Really?" Chomps frowned at the key. "Well, hell. I really thought she was interested. I guess not." Jamming the key back in his pocket, he started to head back up the tunnel.

In unison, the men took casual sideways steps to block his path. "What's your hurry?" the second man asked, all traces of amusement gone from his face.

"You just said she lied to me," Chomps reminded him, letting his expression go confused. "I guess I'll head back and join my squad. We're all supposed to be out there running anyway."

"Yeah, you don't want to PO the CO," the man who'd glanced at his uni-link commented. "That who you were going to call?"

"Huh?" Chomps blinked at him, then produced his very best sheepish grin as he held up his arm. "Oh, *this*? No, no—I was going to call the girl. From the party. She gave me her com combo, so I was thinking I'd ask where the car was. Pretty dumb, I guess."

"Or maybe she just gave you the wrong key, like you said," the other man said. "Go ahead—let's hear what she has to say."

And as Chomps's grandfather used to say, the crapspreader had just reversed gear.

They weren't *completely* sure of what he might or might not have seen, or at least not sure enough to drop him on the spot. But they were obviously suspicious as hell.

And he'd just painted himself into a corner, He could hardly contact the cops now, not while his new playmates were watching and listening. But if he didn't call *someone*, they'd damned well know he'd been playing them.

But who on Casca could he call? No matter how Chomps pitched a story like this, he knew that none of the women in his division would catch on fast enough. If the workmen insisted he put his uni-link on speaker—and as he looked into their faces he realized that was exactly what they were planning to do—the puzzled response from the other end of the conversation would damn him in double-march time.

They might be hesitant about killing an offworlder. In fact, there was a fair chance their insistence that he call his imaginary girlfriend was some stalling of their own. One of the other men back there was very probably having a quick consult with some off-scene boss to decide whether Chomps was ignorant and stupid and could be turned loose or whether he'd seen too much and needed to be silenced.

Either way, this uni-link call could make or break him. If they realized he was playing them, they wouldn't care what he might or might not have seen. They would probably just shoot him where he stood—they were far enough out of the public eye here to get away with it.

On the other hand, if he could somehow produce someone to play the part of the party girl, there was at least the thinnest of possibilities they might just buy his entire story. It was unlikely, but *some* chance was a hell of a lot better than *no* chance at all.

But who could he call?

He could think of only one candidate. Only one person who might offer him a slim, vanishingly small opportunity to pull this off. She was smart, she was quick, and she might at least be stunned into silence long enough for him to somehow clue her in as to what was going on.

The two men were waiting. "Okay," Chomps said, raising his uni-link. "I guess I can't get in any worse with her anyway. I just need to remember—oh, right: *that* was her name." He punched in the code for relay.

"Put it on speaker," the first man ordered.

Chomps gave him a puzzled look, hesitating just long enough for the automated "Manticore relay," voice to come inaudibly through before lowering the uni-link and keying the speaker. "Name?" the automated voice continued.

Chomps braced himself. One way or another, he thought distantly, there was a really good chance he was going to die today. "Donnelly," he said. "Lisa Donnelly."

☆　　☆　　☆

Llyn had made it only three blocks when he discovered he'd picked up a tail.

An extremely amateurish tail. There were two of them, young men, dressed in running gear, with a military look about their faces and hair styling. The Cascan Defense Force? No—it was one of the visiting Manticorans. Their running outfits were identical to the one he'd seen a couple of minutes ago on that other, bigger Manticoran.

The more immediate question was *why*?

The men couldn't have seen him leaving the scene of an obvious crime—surely they'd have called the authorities by now if they had. Had that brief conversation Llyn had had with the Manticoran a few minutes ago somehow caught someone's attention? But unless the big man himself was under suspicion for something, and the tail was just following up on possible contacts, that made even less sense.

Ultimately, though, it didn't matter. Llyn was being tailed, and he would have to deal with it.

There was a gap between buildings coming up on the left, probably leading into a service alleyway. It would do nicely.

Picking up his pace, he headed for the gap.

☆   ☆   ☆

Lisa had just finished going through the breakfast buffet line, and was looking for a good spot to sit down to eat, when her uni-link trilled. Setting down her plate on the end of the counter, she shot her left sleeve and peered at the ID.

It was Missile Tech First Townsend.

Her first, reflexive thought was that something must be wrong, possibly an injury on the exercise run that Commander Shiflett had ordered.

Her second thought was to wonder why in space Townsend was calling *her* about it.

Whatever it was, it had better be important. Clicking it on, she moved it closer to her face. "Donnelly."

"Hey, Lisa, this is Charles," Townsend's voice came on, brisk and cheerful.

And completely and outrageously lacking in proper respect. What the *hell*?

"You remember—we met last night at the party—I'm the guy who was telling you about my trip to Secour—"

Lisa's frown deepened. Townsend hadn't been aboard *Guardian* on the mission to Secour five years ago.

"—and that run-in I had with those rowdies—"

What in the world was he going on about? Had he been trying for some other Lisa Donnelly and been transferred here by mistake?

"—and how my good buddy Mota and I got into deep cow mix when we got back?"

Lisa caught her breath. *Mota*, the murdered pirate from the Havenite recording? How did Townsend even know about that?

"Anyway, I'm trying to find your car like you asked me, only these two guys down here say the key you gave me isn't a car key at all, so I need you to help me out here. Okay?"

There was a muted double finger snap from somewhere across the room, and the low hum of conversation abruptly evaporated. Lisa started, looking up to see Captain Marcello and Commodore Henderson gazing across the table at her, their expressions intent. Something about her face must have clued them in that something odd was happening.

Henderson raised his eyebrows in silent question. Lisa shrugged her shoulders in silent response, touched her finger to her lips, and held out the uni-link as she keyed it to speaker. "Sure, Charles, I remember you," she said. "Little fuzzy on the details of last night, though. What's this about a car key?"

"Yeah, sorry about that," Townsend said.

And in his voice Lisa could hear a subtle lowering of tension. Something strange was going on, all right, and he was clearly relieved that she hadn't simply lowered the boom on him.

"Not surprised, the way you were drinking last night," he continued. "Like there was no tomorrow."

No tomorrow? Did that sound as serious as she thought it sounded? "You weren't exactly falling behind," she said, trying a little probe. It wouldn't hurt to play along—if this was a practical joke, or he was trying to win some bizarre bet, she could always bust him to spacer third class later.

"That's for sure," he agreed. "I sometimes drink like it's my last night on Earth."

Lisa shot a look at Marcello and Henderson. Both men were frowning in concentration.

"Anyway, you asked me to pick up your car this morning from

the parking garage," Townsend continued. "But like I said, these two guys say this isn't a car key. Did you maybe give me the wrong one by mistake?"

"Let me think," Lisa said, stalling for time. So Townsend wasn't alone. Were the two men with him listening in on the conversation?

"Because it looks the same size as the key to my Zulu Kickback back home," Townsend said. "So, you know, it could just be a case of mistaken identity. You know—mistaken key identity. That's why I didn't notice anything was wrong."

A shiver ran up Lisa's back. *Zulu*. The stress on the noun had been very slight, but she was sure she hadn't imagined it. *No tomorrow ... last night on Earth ... and now Zulu. ...*

This was no practical joke. Townsend was in trouble. Serious trouble.

There was a movement to her side, and Lisa looked over as a tablet was held up in front of her with a message scrawled across it. *Uni-link locator being blocked—get his position.* She looked over the top of the tablet to see Commander Shiflett gazing back at her. So the XO had caught on, too. "Okay, for starters, you've got to learn to listen," Lisa said. "The key isn't to the *car*—it's to the key box under the hood. Remember all the car thefts I told you about?"

"Oh," Townsend said, sounding embarrassed. "Right. The box has a kill switch inside."

"*And* the actual key," Lisa said, wondering if any of this even made sense with Cascan technology. If it was completely off the wall, whoever was listening in would call fraud in double-quick time.

"Right," Townsend said. There was a slight pause, and Lisa caught the hint of a murmur, as if someone just out of hearing range was giving him instructions or a prompt— "It was a light-green Picasso Rey, right?"

Across the table, Henderson lifted an urgent finger from his tablet. "*Black*," he murmured urgently. "Picasso Reys don't come in light green."

Lisa nodded. "No, my *first* car was light green," she said, trying to put strained patience into her voice. Henderson and Marcello were murmuring together, she saw, Marcello watching closely as Henderson worked rapidly on his tablet. "You're looking for a *black* Picasso Rey. Jeez, Charles, are you even in the right *place*?"

"Sure I am," Townsend said with an attempt at wounded dignity. "Three apartment garages in a row; I'm down in the first one."

"No, you're down in the *second* one," Lisa corrected. "I *swear* you are utterly useless. Do you need me to come down there and show you?"

"No, no, don't do that," Townsend said hastily. "You don't want to be anywhere near me before I've had my morning coffee. You want me to bring it to your place when I get it?"

"Well, that *was* the idea of sending you," Lisa growled. "Are you going to have to drive all over town until you remember where I live?"

"No, no," Townsend said with an air of wounded dignity. "*That* I remember just fine. You're four doors down from your office at Tinsdale Range Runners."

"Right," Lisa said. If that meant what she thought it did...

"Great," Townsend said. "I'll be there as soon as I can. Bye."

The connection broke. "With all due respect, Commander," a Cascan civilian who Lisa hadn't yet been introduced to said, "what in the Holy Name was *that* all about?"

"One of our people is in trouble," Lisa told her. "Something serious."

"You sure he's not just playing games?" the civilian pressed. "Sure sounded like a game to me."

"Missile Tech Townsend doesn't play that kind of game," Shiflett told him.

"And Case Zulu's not something our people make jokes about," Marcello added. "Especially not to their superiors. Commodore? Anything?"

"Maybe," Henderson said. "Three apartment buildings in a row with underground garages...I've got four possibles within two klicks of the Hamilton Hotel."

"Any of them have an address of three-eleven something?" Lisa asked.

Henderson blinked. "Three-eleven Marsala Avenue," he said. "Four blocks from the Hamilton. How did you know?"

"The Tinsdale 315 is one of the components in *Damocles*'s weapons ranging sensor," Lisa said. "Four down puts it at 311."

Henderson grunted. "This guy's quick on his feet," he said as he tapped rapidly on his tablet. "It's like Secour all over again. Must be something in Manticore's water. Okay; police alerted—emergency one level—signaling they're on their way. What is this Case Zulu thing, anyway? I assume it's not actually a Manticoran car model."

"Hardly," Marcello said grimly. "After Secour, First Lord of the Admiralty Cazenestro decided our personnel needed more hands-on combat training. Originally, the final stage in that training was called 'Zulu Omega': a full-bore combat scenario, some of it live-ammo, as intense and realistic as we could make it without actually killing anyone."

"Some recruits have nightmares for weeks afterward," Shiflett agreed.

"Yes, they do," Marcello said. "Believe me, it leaves an impression. But after a while, our people started calling that stage just 'Zulu' or 'Case Zulu.' It's turned into a sort of shorthand for 'everything's going straight to hell and we're all going to die.' Like I said, it's not something an experienced noncom like Townsend would use to his department head on a whim."

"The captain's right, Sir," Shiflett confirmed. "Either Townsend is facing guns, or thinks he soon will be." She looked at Lisa, inclining her head slightly in salute. "Nicely done, TO."

"Thank you, Ma'am," Lisa said. "I just hope we were reading him right."

Shiflett's lip twitched. "I guess we'll find out."

☆   ☆   ☆

"Man, I'm just running on half-hydraulics today," Chomps said, slathering on all the embarrassment he could as he keyed off his uni-link. At least they hadn't pulled out their guns yet. Maybe they'd bought the act.

Or maybe they were still waiting for a thumb's-up or thumb's-down from their boss. Either way, time to try for a graceful withdrawal.

"Guess I'd better get next door and find her damn car." He took another step up the tunnel—

"You don't have to go outside," the first man said. He gestured behind Chomps. "There are connecting doors between the three garages."

"Really?" Chomps asked, frowning.

"We do a lot of work in this part of town," the second put in. "Most of these side-by-sides have a second exit."

"Safety regulation," the first man explained. "Come on—I'll

show you." He brushed past Chomps and started toward the lines of cars, leaving only the second man between Chomps and the street.

Or rather, leaving the second man plus all the others working up there. Wincing, Chomps turned and followed the first man toward the cars. Trying fervently to figure out what he was going to do.

Were they really just going to show him a way out and let him go? That would imply that they'd bought the little impromptu he and Donnelly had put on. It would also imply they were extremely trusting souls, which Chomps didn't believe for a minute.

But if they'd decided to kill him after all, why go any deeper into the garage? Why not just shoot him here and be done with it?

He felt his stomach tighten. Because once among the rows of cars they could drop him and not have his body discovered for hours. Ten meters ahead was a panel truck with a slightly curved windshield, and in the distorted reflection Chomps saw the second man fall into silent step behind him.

Keep it together, Chomps ordered himself silently. The two men were undoubtedly armed, and they were both out of grabbing range. Even if he was able to get to one of them, trying to use him as a human shield against the other would be useless. With his broad Sphinxian build, he might as well try to hide behind a flagpole.

Keep it together. How would they do it? Certainly the safest method would be to simply shoot him in the back. He'd already seen that gunshots didn't seem to spark any notice from the locals. A nice, quick shot, and they could get back to the main business of the day.

But people who didn't like leaving loose ends typically didn't like taking any other unnecessary risks, either. And if they preferred not to risk someone calling in a fresh gunshot, the next likely approach ...

He was watching the truck windshield closely when the man behind him slid a knife from inside his shirt and picked up speed, closing the gap between him and his victim.

It was all Chomps could do not to react. But he kept walking, forcing down the urge to turn and face his attacker. The man was moving into stabbing range, but he would probably wait until the group was at least within the first line of cars before he made his move, if only so that he and his partner wouldn't have to drag the body so far.

Chomps let the man get to within half a meter. Then, he jerked to a halt, spun around, and slashed his left arm diagonally down and outward through the space between them like he'd been taught in the Casey-Rosewood salle.

To his astonishment, and probably that of his attacker, it worked. Chomps's wrist caught the man's knife hand across the forearm, knocking the weapon out of line.

Follow-up! Lunging forward, Chomps made a grab for the deflected wrist.

But his attacker had recovered from his initial surprise and snatched the hand back out of Chomps's reach. His follow-up would probably be to make some sort of feint and then take another shot at burying the knife in Chomps's torso.

There was no way Chomps would be lucky enough to block the next attack. That left him only one counter. Grabbing the man's collar with his left hand, he reached down and got a grip on the man's belt with his right—

And with a grunt of effort he lifted the attacker off his feet, turned halfway around, and hurled him into his partner.

The man in front had already turned back to face the fracas, his hand digging into his shirt for his own knife or gun or whatever weapon he had in there. He had just enough time to rearrange his expression into stunned disbelief before the incoming human missile rearranged everything else and sent the pair of them crashing to the pavement.

A trained operative, Chomps reflected, would probably take advantage of his opponents' temporary disadvantage to make that condition permanent. But Chomps wasn't trained, his attackers were rapidly sorting themselves out, and if he screwed up the only permanence he was likely to achieve was that of his own death.

And so he charged straight past the tangle of bodies and limbs, reached the first line of vehicles, and ducked in alongside the panel truck, running sideways through the narrow gap between the truck and the next car over. His only chance now was to go to ground, call the police, and hope he could play hide-and-seek with the killers until they arrived.

He had reached the gap between the first two lines and ducked around the truck, looking for the next nearest vehicle that would hide his bulk, when there was the *crack* of a gunshot behind him.

His first impulse was to take a quick, panic-edged inventory of his skin and body parts. He'd heard once that terrible pain didn't always register right away—maybe he was half a minute from death and just didn't know it. But he seemed to be uninjured—

"Freeze, everybody!" The stentorian bellow echoing through the underground structure could be produced only by the sort of portable amplifiers police forces throughout the galaxy used. "Hands where we can see them. *Now!*"

Carefully, aware that his arms and legs were still trembling with adrenaline and not at their most reliable, Chomps came to a stop and crouched down.

Twenty seconds later, a half dozen gray-clad figures came charging from the tunnel, their guns drawn and ready.

Chomps took a couple of deep breaths to steady himself. Then, raising his arms, he stood up and started toward them through the line of cars. Good cops, he knew, wouldn't simply accept his word that he wasn't one of the bad guys. Good cops would grab everybody in sight, throw on the cuffs, and haul them down to the station house to be sorted out at their leisure.

In fact, good cops would probably be *very* hands on throughout the procedure, possibly to the point of making everyone eat pavement while they passed out the restraints.

The Quechua City cops, as it turned out, were very good cops indeed.

CHAPTER EIGHT

KHETHA'S SHUTTLE WAS EXACTLY WHERE Ulobo's tablet had said it would be. The flight systems were cold—the Supreme Chosen One probably hadn't used the vehicle for months—but they came up with gratifying speed. A quick check of the computer as the reaction thrusters did their self-check revealed a quasi-diplomatic priority launch code for the vehicle. The relationship between the Cascans and Khetha's alleged government-in-exile, Llyn reflected, must have been an interesting one. Probably very expensive, too.

But the details didn't matter. If the code got him off Casca in a timely fashion, that was all he cared about.

Meanwhile, Ulobo's tablet had included information on the orbiting ship's startup procedure. It would still be tricky to operate a ship like this alone, but as long as nothing serious happened with the engineering he had no doubt he could handle it. The only other option was to collect the pick-up crew he'd tentatively reserved over the past week and make this journey a group effort.

But he'd already killed enough people for one trip. Besides, a man like Khetha would be sure to keep everything in top-level shape. Leaning back in his seat, keeping an eye on the shuttle's readouts, Llyn settled in to work through the manual.

☆　☆　☆

"...and then they brought me down here," Townsend finished.

"I see," Quechua City Police Detective Dolarz said, nodding. "Okay. Let's go back to the part where you first heard the gunshots—"

"Look, I know that's the stuff you're supposed to be asking me about," Townsend interrupted. "But there's another killer out there, remember? Maybe the guy who killed those other eight men, too."

"Yes; your man with the criminal smile," Dolarz said, his voice strained. "We'll get to him soon enough."

Townsend sent a frustrated glance at Lisa, sitting silently behind the detective, and for a moment she thought he was going to appeal to her.

But he didn't. Which was just as well, because there was nothing she or the entire Navy could do for him right now. At this particular moment, Missile Tech Charles Townsend was about as deep in this growing firestorm as he could get.

Eight murders, right in the middle of Casca's capital city. It was horrifying, it was virtually unheard of on this world, and the police were already apparently starting to feel high-level government heat over it.

They were searching frantically for answers. And if answers weren't forthcoming, they might be willing to settle for scapegoats.

Lisa's uni-link vibrated: Captain Marcello wanted to see her. Silently leaving her chair, she opened the interrogation room door behind her and slipped out.

Marcello and Commodore Henderson were waiting in the briefing room, along with a stiff-backed woman wearing a senior police officer's uniform. Her eyes were fiery as she eyed the newcomer, but Lisa could also sense a bit of hunted animal in her face. "Commander Donnelly," Marcello greeted her gravely. "This is Lieutenant Nabaum. She's currently overseeing the investigation."

"Ma'am," Lisa said, exchanging nods with the other woman. "I hope the rest of the case is coming along better than Missile Tech Townsend's interrogation."

"Your petty officer is not exactly smelling like a garden rose at the moment," Nabaum said acidly. "And yes, we're making progress. We've identified the hit squad—they're members of a criminal organization called Black Piranha. Very nasty group— we've been trying to wipe them out for over thirty T-years. As far as we know, though, this is the first time they've been involved in something with interstellar implications. Maybe this will finally give us the opening and leverage we need to take them out for good."

"You're sure they made the hit?" Henderson asked. "I understood from Townsend's testimony that they didn't arrive on the scene until *after* the gunshots."

"You may also have noticed from Townsend's testimony that he claims to have heard only two shots," Nabaum countered. She waved a hand impatiently. "All right, granted—the room where the other six bodies were found was soundproofed, so forget the numbers. But his claimed timing is still suspicious. Especially since that ridiculous smiling-man theory of his is looking more and more like a deliberate red herring."

"How do you conclude that?" Lisa asked.

Nabaum smiled thinly. "Because we found the message that was sent to the Piranhas, specifying that address and ordering them to deal with whoever they found inside. That order came in via the Havenite mail packet, which means it came in from off-world, which means it was put into motion at least a year ago. That pretty well eliminates the possibility that anyone aboard *Soleil Azur* was involved."

"It does?" Marcello asked, frowning. "I was under the impression that the room where the bodies were found was pretty much an unused storage area. How could whoever sent the message have known the victims would even be there?"

Nabaum lifted fingers. "One: it might have started life as a storeroom, but it was rented three years ago and renovated as a private meeting room. Two—"

"Rented by whom?" Henderson asked.

"We're still running that down," Nabaum said. "We've worked through three layers already—no idea how many more there are. My money's on someone connected with the Piranhas, though. Two: a private meeting room is typically the site of, not surprisingly, meetings. Often those meetings run on a regular schedule, which they apparently did and someone apparently learned. I know that because, three: the message listed no fewer than *twelve* possible dates and times for the Piranhas to do the deed, of which today was the fourth. Clearly, whoever set up the killing was well informed about his intended victims' movements and plans, which means there was no reason he would need to be on Casca, let alone that he actually was."

Marcello's uni-link trilled. He raised his wrist and keyed it on. "Marcello."

He listened a moment, and his already grim expression went

a little grimmer. "Thank you, Commander. Bring it down here, will you?"

He put the uni-link away. "I had Commander Shiflett go to Townsend's room at the Hamilton and take a look at that personal he brought from the ship," he told Lisa. "She found a copy of the Mota murder recording on it."

Lisa winced. So along with whatever Nabaum was considering charging Townsend with, he was also on the hook for the system hack Peirola had spotted last night. "So he was Commissioner Peirola's hacker?" she asked.

"Looks like it," Marcello said. "One other bit of information you don't know: Commodore Henderson ordered a fresh facial-comparison scan run between the recording and *Soleil Azur*'s passengers and crew. The closest any of them come is thirty-eight percent."

"What if the murderer wore a disguise?" Lisa suggested. "A wig, false mustache, and some facial builds could change his appearance that much, couldn't they?"

"Of course they could," Nabaum put in. "But why bother with a disguise when he was going to scramble the security recordings and retrograde the guards' memories anyway?"

"Maybe he likes covering his trail with more than one layer of dirt," Lisa said.

Nabaum puffed out a sigh. "Look, Commander. I realize Petty Officer Townsend is a fellow shipmate, as well as being a close friend. But the facts are—"

"Excuse me," Lisa interrupted reflexively, the RMN rules on chain-of-command fraternization blurring across her vision. "Missile Tech Townsend is *not* a close friend. He's a competent petty officer under my command, and that's all."

"Then why were you the one he called with his little verbal game?" Nabaum countered, a knowing look in her eye.

"I have no idea," Lisa said, painfully aware of her captain listening silently to all this.

"Well, we'll make sure to ask him about it later," Nabaum said placidly.

"What about the victims?" Marcello asked. "Any luck identifying them?"

Nabaum's *gotcha* expression soured. "Not yet," she admitted. "The killers had already loaded the bodies into denature bags—standard predisposal practice among the more sophisticated of our criminals. Their faces, prints, corneas, and retinas were already too far gone for computer match, and their DNA was well on its way. We were able to retrieve enough to work with, but it's going to be a little longer before we can match any names to them."

"I see," Marcello said. "I wonder if we can talk to Missile Tech Townsend privately. Once his interrogation is finished, of course."

"I think that can be arranged," Nabaum said. "If you'd care to wait here, I'll have him sent down as soon as we're done with him. If you'll excuse me, I have other matters to attend to."

She headed for the door. "I need to head out, too," Henderson said. "There are a couple of angles I want to look into."

"Of course," Marcello said. "A suggestion, if I may: you might want to send *Soleil Azur*'s personnel photos to all commercial ground and air services. Just in case one of them tries to leave Quechua City."

"Along with vehicle rentals," Henderson said, nodding. "Already done. Let me know if you find out anything new."

"I will, Sir," Marcello assured him. "I hope we can get this thing straightened out quickly."

"Amen to that." Henderson smiled faintly. "Because so far, the Manticoran friendship tour is not exactly living up to our expectations. Good luck."

It was another hour before Townsend finally arrived in the briefing room. Long enough for Commander Shiflett to join them. More than long enough for Marcello and Lisa to confirm that a purloined copy of the Deuxième Prison recording was indeed on Townsend's personal.

After the incredible morning Townsend had just been through, Lisa had expected him to show up dragging like a new recruit just in from his first ten-klick run. But while the petty officer's face was drawn, there was a simmering fire in his eyes and a flagpole stiffness to his back.

"I don't know what else I can tell you, Sir," he said when they were all seated around the table. "The smile on this man was the same as the one on the recording. Same lips, same shape, same almost-dimple, even the same hint of upper teeth."

"And you got all this from a single glance?" Marcello asked.

"Two glances, Sir, actually," Townsend said. "And the second time I already knew what to look for."

"A remarkable talent, Missile Tech," Shiflett said in a tone that suggested she didn't believe it for a second.

"I don't know if I'd call it a *talent*, Ma'am," Townsend said. "I just saw what I saw." He looked back at Marcello. "I take it, Sir, that the police aren't taking this seriously?"

"They're convinced that the men you saw disposing of the bodies were also the killers," Marcello said. "Or at least were part of the same group as the killers."

"Do they have any thoughts on motive, Sir?" Townsend asked.

"They don't even know who the victims were," Marcello said. "Let's move on, shall we?" He tapped the cover of Townsend's personal.

Townsend winced. "Yes, Sir. I know this is going to sound strange, but in fact I was asked to break into the Havenite pirate download and record it."

"Were you, now?" Marcello said. "By whom, may I ask?"

"I was asked to keep it strictly confidential."

"To the point of spending the trip back home in the brig?"

"Yes, Sir."

"How about to the point of staying on Casca to face obstruction and possibly murder charges?" Shiflett put in.

Lisa felt her stomach tighten. Surely Shiflett wasn't serious.

She was. Lisa had seen that expression before, and she knew with certainty that the XO was completely, deadly serious.

And on one level Lisa couldn't blame her. As Commodore Henderson had said, the Manticoran visit was on the edge of becoming a public-relations disaster. If it took leaving a marginal petty officer behind to face local charges to bring things back on track, Shiflett might very well be prepared to pay that price.

Townsend knew it, too. He looked at Shiflett, then at Marcello, then at Lisa, then back to Shiflett. "No, Ma'am," he conceded.

He turned to Marcello, squaring his shoulders. "It was Countess Calvingdell who gave me the assignment, Sir."

At the edge of her vision, Lisa saw Marcello's and Shiflett's eyes perform a synchronized widening. "The *Defense Minister*?" Marcello demanded.

"Yes, Sir," Townsend said, as painfully uncomfortable as Lisa had ever seen him. "She noticed there were some odd glitches in the Haven pirate data coming in via Casca, and wanted to know whether the glitches were in the original Havenite encryption or

in the extra layer that the Cascans put on it. Since we were going
to be here when one of the packets arrived, she asked me to
pull a copy of the original data and encryption so that we could
compare it with the version that Casca then sent back with us."

"Ridiculous," Shiflett said flatly. "If she wanted a direct copy,
why not just ask Captain Marcello to get her one? Why go to
you in the first place."

Lisa had been wrong. Townsend was capable of at least one
deeper layer of discomfort. "I think, Ma'am, that she was also
concerned the glitches might be coming from somewhere in the
Navy. Possibly even from inside her own office."

For once, even Shiflett seemed to be at a loss for words. "All
right," she said at last, some of the antagonism gone from her
voice. "Again, why *you*?"

"One of my uncle's friends was part of the Intelligence department of the Meyerdahl System Defense Force before he emigrated
to Sphinx," Townsend said. "He's advised the countess before on
clandestine operations, and suggested that I be given the job."

"You have any proof of this?" Marcello asked. "Aside from our
going back and asking Calvingdell, that is?"

"Nothing that would satisfy a Cascan court," Townsend admit-
ted. "And I'd ask, Sir, that you not tell them about this. Please.
Countess Calvingdell's instructions were *very* explicit on that point.
I think she was worried about possible political repercussions."

Marcello grunted. "I'll just bet she was."

"But there *is* a hidden clause in your own orders, Sir, which
the countess put in," Townsend continued.

"Really," Marcello said, his voice dropping half an octave. "I
don't recall seeing anything in there aside from the standard
collection of contingency files."

"It's not just locked, Sir, it's invisible," Townsend said. "You
can't even see that it's there unless you put in the password
donnybrook."

Marcello and Shiflett exchanged glances. "We'll see," Marcello
said.

"Thank you, Sir," Townsend said. "But with your permission,
Captain, we can't afford to wait until you get back to *Damocles*
and confirm that. Let me offer you some indirect evidence right
now. If you look through the record of my incursion, you'll see
that I was using the Havenites' own decryption process. The only

way I could have gotten hold of that is via a senior member of the Defense Ministry."

"Or else you stole it," Shiflett said.

"That's possible, Ma'am," Townsend conceded. "But a thief who'd obtained an official Havenite military encryption probably wouldn't bother using it for a relatively noncritical file like this. He would more likely find a buyer and retire in luxury."

"Maybe that was next on your list," Shiflett suggested darkly. "In fact, maybe your smiling man was part of that deal."

Lisa stiffened as a sudden thought flashed across her brain. If Townsend had copied more than just the Havenite data... "Excuse me," she said as Townsend opened his mouth to reply. "Did you record anything besides the pirate data?"

Townsend's lip twitched. "I got some of the rest of the packet, yes, Ma'am," he said. "I wasn't snooping—I'd seen the recording of the murder, and thought there might be more information elsewhere in the packet."

"You have something, TO?" Marcello asked.

"Maybe," Lisa said. "With your permission, Sir?"

Marcello waved a hand in silent assent. Lisa pulled the personal over to her, turned it on, and swiveled it around to face Townsend. "See if you got a message for a criminal group called—no, wait. Of course they wouldn't have used their real name. Let me think how to do this..."

"Are you talking about the Black Piranhas?" Shiflett asked, pulling out her tablet. "Hang on—Nabaum gave me the original of that file. It was in the *will-call* folder, number—well, here." She turned the tablet so Townsend could see it. "See if you have this one."

"Yes, Ma'am." For a few seconds Townsend worked the keyboard, frowning intently at the display. Then his face cleared. "Got it," he said. "But it's encrypted, and I haven't got the key."

Shiflett gestured toward him. "Send it to me. I should be able to run it through the same decryption system the police used on the original."

"Yes, Ma'am," Townsend said. "Sent."

"Got it," Shiflett said. "Let's see if this works."

"What exactly are you looking for, TO?" Marcello asked quietly into the silence.

"I'm not sure, Sir," Lisa confessed. "Lieutenant Nabaum said the kill order had come in the packet from off-world. I'm thinking that if she's wrong about that, maybe there'll be something different between it and Missile Tech Townsend's version."

"Well, well," Shiflett said, her voice suddenly intrigued. "Would you look at this? The version on the personal is just like the one the police have ... *except* that the location of the hit is missing. Hello—so are those twelve date and time stamps she was so impressed by."

"Interesting," Marcello said. "So it's possible that someone had the template in place in the packet, then added the location and time before the Piranhas picked it up?"

"That would certainly fit, Sir," Shiflett said. "That way, the killer wouldn't have to know in advance where the meeting would take place. Even if the victims were cagey enough to switch the place or time at the last second, he could insert the data into the message and it would still read out as having come from off-world."

"So either the Piranhas were really quick on the uptake," Lisa said, "or else the men you saw were just the clean-up squad."

"It has to be the latter," Townsend said. "I only heard two shots, which had to be the two outside men. That means the six inside had already been killed, which implies the killer was at the meeting by invitation."

"Unless he shot the two outside men first and then went in and shot the others," Lisa suggested.

Townsend shook his head. "You wouldn't charge into a room and wait until you'd closed the door behind you before you started shooting, Ma'am," he pointed out. "Even if you tried, your intended victims certainly wouldn't give you that much time before they started shooting back."

"Point," Marcello said. "So when the message says to *deal with* whoever they found inside, it's just referring to body disposal?"

"Apparently," Shiflett said. "And contrary to how Nabaum's reading it." She gave a little shrug. "Nice plan, really. If Townsend hadn't stumbled on them, and they'd gotten the bodies out of there, the murders would have just gone down as unsolved disappearances."

"And even if they *did* get caught, there's a complete disconnect between them and the actual killer," Marcello agreed. "As an extra bonus, by making it look like the order came from off-planet, it could take months or years for the Cascans to back-track the message and pin down his identity."

"If they even had the resources to try, Ma'am," Townsend added.

"Gimmicking the Havenite packet that way couldn't have been easy, though," Marcello pointed out.

"He's already screwed with a maximum-security prison's recording system," Shiflett pointed out. "This can't be any harder."

"Excuse me, Sir," Townsend said. "But now that we know that Mr. Smiley might be involved, shouldn't we ask the Quechua City Police to pick him up?"

"Afraid you haven't given them much to go on," Shiflett said.

"What about the picture?" Townsend asked. "Redko got you and the cops a picture, didn't he?"

"What are you talking about?" Shiflett demanded.

"I pointed him to the killer and told him to get a picture," Townsend said, sitting up straighter in his chair. "He didn't—? Oh, no. *Damn* it."

Shiflett had already keyed her uni-link. "Lieutenant Nabaum," she ordered, her eyes smoldering. "When was this, Townsend?"

"Just before I got grabbed by the clean-up crew," Townsend said between clenched teeth. "I sent them in pairs—he should have had someone with him."

"His locator's not registering," Marcello muttered, glowering at his own uni-link. He shot a look at Shiflett, still waiting impatiently for Nabaum to answer, then turned to Lisa. "TO, get our people out there," he ordered. "Get them on the streets and have them start a search. Starting at—" he gestured to Townsend.

"Barclay Street and Marsala Avenue," Townsend supplied.

"Starting there," Marcello said. "Have them look everywhere a human being could be hidden. Tell them they're looking for EW Tech Redko." His lips tightened. "Or," he added quietly, "his body."

☆   ☆   ☆

It took the *Damocles* crew and, eventually, most of the Quechua City police force a solid hour to find Redko. He and a Spacer Second Class named Aj Krit were taped to the back wall of a dumpster in a service alley four blocks away from the corner where Chomps had left them, with a couple of trash bags strategically placed to hide them from view.

To Chomps's surprise and infinite relief, they were alive.

According to the petty officer who found them, Redko swore for three solid minutes after they got the tape off his mouth while they were untaping him from the dumpster. By the time

Chomps and Commander Donnelly arrived he had apparently run out of curses.

But from the look in his eye Chomps was pretty sure he was ready to do a repeat performance.

"About freaking time," he bit out as he spotted Townsend. His eyes flicked to Donnelly, and Chomps could see him revising his vocabulary now that a senior officer was present. "I was starting to think you were going to let me get a private tour of the Quechua City garbage sorter. What the hell kept you?"

"It got complicated," Chomps said, some vocabulary of his own very much wanting to come out. "What the hell happened?"

"What do you *think* happened?" Redko said bitterly. "He got the drop on us, that's what. We never even saw him coming."

"And how exactly was there even a drop he could get?" Chomps demanded. "You were supposed to take a picture. *One.* From a safe distance."

"Well, I couldn't, could I?" Redko shot back. "He never gave me a clear shot. So we figured we'd follow him, just for a minute or so, and try to get at least a solid profile on him." He nodded back over his shoulder at the dumpster. "Only next thing I knew, we were wrapped up like bargain-priced mummies and plastered against the back of that thing. Plastered solid—I couldn't even kick the sides to try to get someone's attention."

"Consider yourself lucky you're able to complain about it," Donnelly advised tersely. "We think the man you were tailing killed eight other men."

"I was thinking—" Redko broke off. "Did you say *eight*, Ma'am? But—" he looked back at Chomps.

"Eight," Chomps confirmed. "The two shots we heard were the last of a string. As Commander Donnelly says, consider yourself lucky."

"Yes, Ma'am," Redko said, in a considerably more subdued voice. "Well...did you get him?"

"Not yet," Donnelly said. "But the police have an alert out, and Commodore Henderson has the CDF checking all shuttle flights he might have been able to catch."

"They'll get him," Chomps promised. "In the meantime..." He looked at Donnelly.

She nodded. "The hospital for a quick check, then to the police station for a debriefing."

"Yes, Ma'am." Chomps gestured. "Come on, Reddy. I'll help you to the car."

☆   ☆   ☆

The diplomatic code from Ulobo's tablet worked like a charm. Quechua City Space Control let Llyn leave orbit, their instructions and confirmations filled with the sort of stiff formal phrases that must have come straight from the official rule file. By the time of their second, much less serene call, he'd built up a twenty-one-second time delay's worth of distance.

It made the conversation even more awkward than it otherwise would have been.

"Diplomatic courier ship *Score Settler*, this is Quechua City Control," a harsh voice came over the bridge speaker. "Commodore Henderson of the Cascan Defense Force requests that you abort your trip and return immediately to Casca."

Llyn touched the mike control. "Quechua City Control, this is *Score Settler*," he replied. "Captain Ulobo speaking. My apologies, but I'm afraid it will be impossible to accede to your request. General Khetha has received a message requesting him to come at once to Zuckerman, and is determined that that obligation be met."

He counted out the seconds of the time-delay; and right on target—

"Captain Ulobo, this is not a request," a new, even harsher voice came on. "You are ordered to return to orbit immediately."

Or what? Llyn thought back with a tight smile. He'd carefully checked the locations of the CDF's ships—all four of them—on his way out of orbit, and had confirmed that none of them was in position to come after him.

But there was nothing to be gained by pointing that out. Besides, gloating wasn't Llyn's style. "I'm sorry, Quechua City Control, but that simply isn't possible," he said. "If all goes well, General Khetha will be back in three months. He'll be happy to sit down with Commodore Henderson then."

"Captain Ulobo, I don't think you fully understand the situation," the man said. "If you refuse to comply, you *will* be brought back by force."

Llyn opened his mouth to reply—

And stopped as one of the displays belatedly caught his eye. It was an ID map of everything in orbit around Casca, all the ships that might be close enough to head off after him. He'd taken all of the CDF warships into account, and dismissed them as any threat.

But he'd forgotten about the Manticore destroyer. And if they started bringing up their impellers right now...

Quickly, he ran the numbers. It would be close—it would be damn close. But if they really, *really* wanted him, they could indeed have him.

And as if in response to that sudden revelation— "*Score Settler*, this is Captain Marcello of the Royal Manticoran Naval Ship *Damocles*," a new voice came from the speaker. "The Cascan Defense Force has authorized me to pursue and detain or destroy you. Bring your ship around and return to Casca or we will do so."

Llyn cursed under his breath. He had just one option, and it wasn't a pretty one. Keying for impeller control, he ran his acceleration and inertial compensator to ninety-five percent.

It wasn't something he did lightly. It wasn't something *anyone* did lightly. Especially not someone whose impeller room was running on full automatic, with no one watching to make sure nothing went wrong. Eighty-five percent was considered the upper limit for safe travel, and virtually no one except warships in combat ever crossed that line.

But Llyn needed more of a lead if he was to stay ahead of *Damocles* and her missiles. An hour at ninety-five percent should do the trick. Even if Marcello decided to push his own ship to the same limit.

And if he did...well, then it would be a race.

☆　　☆　　☆

"CIC confirms, Captain," Lieutenant Nikkelsen's voice came from Marcello's uni-link. "*Score Settler* is running at ninety-five percent maximum acceleration."

Lisa shivered. Ninety-five percent. Whoever was aboard *really* didn't want anyone catching him.

"Well, that pretty much confirms it's our boy, doesn't it?" Commodore Henderson said sourly.

"I would say so, Commodore," Marcello said, just as sourly, as they all watched the departing icon on the CDF Command Center display. "I was wishing mightily that we hadn't taken those two beta nodes off-line for inspection last night, but I see now that it wouldn't really have mattered whether we had or not."

"Not unless you were willing to red-line your systems, too," Henderson agreed. "Which I assume you weren't?"

"I wouldn't have been, no," Marcello said. "But seeing that *he* was willing might have changed my mind." He gave a little snort. "One more big fat zero for our collection."

At the rear of the group, Townsend cleared his throat. "If I may, Sir?" he said tentatively. "We also know now that the murderer hasn't got a tap into high-level CDF files."

"How do you figure *that*?" Shiflett asked, frowning.

"Because if he did, he'd have known *Damocles*'s forward ring was down and she couldn't give chase," Townsend said. "I assume that maintenance plan was logged into the Cascans' system?"

"It was," Marcello confirmed, nodding. "It also means he hasn't got an ally tucked in among CDF personnel who could have found that out for him."

"Yes, Sir."

"I suppose that's worth something," Henderson said.

"It's worth a lot," Marcello said. "A traitor in your midst could have made for serious future trouble."

"Agreed," Henderson said. "On the other hand, a traitor would have been a lead we might have been able to ferret out. This way, we've again got zero."

"Yes," Marcello murmured. "Whoever this guy is, he's damn smooth." He gazed at the display another moment, then turned to Townsend. "And now, I think it's time we headed back to the ship," he continued, a slight edge to his voice. "There's apparently some new reading I have to do."

Lisa looked at Townsend, too. The big Sphinxian's face was a little pale, but there was no hint of panic in his expression. Whatever these supposed secret orders were, she had no doubt they really did exist.

What Marcello would choose to do with them, of course, was another matter. Orders were orders, but long-distance ones like this usually included a degree of latitude that ship's commanders could invoke in case of unforeseen circumstances.

"Of course," Henderson said. "We'll continue monitoring him from down here, and *Chachani* will continue bringing up her impellers, just in case he has a malfunction before he hits the hyper limit. Unless that happens, though, I'm afraid he's clear and gone."

"Yes," Marcello murmured. "I wonder what a megalomaniac like Khetha had—or knew—that could possibly make this whole thing worth this much effort."

Lisa swallowed. This much effort, and this many lives.

It was a big galaxy, but she couldn't quite rid herself of the suspicion that the Haven Sector might someday find that out.

It was unlikely to be an enjoyable experience.

☆   ☆   ☆

The timer Llyn had set ran to zero...and with that, there was no longer any even theoretical possibility that the Cascans, Manticorans, or Manticoran missiles could catch him.

With a huff of relief, he quickly ran the impellers back to the standard eighty-five percent. He'd half expected *Damocles* to try anyway, running her own impellers as high as she had to in order to burn off Llyn's lead.

But Captain Marcello hadn't been that crazy. And really, who could blame him? He shouldn't be expected to risk his ship and crew that way, certainly not when all they could even suspect Llyn of was an assault on those two nosy Manticorans he'd caught following him.

And so, for want of a little courage, the captain of *Damocles* had forfeited his chance to save his worlds.

And the real pity was that he would never know it.

CHAPTER NINE

LISA DONNELLY HAD CALLED from the shuttle landing field to let Travis know that she was ready to come pick up her dog, and to make sure he would be home.

Travis was home, was ready, and had nervously paced exactly one hundred seventy-four circuits around the room by the time the door chime finally rang.

To his relief, the anticipated awkwardness didn't materialize. Lisa walked in with a smile and a casual greeting, and then dropped into a crouch and whistled for Crumpets. By the time the Scottie came racing from the bedroom on her little legs, and she and Lisa had had their joyous reunion, any hint of discomfort had long since passed.

And if it hadn't, Lisa's next smile would have done the trick. "Thank you so much, Travis," she said, standing up again with the dog resting in the crook of her arm. "You have no idea how much this means to me."

"It was no trouble," Travis assured her. "Crumpets is a great little houseguest."

"Well, good guest or not, I owe you one," Lisa said. "Thanks again."

"No problem," Travis said, bracing himself. "Um . . . you might not know, just coming in today, but there's supposed to be an announcement from the Palace in about—" he checked his chrono "—an hour. If you leave now, you may not get home in time to watch it live. You're welcome to wait and watch it here if you'd like."

"That's all right—if I don't make it I can listen in the car," Lisa said. "I don't want to impose."

"You're not imposing," Travis assured her, trying to keep the sudden desperation out of his voice. He'd been preparing for this moment—and thinking of ways to prolong it—practically since *Damocles* left Manticoran orbit. "I've got some strawberries fresh from this morning's farmers' market, and I was going to make some chocolate fondue to dip them in. And you can tell me about Casca while we wait for the broadcast."

"Oh, Casca was a trip and a half," Lisa said soberly.

"In a good way, or a bad way?"

"Definitely the bad way." She hesitated. "I probably shouldn't be telling you any of this—it's not exactly classified, but Captain Marcello wanted it kept as quiet as possible. But with your sideways way of thinking...and you *do* know how to keep a secret. The *Phobos* thing showed that much."

"Uh-huh," Travis said, a twinge of guilt pulling at him. He had not, in fact, entirely kept his role in that incident secret. He'd blabbed that one critical detail to his half-brother, Gavin.

At the time, of course, he'd been frustrated and aching and fully intending to leave the Navy once his five-T-year hitch was up.

He'd never known what use Gavin had made of that indiscretion. He'd expected it to come back to haunt him, though, and had walked on eggshells for several months afterward, waiting for the inevitable official fallout.

No such fallout had ever come. But that didn't mean he didn't occasionally still feel it looming silently over his head.

Regardless, he'd learned his lesson. Whatever Lisa told him would stay strictly between them. Especially if it meant spending a few more minutes with her this afternoon.

"Why don't you go into the living room and sit down?" he suggested. "I'll go get the fondue going."

"Let me come help," Lisa volunteered. "Years of eating fondues, and I've never yet seen anyone set one up."

"You may be disappointed to find out how incredibly simple it is," Travis warned.

"I'll take my chances," Lisa said. "Come on. Let's melt some chocolate into submission, and I'll tell you all about Casca."

☆　　☆　　☆

Winton family dinners, Edward reflected, didn't happen very often anymore. And the depressing fact was that when they did they were far too often of this sort.

Bleak. Painful. Quiet.

Heart-rending.

He looked around the table, trying to envision how his family had looked in happier times. But for some reason, his brain found it impossible to bring up those images. All he could see was what was, with perhaps a shadowing of what was to come.

At the head of the table sat his father, King Michael, eating mechanically, his gaze a million light-years away. Beside him was his wife Mary, her own gaze alternating between her husband and the plateful of food she was barely picking at. At Edward's own sides were his wife Cynthia and his son Richard, neither of whom were making any more headway on their meal than anyone else. On Cynthia's other side was their daughter Sophie, who was probably trying harder than anyone else in the family to exude some cheerfulness, and failing miserably.

And directly across from Edward was his sister Elizabeth.

Edward was trying hard not to look at her. Probably everyone at the table was, if only from a desire to offer her whatever degree of privacy they could while sitting bare meters away. But perversely, and despite his best intentions, Edward found it impossible to keep his eyes turned away for long.

There was just something about widow's garb that irresistibly drew people's attention.

In her place, Edward reflected, he probably would have opted to skip this event entirely. No one would have blamed her. The King certainly hadn't commanded her presence.

But Elizabeth had a strength of will far beyond Edward's own, as well as a stubborn streak a kilometer and a half wide. Both qualities had driven him crazy in the past, back when he was the teenaged heir to the Manticoran Throne and she was just a smart-mouthed kid who felt it was her sacred duty to keep her half-brother from feeling too comfortable.

The two of them had butted heads countless times over the years. But there'd never been any doubt in his mind that she loved him dearly, just as there was never any doubt that he loved her.

And now, to see her sitting there like a bag of broken glass...

Perhaps sensing his troubled gaze, she looked up from her

plate. Their eyes met, and for a brief eternity a wordless flicker of empathy and understanding flowed between them. Then her eyes closed in a slow blink, and when they opened again the moment had passed. She was again his younger half-sister, a wounded bird, standing defiantly against the pain. "It's all right, Edward," she murmured, just loud enough for him to hear. "It's not about me. Not today."

Edward nodded. Understanding or agreement, she could take it whichever way she wanted.

He turned his attention to the three children seated on her right and left. They, too, were trying to be brave and grown-up. But to him they looked like baby chicks huddled beneath their mother's wings. They hadn't been present at the horrific hunting accident that had taken their father, so unlike Elizabeth they wouldn't have those images etched eternally across their retinas.

But they would never forget the day they'd been given the news. They would never forget the words their grandfather and grandmother had used in that terrible and life-changing moment.

Just as Edward himself would never forget his own ill-considered and morbidly prescient words bare weeks before the tragedy.

Mary and I will be watching them, the King had said, referring to Elizabeth's step-children as she and her husband Carmichael prepared for their Sphinxian hunt.

So trading off a potential mauling versus guaranteed and unabashed spoiling? Edward had flippantly replied.

He hoped desperately his father hadn't repeated those words to Elizabeth. Bad enough that he would have to remember them the rest of his life. It would be too much to bear if he knew Elizabeth would also associate her husband's death with her half-brother that way.

"Edward?"

The word, crashing in upon the silence, was startling. But Edward had had words unexpectedly thrown at him by senior officers over the years, and his body managed not to flinch. "Yes?" he answered, looking up.

His father was gazing at him from the head of the table, his eyes older and wearier than Edward had ever seen them. "It's time," the King said gently. "We need to get ready." He nodded to Edward's son. "You, too, Richard."

Edward gave his sister one last glance as he rose from his seat, feeling as he did so his wife Cynthia's brief reassuring squeeze on his arm. "Yes, Sir," he said.

It's not about me. Elizabeth's quiet words echoed through Edward's mind as he and his father left the dining room and made their way down the Palace hallway. She'd been right. Tonight was about their father, and about the future of the entire Star Kingdom.

Edward swallowed hard. *God help us*, he prayed silently. *God help us all.*

☆   ☆   ☆

"Hurry up, Gavin," Breakwater snapped from across the room. "We're going to be late."

"Yes, My Lord," Winterfall said, peering into the mirror and making a small adjustment to his jacket. He could understand the Chancellor's impatience; it wasn't often these days that King Michael asked to address a session of the House of Lords. And it was practically unheard-of for him to ask that the session be broadcast live.

Naturally, Breakwater suspected something underhanded was about to happen. And given that today was also supposed to be the day that the first two of the *Pegasus*-class corvettes would be formally handed over to MPARS, the focus of the Chancellor's suspicions were leaning that direction.

Winterfall wasn't ready yet to buy into Breakwater's current conspiracy thoughts. Certainly not about the corvettes and MPARS. For one thing, the Navy didn't have a whole lot of wiggle room in that deal, especially given that the King had officially signed off on it. For another, there was no way Michael would be crazy enough to try to renege on the arrangement in full sight of God, Parliament, and the entire population of Manticore.

In fact, especially given that the Palace had announced Crown Prince Edward would also be there, there was only one possibility Winterfall could see that would jibe with Breakwater's fears.

And that possibility was a frightening one. If the King had decided that MPARS was chipping too strongly at the RMN, what better solution than to take control of the service away from the Exchequer and make it into its own, independent department? And if he did, who better to hand it off to than his own Navy-trained son?

That scenario apparently hadn't occurred to Breakwater, and

Winterfall had no intention of bringing it to his attention. Still, it was the most likely possibility he'd come up with. And of course, by making the announcement as publicly as possible, the King would give Breakwater a choice: sit silently by in apparent assent, or go ballistic in full view of the entire Star Kingdom.

Winterfall didn't know what was about to happen, or what Breakwater was going to do in response. But no matter what went down in the next few minutes, Winterfall was determined that he himself would come out looking as good and as professional as possible.

"Gavin?"

Winterfall gave his neck scarf one final pat. "Yes, My Lord," he said. "I'm ready."

☆   ☆   ☆

"Are you ready?" King Michael asked.

Edward gave a final tug at his collar. "Almost," he said. "Just one more minute."

"*One more minute?*" His father gave him a small smile. "Really, Edward. That was the same line you gave me when you were eight and were trying to stall your way out of something you didn't want to do."

"Consistency is a virtue," Edward said reflexively, his mind still back in the dining room.

"Only if you're consistently right," Michael countered. "Otherwise, it's the granddaddy of all vices." He paused. "She'll be all right, Edward," he said more quietly. "She's strong, and she has all of us to help her get through it. The more important question is whether *you're* going to be all right."

Edward looked sharply at him. Was his father really going to bring up those horribly ill-advised words?

No, of course not. He was merely referring to the next few minutes.

And to the many, many minutes beyond.

"I'll be fine," he said. "You've prepared me well. Despite my best efforts to the contrary."

"You did fine," Michael assured him. "It just took you a while to hit your stride." He raised his eyebrows. "Do try to hit it a bit faster this time."

"I will," Edward promised. He hesitated. "They're not going to like this, you know."

Michael shrugged. "Some won't. At least not at first."

"Chancellor Breakwater?"

"His was one of the names that came to mind," Michael agreed. He shifted his shoulders. "And with that, I believe your minute is up."

Edward forced a smile. "Which was *your* consistent line," he reminded his father.

"You asked for a minute; I gave you a minute," Michael said with another smile. "The art of compromise." He sobered. "Just remember that compromise never means giving away your core values. Ever."

"I know," Edward said softly.

"Good." Michael straightened up—

And suddenly, he was once again King Michael, ruler of the Star Kingdom of Manticore. "It's time. Let's do this."

He headed across the Royal Sanctum toward the door. Edward followed.

Wondering if the collar would be less uncomfortable if it wasn't for the lump in his throat.

☆　　☆　　☆

"Wow," Travis said when Lisa reached the end of her story. "That was...just wow. You're all lucky someone didn't get killed."

"Someone *did* get killed," Lisa reminded him.

"I meant someone from *Damocles*," Travis said hastily, feeling his face warming.

"I know," Lisa said. "Though from what Commodore Henderson told us about General Khetha, I don't feel as sympathetic as I did at the beginning."

"They're sure that was who it was?"

"Very sure," Lisa said. "Once they knew his ship had been stolen, and found out from the people at his mansion exactly who had gone missing, they knew who to test for. After that, it was just a matter of putting together enough surviving DNA for a positive ID." She took another strawberry from the bowl Travis had placed in front of her end of the couch, which she'd been mostly ignoring while she told her story. "And of course, once the police pulled up what they knew about the Canaan situation, and what he'd done before he was kicked off the planet, they wrote the whole thing off as revenge."

"I don't believe it," Travis said. "There's something else going on."

"See, that's what *I* thought," Lisa said, her face brightening.

"But Henderson and Nabaum—that's the police lieutenant who handled the case—seemed to think that was all it was. They said it wasn't for any of the treasure he stole, because the mansion wasn't touched, and he didn't have anything in banks or safe-vaults."

"That they know of," Travis pointed out. "Maybe he had something stashed away and the killer needed an access code or something."

"His people say no," Lisa said. "Though of course they could be lying through their teeth."

"Yeah," Travis said, searching for a different topic. Talking with Lisa was always enjoyable, but he'd hoped to avoid talking shop tonight. "Speaking of teeth, you may have noticed that Crumpets has a new chew toy."

"Yes, I did," Lisa said, reaching down and retrieving the half-eaten hybrid of colorful cloth and more durable rawhide. "Did she lose the old one, or just eat it wholesale?"

"Good question," Travis said. "I'm guessing the latter, since I've searched this place fore to aft and haven't found any trace of the old one."

Lisa waved a hand at the couch she was sitting on.

"Did you look between the couch cushions? Not *under* the couch, but between the cushions?"

For a moment Travis stared blankly at her. How in the world would a dog that size—?

"No, I didn't," he confessed, standing up. "Uh..."

"Allow me." Smiling, Lisa stood up, made a magician's abracadabra gesture, and lifted up the cushion she'd been sitting on.

And there it was. Slightly more bedraggled than the last time Travis had seen it, but it was indeed Crumpets' old chew toy.

"I'm not even going to ask," he said.

"Probably just as well," Lisa said, replacing the cushion and resuming her seat. She wiggled the toy at Crumpets a moment then tossed it over her head, sending the little animal scurrying after it. "Our best guess was that she liked smelling it nearby when she was on the couch with us."

"Ah," Travis said, feeling his throat tighten. *Our. Us.* How did Lisa's ex always manage to intrude on these conversations? "Well, I guess now she's got two of them."

"Trust me: a dog can never have too many chew toys," Lisa said. "You have any idea what this big broadcast is about?"

"Nope," Travis said, watching as Crumpets trotted back with her newly rediscovered treasure. She settled down at Lisa's feet and started gnawing it. "I was hoping you might."

Lisa shook her head.

"Not a clue."

There was a chime from across the room, and the vidscreen came on. "Ah—here we go," Travis said, swiveling around in his seat.

"You'll see better from here," Lisa suggested, pointing to the other end of the couch.

"Thanks," Travis said. Feeling a little odd, he got up and sat down near her. Not too near, of course, but not so far away as to be insulting.

On the screen, King Michael stepped to a podium adorned with the Royal Seal of the House of Winton. Dressed in his full regalia of state, he looked every millimeter a monarch.

"*My people,*" he said into the pair of microphones on the podium, his voice deep and confident.

And yet, behind the richness of his tone, Travis sensed a hint of weariness.

"*Citizens of Manticore, Sphinx, and Gryphon; Members of Parliament; My Lords and Ladies.*"

There was every reason for him to be weary, of course. The daily wrangles with Parliament; the decisions necessary to keep the Star Kingdom running smoothly; not to mention the continual squabbles for power between the RMN and MPARS.

"*In the eighteen years that I've been privileged to be your king, the Star Kingdom of Manticore has experienced unprecedented growth. We've continued to move along the path of recovery from the devastation of the Plague, and with the additional citizens who have come to us via the assisted immigration program we have become a stronger and more vibrant society. The Royal Manticoran Navy has guarded us against external threat, while the Manticoran Patrol and Rescue Service has risen to the challenge of securing the safety of travel within our borders.*"

The image went to split screen, the second image showing a slow pan across the assembled Lords. Chancellor Breakwater was prominent among them, his face studiously neutral. Two seats down from him, Travis spotted his brother Gavin, wearing the same expression.

"We have begun building our own merchant marine, and our industrial capacity continues to flourish. You have worked together with fortitude and patience, and I have no doubt that we have a bright future ahead of us."

"But that future will not be mine to oversee."

Travis felt a sudden tightness in his chest, the weariness in the King's face suddenly taking on an ominous edge. Was he ill? Discouraged?

Dying?

"For reasons which must remain private, I have decided that I can no longer lead the Star Kingdom of Manticore. Accordingly, I am today declaring my abdication from the Throne in favor of my son, Crown Prince Edward."

Travis felt his eyes widen with disbelief. King Michael was *abdicating*? Beside him, Lisa said something shocked-sounding under her breath. Travis barely even noticed.

"I have no doubt that he will lead you with dignity and strength, and I know that you will accept him with the same loyalty and honor you have always shown me.

"Thank you, and may God be with you all."

With that, he stepped away from the podium.

And was gone.

For a long moment, Travis just stared at the screen. The camera belatedly turned to follow the King—the former King—from the stage and into the wings, then shifted back to a view of the Lords.

They looked as stunned as Travis felt.

King Roger had died in office. So had his daughter, Queen Elizabeth. Travis had grown up assuming that was the way of things, that Manticoran monarchs gave their entire lives for their people and for the crown. *The king is dead; long live the king.*

Now, without warning, all that had changed. The Star Kingdom was entering uncharted territory.

And Travis had never liked uncharted territory.

"Travis?"

He started, turned to look to his side. Lisa was still sitting there, gazing at him with what looked like concern on her face. "You all right?" she asked.

Travis forced a nod. "Sure," he said. "It's just...that was about the last thing I expected."

"You and the rest of the Star Kingdom," Lisa said darkly. She nodded at the TV. "Looks like Crown Pr—like *King* Edward is going to speak."

Travis looked back. With his father now gone from the stage, Edward had stepped to the podium. In the background behind him was his son, Richard Winton, resplendent in his black and gold Academy cadet uniform.

Only now they were King Edward and Crown Prince Richard.

Travis took a deep breath. He'd survived uncharted territory before. He would survive this one, too.

Lisa had set Crumpets down on the couch between them. Absently scritching the dog behind her ears, Travis braced himself for this new and unexpected future.

BOOK TWO

1541 PD

CHAPTER TEN

"...AND AS ALWAYS I WISH YOU safe journeys," the middle-aged man on the display said. "Godspeed, Lorelei. Come home to me soon."

The message ended. For a long moment Senior Chief Fire Control Tech Lorelei Osterman stared at the empty display, her emotions pinballing between the familiar and rock-solid warmth and love for her widowed father, and her extreme annoyance at the position he'd just put her in.

Watch over young Locatelli was what he'd said. *Babysit the snot-nosed nephew of the Navy's Commanding Officer of System Command* was what he'd meant.

Blast him for putting her into this position, anyway.

Still, she should have expected it. Her parents had been long-time friends of Admiral Locatelli and his wife before Osterman's mother passed away six T-years ago. When she heard that Locatelli's nephew and four other freshly minted ensigns had been assigned to *Salamander*, it was only logical that Locatelli's father would call her father, who would message her.

There was still some hope that the kid would be assigned to aft weapons instead of Osterman's forward weapons division. But given that the elder Locatelli knew she was aboard, the odds were depressingly good that the admiral had pulled whatever strings were necessary to put him in her part of the ship.

And thus continued the Royal Manticoran Navy's slide into hell.

The sudden abdication of King Michael two years ago had

been the first knell. Not that Edward was a bad king. Far from it. On top of that, he'd been an RMN officer, which meant he understood the needs of the Navy even better than his father had.

The problem was that Chancellor of the Exchequer Breakwater was still hell-bent on draining every drop of blood from the Navy that he could and transfusing it to his private MPARS fiefdom, and so far Edward hadn't found the backbone to stand up to the man.

Complicating that hemorrhage had been Knell Number Two: the abrupt and equally unexpected resignation of Defense Minister Calvingdell shortly after *Damocles*'s return from Casca.

The rumor mill had worked overtime on that one, without ever reaching any solid conclusions. But there had been hints. In the weeks after *Damocles*'s return from the Cascan fly-by Osterman's private sources had marked several high-level, closed-door meetings between Calvingdell, Prime Minister Burgundy, and First Lord of the Admiralty Cazenestro. Sometimes those meetings had included one or more of *Damocles*'s officers and petty officers, and King Edward himself had joined the group for at least two of them.

The rumors surrounding the Cascan trip itself were just as murky and equally unsatisfying. The official news reports spoke of a multiple murder that had occurred in Quechua City while *Damocles* had been there, but no one seemed to know how or why the RMN and the Star Kingdom were involved.

All Osterman knew for sure was that when the round of meetings was finally over, Calvingdell was no longer Defense Minister. Unfortunately, Breakwater had been Johnny-on-the-spot there, too, somehow managing to pressure Prime Minister Burgundy into reinstating Earl Dapplelake to that position.

Osterman had liked Calvingdell. The woman had been elegant, articulate, and a good foil for Breakwater's schemes. She'd persuaded Parliament to authorize out-system pirate hunts and good-will visits, all of which had not only been the absolutely right proactive response to Secour, but had also raised the Star Kingdom's visibility and prestige among its neighbors.

Dapplelake, in contrast, had been the Defense Minister who had authorized the *Mars* debacle.

And now, here was the third knell: the rebirth of nepotism.

Calvingdell had stopped that, too, or at least had slowed it down. The brief resurgence in funding and enlistment had allowed the

Navy to go for quality, not just cater to the vicarious military dreams of the Lords and Ladies lying thick upon the ground.

Her uni-link signaled. Bracing herself, Osterman clicked it on. "Osterman."

"Todd," the voice of Commander Maximillian Todd, *Salamander*'s XO, came tersely. "Captain wants to see you in his office."

"Aye, aye, Sir," Osterman said, suppressing a sigh. Three guesses as to what *this* was about.

Sure enough, Ensign Locatelli was waiting with Captain John Ross, Baron Fairburn, when Osterman arrived in his office.

"Senior Chief," Captain Fairburn said, nodding to her. "I want to introduce you to *Salamander*'s newest officer. Ensign Fenton Locatelli; Senior Chief Lorelei Osterman."

"Pleased to meet you, Senior Chief," Locatelli said, giving her a brisk nod of his own. The nod was so obviously an attempt to imitate the mannerisms of his famous uncle that Osterman had to consciously suppress a wince. What looked good and proper on a face lined with long naval experience looked ridiculous and pretentious on a kid barely a third his age. "I've heard good things about you from my father and uncle. I'll look forward to having you serving under me."

"Thank you, Sir," Osterman said. *Serving under me.* Not *teaching me how to do my job* or even *serving with me.*

Even senior officers who'd earned the right to speak that way almost never did. Only ensigns came wrapped in such confident arrogance and oblivious ignorance.

Fairburn was watching her closely, clearly hoping she would verbally fawn a little. Unfortunately for him, Osterman had no intention of doing so. After a couple of seconds of silence, the captain's lip twitched with resignation and he nodded again. "Very well. Ensign Locatelli, you're dismissed. Senior Chief, a word, if I may."

He didn't speak again until the door had sealed behind the ensign. "I have the sense, Senior Chief, that you don't care for the new addition to our little family."

"I'm sorry you were left with that impression, Sir," Osterman said. "I have nothing against Ensign Locatelli."

"Except that he's an ensign? *And* a Locatelli?"

"Neither has anything to do with the situation, Sir."

"So pleased to hear that, Senior Chief," Fairburn said acidly.

"You *are* aware, I trust, that Admiral Locatelli is the main reason you're wearing a Navy uniform right now and not an MPARS one."

Osterman made a face. But he was right. After *Mars*, they certainly couldn't count on the Defense Minister's judgment and backbone. The only person standing between the Navy and Chancellor Breakwater these days was indeed the System Commander. "Yes, Sir," she conceded. "I just...permission to speak freely, Sir?"

"Of course."

"What you just said is true," she said. "Furthermore, everyone aboard knows it. I'm concerned that he might therefore be treated differently than if he were Ensign No-Name."

Fairburn's eyes narrowed. "Rest assured, Senior Chief, that neither I nor anyone under my command is going to treat him as anything more than a brain-dead wet-ear who needs petty officer help to find his boots in the morning."

"I hope that will be the case, Sir," Osterman said. "Will that be all, Sir?"

"For now." Fairburn raised his eyebrows. "Just make sure you don't backflip the other direction and lean on him harder than you would your Ensign No-Name."

"No, Sir, I won't." Osterman dared a small smile. "Even if that was possible."

Fairburn gave a little snort. "Of course, Senior Chief. What in the world was I thinking?" He waved a hand. "Dismissed."

☆   ☆   ☆

"Glad to meet you, Mr. Llyn," Cutler Gensonne said, the prominent and self-awarded admiral's bars glinting on his shoulders as he seated himself behind his desk. "My apologies if the journey was a bit more than you were expecting."

"Not a problem," Llyn assured him.

Which wasn't to say he was pleased by the delay, of course. The Volsung Mercenaries' headquarters was right where Ulobo's data had put it: in the city of Rochelle on the planet Telmach in the Silesian Confederacy. Once Llyn had collected a proper crew from the covert section of Axelrod's mining operation in Minorca, which had allowed him to use the full capabilities of General Khetha's modified courier ship, he'd arrived at Rochelle less than six months after his rather hurried escape from Casca.

Only to find that Gensonne and several of his ships had headed off elsewhere in the Confederacy.

The liaison who'd been left to man the office had said they would probably be away for a year, possibly two. Llyn, with no intention of waiting that long, had reboarded his ship and headed off to track them down.

That trip had eaten up much of the time he'd saved by the serendipity of Khetha being on Casca. But that was all right. There was still one more test Axelrod's people needed to make anyway before Llyn could greenlight the invasion. "I hope I'm not interrupting anything important," he added.

"Not at all," Gensonne assured him. "Actually, our business here went faster than I'd expected. Another month or two, and we'll be ready to look at your job." He cocked an eyebrow. "Assuming it proves to be worth our while."

"Let's find out," Llyn suggested, handing a tablet across the desk.

Gensonne accepted it with a grunt and settled back to read.

As he did so, Llyn took the opportunity to study the man.

Gensonne was pretty average-looking, as mercenary chiefs went. Light-skinned and blond, with blue eyes, he had the near-focus look of a man who had spent most of his life aboard ships.

His history was far more colorful than his bland looks would suggest. He'd served for several years with Gustav Anderman, and had been on hand when Anderman defeated Ronald Devane and added the Nimbalkar system to his growing empire. For a while, as Anderman settled into his new role of emperor, it had looked like Gensonne might be in line to take up a significant and senior role in Anderman's navy. There were indications, as well, that Gensonne might be hoping to emulate his boss's successes, with his sights set on a couple of other small colony worlds in the region that could be added to Anderman's empire.

But then, without explanation—or at least none that Llyn had found in the files he'd read on the trip to Rochelle—Anderman had abruptly pulled the plug on Gensonne's ambitions. Gensonne had apparently responded by taking his core crew, and a couple of small ships Anderman gifted him, and going home. He'd ended up on the fringes of the Solarian League, where he'd started to build an organization of his own, one without Anderman's inconvenient list of scruples. Eventually, he'd relocated into Silesia, with his growing collection of ships and men, and ever since had been taking on the kind of jobs Anderman would never have touched.

Llyn didn't know why Anderman and Gensonne had parted

company, though he had his suspicions. Still, Gensonne's record was one of competence, certainly enough to handle the subjugation of the Star Kingdom of Manticore. At the end of the day, that was all that mattered.

And in fact, the Anderman connection made things perfect. An investigation in one direction would dead-end at the late General Khetha and his homecoming ambitions, while an enquiry in the other direction would conclude that Gensonne had been inspired by his former chief's example to try his own hand at the whole planet-conquering game. Either way, Axelrod's name would be completely out of it.

Across the desk, Gensonne stirred in his seat. "Interesting," he said, with his eyes still on the tablet.

Llyn waited a moment, wondering if there would be more. But Gensonne just flicked to the next page, his eyebrows pressed together in concentration. "Is that a good interesting, or a bad interesting?" Llyn asked at last.

"Well, it sure as hell isn't good," Gensonne growled. "You realize this is a star nation that can conceivably field somewhere in the vicinity of *thirty* warships? Including six to eight battlecruisers?" He cocked his head. "That's one hell of a fighting force, Mr. Llyn."

Llyn smiled. It was a standard gambit among mercenaries, one that had been tried on him at least twice before. By inflating the potential risks, the bargainer hoped to similarly inflate the potential payment. "You apparently missed sections fifteen and sixteen," he said. "The bulk of that fleet is in mothballs awaiting the scrapyard. What's left is either half armed or half crewed or both. Our estimate is that you'll be facing no more than eight to ten ships, with maybe *one* of those ships a battlecruiser."

"I *did* read sections fifteen and sixteen, thank you," Gensonne countered. "I also noted that the most recent data here is over fifteen months old."

"I see." Standing up, Llyn reached across the table and plucked the tablet from Gensonne's hands. "Obviously, you're not the group we're looking for, Admiral. Best of luck in your future endeavors."

"Just a moment," Gensonne protested, grabbing for the tablet. Llyn was ready for the move and twitched it out of his reach. "I never said we wouldn't take the job."

"Really?" Llyn said. Time for a little gamesmanship of his

own. "It certainly sounded to me like you thought the job was too big for you."

"There *is* no such job," Gensonne said stiffly, standing up as if prepared to chase Llyn all the way through his office door if necessary to get the tablet back. The fact that Llyn was making no move to leave seemed to throw him off stride. "I was simply making the point that your intel was stone cold, and that *any* merc commander would want an update before taking action."

"Was *that* what you were saying?" Llyn said, feigning a puzzled frown. "But then why did you imply that the odds—?" He broke off, letting his frown warm to a knowing smile. "Oh, I see. You were trying to amp up your price."

Typically, Llyn knew, people hated to see their stratagems trotted out into the sunlight. But Gensonne didn't even flinch. A bull-by-the-horns type, with no apologies, no excuses, and no regrets, nicely consistent with Llyn's analysis of the man. "Of course I was," he said. "I was also looking for more information." He gestured to the tablet. "We can handle the job. Trust me. The question is why we should bother."

"A good question," Llyn said. As if he was really going to let a mercenary leader into Axelrod's deepest thoughts and plans. "You'll forgive me if I respectfully decline to answer."

Gensonne's eyes narrowed, and for a moment Llyn thought the other was preparing to delve back into his bag of ploys and tricks. But then the admiral's face cleared and he shrugged. "Fair enough," he said. "You're hiring mercenaries, after all. Not fishing for investors."

"Exactly," Llyn said, his estimation of the man rising another notch. Gensonne knew how to play the game, but he also knew when to stop. "So. Are the Volsung Mercenaries the ones for this job? Or would you rather keep on hitting small mining colonies and helpless freighters?"

Again, Gensonne's eyes narrowed. But this time it was the narrowing of a predator's eyes as the animal prepared to spring. "What's that supposed to mean?" he asked, very softly.

"Oh, don't worry—I'm not planning to tell anyone," Llyn assured him, rather surprised that his piracy shot in the dark had drawn some blood. The thought had only occurred to him a few days ago as he contemplated all the attention Manticore and Haven were putting into their pirate hunt.

Though of course there was also the whole general drying-up of jobs all across the galaxy that were available for under-the-radar groups like Gensonne's. The predator was still there, but it was an increasingly hungry and desperate one.

And desperation was an emotion Llyn was quite adept at playing.

"I understand that it's hard for an honest mercenary to make ends meet these days," he continued. "I'm merely suggesting you might find this job more lucrative as well as more satisfying than simple piracy."

For another moment Gensonne continued his predator's stare. Then, he gave a little shrug. "Probably," he said. "But you're missing the point. The freighters aren't supplementary income. They're practice."

"Practice?"

"Running down ships is an art, Mr. Llyn," Gensonne said. "One that needs constant practice to maintain. All the training and drills I can give my men can only take them so far. In the end, you need to face someone who genuinely and desperately wants to get away."

"Ah," Llyn said, suppressing a shiver. Suddenly, he was starting to see exactly why Anderman had kicked this man off his team.

"You disapprove?"

"I have no opinion one way or the other," Llyn said. "All I care about, as I said, is whether you're the ones for my job."

Gensonne smiled grimly. "The Volsung Mercenaries are very much the ones for your job, Mr. Llyn," he said. "Have a seat, and let's talk money."

☆　　☆　　☆

Missile Tech Chief Charles Townsend had been aboard HMS *Phoenix* for a full week before Travis was finally able to carve out time during midwatch to head back to Aft Weapons and see his old boot camp friend.

The meeting did not go exactly the way he'd expected.

"Lieutenant," Chomps said formally, floating at attention in the autocannon monitor station. "I'm pleased to see you again, Sir. It's been a long time since our days at Casey-Rosewood. Congratulations on your success at OCS and your promotion."

Travis was still trying to think how to react to the other's unexpectedly cool correctness when Chomps's face split in a huge grin. Grabbing Travis's arm, he yanked him close and enfolded him in a big bear hug. "You son of a yard dog," he said in Travis's ear. "*Man*, it's good to see you, Rule-Stickler."

Travis was still trying to think how to react to *that* when Chomps pulled back as quickly as he'd moved in and was once again floating in the kind of formal posture a petty officer was supposed to present to a superior. "I mean, man, it's good to see you, Rule-Stickler, *Sir*," he corrected.

"Nice to see the years haven't degraded your sense of humor," Travis managed, still trying to get his brain leveled after the double blindsiding. "If that's how you typically greet officers, I'm surprised you haven't been busted to Spacer Third by now."

"Or lower," Chomps agreed. "They *could* bust me to MPARS, you know. Don't worry—I have a *bit* more discretion than that."

"Good," Travis said, his thoughts flashing back to the awkwardness of his first meeting with Lisa Donnelly when she'd bounced back into his life a couple of years ago. For obvious reasons, of course, this acquaintance renewal felt completely different from that one. "So how've you been?"

"Slogging my way up the chain," Chomps said, dropping into the kind of semiformality that Travis had seen between other officers and petty officers who were also friends. "Due to some apparently chronic glitch in the BuPers computer system, they keep promoting me. And now—" he waved a hand expansively "—here we are, together again."

"My son, who done good," Travis said.

Chomps smiled, but there was a seriousness about his eyes. "Thanks to you. I don't know what would have happened if you hadn't taken the heat for me when you did."

"Probably the same thing that happened to me," Travis said, trying for a light tone. "A slap on the wrist, then business as usual."

"Maybe," Chomps said. "Maybe not." He pursed his lips. "I know I thanked you at the time...but as the years pass and I get older and wiser, I'm able to see even more clearly the risk you took. So again, thank you."

"You're welcome, Chief," Travis said. "Provided we make this the last time you mention it. Officers are used to being cursed out by petty officers. Getting thanked by one plays havoc with our timing."

Chomps grinned. "Aye, aye, Sir," he said. "So; hyper limit patrol. Exciting stuff."

"Certainly less exciting than Casca, anyway," Travis agreed.

"So you know about that?" Chomps said, his forehead furrowing slightly.

"As least as much as anyone else does," Travis said suppressing a wince. In the rush of old camaraderie he'd completely forgotten that, while the subject wasn't exactly classified, Lisa had asked that he not bandy it about. Still, if there was anyone aboard *Phoenix* with whom he could talk about it, Chomps was certainly it. "Seems to me you're lucky to be alive."

"You got that right," Chomps agreed, his nose wrinkling. "If it hadn't been for Commander Donnelly—"

He broke off at a sudden violent klaxon blared from the intercom. "General Quarters, General Quarters," the cool voice of *Phoenix*'s Weapons Officer, Lieutenant Commander Bajek, came from the speaker. "Set Condition Two throughout the ship. Repeat: set Condition Two throughout the ship."

Travis felt a sudden tightness in his stomach. Readiness *Two*? Sixty seconds ago *Phoenix* had been at Readiness Five.

What the hell had just happened?

"Looks like I spoke too soon about this being boring, Sir," Chomps said, the easy familiarity abruptly gone.

"I guess we'll find out, Chief," Travis said, hearing the same military precision and formality in his own voice. "We'll talk later."

"Yes, Sir."

Travis found Lieutenant Brad Fornier, commander of *Phoenix*'s Missile Division, hovering off to the side in Forward Weapons, watching silently as the partial crew summoned by the Readiness Two order glided in and strapped into their consoles. "Bit late, Long," Fornier commented as Travis joined him.

"Sorry, Sir," Travis said, running his eyes over the monitors. Forward Weapons wasn't ready, but the systems were coming up with gratifying speed.

Those that *would* be coming up, anyway. One of the tracking sensors and one of the fire-control repeaters were dark, and the electronic warfare assembler was hovering on the edge of failure. Like every other ship in the Navy, *Phoenix* didn't have enough spare parts or people to keep everything together. "What do we have here, a drill?"

"Doesn't sound like it," Fornier said. "Apparently, CIC's reporting a hyper footprint on a least-time course from Casca."

"Could be the Havenite freighter that's scheduled to be in next week," Travis suggested.

"If it is, it's early," Fornier said. "Not unheard of."

"But not common."

"No."

Travis scowled as the assembler flickered and died. "There it goes."

"Damn," Fornier muttered. "Skorsky?" he called. "Get that assembler back up."

"Yes, Sir."

"Anyway, it sounds like the captain's not in a particularly trusting mood," Fornier continued. "We're moving to intercept."

Travis squinted at the range display, running a quick calculation. About ten minutes to com range. "Well, we should know something soon."

"*If* the captain decides to hail her as soon as she's in range," Fornier pointed out. "He might prefer to wait until we've closed a little more distance."

"He won't," Travis said. "She's already spotted our wedge and knows we're heading her way. If we don't hail as soon as we can she may figure we're a pirate and run."

"Which would be pretty much the same response she'd show if she *was* a pirate," Fornier conceded. "Which means we wouldn't learn a thing by doing that."

"Right."

"Let's see if the captain follows your logic," Fornier said. "Not to mention regulations. Pull up a chunk of bulkhead, and make yourself comfortable."

CHAPTER ELEVEN

"I ASSURE YOU, CAPTAIN CASTILLO," Captain Shresthra said, a layer of sweat sheening his little brown face, "that there is nothing at all irregular about my ship, my crew, my passengers, or my cargo. I had no idea that traffic to the Star Kingdom of Manticore was so rigorously monitored and controlled."

Floating behind him in the *Izbica*'s cramped bridge, the man who called himself Grimm watched silently while Shresthra's engineer, Pickers, ran a diagnostic probe along the circuits of one of the switching boards. There was nothing seriously wrong with the board—or the entire computer, for that matter—but Grimm had made a point of introducing the occasional harmless hiccup into the system over the year that he and his two colleagues, Bettor and Merripen, had been aboard. There was a good chance he would need to engineer a major collapse sometime in the next couple of weeks, and he needed to make sure the problem was adequately set up in the crew's minds.

Shresthra finished speaking, and the long time delay to the *Phoenix*'s reply began. "You don't suppose he'll want to board us, do you?" Pickers asked nervously. "We're behind schedule enough as it is."

"Now, now—he sounds like a reasonable enough man," Shresthra soothed. "Still, I have no doubt he'll do whatever he chooses. It's small-world mentality. They tend to lord it over people from more advanced systems when they have the opportunity."

Grimm smiled to himself. Like Shresthra had any right to

talk. The Solarian League might be the undisputed big dog on the street, but not all of the League's worlds were up to that exalted standard. As far as Grimm was concerned, Shresthra's own homeworld of Berstuk was definitely one of those holding the average down.

"But besides possible damage to our schedule, this presents no real difficulty," Shresthra continued. "It's Mr. Grimm and his friends who have the most to lose."

"Indeed we do," Grimm agreed, turning to face the captain. Shresthra was right on the money, though he had no idea how right he was. "We can only hope that Captain Castillo will accept and honor our documents, should he choose to send boarders."

"And if he doesn't?" Shresthra pressed. "Will the Minorcan government invoke their penalties even if a disclosure isn't your fault or your doing?"

"I certainly hope not," Grimm said. "Unfortunately, the non-disclosure agreement makes no specific allowance for such things, so it will be entirely at their discretion." He nodded toward the gravitic display and the mark that indicated the *Phoenix*'s position. "Even more unfortunately, Manticoran meddling would be the worst meddling of all."

"I can imagine," Shresthra said, nodding.

"Actually, you can't," Grimm said, putting some iron into his voice. He doubted Castillo would bother chasing down and boarding a clearly harmless freighter, and with their equipment still packed away in their crates a simple Navy spacer wouldn't see anything suspicious.

But Grimm's policy was to avoid even small risks; and if the Manticorans decided to board, he wanted Shresthra to be as solidly on his side as he could make the little man.

"I'll tell you this much," he continued. "What we have in the hold is a completely revolutionary system of—well, I can't really say. But the fact that the Minorcans will be the only ones in the region with it will translate into huge profits over the next few years. If a nation with Manticore's industrial base and funding was able to get even a hint of what it is and what it can do, they could conceivably undercut Minorca's monopoly and its future profits. With a world their size, that would be a financial disaster."

"Understood," Shresthra said, importing some of Grimm's iron into his own tone. "Do not fear. Even out here, Solarian-flagged freighters have certain rights. Rest assured that I will do every-thing in my power to make sure your secret cargo remains secret."

"Thank you," Grimm said, bowing his head. "Not just for us, but for the people of Minorca."

He looked back at the computer. "And speaking of our cargo, if you'll excuse me, I'd like to go check on it."

"Of course," Shresthra said. "Again, have no fear. I'm sure we'll be fine, and that this Manticoran won't cause us any further delays."

Grimm's two companions were inside Number Two hold when Grimm arrived. "How's it look?" he asked as he sealed the door behind him and glided over to join them.

"I did what diagnostics I could," Bettor reported. "Everything seems intact. Do you want me to start setting up?"

"Not yet," Grimm said. "There's an inconveniently positioned RMN ship out there asking questions. My guess is that they came out to escort that Havenite freighter that was still loading at Casca when we left."

"Let's hope they stick with that mission and leave us alone," Bettor said.

"I think they will," Grimm said. "Their interest is probably just a matter of traffic being so sparse that *every* newcomer raises eyebrows."

"Maybe," Bettor said. "So we leave things packed until we're clear?"

"Yes," Grimm said. "Shouldn't be more than a few hours at the most."

"Let's hope it's less," Grimm warned. "We're cutting it close enough as it is, time-wise, especially if you want me packing up again before we hit orbit. A few lost hours out here could be awkward at the other end of the trip."

"You'll be all right," Grimm soothed him. "Unless Shresthra manages to really raise their suspicions, they'll probably let us go and continue to wait here for the other freighter." He looked at Merripen, lifting his eyebrows in silent invitation to weigh in.

But Merripen just shrugged. He was a man of few words, Grimm had long noted. On a voyage of this length, that was more of a plus than a minus.

"So what kind of warship is it?" Bettor asked.

"Destroyer," Grimm said. "HMS *Phoenix*. I'll let you know when you can start setting up."

"Okay," Bettor said. "But I meant what I said about the timing. It's going to take all the way in, plus whatever time you can get Shresthra to spend hustling for cargo, plus all the way back out. Even all that might not be enough. Especially with this extra delay."

Grimm wrinkled his nose. But it couldn't be helped. The incredibly delicate, double-incredibly expensive equipment they'd brought aboard should theoretically map the gravitational subtleties in the Manticore system well enough to nail down once and for all whether or not there was a wormhole junction here.

But as Bettor had pointed out, such things took time, and distance, and then more time.

"Just make sure you stay on top of it," he said. "By the time we leave orbit, I need to know how much extra time you'll need."

"You'll know when I do."

"Good enough."

And one way or another, Grimm reminded himself, by the time the *Izbica* left the Star Kingdom they would know whether or not a Manticore junction existed.

One way, or another.

☆   ☆   ☆

Three hours later, *Phoenix* returned to the humdrum boredom of Readiness Five. Apparently, Travis concluded, whatever concerns Captain Castillo had had about the unexpected visitor had been satisfactorily resolved.

Resolved enough, in fact, that *Phoenix* was apparently also going to return to her patrol duty and let the visitor head in toward Manticore without escort.

Travis was of two minds about that one. On the one hand, their orders were to patrol the hyper limit, and such orders weren't to be discarded without good cause. On the other hand, he wasn't sure it was wise to allow an unknown ship free and unfettered access to Star Kingdom space. Especially not when *Phoenix* had barely gotten close enough for a full sensor scan.

Still, in the year since Travis had come aboard, he'd found that Captain Castillo generally knew what he was doing. Presumably he did here, as well.

It was four days later, as Lieutenant Commander Bajek took advantage of the ship's idle time to run her weapons crew through combat drills, that Travis received a message to contact Chomps at his earliest convenience.

In this case, Travis's earliest convenience turned out to be six hours later.

"Thanks for coming, Sir," Chomps said as Travis floated through the doorway into the Aft Weapons monitor room. His tone, Travis noticed, was back to formal officer/petty officer mode.

And there was something odd displayed on the station where he'd been working when Travis entered.

"I wanted to run something past you," Chomps said, casually reaching over to blank the display. Maybe a little *too* casually... "Can you first tell me what you know about the League freighter we let pass four days ago?"

"All I know is what Captain Castillo has released to the rest of the ship," Travis said. "Her name is *Izbica*, out of Beowulf, carrying a chartered cargo for Minorca. She's been tramping a few stops along the way to try to pull some extra business. Why?"

"I was hoping I could run a theory past you," Chomps said. "It's a bit...odd...and I know you're pretty good at outside-the-line thinking."

"Sure. Go ahead."

"Okay." Chomps took a deep breath. "Here's the thing. I'm wondering if that exiled dictator from Canaan—General Khetha—might still be alive."

"I thought the Cascans said Khetha was one of the men who was murdered."

"They also thought the murderer was blond with a mustache," Chomps pointed out. "And even the Cascans admit the victims' DNA was degraded, and that they only identified one of the samples as Khetha's after they knew what to look for. Who's to say it was actually him?"

"Let's assume for sake of argument that you're right, that Khetha's still alive," Travis said. "I assume you have more theory to go along with it?"

"Yes, Sir," Chomps said. "Okay. Khetha kills someone—probably a random guy in the street—who's close enough in height and build to pass as him after some time in a denature bag. Maybe he substitutes the guy's DNA for his own in his mansion's records; maybe he just assumes the degrading will be enough to do the trick. In that case, it could have been *Khetha*, not the killer, who took the courier ship and made a run for it."

"Or else they're both aboard?" Travis suggested.

"The Cascans said the security cams show only one man getting aboard the shuttle."

"Any description?"

"None they shared with us."

Travis nodded. "Okay, so now it's Khetha and not the killer who escapes from Casca. Go on."

"The killer now goes to ground on Casca for a couple of years," Chomps said. "Not impossible if he's prepared the papers and has enough money. Somewhere along the way, Khetha decides there's something he needs from Canaan, either more looted treasure or something else. So he sends a message to someone in the League, who then charters *Izbica*. This someone and a buddy come aboard as passengers. The freighter heads to Canaan, bouncing around a few more ports on the way just to muddy the waters, where Khetha's agents pick up the goods. Then they head to Casca."

"Hold on a second," Travis said, quiet alarm bells going off in the back of his head. He hadn't heard anything about passengers, and he certainly hadn't seen a copy of the freighter's itinerary. How was it Chomps knew all this? "So they just pick up these gold bricks or whatever and stash them aboard?"

"*Izbica*'s passengers have taken over two of the holds and loaded them with a secret cargo," Chomps said. "Supposedly running under diplomatic privilege via the Minorcan government. The treasure or whatever could be in there. So they head to Casca, where they do a little more trading and add the killer to their party. That now makes it the party of three that *Izbica* shows on their personnel list." He lifted his hands. "Does this make any sense? Or am I just spitting at a radiator?"

"I think you've been reading too many thrillers, Chief," Travis said. "Why would Khetha go to all that trouble? And I mean as far back as Casca. The courier boat was *his*—he could have just taken off whenever he wanted."

"Unless he was also conning his own entourage," Chomps said. "If he was running out on them too, or else trying to throw off other enemies, going to ground on Minorca is about as deep a hole as you can find to lose yourself in."

"It's still way more complicated than necessary," Travis said. "New topic. How exactly do you know so much about *Izbica* and her particulars? *I* don't even know all that."

"I have sources," Chomps said evasively. "If you think it's too complicated, then I'm probably blowing smoke into—"

"Hold it," Travis cut him off as the visual memory of that blanked display suddenly bounced back into his mind's eye. "What did you just have on that display?"

"It was nothing," Chomps said, a little too quickly. He pushed off the side of the compartment with one of his large fingers and began floating almost imperceptibly toward a spot directly between Travis and the display. "Just some stuff I was working on."

"Like hell," Travis bit out. "It was confidential ship's data, wasn't it?"

Chomps's face had gone wooden. "No, Sir."

"Don't lie to me, Chief," Travis warned, pushing off the bulkhead toward the display.

Chomps got there first. "I can't let you see this, Sir."

"Why not?" Travis demanded. "Because I'd report it?"

"Yes, Sir, you would," Chomps said. "And that would be bad. For both of us."

"Chief—"

"Sir." Chomps's throat worked. "Travis. Please. I need you to trust me. Like you did back in boot camp."

"That wasn't about *trust*, Chief," Travis bit out. "That was about me sticking up for someone in my squad."

"It still is, Sir." Chomps braced himself. "What are you going to do?"

Travis felt his gaze slip to Chomps's shoulder, trying desperately to come up with a solution that would let his friend off the hook. He'd done it once, back in boot camp. Surely he could do it here, too.

Only he couldn't. Then, it had been a question of dangerous malnutrition, and Travis had been able to see his decision as the morally right thing to do.

But there was no such moral gray area here. Someone—Chomps or someone else—had hacked into *Phoenix*'s records and accessed confidential information. That was a clear violation of Naval Code.

And unfortunately, it put Chomps's actions over the line.

"I need to know who gave you that information, Chief."

Chomps's face hardened even more. "No one, Sir," he said. "I accessed it by myself."

"How?"

"I'd prefer not to go into the details, Sir."

And unless Travis was willing to call for an official enquiry, he was at a dead end. "Very well, Chief," he said. "Return to your duties."

"Aye, aye, Sir," Chomps said. To Travis, he looked like a man who'd just lost his best friend.

Maybe he had.

Later, as Travis sat in his cabin, the stillness of the midwatch broken only by the sound of gentle snoring from Fornier's rack, he spent an hour trying to find the least damning way to write up Chomps. Finally, he settled on *unauthorized access to ship's computer records*. If he—and Chomps—were lucky, it would just be passed over as something small and ridiculous from Rule-Stickler Long and no one would bother to follow up on it.

Still, it would remain in Chomps's record. At any point from now until the heat-death of the universe someone could call Travis in front of a board somewhere and ask why he hadn't provided any details, and what exactly those details were. When they did, he would have to tell them.

And at that point, he and Chomps would both accept the consequences.

With a touch of his finger, he sent the report into the depths of *Phoenix's* computer. Sometime tomorrow, Commander Vance Sladek, *Phoenix's* XO, would pull up the various reports and read or skim through them.

Until then, Travis would hit his rack, try to put this out of his mind, and get whatever sleep he could. *Sufficient unto the day*, he quoted tiredly to himself, *are the troubles therein*.

☆   ☆   ☆

There was no summons to the XO's office the next day. Nor was there one on the second day, nor the day after that. By the fourth day, Travis was finally beginning to breathe a little easier. Surely by now the press of other business had safely buried Travis's report until such time as everything was transferred en masse to Manticore and BuPers' even more massive computer system.

On the fifth day, Travis was abruptly called to Commander Sladek's office.

The meeting was short and about as unpleasant an encounter as Travis had had in the seven T-years since Secour. He was warned about burying reports that should have been promptly brought to the XO's attention, told to stay away from idle gossip and wild theories, and told in no uncertain terms that the next time something like that happened it would go on his record. When Travis dared to ask about Chomps, he was told that it was none of his business.

But a later check of ship's records showed that his old friend had been dropped a rank to Missile Tech First.

From that time on, Chomps never again spoke to Travis aboard *Phoenix* except when absolutely necessary, and then in full formal speech.

Perhaps Chomps had indeed lost his best friend.

Perhaps Travis had, too.

CHAPTER TWELVE

MANTICORE HAD COME AND GONE, and was no more than a faint dot in the *Izbica*'s aft viewer.

And Captain Shresthra, in the quaint old vernacular, was not a Happy Camper.

"You said there would be bales and bales of cargo to be had at Manticore," he grumbled yet again to Grimm, punctuating his rant with an accusing finger. "You remember? That was exactly what you said: bales and bales."

"I know," Grimm said in as apologetic a voice as he could muster. It wasn't easy, when what he really wanted to do was take hold of that jabbing finger and break it off. *Patience*, he reminded himself firmly. "But that really *was* how things worked eight years ago, when I last passed through this region. There was no way I could have known that freighter traffic had picked up so much since then."

Shresthra gave a contemptuous sniff. "A dozen or so ships a year hardly qualifies as *traffic*, Mr. Grimm. At the very least you should have asked the Havenite freighter at Casca whether he and the other freighters had this route sewn up. If I'd known, we could have gone directly to Minorca instead of wasting three weeks with this side trip."

"I know," Grimm said again, doing his best verbal grovel in front of the annoying little man. In fact, he *had* talked to the Havenites, learned that Manticoran trade was indeed well covered, and had been careful to leave them with the impression that he would pass on any relevant information to the *Izbica*'s captain and crew. But the visit to Manticore was the whole reason Grimm and his partners were aboard; the last thing he'd wanted was for Shresthra to bypass the system.

Just as the last thing he wanted right now was for Shresthra to make a stink that would force him to kill the little man and his crew. They were still close enough to the planet—and more than close enough to the ships plying the route between Manticore and Sphinx—that there might still be some need for communication. There was nothing like an abrupt switch to a new and unfamiliar voice to make people curious.

"But there *is* also the planet Gryphon," he continued, gesturing outward. "Not to mention all the Manticore-B mining operations. We could make a quick microjump over there, send out a query to the mining factories, and see if they've got some product they want to sell."

"No," Shresthra said firmly. "The Star Kingdom had their chance. We hit the hyper limit, we're heading straight to Minorca."

Damn. "Certainly, if that's what you want," Grimm said. "I was just trying to salvage something useful from this trip."

"You want to salvage something, salvage your breath next time you have a bright idea," Shresthra growled. Grabbing a handhold, he spun himself around in midair and gave himself a pull toward the bridge.

Grimm waited until he'd floated out of sight. Then, glowering, he headed back to the hold.

Bettor was floating in front of the analyzer, watching as it ran the latest batch of data though its electronic hoops. "Well?" he asked.

"We're going to Minorca," Grimm told him. "Do we care?"

"Afraid we do," Bettor said. "Rough estimate is that we'll need ten to twelve more hours than we're going to get if we leave on the *Izbica*'s current schedule."

"*Twelve?*" Grimm echoed, frowning. "I thought it was only six at the most."

"That was before Shresthra had Pickers goose a few more gravs out of the impellers," Bettor said. "The man's serious about trying to get back on schedule." He raised his eyebrows. "Time to let loose the Merripens of war?"

Grimm pursed his lips, seriously tempted. But his earlier concern about changing personnel in possible future communications was still valid. "Not yet," he said. "I've already gimmicked the interface with the hyperdrive. That should buy us the rest of the time you need. Once you're finished, I'll find the magic fix, and Shresthra can make course for wherever he wants."

"Sounds like a plan," Bettor agreed. "Let's just hope he doesn't figure it out."

"He won't," Grimm said. "We've introduced enough glitches on this trip for him to put it down to yet another bit of balky equipment."

"If you say so," Bettor said. "Just be ready if he isn't as naïve as you expect."

"Don't worry," Grimm said. "I'll be as ready as Merripen is."

"And Merripen's always ready?"

Grimm smiled grimly. "Yes. Always."

☆   ☆   ☆

"This is a drill," Captain Castillo's voice boomed across *Phoenix*'s intercom system. "General Quarters, General Quarters. Set Condition Two throughout the ship. Repeat: set Condition Two throughout the ship. This is a drill."

Travis was the second of his crew to reach their station in Forward Weapons, right after Spacer Second Skorsky. The rest of them were no more than two minutes behind him. Luckily for them.

Two minutes and twelve seconds after that, the missiles, beam weapon, and all of the functional support equipment showed green.

"Nice," Fornier commented, checking his chrono. "I make that as a hair under an eight percent improvement. Excellent work, Lieutenant Long. At this rate, you'll be dropping that awkward *jay-gee* from your rank within a couple of months."

"Thank you, Sir," Travis said, scowling a little to himself. That eight percent might look good on paper, but the bottom-line fact was that the improvement was mainly due to *Phoenix* now being down to a single forward tracking sensor, several major components of the second system having been cannibalized to fix the balky EW assembler.

And it took zero time to bring up, check, and confirm a system that wasn't working in the first place.

All of which Fornier knew, of course. But like everyone else in the Navy, he'd learned how to put good spin on anything capable of being spun.

"Sounds like the aft autocannon's still coming up," Fornier

continued, cocking his ear toward the commentary stream coming from the intercom. "Let's try giving the tracker something to track."

"Yes, Sir," Travis said. Grabbing a handhold, he gave himself a pull and floated over to the main display.

As usual, there wasn't much out there. There were three contacts showing in the inner Manticore-A system—a couple of local transports, plus HMS *Salamander*, out on some kind of training cruise.

And between *Salamander* and the transports was a single contact: the Solarian freighter *Izbica*, heading out from her cargo-hunt on Manticore.

She would do nicely.

"Give me a track on bogey bearing one-four-six by two-two-nine," he called toward his crew.

"A track, Sir?" Skorsky asked, sounding confused. "Sir, she's way out of range for that."

"She's out of range for radar and lidar, yes," Fornier said with an edge of deliberate patience. "They're also blocked by the aft quarter of the dorsal wedge. So what else have you got?"

"Gravitics, Sir," Skorsky said, belatedly catching up. "Yes, Sir. Tracking via gravitics."

"And don't think this is just make-work," Fornier added, raising his voice so the whole compartment could hear. "Yes, tracking is usually CIC's or the bridge's job. But there might be a time down the road when communications get cut off, and you're on your own."

"Understood, Sir," Skorsky said briskly. "Track plotted and on the board."

Travis craned his neck to look at the display. *Izbica*'s position and a rough estimate of her vector were now displayed, within the limits of the gravitic data for something that far away. He ran his eye down the numbers...

And frowned.

"Confirm position," he ordered.

"Confirm position, aye."

"Trouble?" Fornier asked quietly from behind him.

"I don't know," Travis said. "Look where she is."

"Outside the hyper limit," Fornier murmured.

"*Considerably* outside the hyper limit," Travis agreed. "A good three hundred thousand kilometers, and she hasn't made her alpha translation yet. She's not accelerating, either."

"She does seem to be just coasting," Fornier agreed. "You think she's in trouble?"

"Could be," Travis said. In the back of his mind, he could hear the echo of Chomps's voice as he laid out his theory about the Cascan mass-murderer being aboard the freighter. Could he have been right?

No. The theory had been ridiculous. And even if it hadn't been, that could hardly have anything to do with this current situation. The last thing a killer on the lam would want was to draw attention to himself by fiddling with his ship's operation. Especially not this close to an inhabited system.

But while Travis might not know much about freighters, he *did* know that they lived by their schedules. No captain would waste time doodling along past the hyper limit unless he didn't have a choice.

"You think we should signal *Salamander*?" Travis suggested. "She's in range to head over and see what's going on."

"She's also got the same sensor suite we do," Fornier reminded him. "Don't worry—if there's anything worth investigating, Fairburn's already on it."

"I hope so."

In the background, the XO's voice came on the intercom: *Phoenix* was now at full Readiness One.

"Meanwhile, we have a drill to run," Fornier said. "Let's get to it."

☆   ☆   ☆

"I assure you, Captain Lord Baron Fairburn, we have no need of assistance," the voice of *Izbica*'s captain came over *Salamander*'s bridge speaker.

Captain Fairburn, Fairburn corrected him silently. *Or Baron Fairburn. Or Lord Fairburn. Pick one and stick with it.*

Maybe the man assumed *Baron* was Fairburn's given name. Maybe he was just an idiot who didn't bother to read up on the proper protocol for the places he was going to visit.

Fairburn was betting on the second option.

"One of our passengers has seen this before," Shresthra continued. "He says it's just a matter of taking the interface apart, cleaning it and checking all the connections, and reassembling it. A few hours, and we'll be on our way again."

"Very well, Captain Shresthra," Fairburn said. "Again, we're only a couple of hours away from you. Don't hesitate to call if you decide you'd like us to look over your equipment."

It would be another minute and a half before there was any response. But Fairburn wasn't expecting anything except a polite farewell from the freighter. Shresthra apparently had everything under control, and the matter was closed.

And yet...

"Com, were you able to find that report?" he asked.

"Yes, Sir, I think so," Chief Marulich replied from the com station, touching a key on her console. "Is this it?"

Fairburn peered at the report. It was a couple of weeks old, filed with System Command by *Phoenix*'s XO, Commander Vance Sladek. Someone aboard had come up with some scatterbrained idea about the Cascan mass-murderer being aboard *Izbica*. For some reason Sladek had thought it plausible enough to kick an enquiry back to Manticore. "That's the one," he confirmed. "Did you find any follow-up?"

"Not much of one," Marulich said, peering at her display. "It looks like Customs checked *Izbica*'s backtrack and then compared her crew and one of her passengers to the image of the Haven murderer. No matches, so it was marked concluded."

Which was all Customs could reasonably be expected to do, Fairburn knew, especially given the source of the suspicion. He'd heard his share of ship's scuttlebutt over the years, and was surprised that the theory hadn't included the Flying Dutchman among *Izbica*'s secret passengers. And without anything more solid, Customs certainly wouldn't have called in their big brothers in MPARS to board the vessel.

On the other hand...

"How many passengers are there?" he asked.

"The personnel file lists three."

"And Customs only checked *one* of them?"

"The other two never came down to the planet, so they were never scanned."

Fairburn frowned. *Izbica* had been a full week in orbit, and he'd never seen a freighter crew yet where everyone wasn't off the ship and on the ground as fast as they could physically get there.

Yet two of *Izbica*'s passengers had *never* left? "She came from Casca, right? Do we know if those two passengers left ship while she was there?"

"I can check, Sir," Marulich said doubtfully. "But I doubt we have that information."

"And Shresthra said it was one of the passengers who was working on the hyperdrive interface," Commander Todd murmured from behind Fairburn.

"Meaning?" Fairburn asked.

"No idea, Sir," the XO admitted. "It just seems odd that Shresthra would be letting a passenger into the guts of his ship."

Fairburn ran a finger over his lower lip. Odd. Not threatening or suspicious, just odd. Certainly nothing *Salamander* had reason to look into.

Then again, there was also no reason why she *couldn't* look into it.

"Helm, plot me a zero-zero intercept course to *Izbica*," he ordered. "Make acceleration one point two KPS squared."

He swiveled around and eyed his XO. "Let's go be neighborly."

☆   ☆   ☆

"How much longer?" Shresthra asked, his hands opening and closing with barely controlled impatience.

"Two minutes less than when you asked two minutes ago," Grimm said as soothingly as he felt like being right now.

Which wasn't very much. He understood Bettor's need to continue compiling data and was fully prepared to drag out this interface project as long he needed to. But that didn't mean he wasn't starting to wish Shresthra wouldn't keel over from a heart attack or something.

"You said it would take three hours," Shresthra bit out. "It's already taken four, and you've barely started."

"You *did* say it would only take three," the engineer, Pickers, added.

"That was before I realized how filthy everything in here was," Grimm countered, waving the board he was working on for emphasis. "I don't think either of you appreciates just how much this amount of caked grime can affect the current flow. These things are extremely delicate—"

"Captain?" the voice of the helmsman, Nguema, boomed from the crawlspace intercom. "That Navy ship—the *Salamander*?—it's heading our way."

Grimm felt his stomach tighten. What the *hell*?

"What for?" Shresthra asked. "Damn it all—I *told* them we don't need any help."

"They know," Nguema said. "They say they're just running crew drills and might as well run them this direction."

"Very convenient," Grimm said, his mind racing. At all costs he had to keep that Navy ship out of here. If they came aboard, for any reason, they might take it into their pointy little heads to look into the cargo holds.

And with Bettor's sampling equipment unpacked, assembled and sucking in data, that would be a disaster. The very fact that someone was running a secret experiment would be enough of an excuse for Captain Fairburn to commandeer the freighter and haul it back to Manticore for further study.

"Also potentially very pricey," he added. "Some systems charge a fee for rescues, you know."

"We don't *need* a rescue," Shresthra insisted.

"Of course we don't," Grimm said. "We'll have this back together in no time." But not before the *Salamander* arrived, he knew. Not unless the *Izbica* got off her rear and opened up a little more distance. "Best way to show them that would be to throw a few gravs on the fire and get moving. Sooner or later, they'll get tired of chasing us."

"Don't be ridiculous," Nguema scoffed. "I'm not going to blow off energy for that."

"They're not going to charge anything anyway," Pickers added. "The fee-for-rescue thing is a myth."

"And there's no point in getting any farther out than we already are," Shresthra concluded. "Especially if we find out you *can't* put that back together." He jabbed a finger at the disassembled interface.

Grimm clenched his teeth. He hadn't wanted to do this, certainly not here and now. But the very fact that the *Salamander* was heading in their direction showed that something had made the captain suspicious. And once the destroyer was alongside there would be nothing he could do except hope and pray that the Manticorans didn't find Bettor's precious instruments.

And Grimm had never been much for praying.

"We need to get moving," he told Shresthra, keeping his voice low and calm. Merripen would be on the bridge, he knew, keeping track of things up there. "Please."

The captain's eyes narrowed. "Do we, now?" he said, matching Grimm's volume. "Why exactly is that?"

"That's not important," Grimm said. "Just call Nguema and have him get us moving."

"I see." Shresthra took a deep breath. "Nguema?"

"Yes?"

"Shut down the impellers," Shresthra ordered. "I repeat: shut down the impellers. Then call the *Salamander* and request—"

"Merripen?" Grimm cut him off.

"I'm here," Merripen's voice came faintly from the intercom.

"Do it."

Shresthra frowned at Grimm. "Do what—?"

He broke off at the soft, distant-sounding *crack* from the speaker.

"Nguema?" he called. "*Nguema?*"

"I'm sorry," Grimm apologized. "But I *did* say please."

And before the captain could do more than open his eyes wider in a disbelieving stare, Grimm drew his own gun and shot him. Pickers had just enough time for a surprisingly feminine squeak before Grimm shot him, too.

"Merripen?" he called again.

"Bridge is secure," Merripen's voice came back, as stolid and emotionless as always. "He didn't get the wedge down. Want me to get us moving?"

"Immediately," Grimm confirmed, slipping the half-cleaned board back into its slot in the interface. "Then go finish off the rest of the crew. I'll send Bettor to the bridge to watch things while you do that."

"Right," Merripen said. There was a short pause. "Okay, we're up and running—eighty gees acceleration. How soon before you get that thing back together?"

"A couple of hours at least," Grimm said, wishing now that he hadn't been so thorough in his disassembly. "You just worry about your part of the job."

"On it."

Keying on his uni-link, Grimm punched for Bettor. "Status report."

"It's coming along," Bettor said, his voice tight. "Was that a shot I just heard?"

"It was," Grimm confirmed. "That RMN ship—the *Salamander*—decided they needed to get up close and cozy. Shresthra wouldn't get us moving, so I relieved him of command."

"And we're moving now?" Bettor growled. "Great. *That's* not going to look suspicious or anything."

"Bottom line for you is that we may have to cut your sampling time short," Grimm said, ignoring the dig. "Will two or three more hours be enough?"

"I guess we'll find out. You want me to lock down here and go to the bridge?"

"Yes, at least until Merripen finishes his sweep."

"Okay. What do I do if the Manticorans call?"

"Just pipe it down here," Grimm said. "I'll handle it."

☆   ☆   ☆

"They're *running*?" Fairburn demanded, part of his brain refusing to believe the evidence of his eyes.

"Confirmed," Tactical Officer Wanda Ravel said. "She's up to point eight KPS squared. Seems to have leveled off, though a ship of that class ought to have another few gravities in reserve."

"Probably waiting to see our response," Todd murmured.

Fairburn scowled at his displays. There was no reason for *Izbica* to be doing this. None. She was a *freighter,* damn it, and freighters had only one purpose in life: to fly cargoes back and forth and make money doing it. *Izbica* was beyond the hyper limit and on her way to Minorca, and the next item on her checklist would be spinning up her hyperdrive and hitting the Alpha band. This extra n-space acceleration made zero sense.

Unless her new purpose in life was to get away from *Salamander.*

Smugglers? Ridiculous. *Izbica* had been in Manticoran orbit for nearly a week, with every hour bringing the possibility that Customs would suddenly decide to drop in and take a look at her cargo. Granted, the probability that anyone would do something like that was pretty small, but it was still possible. If Captain Shresthra hadn't been worried about an examination then, why would he be worried about one now?

The Cascan mass-murderer? Same logical problem.

So why run from *Salamander*? And why run *now*? Could it be because Fairburn, unlike Manticoran Customs, was *definitely* talking about boarding her?

Mentally, he shrugged. He could speculate all day without coming up with anything. Sometimes the best way to an answer was just to ask.

"Increase acceleration to one point four KPS squared and

recalculate zero-zero," he ordered. "Com, get me a laser on *Izbica*. Let's see if Shresthra has a logical explanation."

"And if he doesn't?" Todd asked.

"Then we'd best be ready, hadn't we?" Fairburn countered. "Bring us to General Quarters, if you please." He smiled tightly. "We're on a training exercise, after all. Might as well run the crew all the way up."

☆   ☆   ☆

"Damn," Grimm muttered.

"Yeah, I think *damn* pretty well covers the situation," Bettor's tight voice came from the intercom. "*Now* what?"

"Let's not panic," Grimm soothed as he eased the board he'd just finished back into position. Just three more to reassemble and replace, and the interface would be up and running again. "They can't possibly catch up with us before we're ready to get out of here."

"They could still fire a missile."

"They won't," Grimm assured him. "They have no reason to attack and nothing to gain. And missiles are damned expensive."

"Yeah." For a moment Bettor was silent. "Though, you know... maybe we should give them a reason."

Grimm blinked. "Come again?"

"I'm trying to come up with a good reason why we're running," Bettor said. "I mean, a reason from their point of view. We can't be smugglers—if we weren't worried about Manticoran Customs finding some special cargo a week ago, we shouldn't be worried about the *Salamander* finding it now. We can't be accelerating just for the fun of it—merchant ships run too close to the margin to waste energy that way. What's left?"

Grimm pursed his lips. Unfortunately, Bettor had a point. It would take a huge leap of intuition for the Manticorans to guess that the *Izbica* was secretly collecting data on a wormhole junction that no one even suspected was here. But in the absence of any other reason, someone could conceivably wander off down that path.

And Grimm's team's job wasn't just to collect data, but to make sure no one knew that they were collecting it.

"I guess what's left is the most obvious one of all," he told Bettor. "They still waiting?"

"Yes."

"Okay. Patch me through."

There was a brief pause— "You're on."

"Hello, Captain Fairburn," Grimm called toward the intercom. "This is Captain Stephen Grimm of the Solarian Merchantman *Izbica*. How can I assist you?"

There was a long silence, longer than the normal light-speed time lag for their current distance would account for. Grimm had the third-to-last board halfway reassembled by the time the *Salamander* finally responded. "Apparently, our records are in error," Fairburn's calm voice came over the speaker. "We have Stephen Grimm listed as a passenger, not the captain."

"There's been a slight shake-up in the chain of command," Grimm told him. "None of your concern. What do you want?"

Silence descended as his words began their slow, speed-of-light journey to the distant RMN vessel. "What exactly are we going for here?" Bettor asked. "You hoping to convince him we're pirates?"

"That's the big buzz word around here these days," Grimm reminded him. "Shouldn't be too hard to get them to that conclusion. Once they do, they won't look for other possibilities."

"What are you going to do if he asks why we didn't take the ship sooner?"

"Probably spin some nonsense about hoping Shresthra would pick up some high-tech stuff at Manticore we could add to our loot," Grimm said. "But I doubt he'll ask. Their focus now should be on doing whatever they can to catch us."

"But they *can't* catch us, right?" Bettor asked, his voice sounding just a little apprehensive. "You're going to have that interface finished in time, right?"

"Don't you worry your little head," Grimm soothed. "A *Salamander*-class destroyer can pull a maximum of two hundred gees, but they're not going to go over one-seventy. We can safely do about eighty. At our current vector differential—look, you can run the numbers yourself if you want. Bottom line: we'll be out of here before they can get even close to a zero-zero."

The speaker hissed with a sigh. "If you say so," Bettor said. "You'd just better be right."

☆   ☆   ☆

Grimm's—*Captain* Grimm's—message ended, and for a long moment *Salamander*'s bridge was silent.

Not for lack of anything to say, Fairburn knew. But merely because everyone was thinking the same thing.

Izbica had been hijacked. And there was only one reason why a simple freighter with no ransom-worthy people aboard would be seized.

Grimm and his fellow passengers were pirates.

Pirates.

The word seemed to hang in front of Fairburn's eyes. After all these years of sifting through flight data, listening to rumors, and traveling across interstellar space, he and *Salamander* finally had found real, living, breathing pirates.

And unless he did something fast, those pirates were going to get away.

He squared his shoulders. "Increase acceleration to one point eight KPS squared," he ordered, wishing briefly that his voice was the deep, resonant type. This was history in the making. "And recalculate for zero-zero."

There was a brief silence, and he knew what they were all thinking. Eighty percent of maximum acceleration was one point six KPS squared, and standing orders were to stay below that line unless at dire need.

But *Izbica* held the proof that would finally and permanently shut up Chancellor Breakwater and the rest of the doubters in Parliament. There was no way in hell that Fairburn was going to let that proof get away.

The rest of the bridge crew knew that, too. That, or they knew better than to argue with their captain. "One point eight KPS squared, aye," the helm confirmed.

"Recalculating zero-zero," Ravel added.

"Good," Fairburn said. "And go to Readiness One," he added. "*Izbica* appears to have been taken by pirates." *History in the making...* "We're going to take her back."

CHAPTER THIRTEEN

READINESS TWO.

The words echoed through Osterman's mind as she carefully slid her rebuilt circuit board back into the Forward Missile capacitor-charging monitor. Captain Fairburn hadn't bothered to explain what was going on, and Osterman suspected most of the crew thought it was just part of the training exercise.

But all her years in the Navy had honed Osterman's instincts into fine-tuned sensors in their own right. She could feel the subtle tension in the air, the slight edge in the sporadic orders and communications emanating from the bridge.

Something was definitely going on.

But what? A rescue mission? An attack on the Star Kingdom? Pirates?

Readiness Two.

Out of the corner of her eye, she saw a figure float swiftly past the compartment doorway. She glanced over just in time to see that he was carrying something fist-sized in his hand. An electronic module, her brain automatically identified it, probably a hex.

Which in itself wasn't unusual. Ever since general quarters had been called, officers, petty officers, and spacers had been scrambling like mad to get half-working systems up to full operating capacity. Forward Weapons was no exception, and Osterman had nearly been mowed down at least twice by spacers maneuvering racks and large components through the zero-gee at unsafe speeds.

What made this current sighting odd was that there were no

storerooms or component bins in the direction the spacer had come from.

Which strongly implied that the hex clutched in the spacer's hand had been borrowed from somewhere else.

Osterman had pushed her way out of the compartment and sent herself flying down the passsageway almost before the analysis had fully worked its way through her brain. Midnight requisitions were hardly unheard of aboard *Salamander*—indeed, they were depressingly common, given the chronic shortage of equipment. But there was a big difference between borrowing from a secondary system and from a vital one. Wherever the spacer was going with that hex, she was damn well going to find out where he'd gotten it.

She caught up with him two turns later, and to her complete lack of surprise saw that it was Spacer First Class Hugo Carpenter. "Hold it," she called as she hurried to catch up. "Carpenter? I said hold it."

For that first second it had looked like he might try to ignore the order and make a break for it. But the use of his name had apparently convinced him that running would be both useless and foolish. Catching hold of a handhold, he brought himself to a clearly reluctant halt.

"Yes, Senior Chief?" he greeted her carefully as he turned around, pressing the hex close to his side. Maybe he was hoping she wouldn't notice it there.

Fat chance. Even on a ship full of scavengers, Carpenter was something of a legend among the petty officers.

"Something seems to have attached itself to your hand," Osterman said. "I thought you might need help getting it removed."

The majority of people didn't blush in zero-gee. Unfortunately for Carpenter, he wasn't one of them.

"Uh..." he stalled, his face reddening.

"Come on, we don't have time for this," Osterman growled, gesturing to the hex. "Where'd you get it?"

Carpenter sighed.

"Ensign Locatelli ordered us to get the tracking sensors up and running," he said, reluctantly holding up the hex.

"What, all three systems?" Osterman asked, frowning. One of His Majesty's ships these days was lucky if it had even two of the tracking systems running. Most of the time they had to make do with one.

"All three," Carpenter confirmed, giving her a wan smile. "He said he didn't care how we pulled it off, but that by God we would."

Osterman suppressed a scowl. That sounded like Locatelli, all right. Still trying to wield the kind of authority he wasn't even close to actually possessing.

"Where'd you get it?" she asked.

"The laser temperature sensor," Carpenter said. "I figured that since the system has been down for weeks, and these components were just sitting there—"

"Yeah, yeah, I know," Osterman interrupted, plucking the hex out of his hand. With the lack of a functioning X-ray emitter having put the beam weapon semi-permanently out of commission, the rest of its associated equipment had become a sort of happy hunting ground for *Salamander*'s scroungers.

And indeed, Carpenter's hex looked damn near fresh out of the box. There were no kluges, no rebuilds, and only a couple of casing scratches around the mounting bolts where careless techs had missed the mark with their screwdrivers. Definitely a component that hadn't seen much use.

"You put your old hex in its place, I assume?"

"Yes, Senior Chief," Carpenter said. "Ours wasn't broken, exactly, just a little iffy, and I wasn't sure it would hold up to one of Ensign Locatelli's one-ten tests. If it didn't—well, you know what he's like."

"Not sure I like your tone, Spacer," Osterman warned. "That's an officer you're talking about."

"Sorry, Senior Chief."

Osterman grunted. Tone notwithstanding, Carpenter had a point. Locatelli the Younger was famous for pushing people and equipment past their limits, and had little patience when the results didn't match up with his expectations.

In a navy with infinite money and resources, pushing components to a hundred and ten percent of their normal operating ceilings was a good way to weed out those that might fail under the added duress of combat. In a navy with extremely finite quantities of both, that kind of limit-pushing was just begging for trouble.

But nobody could tell Locatelli anything. More depressingly, nobody *would* tell him anything. Not with the shadow of his powerful uncle looming over him.

Still, this kind of poaching wasn't something a senior chief ought to turn a blind eye to. Osterman was trying to decide whether to simply tell Carpenter to return the hex, or to take the time to accompany him to the beam monitor compartment to make sure he did it, when the ship's klaxons abruptly began wailing. "Battlestations! Battlestations! All hands to battlestations. Set Condition One throughout the ship."

Osterman swore under her breath. Battle stations. Whatever the hell was going on out there, it had just gotten real.

"Here," she said, thrusting the hex back into Carpenter's hands. "Get the tracker back together before Locatelli skins you alive."

"Yes, Ma'am," he said tensely. Shoving off the handhold, banging his shoulder against the bulkhead in his haste, he headed back toward Forward Missiles.

And in the meantime, Osterman still had the rest of the capacitor-charging system to double-check. Shoving herself the opposite direction, she flew down the passageway.

Wondering what the hell Captain Fairburn was up to.

☆　☆　☆

"I'm sorry, Sir," Ravel said. "Even if Captain Shresthra was telling the truth about the hyperdrive interface being disassembled, there's just no way to know how disassembled it was when this Grimm character took over. And without that data, there's no way to know when *Izbica* will be ready to translate."

Fairburn glared at the gravitics display. *Izbica* was still far ahead, with the TO still putting their zero-zero rendezvous half an hour away.

And *that* assumed the freighter didn't increase her acceleration again. *Salamander* was already pulling more gees than Fairburn liked, and he really didn't want to push his compensator any further than he already was.

Besides, for all they knew, *Izbica*'s hyperdrive might already be ready to spin up. Grimm could be one of those sadistic SOBs who would let *Salamander* get almost in reach before making his move.

In theory, assuming *Salamander* made it far enough outside the hyper limit, Fairburn could follow the target into hyperspace. But *Salamander* was still close enough to the edge to make that a bit risky. If *Izbica* got even a minute's head start, all Fairburn would have to show for his trouble would be a single sarcastic communication, some useless sensor readings, and a double handful of nothing.

And Chancellor Breakwater and his allies would continue their campaign of scorn and contempt for the Navy.

Fairburn couldn't let that happen. Not now. Not when *Salamander* was so close.

Not when there might be a way to make sure that pirate ship stayed put.

"TO, what's our range and position vis-à-vis a missile launch?" he asked.

Even without looking, he could sense the sudden tension on the bridge. "Excuse me, Sir?" Ravel asked carefully.

"Relax—I'm not planning to shoot her out of the sky," Fairburn said, swiveling to face her. Ravel's expression was just as rigid as her voice. "What I want is to send a missile *past* her wedge, detonating the warhead in front of her. Close enough for the blast to cause some damage to sensors, maybe glitch the hyperdrive or impellers if we're lucky, but far enough away not to instantly vaporize her. Can you set up a shot like that?"

"Yes, Sir, I think so," Ravel said, her voice going even more stiff and formal. "But even with close-control telemetry I can't guarantee the blast will damage *Izbica* enough to disable her. If the error's on the other end, it may destroy her outright."

"Understood," Fairburn said. "But actually disabling her may not be necessary. Once we've proven we have the will and the ability to destroy her, Grimm may be more willing to surrender."

"That may be, Sir," Commander Todd spoke up, his expression and tone as formal as the TO's. "For the record, Sir, I'm obliged to remind you that a missile is an expensive and valuable part of the Star Kingdom's arsenal. To spend one on what is little more than a warning shot could be construed as wasteful."

And Breakwater would indeed construe it that way, Fairburn knew. Firing a missile at *Izbica* would be a huge gamble, on several levels.

"I must also remind you, on the record," Todd continued, "that standing orders require that all expenditures of missiles and other restricted ordnance be fully justified by the situation, and can only be done in consultation with the Executive and Tactical Officers."

"So noted," Fairburn said, an eerie feeling creeping along his spine. He'd read this order when it first came out five T-years ago, and remembered feeling the same black cynicism that probably every other officer in the Navy had felt at the time. Here and now, though, the words didn't sound nearly so ridiculous. "For the record, I note in turn that I am consulting Executive Officer Commander Todd and Tactical Officer Lieutenant Commander Ravel. Have either of you anything to say?"

Todd and Ravel exchanged looks. Neither seemed exactly thrilled at the plan, Fairburn could see. But neither did they want to go down in Star Kingdom history as the ones who'd ruined the Navy's first chance to finally nab a real pirate.

"I agree with Captain Fairburn's assessment of the situation," Todd said formally. "The circumstances justify the expenditure of a missile."

"I also agree," Ravel said.

"So noted and logged," Fairburn said. And thanked God that Breakwater hadn't added language that would have required them to ask his personal permission to do their damn jobs. "Weapons Officer, prep me a missile. TO, plot me a warning shot.

"Let's take these bastards down."

☆   ☆   ☆

The last board was half reassembled, and Grimm was starting to breathe a little easier, when a sudden curse came from the intercom. "Grimm—they've launched on us," Merripen bit out.

Grimm felt his heart skip a beat. "You mean a *missile*? They've launched a *missile*?"

"No, a cupcake," Merripen snarled. "*Yes*, a damn missile. What the hell do I do?"

"You start by not panicking," Grimm said, thinking fast. Unless the destroyer had increased its acceleration significantly—and Bettor had given Merripen strict orders to watch for that when the latter took over bridge duty—they still had several minutes before even a fast-track missile could reach them. "You'll want to do a pitch, either up or down. Twenty degrees ought to be enough. Can you do that?"

"Yeah, sure, I can do that," Merripen said. "But if I do, I won't be able to see the *Salamander* anymore."

Grimm frowned. That side effect of the maneuver hadn't occurred to him. But Merripen was right. Blocking the incoming missile's path with the floor of the *Izbica*'s wedge would also block their view of the *Salamander*.

Could that be exactly what Captain Fairburn was going for? To force the *Izbica* to lose track of it while it—?

While it what? Fired another missile, this one angled and arcing to run straight up the *Izbica*'s kilt? Or kicked up to a pursuit acceleration that was far greater than its listed limits?

Both scenarios were damn unlikely. But neither was completely out of the question.

But Grimm and the others had no choice. There was a missile incoming, and no matter what Fairburn had planned for after that, it would all be irrelevant if the missile blew the *Izbica* to atoms.

"Just do it," he growled toward the intercom.

"Fine," Merripen growled back. "You just get that interface the hell back together, okay? Suddenly, this isn't looking like such a good neighborhood."

"Yeah, yeah," Grimm said, feeling fresh sweat working its way onto his skin. "Working on it."

☆   ☆   ☆

The missile had been launched, *Salamander* had cut her acceleration long enough for the solid booster to get the weapon clear enough of the ship, and as the missile's wedge came up *Salamander* resumed her own acceleration.

"They did it," Forward Gunnery Officer Lieutenant (jg) Pascal Navarre murmured from behind Osterman. "They really *did* it."

Osterman nodded silently. Captain Fairburn had actually fired one of *Salamander*'s missiles.

Or rather, *Salamander*'s senior officers had launched it. She'd seen that ridiculous committee order when it first came down, requiring a vote of the senior officers before a ship's captain could spend any of the Navy's precious ordnance.

Clearly, all of those officers had agreed.

What the *hell* was going on out here?

Osterman hadn't the faintest idea. But given the situation, maybe Ensign Locatelli's loud insistence that all three of his tracking systems be functional might not have been such a stupid order, after all.

An instant later, a dull *thud* sounded faintly in the distance.

And the telemetry section of the status board went solid red.

"Telemetry," Navarre snapped unnecessarily. "Damn. Crash kit?"

"Probably not," Osterman said, grabbing a handhold and pulling herself into the passageway. "I'll get the one from Autocannon."

"No—I'll get it," Navarre said. "You get to telemetry."

"Aye, aye, Sir," Osterman said. Leaning into the handhold and her own inertia, she changed direction and headed toward the telemetry compartment.

She had the face off the main panel when the sound of someone tumbling through the hatchway came from behind her. "Report," Ensign Locatelli ordered tartly.

"Telemetry is down, Sir," Osterman said, her teeth clenching around the last word as she spotted the problem. "Looks like a hex blew."

She spared a glance at him as she shoved off the deck toward the crash kit. But there was no recognition of reality in Locatelli's eyes, no connecting of the blatantly obvious dots. All he saw was a dead component, and a job for his senior chief petty officer. "Then we'd better replace it, hadn't we?" he said.

"Yes, Sir," Osterman said, consciously unclenching her teeth. This was no time for revelations or recriminations. One of *Salamander*'s missiles was running free, and with the telemetry system crashed there was no way for anyone to guide or otherwise control it. All the missile had right now was its own internal hunting programming, and that might not be the proper setup for whatever Fairburn had in mind. "Can you get the face off the aux panel, Sir?" she called back over her shoulder.

At least Locatelli knew how to move when he needed to. By the time Osterman got back with the crash kit he had pulled off the auxiliary panel's face and set it out of the way. Osterman braked to a halt with her feet against the supports and popped open the kit.

Crash kits were supposed to be the emergency supply boxes, theoretically holding a spare or two of all the major components for a given electronics or hydraulics system. Unfortunately, they were as subject to pilferage as all the rest of the ship's equipment. As Osterman had predicted to Navarre, the telemetry crash kit was woefully incomplete, with barely a third of its untouchable contents having actually remained untouched.

Among the missing items, of course, were the two hexes that were supposed to be there.

"Damn," Locatelli growled as he peered into the box. "Now what?"

"We first get the bad one out," Osterman said, grabbing the

eight-mil wrench from the tool tack strip and getting to work on the hex. "The lieutenant's getting the crash kit from Autocannon. Maybe it'll have a hex."

"If it doesn't?"

"Then you'd better have Carpenter pull the one he stole for your Number Three tracking system, hadn't you?" Osterman countered. It wasn't the smartest thing a petty officer could say to an officer, but she wasn't much in the mood for tact right now.

"I have no idea what you're talking about," Locatelli shot back. "My people don't steal equipment. They get it from Stores, and through proper channels."

Osterman felt her teeth clenching up again. Either the man was as dumb as paint, or he was deliberately turning a blind eye to the inevitable consequences of his *or-else* orders. "Unless Stores doesn't have what's needed," she said. "In which case—"

She broke off as Navarre came caroming in off the edge of the hatchway. "Got it," he puffed. "What do you need?"

"A hex," Osterman told him, mentally crossing her fingers.

Crossing them uselessly. There were no hexes in Navarre's kit.

"Now what?" Locatelli demanded.

Dumb as paint. Leaning past him, Osterman jabbed the intercom.

"Forward Tracking; Telemetry," she called. "Osterman. Shut down one of your tracking systems, pull out a hex, and bring it to me here."

"*What?*" Locatelli said. "Wait—"

"Meanwhile, Sir," Osterman put in as she cut off the intercom, "may I suggest you and Lieutenant Navarre start calling the other stations nearby and see if any of them has a crash kit with a spare hex."

"Senior Chief—" Locatelli began, his voice dropping into Authority Zone.

"Good idea, Senior Chief," Navarre interrupted. "Ensign, you start with Electronic Warfare and Sensors—use the intercom in the next compartment. I'll call Gravitics and Forward Impellers from here."

"Sir—"

"*Move* it, Locatelli."

Out of the corner of her eye, Osterman saw Locatelli throw a glare in her direction. But he merely nodded and swam his way out the hatchway.

"Thank you, Sir," Osterman murmured.

"Just doing my job," Navarre rumbled, moving over to the intercom. "Meanwhile, better make sure the hex didn't cascade anything else when it died."

"Already on it."

☆   ☆   ☆

The seconds crept by. Slowly, they turned into a full minute.

And the missile was still rogue.

Fairburn consciously forced open his hands, which had somehow closed themselves into fists when he wasn't watching. A rogue missile might not be a commander's worst fear, but it was pretty damn high on the list.

And still the missile flew. How long did it take to repair a damn telemetry transmitter, anyway?

"Tracking reports missile still on kill course, Sir," Ravel said tautly.

Fairburn's hands again closed into fists. Kill course. Not the overshoot-and-explode in the wide open area in front of *Izbica* that he'd planned for it. With its telemetry link to *Salamander* gone, the missile had shifted to internal guidance.

And the default programming was to go for the kill.

Whether the missile would be able to carry out its new goal was still in question, of course. At its current flight angle, *Izbica*'s floor was blocking a direct intersect vector, and as the missile gained speed it progressively lost its already limited maneuverability. At this point it really had only three possibilities: impact on *Izbica*'s floor, make it past the edge of the floor and impact on the roof, or split the difference and detonate during the split-second it was between the two stress bands.

The first two scenarios would accomplish nothing except the waste of the missile itself. The third would probably vaporize the freighter.

If Grimm had killed Shresthra and the rest of the crew, *Izbica*'s destruction could be viewed as a form of summary and unprocessed justice on a group of murderers. If the pirates had merely confined the crew, Fairburn would be guilty of murder himself.

"Telemetry's back up," Ravel snapped abruptly. "Retaking control."

Fairburn glanced at the timer. Two minutes four seconds had passed since the missile took off. Fifty-six seconds to go before its wedge burned out.

"Can you get it back on track?" he asked.

"Working on it, Sir," Ravel said. Fairburn counted off ten more seconds— "No, Sir," Ravel said. "It's too far along on its kill course. I might be able to get it to detonate between *Izbica's* stress bands, but the timing would be tricky."

Fairburn looked at the tactical display. His eyes followed the missile's track as it converged on *Izbica's*...

"Shall I send the self-destruct code?" Ravel prompted.

"No," he told her. "Run it into *Izbica's* wedge. Try to get it to detonate just before it hits. But if you can't, just let it hit her wedge."

"If we detonate between bands, we can still pretend it was a deliberate warning shot," Todd pointed out.

"Too close, XO," Fairburn said. "Even if Commander Ravel can pull off the timing, we stand a good chance of killing everyone aboard."

Todd cleared his throat.

"Understood, Sir," the XO said, lowering his voice. "May I point out that the whole point of the warning shot was to demonstrate that we had the skill to put a missile exactly where we wanted it? Running it into their wedge hardly sends that message."

"Sir, *Izbica* has gone to full-bore acceleration," CIC reported. "Pushing their compensator to the limit."

"She's pulling away," Todd confirmed. "Shall we increase our own acceleration to compensate?"

"Negative," Fairburn growled. In theory, *Salamander* had more than enough gravs waiting in reserve. In practice, the iffy state of her compensator made any such increase far too dangerous to attempt.

Fairburn had already taken one gamble. His ship had failed him. He wasn't about to tempt fate with another roll of such badly loaded dice. "We could try another warning shot," Ravel offered quietly. "We might still have time."

"With our telemetry probably being held together with packing tape?" Fairburn shook his head. "No. At best, we're one for two—hardly the convincing argument we'd hoped to deliver. At worst, we kill them all."

"They *are* pirates, Sir," Todd reminded him.

"I know," Fairburn said. "But bodies alone prove nothing. If we can't take them alive, there's no point in taking them dead."

There was a slight pause. "Yes, Sir," Todd said.

"Everyone stand ready to follow when *Izbica* jumps into hyperspace," he ordered, raising his voice again so that the entire bridge could hear. "We may yet be able to run them down."

There was the usual murmur of acknowledgments.

But Fairburn hardly heard them. It was still history in the making, certainly. But not the glorious historical victory he'd envisioned.

It might even be the beginning of the end of the Royal Manticoran Navy. Breakwater would certainly be all over this once he heard about it. It was conceivable that a fiasco of this magnitude would be the straw that would persuade Parliament to let the Chancellor take the Navy apart and fold it into MPARS.

Even if that didn't happen, it was certainly the end of the career of one Captain John Ross, Baron Fairburn.

☆   ☆   ☆

"Crap, crap, *crap*," Merripen's muttered voice came from the intercom. "They hit us, Grimm. The damn Manticorans fired a missile and *hit* us."

"Yes, I know," Grimm said with all the patience he could manage. He'd seen the result of that impact on the repeater displays.

That result being exactly nothing. The *Izbica*'s wedge had made short work of the weapon, exactly the way stress bands were supposed to. There'd been a bit of a power flutter, but that was all.

"So are we dead?" he asked Merripen.

"What?" Merripen asked. "No, of course we're not dead."

"Then shut up about it," Grimm said. "We still pulling ahead of them?"

"Yeah. For the moment."

"That's all we need," Grimm said. "Relax—we're almost ready. Did you call up the Number One course package like I told you?"

"Yeah, it's plugged in," Merripen growled. "You *do* realize they're outside the hyper limit, right? And that there's no way in hell we can outrun them in this thing?"

"Trust me," Grimm said with a tight smile. He made the last connection— "Ready," he said, plugging the board into the interface and keying for a self-test. "Don't touch anything—I'll be right up."

The self-test had finished by the time Grimm reached the bridge, with everything showing a satisfactory green. "I hope you've got a really good hole card on this one," Merripen warned with a grunt as he moved away from the helm station. "Fairburn's called twice with orders to surrender."

"Why didn't you pipe it down to me?" Grimm asked, keying up the board.

"'Cause you were busy," Merripen said. "I didn't think you had time to gloat."

"There's always time to gloat," Grimm admonished him mildly. "Okay. Here goes..."

☆　　☆　　☆

"There she goes!" Ravel snapped. "Bearing...we've got her vector, Sir."

"Go!" Fairburn snapped, mentally crossing his fingers. If *Salamander*'s hyperdrive was in the same sorry shape as her telemetry system, this was going to be a very short trip.

Fortunately, it wasn't. Without even a flicker of a problem, *Salamander* translated into the alpha band.

Only to find that *Izbica* had vanished.

"Where did she go?" Fairburn demanded, running his eyes back and forth over the sensor displays, as if he could will the freighter's image into existence by sheer willpower. "There's no way she could have gotten out of range that fast. Could she?"

"No," Todd said grimly. "Best bet is that she did a microjump and got back to n-space just as we were leaving it."

Fairburn clenched his teeth. Todd was right. It would take precise timing, but that had to be the answer.

"TO, calculate how far *Izbica* would have gotten if she'd translated down just as we translated up," he ordered. "Helm, get us back to n-space as close to that spot as you can. CIC, I want a full-sensor scan as soon as we translate."

"Got it," Ravel reported. "Sending coordinates to the helm."

"Ready to translate," the helmsman reported.

"Go," Fairburn ordered.

Izbica wasn't there. *Izbica* was nowhere.

Salamander spent the next six hours not finding her.

☆　　☆　　☆

Bettor lifted a glass of the wine Merripen had found in the late Captain Shresthra's private stores.

"That," he said flatly, "was about as crazy a trick as I've ever seen."

"Not crazy at all," Grimm said mildly, taking a sip from his own glass. Whatever else Shresthra had been, he'd had excellent taste in alcoholic beverages. "It's all in the timing. Plus a certain degree of willingness to push the envelope when making one's translations. Don't forget, I spent a lot of time studying this ship during the voyage. I knew exactly what it could and couldn't do."

"I still think it was crazy," Merripen said. "But I guess you can't argue with success."

"Especially when success pays so well," Grimm said. "Speaking of which, I hope you were able to get all the data you needed, because we sure as hell aren't going back."

"I got enough," Bettor assured him. "Another couple of hours would have been nice, but I should have enough to confirm the junction's existence *and* give us a close approximation as to where it's lurking."

"Good enough," Grimm said.

"And meanwhile," Merripen rumbled, "the Manticorans now know there are pirates working the area."

Gently, Grimm swirled the wine in his glass. Yes, that was indeed the downside of all this. In retrospect, he probably should have just ignored *Izbica*'s hails and let Fairburn come to the pirate/hijacker conclusion on his own. That was surely all the little man's little brain was capable of. The problem was that, without Grimm's declaration on record, a more clever brain might have started thinking outside the lines and wondering if there might be another reason behind the *Izbica*'s passengers' visit.

The odds that someone was searching for wormholes in their system were extremely low, of course. But low odds were not zero odds; and if the Manticorans even suspected what it was they were sitting on, there would be a mad scramble to get all those mothballed ships back into service to defend themselves and their incredible asset.

But pirates weren't nearly such a serious threat, certainly not to a system with this many warships already in service. The most likely response to *Izbica*'s hijacking would be a beefing-up of their customs personnel and procedures, and maybe more escort runs.

Of course, the best-case scenario would have been to continue on to Minorca without causing any ripples whatsoever, leave the *Izbica* peaceably, and catch the Axelrod freighter that would be arriving on carefully unrelated business. That would have left everyone blissfully unaware of what had happened, and given no one any reason to look at this ship, her passengers, or her cargo ever again.

But what was done was done.

And really, the repercussions were unlikely to be anything serious.

"Not a problem," he assured Merripen. "They'll probably tighten up scrutiny on incoming passengers, but that'll be the end of it."

"You don't think they'll beef up their Navy?"

"Against the vague threat of some pirates?" Grimm shook his head. "Not a chance. I mean, come on—they already have all the hardware they need for that."

"The Navy will want more anyway," Merripen said. "Navies always do."

Grimm snorted. After spending a week in Manticore orbit reading the newsfeeds, skimming the recent history, and generally getting a feel for the Star Kingdom, he could answer that one with complete confidence. "Of course they'll want more," he said. "But they won't get it. Not here."

"You sure?" Merripen persisted.

Grimm lifted his glass in salute, the transcript of Chancellor of the Exchequer Earl Breakwater's last speech in Parliament floating before his eyes. "I guarantee it."

CHAPTER FOURTEEN

THEY WEREN'T THE WORDS CAPTAIN FAIRBURN wanted to hear, Osterman knew. For that matter, they weren't the words she wanted to say.

But she had no choice but to say them.

"No, Sir," she said, feeling the pain in her throat. "In all good conscience, I can't place the blame on Ensign Locatelli."

"You *can't?*" Fairburn demanded. "Excuse me, Senior Chief, but didn't you just testify that he ordered his crew to find replacement parts for his tracking systems in any way they could?"

"Yes, Sir," Osterman said. "But unless Ensign Locatelli specifically said to take the components from other systems—and I have no evidence that he used any such language—then he's personally not liable for the, uh, overenthusiasm of his crew."

"Isn't he responsible for knowing what his crew is doing?" Commander Todd put in.

"Yes, Sir," Osterman said. "But only within reason. In this case, with *Salamander* having gone to Readiness Two, the bulk of everyone's attention was on bringing systems to full operational status, not on wondering where replacement parts had come from."

"Then at the very least a charge of negligence should be put on his record," Fairburn pressed.

Osterman felt a stirring of annoyance. That wasn't in any way what she'd just said. Was he even listening to her?

Probably not. Fairburn had spent an expensive missile for nothing, and he was clearly desperate to share the blame for that fiasco with someone. And if that someone was well-connected, so much the better.

Osterman could sympathize. She could also agree that Locatelli was a pain in the butt.

But there were lines she wasn't ready to cross. This was one of them.

"Ensign Locatelli was occupied with the preparation of his equipment for combat, Sir," she said. "As, I daresay, was everyone aboard *Salamander*." She hesitated; but this, too, had to be said. "Furthermore, the action of Spacer Carpenter in swapping out the hex is not what caused the telemetry system to fail. That was the fault of whoever subsequently swapped out the telemetry hex for the unreliable one Spacer Carpenter had put into the temperature sensor."

Fairburn frowned. "There was *another* component switch made?"

As if such switches weren't the norm aboard his ship. "Yes, Sir, as near as I can tell," Osterman said. "I did a check on the serial numbers, and while some of that data is...foggy...it supports my conclusion."

"Then it was whoever did *that* swap who's responsible," Fairburn said.

"Except that he or she would have no way of knowing the hex in the temp sensor was used," Todd murmured reluctantly. "As far as they would have known, it was the original temperature sensor component."

Fairburn opened his mouth, probably preparing to point out that the spacer should have done a complete system check once the new hex was in place.

He closed it again, the words remaining unspoken. Of course there hadn't been time for anything but the most cursory check before *Salamander* went to Readiness One and launched the missile.

There was plenty of liability here, Osterman knew. More than enough to go around. But it was so evenly shared among so many people that there was no way Fairburn would ever be able to gather enough to tar any one person.

She could understand his desire to find a scapegoat. But it wasn't going to happen.

More than that, Fairburn was *Salamander*'s captain. That was the bottom line. He was her captain, and the ultimate responsibility for what happened aboard her rested with him.

Fairburn took a deep breath. "I see," he said. And with that, Osterman knew, the witch-hunt was over. "Commander, close the record."

Todd keyed off the recorder, a frown creasing his forehead. Apparently, this wasn't part of the usual interrogation procedure. "Record closed, Captain."

Fairburn's eyes locked onto Osterman's. "This stays between the three of us, Senior Chief," he said. "I will be ending this investigation, and will reluctantly be leaving the records of those involved intact. But I'm not putting up with him and his posturing anymore. I've done my time, and I want him off my ship."

Osterman glanced at Todd, saw her surprise mirrored there. Clearly, this was news to him, too. "Ensign Locatelli, Sir?" she asked.

"Who else?" Fairburn countered. "I've spoken with Admiral Locatelli, and Captain Castillo's agreed to take him. He can be *Phoenix*'s problem for a while."

"Yes, Sir," Osterman said, breathing a little easier.

"There's just one catch," Fairburn continued sourly. "Admiral Locatelli insists that if his nephew goes, you go with him."

Osterman stared at him. "Excuse me, Sir?" she asked carefully.

"You and Ensign Locatelli are being transferred to *Phoenix*, Senior Chief," Fairburn said. "Effective immediately upon our return to Manticore."

"For how long, Sir?" Osterman asked. "I mean—"

"I know what you mean, Senior Chief," Fairburn said. "And the answer is, God only knows. Until Ensign Locatelli is transferred again, I suppose. Or until he grows up. Your guess is as good as mine."

"I see, Sir," Osterman said, her voice going automatically into Petty Officer Neutral mode. Until Locatelli the Younger grew up. Right.

"That's all, Senior Chief," Fairburn said. "Dismissed." He hesitated as Osterman stood up. "And," he added, "may God have mercy on your soul."

Osterman suppressed a sigh. "Yes, Sir," she said. "Thank you, Sir."

☆　　☆　　☆

Carefully, Breakwater set his tablet on the table. "Extraordinary," he said. "I trust I don't have to tell anyone at this table how much that missile cost the Star Kingdom?"

It was, Winterfall decided, about as rhetorical a question as it was possible to ask. Across from him and Breakwater were Prime Minister Burgundy, Defense Minister Dapplelake, and Admiral Locatelli. At the head of the table was King Edward, himself a former captain in the Royal Manticoran Navy. All four of them would know precisely how much a missile cost.

Not just in Manticoran dollars, but also in Solarian credits, Havenite francs, and number of years' worth of a captain's salary. They knew how much the missile had cost, all right.

"We're quite familiar with the numbers, My Lord," Dapplelake said evenly. "If you don't mind, let's move on to the extra pound of flesh you're hoping to extract."

"Please, My Lord," Breakwater said, in that reproachful tone that managed to be injured and condescending at the same time. "This isn't about penalties or punishment. On the contrary: given Captain Fairburn's incident report, I'm ready to concede that you've been right about pirate activity in the region."

"Really," Locatelli said. "I haven't heard any mention of that in your speeches."

"Nor has there been any such in Parliamentary or committee meetings," Burgundy murmured.

"There's a time for public pronouncements, My Lords, and a time for private discussion," Breakwater replied smoothly. "This is one of the latter." He turned to King Edward. "Your Majesty, I submit that Captain Fairburn's encounter proves beyond a doubt that there are indeed outside dangers that need to be addressed. Accordingly, I would like to again submit my request that the five remaining corvettes be transferred to MPARS."

"And?" the King prompted.

"*And* that they retain their full armament," Breakwater said. "Future pirate activity can only be dealt with if there is a strong, armed presence throughout the Star Kingdom."

"Welcome to our side of the argument, My Lord," Dapplelake said dryly. "Unfortunately, you seem to have forgotten that the problem of crewing those armed ships still remains."

"A problem which would have been eliminated long ago if more slots had been opened up for MPARS personnel at the Academy and Casey-Rosewood," Breakwater countered.

"You have as many slots as we can afford to give you, My Lord," Dapplelake said. "But there may be another way."

Breakwater tilted his head to the side. "I'm listening."

"MPARS already has *Aries* and *Taurus*," Dapplelake said. "Since Baron Winterfall's rescue modules haven't proved all that useful—" he inclined his head at Winterfall, as if apologizing for that assessment "—I suggest we go ahead and reinstall the box launchers. The Navy will supply you with petty officers and gunnery crews to handle them, and we'll try to squeeze a few more slots in those rating tracks for your people."

"That sounds acceptable," Breakwater said. "And the other five ships?"

"Again, we can reassign their current missile crews to MPARS," Dapplelake said. "Unfortunately, we can't spare the rest of the crews, so you'll have to supply those yourselves. At current enlistment and graduation rates, I imagine you can get all of them up and running within the next three to four years. Does that work for you?"

"Not entirely," Breakwater said, a frown creasing his forehead. "You say you can't spare the rest of the crews. Why not? The corvettes already have full crews you could transfer to us. After all, those are men and women you don't need elsewhere."

"Hardly, My Lord," Dapplelake said. "Most of the Navy's ships are badly undercrewed, including the corvettes themselves. Even at Casey-Rosewood's current graduation rate we're only slowly filling those slots. More significantly, we're going to need all the personnel we can get—" he paused, overly dramatically in Winterfall's opinion "—since we're about to bring the battlecruisers *Swiftsure* and *Victory* out of mothballs and back to full operational status."

Winterfall felt his eyes widen, a small part of his mind noting in retrospect that Dapplelake's pause hadn't been *overly* anything. If anything, he'd underplayed the drama.

"That is, of course, ridiculous," Breakwater said. The verbal bombshell had clearly caught him as much by surprise as it had Winterfall, but he was quickly recovering his balance. "We've been through this, My Lord, many times. Those ships aren't needed, and the Star Kingdom simply doesn't have the money or manpower to operate them."

"I think we do," Dapplelake said. "More importantly, so does the King."

Breakwater's eyes turned to Edward . . . and in the Chancellor's face was something Winterfall hadn't seen in a long time.

Something that was almost as stunning as Dapplelake's own pronouncement.

Uncertainty.

"Your Majesty?" Breakwater asked carefully.

"You heard correctly, My Lord," Edward said. "If there are indeed pirates working this part of space—and you yourself have just conceded that point—then they must have a base nearby. We can't simply wait for them to come after us and our neighbors. We have to go find them and deal with them."

"And that requires more large ships than we have available," Dapplelake added. "Hence, the reactivation."

For a long moment Breakwater's eyes flicked back and forth between the Defense Minister and the King. Then, he drew himself up. "I'm sorry, Your Majesty; My Lord," he said. "But I cannot in good conscience support such an action. My responsibility—*your* responsibility—is to defend and protect our three worlds, not to send our men and women charging off on some grand adventure to right all wrongs in the galaxy. We're not the region's police force, and I have no intention of letting us become one."

"You intend to stand against us, then, My Lord?" Burgundy asked. "Because if you do, I tell you right now that you *will* lose."

For a moment the two men locked eyes, and Winterfall found himself holding his breath. There was a sizeable group of Lords who supported Breakwater or who at least tended to follow his lead. But it wasn't nearly big enough to force a no-confidence vote and take down Burgundy's government. Even if it was, the King would undoubtedly offer Burgundy whatever time he needed to work out a new coalition and form a new government.

The other obvious option, that Breakwater would threaten to take his case directly to the people, was even worse. Not only did the King enjoy the support of a sizeable majority of the populace, which would probably doom such an approach anyway, but Edward and Burgundy could never let such a challenge go unanswered. Even just the threat alone would probably get the Chancellor unceremoniously booted out of his job.

Or would it?

Because by all logic Breakwater should have been booted already. Like everyone else in the Cabinet, he'd submitted his resignation when King Michael abdicated and King Edward ascended the Throne. Edward had reappointed Burgundy and most of the others, but the common wisdom at the time had been that he would take the opportunity to remove Breakwater's perennial thorn from the Monarch's side.

Only he hadn't. After a series of closed-door meetings at the Palace, Breakwater had been reinstated to his position.

And as far as Winterfall knew, no one knew why.

There were theories, of course. Lots of theories. One was that Breakwater *did* have enough support to take down Burgundy's government, and the Chancellorship had been the price for his grudging support. Another was that he knew where too many political bodies were buried, and his appointment was again the price of silence.

Personally, Winterfall subscribed to the statesman theory: that however annoying Breakwater might be to Burgundy and his government, the man was so good at his job of running the Exchequer that the Prime Minister was able to rise above the politics of the situation and do what was best for the Star Kingdom.

Of course, none of the theories left Breakwater so steel-clad that he still couldn't blow it. He most certainly could.

And he could do it right here, and right now. Fortunately, he knew how and when to choose his battles.

"Of course I would not stand against the express will of my king," Breakwater said at last, bowing his head slightly toward Edward. "If he truly believes this is necessary, I will accept his decision."

He shifted his gaze to Dapplelake. "I trust, My Lord, that the weapons and crews you promised will be delivered to my other corvettes in a timely manner?"

"They will," Dapplelake said. "As has already been noted, we all have the same interest in adding more armed vessels to the Star Kingdom's spaceways."

"Then I believe we are adjourned," King Edward said gravely. "Thank you all for coming. My Lord Burgundy, a moment more of your time, if you please."

Breakwater remained silent as he and Winterfall walked from the palace to their waiting car. With every step Winterfall felt his own tension ratcheting upward as he waited for the inevitable explosion, and wondered how much of it would be directed at him.

Because he should have seen this coming. He really should. He'd noted the sudden flurry of private meetings over the past few days between the Prime Minister, Defense Minister, and members of the Admiralty. But he'd put it down to an attempt at damage control in the wake of *Salamander*'s less than impressive encounter with *Izbica* and the men who'd commandeered her.

He'd accepted the scenario of Burgundy and Dapplelake scrambling to shore up support. It had never occurred to him to think they might pick that moment to go on the offensive.

They reached the car and got in. Breakwater closed the door behind him, and Winterfall braced himself.

"Interesting," the Chancellor murmured.

Winterfall shot him a sideways look. Breakwater's profile was no angrier than his voice. "Excuse me, My Lord?" he asked carefully.

Breakwater smiled tightly. "Relax, Gavin—I'm not angry with you," he assured the younger man. "Surprisingly, I'm not even angry with Burgundy and his sledgehammer tactics. Intrigued, but not angry."

Winterfall frowned. He hadn't seen anything from the Prime Minister that could be construed as sledgehammer.

"I'm not sure I understand, My Lord."

"Oh, come on," Breakwater chided. "Surely by now you're able to read between the man's lines. He was prepared to go to the mat for those battlecruisers. Including, I dare say, calling in years' worth of favors." He lifted a finger. "The question is why? And why *now*?"

"I presume because the King wants them reactivated."

"Yes, but *why*?" Breakwater persisted. "To pay off supporters? To spite me?" He shook his head. "No. Burgundy might do something like that. Not the King."

"Personally, I wouldn't have thought Burgundy capable of much of *anything*," Winterfall murmured.

"That's because you didn't know him before King Michael," Breakwater said ruefully. "He was quite the politician during Elizabeth's time, with a firm grasp of his opponents' weaknesses and a clear eye for pushing through whatever laws or policies his sovereign wanted." He shook his head. "I'd assumed that age and the lack of a strong monarch had simply sapped his strength. I appear to have miscalculated."

Winterfall turned that one over in his head. Only minutes ago the Chancellor's faction had been striding fearlessly through the Star Kingdom's political waves. Now, suddenly, they seemed to have fallen in over their collective head. "What are you going to do?"

"I'll tell you what we're *not* going to do," Breakwater said. "We're not going to make our stand on this issue. This smells too much like the aftermath of the Secour incident, and I have no intention of going through that kind of humiliation again. No, I think that for the moment we'll support their move."

"*Support* it?" Winterfall asked, frowning. "You mean actively, as opposed to staying on the sidelines?"

"Very actively," Breakwater assured him. "For one thing we're in the middle of a pirate crisis. For another, playing that card also all but requires them to turn over those remaining corvettes to us in a timely fashion." He cocked his head. "In fact, if we work it properly, we may be able to make the cause and effect run backwards. That is, we make it look like the Navy gave us the corvettes in exchange for graciously allowing them to reactivate the battlecruisers."

"Not much of a distinction," Winterfall murmured.

"It's all in the presentation, my boy," Breakwater said. "For now, the perception of victory will be enough."

He settled back against the cushion. "And sooner or later, Edward will have to show his hand. Once we find out what this is *really* all about, we'll find a way to turn it to our advantage."

Winterfall exhaled a huff of air. "I hope so."

"Trust me," Breakwater said. "Burgundy may be an excellent politician. But I'm better.

"Much, much better."

☆　　☆　　☆

The door closed, and it was once again just the two of them. "So you're not going to tell them?" Burgundy asked.

"Not yet," Edward said, feeling some of the tension draining away. He'd tried to hide it from Burgundy and Dapplelake, but he'd dreaded this confrontation. Dreaded what Breakwater and his allies would do in the face of Burgundy's effective coup d'état.

And it wasn't over yet. Not by a long shot. On the surface, Breakwater had committed to supporting the Crown and the rest of the Cabinet. But Edward didn't believe for a minute that that would be the end of it. Odds were that the Chancellor was merely treading water while he analyzed, considered, and strategized for his next move.

What that move would be Edward didn't know. But it wouldn't be good. Not for him, not for Burgundy, and not for the Star Kingdom.

"Then when?" Burgundy pressed. "This is a serious threat, Your Majesty."

"I almost wish it was," Edward said with a sigh. "Threats can be faced and dealt with. The problem is that all we have are *possible* threats, and that argument isn't going to get us anywhere. Not with Breakwater."

"I'd say Gustav Anderman's newly enlarged empire is more than just a *possible* threat, Your Majesty," Burgundy countered. "I know he keeps saying he's not in the expansion business, but somehow his territory keeps expanding. Add to that Haven's assessment that the Silesian Confederacy is starting to look outside its borders, and we need to be rethinking the Star Kingdom's security needs."

"I *do* understand the problem, Davis," Edward said mildly.

Burgundy ducked his head. "My apologies, Your Majesty," he said. "I'm just . . . Anderman's forces could conquer practically anyone in the area. Even Haven would have a serious fight on its hands. I'm just suggesting that reactivating our battlecruisers without Breakwater being totally on board will be like driving a car with the brakes still on."

"I understand that, too," Edward said. "And if I could be sure he would be on our side I'd bring him aboard in a heartbeat. The problem is that if he adds up all the *ifs* and gets zero, it would be worse than simply having the brakes on. He'd be hitching up a tow truck and pulling the opposite direction, back toward focusing all our efforts and resources on MPARS."

Burgundy was silent a moment.

"I suppose you're right, Your Majesty," he said at last. "He doesn't have the strength for a serious challenge, but he could still roil the waters and make things more difficult. As long as he isn't demanding explanations, we might as well let sleeping dogs lie." He eyed Edward closely. "But sooner or later, you'll have to tell him."

"Sooner or later, I will," Edward assured him. "But he'll keep for the moment." He smiled. "Besides, Daddy just promised him a whole set of shiny new corvettes. With luck, he'll take them back to his favorite corner and play with them for a while."

"I hope you're right, Your Majesty," Burgundy said doubtfully. "If you're not, there *will* be hell to pay."

☆　　☆　　☆

"You're kidding," Redko said, craning his neck to look over Chomps's shoulder. "They're sending you to *MPARS*?"

"That they are," Chomps confirmed sourly, running his eyes down the tablet again. This was *not* what he'd expected.

> *08-5-76*
> *BuPers Order 76-7762*
>
> *(1) MT 1/c Townsend, Charles, RN01-962-1183, hereby detached RN duty effective 00:01, 22-5-76.*
> *(2) MT 1/c Townsend, Charles, RN01-962-1183, assigned Temporary Duty MPARS, effective 00:01, 22-5-76.*
> *(3) MT 1/c Townsend, Charles, RN01-962-1183, hereby assigned HMS Aries, CT05 effective 001:01 22-5-76.*
> *(4) Transport MT 1/c Townsend, Charles, RN01-962-1183, to HMS Aries, CT05 hereby authorized, to be arranged BuPers/MPARS liaison at the convenience of the Service. (See attachment No. 1.)*
>
> *LT CMDR George Sukowski*
> *By direction of*
> *ADMR Anastasiya Dembinski*
> *BuPers RMN*

"Hell on wheels," Redko murmured, shaking his head. "I'm so sorry, buddy."

"Hey, it could have been worse," Chomps soothed. "I could have been tossed out completely."

"You *have* been tossed out. Just like Calvingdell was."

"Not exactly the same thing," Chomps murmured. The last person he wanted to talk about right now was Countess Calvingdell.

"No, you're right," Redko said scornfully. "All that happened to *her* was that she got kicked out of the Defense Ministry and had to go back to a life of ease in Parliament."

Chomps looked sharply at him. But Redko was still gazing at the orders on Chomps's tablet, with no hint of secret knowledge or insight in his face.

"But I suppose they needed you to work on their new missiles," Redko continued. He hesitated. "You know...I never thanked you for keeping my name out of things back at Casca."

"Not a problem," Chomps assured him. "The captain was ready to chew nails. No point in both of us catching the shrapnel."

"I still appreciate it," Redko said. "Especially—" he waved at the tablet "—with this."

"Not a problem," Chomps said again. "You know, I do have two more weeks before I have to report."

"Right," Redko said. "Maybe the orders will be countermanded."

"Could happen," Chomps said, knowing damn well that they wouldn't. "Maybe MPARS will collapse."

"Or maybe we'll all die in an asteroid collision."

"*You're* a cheery one," Chomps said. "I was thinking more along the lines that you'd have plenty of time to buy me a drink."

"More than just one," Redko said. "In fact, let's start right now. We're off-duty, right?"

Chomps checked his chrono. "Seven more minutes."

"Seven minutes, then," Redko said. "Start the clock. And if you ever need anything—anything at all—don't hesitate to ask."

"I will," Chomps assured him. "And rest assured that I *will* collect. You can count on it."

CHAPTER FIFTEEN

"LIEUTENANT LONG?" the gruff voice echoed down the passageway of HMS *Phoenix*. "Sir?"

Travis came to a reluctant halt, taking the calming breath he'd taught himself to do at times like this. Senior Chief Osterman was a major pain in the butt, on a ship much of whose officer corps and enlisted personnel seemed to take a special pleasure these days in competing for honors in that position.

"Yes, Senior Chief?" he replied, catching one of the passageway handholds and bringing himself to a floating stop.

Osterman was about twenty meters away, moving from handhold to handhold toward him, deftly avoiding collisions with the other crew members also moving through the narrow space. *Phoenix* had its share of first-tour crewmembers bumbling awkwardly in the zero-gee, but long-time veterans like Osterman made it look quick and efficient.

At the moment, though, Osterman didn't seem to be putting much effort into the *quick* part of that solution. In fact, now that Travis had stopped she seemed to be taking her time closing the rest of the gap between them. Travis waited, cultivating his patience and resisting the urge to order her to snap it up. He'd been on the other side of the line once, back when he was enlisted, and remembered all too well what it was like to have officers barking at you.

Finally, after a few seconds, and in her own sweet time, Osterman reached him. "I just wanted you to know, Sir," she said in a voice that skated the same not-quite-insubordinate line, "that Captain Castillo wants to see you."

Travis frowned, glancing at his uni-link to make sure it was active. It was. "I haven't heard any such orders."

"That's because he doesn't know it yet, Sir," she said calmly. "But I guarantee he's going to."

So even Osterman's department had heard. "Ensign Locatelli brought it on himself," Travis said firmly.

Or tried to say it firmly. Even in his own ears the edge of defensiveness was painfully obvious.

Apparently, it was obvious to Osterman, too. "It was one of *three* separate tracking sensors," she reminded him. "The next shift's diagnostic run would have spotted it in a minute."

"That diagnostic run was two hours away," Travis countered. "What would have happened if you'd had to fire one of your autocannon sometime during those two hours?"

Osterman raised her eyebrows. "At . . . ?"

"At whatever Captain Castillo decided needed shooting."

Osterman's expression was worse than any raised eyebrows could have been. And, to be honest, Travis couldn't blame her.

Because, really, there wasn't anything out there for *Phoenix* to shoot at. There were no invaders, no enemies—foreign *or* domestic— and the last boogeyman who'd shown himself around these parts had vanished into the stardust nearly a century ago. There were supposedly pirates out there, but aside from the incident at Secour nine T-years ago none of them had so much as shown their noses.

There *was* the so-called *"Izbica* Incident" a couple of months ago, which the local newsfeeds and 'faxes had had a field day with. But the truth was that the freighter's theft had been more along the lines of a hijacking than genuine ship-to-ship piracy. As far as any sort of outside incursion went, Manticoran space was about as secure as it was possible to be, and everyone knew it.

Still, what had happened to *Izbica* ought to serve as a wake-up call for everyone involved. If one ship could be hijacked in the Star Kingdom's space, so could a second . . . and the only thing standing in the way of such a recurrence was a Navy staffed with competent people and equipped with fully functioning systems. If anyone could understand that, it really ought to be Osterman.

Besides, men and women who wore the RMN uniform were supposed to *care* about their jobs.

Osterman might have been reading his mind. "And you think you're the only one who's getting it right, Sir?" she asked politely.

"No, of course not," Travis muttered. "But..."

He was saved by the twittering of his uni-link. He keyed it and raised it to his lips. "Long," he said briskly.

"Bajek," the voice of *Phoenix*'s Weapons Officer came from the speaker. "Report to the captain's office immediately."

Travis swallowed. "Aye, aye, Ma'am."

"Commander Bajek?" Osterman asked knowingly as he keyed off.

"Yes," Travis said sourly. Was the smug chief *always* right? "Carry on." Turning in the zero-gee, he gave his handhold a tug and once again launched himself down the passageway.

"Learn to play the game, Lieutenant," Osterman called quietly after him.

Travis glowered. Play the game. It was the same advice everyone else in the universe seemed ready and eager to give him. Learn to play the game. Never mind whether the game was good or bad or clean or rigged. Learn to play the game.

Like hell he would.

☆   ☆   ☆

Osterman watched Long go, not sure whether to be angry, frustrated, or sympathetic.

With a senior chief's ability to walk the balance bar between officers and enlisted, she decided to go with a combination of all three.

Long was a decent officer—no doubt about that. He had the knowledge and the ability, and he knew regulations like nobody's business.

But he needed to learn how to choose his battles and his opponents. Ensign Locatelli, for all the alluring fatness of the target, wasn't one of them. Which Long was presumably about to find out.

He also needed to learn how to understand people. He'd been radiating annoyance like a reactor exchange coil as she worked her way toward him down the passageway, clearly assuming she was dawdling specifically to exasperate him. Apparently, it had never even occurred to him that she was timing her approach to let everyone else clear the space so that the two of them would be alone when she delivered her unpleasant news.

That was a blindspot she wouldn't have expected from someone with his prior enlisted experience. Obviously, he wasn't what her father used to describe as "a people person."

In some ways, that was probably a good thing. Osterman had a high regard for officers who actually tried to do their jobs rather than letting things slide. But there was a balance required, and Long tended to be as subtle as a hammer when it came to accomplishing that. He seemed more tone deaf than most where other human beings were involved.

Even worse, he seemed completely oblivious to the way certain family connections were affecting his own position. Chancellor Breakwater's successful extraction of two of the Navy's corvettes for MPARS hadn't sat well with anyone in the RMN, and the fact that five more were slated to follow sat even more poorly. *Phoenix*'s officers and crew were no exception to that reaction, and the fact that Long's half-brother was one of Breakwater's staunchest allies had resulted in a noticeable cooling in overall attitude toward the young lieutenant.

But unlike everyone else aboard, Long didn't seem to have made that connection.

Of course, the true irony here, though Long would never know it, was that his insistence on Locatelli keeping all three tracking systems up and running was exactly the same attitude that had gotten the ensign himself into trouble back on *Salamander*.

With a sigh, Osterman twisted herself around and headed back toward her duty station. Long was terrific at reading the lines of manuals and regs and orders.

Now, he needed to learn how to read between them.

☆   ☆   ☆

The lift ride through *Phoenix*'s spin section, as usual, was more than a little unpleasant, the rapid shift in effective gravity triggering Travis's sensitive inner ear. He kept his eyes straight ahead during the trip, thinking evil thoughts about whichever law of physics allowed stress bands that could create and mold huge gravitational fields, and compensators that could zero-out more than two hundred gees, but were only just now figuring out how to get a measly one gee pointed toward a warship's decks. Having a half-gee rotating section to live in was better than having to eat and sleep in weightlessness, but floating around the main duty stations like air-breathing fish was a royal pain in the butt.

Bajek was waiting in Captain Castillo's office when Travis arrived. "Come in, Lieutenant," Castillo said, his voice and expression stiffly formal. "I understand you want to write up Ensign Locatelli."

Travis was opening his mouth to answer when the phrasing of the comment suddenly struck him. No, he didn't *want* to write up Locatelli. He'd already done so.

Or so he'd thought. "Yes, Sir, I do," he said carefully. "Is there a problem?"

For a tense second he thought the question had put him over the line. Castillo's expression didn't change, but Bajek shifted her weight slightly in what was, for her, an unusually demonstrative show of discomfort.

"You're aware, I presume, that Ensign Locatelli's uncle is Admiral Carlton Locatelli," Castillo said. It wasn't a question.

"Yes, Sir, I am," Travis replied. For a brief moment he considered asking what Locatelli's genetic makeup had to do with following procedure, but decided he was in deep enough already. Besides, he was pretty sure he already knew the answer.

He was right. "Admiral Locatelli and his family have had a long and distinguished history of service with the Royal Manticoran Navy," Castillo said, in a way that reminded Travis of someone reading from a script file. "His nephew is this generation's representative to that line. The admiral is anxious that he achieve something of the same honor and distinction as his forebears." Castillo raised his eyebrows, forming exactly the same expression Travis had gotten from Osterman a few minutes ago. "Do you need me to spell it out for you?"

Travis took a deep breath. Unfortunately, neither he nor anyone else in the RMN needed it spelled out for them. "No, Sir," he said.

"As you may be aware, there's a strong and growing movement in Parliament to gut the RMN even more than it already is." Castillo's tone was a bit sharper and his eyes were quite a bit harder than Osterman's had been. Apparently, despite Travis's assurances, the captain was in the mood for a spelling lesson. "Men like Admiral Locatelli and their allies are the ones standing up for our jobs. Standing up for *your* job, Lieutenant."

Which would mean a double handful of nothing, Travis thought blackly, if the cost of that protection was staffing the Navy with political animals who either couldn't or wouldn't do those jobs.

But that, too, was part of the spelling lesson. "Understood, Sir," he said.

"Good," Castillo said. "You have a promising career, Mr. Long. I'd hate to have it cut short for nothing." He pursed his lips briefly. "And bear in mind that there are other ways of dealing with incompetence and neglect, ways that don't involve the recipient's permanent record. You'd be well advised to learn them."

"Yes, Sir." In fact, Travis *did* know those other methods. Sometimes they worked. Sometimes they didn't.

"Good." Castillo looked up at Bajek. "Is he still on duty?"

"Yes, Sir," Bajek said, never taking her eyes off Travis.

Castillo nodded and looked back at Travis. "Return to your station, Lieutenant. Dismissed."

☆   ☆   ☆

The rest of the shift was tense, but not as bad as Travis had feared it would be. None of the men and women in his division said anything, though he did catch the edge of a couple of whispered conversations. Locatelli himself had the grace not to smirk. *Never ascribe to malice what can be explained by stupidity*, someone had once told Travis, and it was just barely possible that Locatelli wasn't so much arrogantly indifferent as he was a really slow learner.

Travis hoped it was the latter. Slow learning could be corrected with time and patience. Arrogance usually required something on the order of an exhibition bullwhip.

Still, by the time he started his final check of the systems under his watch, he was feeling more optimistic than he'd been earlier in the day.

Or at least he was until he discovered that the primary tracking sensor for the Number Two forward autocannon was once again miscalibrated.

Maybe, he thought as he headed wearily back to his quarters, it was time to go hunt up that bullwhip.

☆   ☆   ☆

"Freighter *Hosney*, you are cleared to leave orbit," the voice of Manticore Space Control came over the bridge com.

It was an interesting voice, Tash McConnovitch thought, holding shades of both excitement and regret beneath the official tone. Excitement, because in a system where visitors typically dropped in only once or twice every T-month a Solly freighter was a welcome break from the drab routine of the controller's job. Regret, because with *Hosney*'s departure the boredom would settle in again.

Patience, McConnovitch thought darkly in the controller's direction. *You'll be begging for boredom and routine before we're done with you.*

Or possibly not. The last data file Jeremiah Llyn had received from Axelrod's spies had put Manticore's fleet at somewhere around ten warships, with at most a single battlecruiser poised and ready to face combat.

But that data had been old. Dangerously old, as it turned out. For reasons McConnovitch had yet to pin down, King Edward had launched into an ambitious program of pulling RMN ships out of mothballs and pushing the Casey-Rosewood boot camp and the Academy to churn out enough warm bodies to put aboard them.

Still, Edward's revitalization was a work in progress. While the RMN might look impressive on paper, none of the newly refurbished ships were even close to running at full strength. They should still be no problem for the Volsung Mercenaries.

Though of course the Volsungs themselves might not see it that way.

Fortunately, none of that was McConnovitch's concern. His job was simply to deliver the data to the rendezvous system where the mercenary task force was assembling. That snide little man Llyn was the one who would have to make the actual go/no-go decision.

"We're clear of the lane, sir," the helmsman announced. "Course laid in."

"Good," McConnovitch said, and meant it. He was more than ready to show his kilt to this grubby, backwater little system. "Make some gees, Hermie. We wouldn't want to keep Mr. Llyn waiting."

☆   ☆   ☆

"Admiral on the bridge!" the petty officer at Tracking called.

Captain Allegra Metzger swiveled around in her station at the forward end of HMS *Invincible*'s bridge. Admiral Locatelli had just entered and was pulling himself through the zero-gee in her direction.

"Admiral," she greeted him, reaching for her straps. Usually when he came to the bridge unexpectedly it was to take over.

Not that taking over right now would be all that exciting. *Invincible* was on a shakedown cruise, with a bunch of new spacers and petty officers who were just barely starting to learn the ropes. About all Locatelli could do—and all Metzger herself was doing—was to ride herd on the junior officers and make sure no one did anything fatally stupid.

Apparently, the admiral agreed. He waved Metzger back to her position, floated past her, and braked himself to a halt behind the helm station. "You have a position and vector for *Phoenix*?" he asked without preamble.

"Ah—yes, Sir," Lieutenant Tessa Griswold said, her hands moving across her board. "One moment, Sir. There she is. Bearing—"

"Yes, I see her," Locatelli cut her off. For a moment he studied the plot, then gestured to the com officer beside her. "Com, signal to *Phoenix*. I want to speak with Captain Castillo, personally and in private."

"Aye, aye, Sir."

A minute later, the com officer had made contact with *Phoenix*'s bridge and relayed the request. Three minutes later, Castillo was there.

"Good day, Captain," Locatelli said. "You're alone, I trust?"

"Yes, Sir, I'm in my cabin," Castillo confirmed. "And I have my contingencies files laid out."

Out of the corner of her eye, Metzger saw Locatelli smile. Castillo was a good commander, and smart enough to suspect that two ships meeting like this was unlikely to have happened by chance.

"Very good," Locatelli said. "You're hereby authorized to open Order Number Seven. Here's the password." He read off the fifteen-character code. "Let me know when you've read it."

"Yes, Sir."

The com went silent. Metzger counted out twenty-six seconds—

"Understood, Admiral," Castillo said. "May I also say that congratulations are in order. This is the first time in years that I've heard of anyone being actually preauthorized to spend a missile. Even a practice one."

"I credit the *Izbica* Incident," Locatelli said. "I expect the Exchequer's newfound generosity will fade with time. Do you have any questions?"

"No, Sir," Castillo said. "But I do have a request. One of my junior officers is very good with book learning, but I see a certain disconnect with real-world situations. I'd like your permission to have him on the bridge during the exercise and perhaps let him make a call or two."

"That's rather an odd request, Captain," Locatelli said, a frown in his tone. "This is partly a test of your bridge crew. It's not going to be very useful in that regard if someone else is giving the orders."

"If I may respectfully disagree, Admiral, the bridge crew *will* be functioning exactly as they normally would," Castillo said. "I'll be the only one who isn't being tested. Unless that's a specific and important part of the exercise, of course."

"It's part of the test, but not a vital part," Locatelli said. "Otherwise I wouldn't be giving you this head's-up. Rather a deep end of the pool to throw a junior officer into, though. I assume he shows promise?"

"Yes, Sir. If a couple of his rough edges can be knocked off."

"What's his name? Do I know him?"

"Only by reputation, Sir." Castillo's voice had gone a bit dry. "Lieutenant Travis Uriah Long."

There was a long, rigid silence. "Lieutenant Long," Locatelli repeated, his voice studiously casual. "*That* Lieutenant Long?"

"Yes, Sir."

"In that case, Captain," Locatelli said, "by all means, let's give the young man some real-world experience."

"Thank you, Sir," Castillo said. "I think it'll do him some good."

"Let's hope so," Locatelli said. "Return to your bridge, and let's make this happen. *Invincible* out."

For a moment, the admiral continued to float behind the helm station. Then, giving himself a gentle push, he floated back to Metzger.

"Captain, I understand you once served with Lieutenant Long. Is that correct?"

Metzger braced herself. This had the potential to get very awkward. "Yes, Sir, I did."

"Is he as big a prig as he seems?"

"He's very much by-the-book," she said, choosing her words carefully. "But he also has a great deal of ingenuity and the ability to think outside the lines."

"Always thinks he's right, does he?" Locatelli asked. "Thinks he's got all the answers?"

Metzger frowned. That wasn't what she'd said. Was that what Locatelli had heard? "I'm not sure I'd put it quite that way, Admiral," she said.

"Well, we'll see if he's as clever as he thinks he is." Locatelli settled beside Metzger's station in a posture that suggested he was going to be there awhile. "Prepare to call battlestations. Let's see how good this new crew of ours is."

☆   ☆   ☆

Travis had finished unsealing one of his boots and was starting on the other one when Fornier, lolling on the top bunk of their tiny cabin, finally emerged far enough from the depths of his tablet to notice he was no longer alone. "*There* you are," he commented as he peered over the edge of the bunk. "Bajek have you on extra duty today? Or were you just starting the celebration early?"

"What are we celebrating?" Travis asked.

"Our upcoming R and R, of course," Fornier said. "Don't tell me you're not looking forward to a couple of weeks groundside."

Travis shrugged. "Depends on if the Number Two autocannon tracking sensor is slated for replacement. If so, yes. If not, not really."

"Mm," Fornier said. "At least you're not blaming Locatelli for that anymore."

Travis winced. No, he wasn't blaming the young ensign for the sensors' foul-up. At least not directly.

"He still should have spotted the problem and either fixed it or reported it."

"Uh-huh," Fornier said, an annoyingly knowing tone to his voice. "How many people in your section, Travis?"

"Nine, including me."

"And how many of them are useless political appointees like Locatelli?"

Travis made a face. It wasn't hard to see where Fornier was going with this. "Maybe two."

"Maybe two," Fornier repeated. "So let's call it one and a half. One and a half out of eight—make it nine, since you're not political and I assume you consider yourself non-useless. That comes to about seventeen percent. All things considered, that's really not all that bad."

"I suppose not," Travis conceded. Though Fornier was conveniently ignoring the fact that the political problem seemed to get worse the higher up the food chain you traveled. With Breakwater's faction still pushing to defund and dismantle the Navy, the political animals who'd joined for the honor and glory were scrambling to claw their way up the ladder to the coveted command ranks before the rug was pulled out from under them.

Maybe King Edward would turn that around. Certainly his "refit and recruit" program was showing progress. Having the battlecruisers *Swiftsure* and *Victory* back in service was certainly a good sign.

But Travis had seen other such efforts fizzle out over the years. He wasn't really expecting this one to do any better.

And in the meantime, there were way more earls and barons in the command structure than anyone needed.

Maybe that was the end vector of all armed forces during protracted peacetime. Maybe the trend always drifted toward the political appointees, and the people who couldn't figure out what else to do, and the coasters who figured such service would be an easy and comfortable way to wander their way through life. Maybe the only way that ever turned around was if there was a war.

Still, much as it might be interesting to see how those three groups handled a sudden bout of real combat, Travis certainly didn't wish a war on the Star Kingdom. Or on anyone else, for that matter.

"Trust me, it's not bad," Fornier said dryly. "Certainly isn't a *travesty* or anything."

Travis glared up at him. "Not you, too," he growled.

"Sorry," Fornier said, not quite suppressing a grin. "It just suits you so well, that's all. How in the world did you pick up a signature phrase like that, anyway?"

"It's a long story," Travis said, returning his attention to his boots.

"Okay, fine—don't tell me," Fornier said equably. "But seriously, take it from someone who did two years in retail before joining up. You keep track of every vendor, tradesman, bureaucrat, and official you meet during your two weeks groundside. I'll bet you a hundred that you'll find way more than seventeen percent who are jerks—"

Abruptly, the heart-stopping wail of the ship's klaxons erupted all around them. There were two seconds of full volume, and then the cacophony abruptly dropped to a relative whisper. "General Quarters, General Quarters!" the voice of Commander Sladek came sharply over the alarm. "Set Condition Two throughout the ship! Repeat: set Condition Two!"

There was a thud as Fornier hopped off his bunk and landed on the deck. Travis was already at the emergency locker; pulling out the vac suits, he tossed Fornier's to him and started climbing into his own. "Hell of a time for a drill," Fornier said with a grunt.

"If it *is* a drill," Travis warned.

"Sladek didn't say it wasn't."

"He also didn't say it was," Travis countered. "Either way, Bajek will skin us alive if we're late, so move it."

Four of Travis's eight men and women were ready at their combat stations when he arrived. Ensign Locatelli, he noted darkly, wasn't one of them.

"Diagnostics?" he asked, floating over to them in the zero-gee of the ship's bow.

"In progress," Beam Weapon Tech Second Tomasello confirmed. "Number Two's trackers are still coming up twitchy—"

"Long!" Bajek's voice boomed through the cramped space. "Lieutenant Long?"

"Here, Ma'am," Travis said, moving out from the partial concealment of a thick coolant pipe.

"Captain wants you on the bridge," Bajek said shortly.

Travis felt his eyes widen. "The *bridge*, Ma'am?"

"The bridge," Bajek confirmed tartly. "I'm taking over here."

She fixed him with a dark look.

"And move it," she added. "The captain doesn't like to be kept waiting."

CHAPTER SIXTEEN

"YES, MA'AM," TRAVIS SAID, his pulse suddenly pounding.

Maneuvering past her, he pulled his way down the passageway and headed toward the bridge, a sinking feeling joining the resident tension already in his stomach. He had no idea what he'd done now, but for Castillo to be bothering with him at a time like this it must have been something big.

Like the other officers aboard *Phoenix*, Travis had been part of the bridge watch rotation ever since the early days of his assignment. But he'd never seen it during combat conditions, and the first thing that struck him as he maneuvered through the hatch was how calm everyone seemed to be. The voices giving orders and reports were terse, but they were clear and well controlled. Captain Castillo was strapped into his station, his eyes moving methodically between the various displays, while Commander Sladek held position at his side, the two of them occasionally murmuring comments back and forth. All of the monitors were live, showing the ship's position, vector, and acceleration, as well as the status of the two forward missile launchers, the spinal laser, and the three autocannon defense systems.

In the center of the main tactical display was the approaching enemy.

It was a warship, all right. The signature of the wedge made that clear right from the outset. It was pulling a hundred twenty gees, which didn't tell Travis much—virtually any warship could handle that kind of acceleration, and most could do considerably better. The range marker put it just under four hundred thousand kilometers out, a little over twelve minutes away on their current closing vector.

His first reaction was one of relief. There was no way a warship could sneak up that close without *Phoenix*'s sensors picking it up. Fornier had been right: this was indeed a drill.

But what kind of drill required Travis to be hauled away from his station onto the bridge? Was Castillo testing Bajek's ability to run Forward Weapons? That seemed ridiculous.

"Analysis, Mr. Long?"

Travis snapped his attention back. Castillo and Sladek had finished their quiet conversation, and both men were gazing straight at him.

Travis swallowed hard. What were they asking *him* for? "It's definitely a warship, Sir," he said, trying frantically to unfreeze his brain as he looked around the multitude of displays. CIC should have spit out a data compilation and probably even an identification by now, but the screen was still showing nothing except the preliminary collection run-through. Probably another of *Phoenix*'s chronic sensor glitches. "But it's not being overly aggressive," he continued, trying to buy himself some time. "The hundred twenty gees it's pulling is probably around seventy percent of its standard acceleration capability."

"So far, there's been no response to our hail," Sladek said. "How would you proceed?"

And then, to Travis's relief, the sensor ID screen finally came to life. The approaching ship was indeed one of theirs, a *Triumph*-class battlecruiser. Specifically, it was HMS *Invincible*, flagship of the Green One task force.

He had a fraction of a second of fresh relief at the confirmation that this was, indeed, just a drill. An instant later, a violent wave of fresh tension flooded in on him.

Green One was commanded by Admiral Carlton Locatelli. Uncle of Ensign Fenton Locatelli. The junior officer Travis was continually having to write up.

And here Travis was on *Phoenix*'s bridge, being asked advice by his captain while Locatelli charged into simulated battle.

What the *hell* was going on?

"Mr. Long?" Castillo prompted.

With a supreme effort, Travis forced his brain back to the

situation. "Do we know if she's alone?" he asked, again looking around the bridge. Everything he could see indicated *Invincible* was the only vessel out there, but he wasn't quite ready to trust his reading of the relevant displays.

"Confirmed," Sladek said. "There's nothing else within range—"

"Missile trace!" someone barked.

Travis snapped his gaze around to the tactical. *Invincible* was actually firing a *missile*?

A practice missile, obviously, without a warhead. But even so, it was unprecedented to use one in an exercise.

Or, for that matter, to use one at any time, for any reason. Captain Davison had refused to use one of *Vanguard's* missiles even when lives were at stake. Commander Metzger had undergone hours of hearings after using one at Secour, and that situation had been just one step short of a full-on war footing. And rumor had it that *Salamander's* captain had been relieved of command mainly because he'd used one in the *Izbica* Incident.

But a new wedge had definitely appeared on the displays: the smaller, more compact wedge of a missile tracking straight toward *Phoenix*. Either Locatelli had some special dispensation, or he no longer gave a damn what Parliament thought.

"Acceleration thirty-five-hundred gees; estimated impact, two minutes forty seconds," the tactical officer called.

"Stand by autocannon," Castillo ordered calmly. "Fire will commence fifteen seconds before estimated impact."

Travis drew a hissing breath. That was, he knew, the prescribed response to a missile attack. With an effective range of one hundred fifty kilometers, the autocannon's self-guided shells were designed to detonate in the path of an incoming missile, throwing up a wall of shrapnel that could take out anything that drove through its midst, especially something traveling at the five thousand kilometers per second that a missile carried at the end of its run.

At least, that was the hoped-for outcome. Given that the missile would be entering the shrapnel zone barely two hundredths of a second before reaching its target, it was a tactic that either worked perfectly or failed catastrophically. Still, more often than not, it worked. Or at least it worked in simulations.

Only this wasn't a simulation. And *Phoenix's* Number Two autocannon wasn't tracking properly.

"You have an objection, Mr. Long?" Castillo asked.

Travis started. He hadn't realized he'd said anything out loud. "We've been having trouble with the autocannon, Sir," he said. "I'm thinking..." He stopped, suddenly aware of the utter presumption of this situation. He, a lowly lieutenant, was trying to tell a ship's *captain* how to do his job?

But if Castillo was offended, he didn't show it. "Continue," he merely said.

Travis squared his shoulders. He *had* been asked, after all. "I'm thinking it might be better to interpose wedge," he said, the words coming out in a rush lest he lose his nerve completely. "If the missile comes in ventral, there may not be enough autocannon coverage to stop it."

Castillo's lip might have twitched. But his nod was firm enough. "Helm, pitch twenty-six degrees positive," he ordered.

"Pitch twenty-six degrees positive, aye, aye, Sir," the helmsman acknowledged. "Pitching twenty-six degrees positive, aye."

On the tactical, *Phoenix*'s angle began to shift, agonizingly slowly, as the ship's nose pivoted upward. Travis watched the display tensely as the incoming missile closed the distance at ever-increasing speed, wondering if his proposed countermove had been too late.

To his relief, it hadn't. The missile was still nearly twenty seconds out when the leading edge of *Phoenix*'s floor rose high enough to cut across its vector.

"Continue countdown to missile impact," Castillo ordered. "Jink port one klick."

Travis frowned as the helmsman repeated the order. A ship had a certain range of motion within the wedge, particularly at the zero acceleration *Phoenix* was holding right now.

But moving the ship that way was tricky and cost maneuverability. What was Castillo up to?

"Missile has impacted the wedge," the tactical officer announced. "Orders?"

Castillo looked at Travis and raised his eyebrows. "Suggestions, Mr. Long?"

Travis stared at the tac display, where *Invincible* was now rimmed in flashing red to show that her position was based on the foggy gravitic data *Phoenix* was able to glean through the disruptive effects of her own wedge. For the moment, at least, the two ships were at a standoff. *Phoenix* couldn't fire at something she couldn't see well enough to target, and with its wedge floor interposed between them the destroyer was likewise completely protected from any weapon *Invincible* cared to throw at her.

But *Phoenix* was a ship of the Royal Manticoran Navy. Her job wasn't to be safe. Her job was to protect the Star Kingdom's people. Whatever this exercise was all about, and however Locatelli was grading them on it, that grade wouldn't be very high if *Phoenix* continued to hide behind her wedge.

"Recommend we reverse pitch and reestablish full sensor contact, Sir," he said. He hesitated, the regulations against spending missiles pressing like fire-suppression foam against all of his tactical training. Still, if this was an all-out exercise, surely it worked both directions. "I'd also recommend we stand by to launch missiles."

This time Castillo's lip definitely twitched. But he merely nodded. "Anything else?"

Travis frowned. From the tone of Castillo's question, he guessed there was indeed something else they should be doing. Wedge, sensor contact, missiles—

Of course. "I'd also suggest the autocannon begin laying down fire as we approach reacquisition."

"Good." Castillo gestured. "Pitch twenty-six degrees negative; prepare missiles and autocannon."

"Pitch twenty-six degrees negative, aye, aye, Sir."

"Prepare missiles and autocannon, aye, aye, Sir."

Once again, the tac display began to shift. Travis watched, his thumbs pressed hard against the sides of his forefingers. From somewhere forward came a muted rumble as the autocannon began firing. The flashing red rim around *Invincible* vanished as the sensors reacquired contact—

"Missile!" the tac officer snapped.

Travis blinked. The whole thing had happened way too fast for him to see, but the vector line on the tac display showed that the incoming missile had come in right along the edge of fire from the misaimed Number Two autocannon, shot past the wedge floor as it pitched back down, skimmed past *Phoenix* at a distance of eleven kilometers, then continued on to disintegrate against the wedge roof.

He was staring at the line in confusion, wondering how in the world a second missile had sneaked past the sensors—wondering, too, how in hell Locatelli had gotten permission to spend not just one but *two* practice missiles—when the com display lit up and Admiral Locatelli himself appeared. "Well, Captain," the admiral's voice boomed from the speaker, "I believe that gives me the kill."

"Very nearly, Sir," Castillo said calmly. "I think you'll find your missile didn't *quite* make it into full kill range."

Locatelli frowned, his eyes shifting off camera. His smile soured a little, and he gave a small grunt. "Clever," he said reluctantly. "You're still blind, though—your whole tracking radar system would have been destroyed. Telemetry system, too."

"I can still launch missiles," Castillo pointed out.

"Only if there was another ship nearby you could hand them off to," Locatelli countered. "In this case, there isn't." He shook his head. "All in all, Captain, your response was a bit on the sloppy side. I suggest you consider upgrading your tactical officer's training and drill schedule."

"This wasn't my usual tac team, Sir," Castillo said. "One of my other officers was handling the action."

Locatelli sniffed audibly. "Your other officer has a lot to learn."

"Yes, Sir." Deliberately, it seemed to Travis, Castillo turned a studiously neutral look in his direction. "I believe he knows that."

Travis felt a swirl of disbelief corkscrew through his gut. He'd been prepared—almost—to believe that an admiral of the RMN might actually go out of his way to slap down a junior officer who had crossed him.

But for Travis's own captain to join in on the humiliation was beyond even Travis's usual level of reflexive paranoia. For Castillo to single him out this way, in front of the entire *Phoenix* bridge crew...

He swallowed, forcing back the stinging sense of betrayal. Castillo was still his commanding officer, and he was expecting a response. "Yes, Sir," he managed.

"Perfection is a noble goal," Castillo continued, his eyes still on Travis. "We sometimes forget it's a journey, not a destination."

I never claimed to be perfect. Travis left the automatic protest unsaid. Clearly, this was his payback for insisting that Ensign Locatelli do his job, and neither Castillo or the admiral would be interested in hearing logical arguments.

Or pathetic excuses, which was what any comment would be taken as anyway. "I understand, Sir," he said instead. "I'll make it a point to remember today's lessons."

"I'm certain you will." Castillo turned back to the com display. "Any further orders, Admiral?"

"Not at this time," Locatelli said, a quiet but definite note of satisfaction in his voice. "Resume your course for Manticore. I'll want a full analysis of your crew's response to this unscheduled exercise a.s.a.p."

"It'll be ready by the time you return from your training run, Sir," Castillo promised.

"Good," Locatelli said briskly. "Carry on." He reached somewhere off-camera, and his image vanished.

☆ ☆ ☆

And with Locatelli's tap on the com switch, the image of *Phoenix*'s bridge vanished from the display.

"Excellent," the admiral said with clear satisfaction. "We'll want to look closely at the post-action data, but from the looks of it the exercise went quite well."

"Yes, Sir," Metzger said, keeping her voice neutral and making sure her face was turned away from him.

A complete waste of effort. As always, the admiral knew exactly what she was thinking. "You disapprove?" he suggested.

She hesitated. But Locatelli always encouraged his senior officers to speak their minds. "I just think the exercise was flawed, Sir. Captain Castillo's tactical team should have been calling the orders, not some random junior officer."

"In other words, you disapprove of Castillo dealing out an object lesson to Lieutenant Long?"

Metzger winced. Was she really that transparent? "I disapprove of his choice of time and place," she hedged. "This was an expensive exercise. It should have remained focused on its main purpose."

"The purpose of all exercises is to make a better Navy," Locatelli said. "Sometimes they shock officers and crews out of routine and complacency. Sometimes they demonstrate flaws in equipment and tactics. And sometimes they teach valuable lessons." He paused. "Or don't you think your shining Lieutenant Long needs to occasionally learn a lesson?"

Metzger clenched her teeth. Long was smart and innovative, and in her opinion was one of the rising stars of the new generation of Naval officers.

But damn it all, the admiral was right. Long *did* have a

few serious blind spots, and those gaps definitely needed to be filled in.

"Long has enough trouble with human interactions and contacts as it is," she said. "Making him look like a fool in front of his ship's bridge crew won't help with that."

"I disagree that it made him look like a fool," Locatelli said. "But if I assume you're right, it still leaves him with a choice. The same choice one we all have to make on occasion. Sink, or swim."

He gestured toward her board. "And while Lieutenant Long contemplates that decision, you can start collating data on the exercise. I want to know how well *Invincible* performed, preferably before we hear *Phoenix*'s results."

"Aye, aye, Sir," Metzger said.

She watched out of the corner of her eye until he was gone. Then, she turned back forward, indecision gnawing at her gut.

In some ways, Locatelli was right. Long needed some real-world experience, and this was as close to real combat as he would ever actually get.

But for his captain to deliver that experience this way...

Metzger scowled. It wasn't a big deal, she told herself firmly. Humiliation was something that happened all the time in the Navy. Long had certainly had his share of verbal dressings-down, and he would live through this one, too.

But she couldn't shake the feeling that there was something else going on here. Something that maybe she should look into.

She straightened her shoulders. And why not? Long was a good officer, and Castillo was a decent and competent captain, whom she was on good enough terms with. And there was certainly no reason two captains who happened to be within easy conversation range shouldn't have a little chat about things. Especially when both of them were coming off an important exercise.

"Com, send a signal to *Phoenix*," she ordered. "My compliments to Captain Castillo, and ask when it would be convenient for me to have a private discussion with him."

"Yes, Ma'am."

"And," Metzger added, "make sure to emphasize the word *private*."

☆   ☆   ☆

"Secure from Readiness One," Castillo ordered. "Resume course to Manticore, and get the spin section back up to speed."

He turned back to Travis. "First lesson of combat, Mr. Long:

always be ready for the unexpected. In this case, because we weren't accelerating and were on a fairly predictable course, *Invincible* was able to slip a second missile into the wedge shadow of the first. If the attacker is very clever with his timing, he can arrange it so that the rear missile burns out its wedge at the same time the forward one impacts the target's wedge. With nothing showing, a pitched target will have just enough time to resume attitude as the second missile enters kill range."

"Sometimes the tell is a bit of the second wedge peeking through during the drive," Sladek added. "It can also show up as a sluggishness in the first missile's maneuvering as its telemetry control is eclipsed by the one behind it."

"Yes, Sir," Travis said. And if the missile was kicked out with a fusion booster, as most RMN missiles were, there would also be a telltale flare when it was launched, plus a slight decrease in the attacking ship's acceleration to give the missile time to get a safe distance before lighting up its wedge.

All of that had been in his tactics classes back at Division Officer's School, of course. But in the heat of the moment, and with the role of command unexpectedly thrust upon him—

He cut off the train of thought. Rather, the train of excuses. He'd been given a job, and he'd failed. Pure and simple.

And if it hadn't been an exercise, with a practice missile instead of the real thing, he and everyone aboard *Phoenix* would probably be dead. "Yes, Sir," he said again. "I'm sorry, Sir."

Castillo grunted as he unstrapped from his station. "No need to be sorry, Lieutenant. There's just a need to learn." He waved at the tac display. "As I said, that kind of trick takes careful timing and a great deal of skill. But it also requires a fair amount of luck. Your job as an officer of the Royal Manticoran Navy is to cultivate both. And to always assume that your opponent has done likewise."

He floated out of his chair, steadied himself a moment, then gave himself a shove that sent him floating swiftly across the bridge. Quickly, Travis moved sideways to get out of his way. "Mr. Sladek, return ship to Readiness Five," the captain called over his shoulder. "Mr. Long, you may return to your station for debriefing."

"Yes, Sir," Travis said. Lesson delivered, and lesson learned, and the captain was back to business as usual.

Travis would remember the day's lesson, he promised himself. The *whole* lesson.

Very, very well.

☆　　☆　　☆

"Understand, Allegra," Castillo said, "that what I've told you is to remain strictly between the two of us."

"Of course," Metzger said, a sour taste in her mouth. So simple. So obvious.

And really, so inevitable.

Lieutenant Travis Long, an inventive and clever young man, but an absolute rule-stickler, especially where proper maintenance and operational procedure were concerned. Ensign Fenton Locatelli, not inventive at all, driven by a sense of family history toward a greatness that could only be earned and wouldn't be his for years, if it ever was. Of course the two of them would clash. And clashing over maintaining a piece of junk equipment that neither had realized was damaged and *couldn't* be maintained had drawn the attention of the ensign's justly distinguished uncle.

Castillo was a good officer, and a good captain. But he was also acutely aware of how the Star Kingdom worked, and of the turmoil that rumbled at the political intersection of Navy and Lords. Long's ongoing trouble with Ensign Locatelli not only could be played to the advantage of the Navy's opponents somewhere down the line, but it also put Castillo's own position and standing at risk.

And so when the opportunity had presented itself, he'd opted to give Long a reminder that no one was perfect.

Only it wouldn't work, Metzger knew. Long might be cowed for now, but sooner or later his inability to look the other way on these things would reassert itself. And if Ensign Locatelli got in the way, Long wouldn't hesitate to write him up.

Long was a good spacer. But he really had no idea how the political games were played.

And she was pretty sure Castillo knew it, too.

"What are your plans?" she asked.

"Ideally, I'd like to separate them," Castillo said heavily. "Leave one in Forward Weapons and move the other to Aft Autocannon. The problem is that Long is really too qualified to kick back there, and I doubt the admiral would take kindly to me moving his nephew."

"How about simply transferring one of them off your ship?"

"How?" Castillo countered. "I've more or less promised to keep Locatelli for a while—don't ask—and last I checked there weren't any likely Gunnery Officer openings in the fleet where I could put Long."

"How about something on shore?"

"He just came out of BuShips. Sending him back would probably look bad on his record, and I really don't want to do that to him. Personality clashes aside, he's really a pretty good officer."

"And a smart one, too," Metzger said, a sudden thought occurring to her. It would be a bit of a stretch, but nothing so far out of the ordinary that it would raise any red flags. "What was your assessment of Long's performance? Off the record?"

"Off the record, he did okay," Castillo said. "Especially considering he was thrown into it without any warning. A little more experience and training and he'll probably make a pretty fair tactical officer."

"How about right now?" Metzger asked. "Not TO, of course, but ATO?"

"You know an ATO slot that's open?"

"Maybe," Metzger said. "*Casey* is just about finished with her refit. Maybe that slot's still open."

"You must be joking," Castillo said with a snort. "Half the RMN wants aboard that ship."

"Which means it may still be under consideration," Metzger pointed out. "If I were you, I'd send the suggestion directly to Defense Minister Dapplelake."

There was a short pause. "Dapplelake," Castillo repeated, his tone gone a little flat. "Is there something about Long that I should know, Captain?"

"Nothing relevant," Metzger hedged. There were details about the Secour incident that were still known only to the Star Kingdom's top leaders, details which Metzger herself was still under orders not to talk about.

But the Defense Minister knew all about Long's contribution in turning that potential disaster into a slightly tarnished victory. He knew, and King Edward knew. Between them, they should be able to pull all the necessary strings.

"All I can tell you is that the Defense Minister has all the relevant data," she added.

"All right, I'll give it a try," Castillo said. "But only because you've got me intrigued. And if it actually goes through, you're going to owe me a drink."

"Next time we're on Manticore," Metzger promised.

"And," Castillo added, "you're going to owe me an explanation. One that's as every bit as full as my glass."

"Absolutely," Metzger said with a smile. "One half-full glass, on me."

☆   ☆   ☆

For the next five days Travis walked around on figurative eggshells, waiting for the inevitable fallout from his part in the fiasco.

To his surprise, no such fallout materialized. Or at least nothing materialized in his direction. There were vague rumors that Captain Castillo was spending an unusual amount of time in his cabin on the com with System Command, but no details were forthcoming and Travis himself was never summoned into his presence. Given that *Phoenix* was about to settle in for some serious refitting, chances were good that that was the main topic of any such extended communications.

Phoenix was slipping into its designated slot in Manticore orbit, and Travis was finally starting to breathe easy again, when the shoe finally dropped.

☆   ☆   ☆

"You're joking," Fornier said, staring wide-eyed from across the cabin. "After all that, you're being *promoted*?"

"I'm being transferred, anyway," Travis corrected. "I still think the promotion is a mistake."

"Please," Fornier said dryly. "BuPers doesn't make mistakes like that. Or at least, they don't admit to it. Besides, just getting put aboard *Casey* is a hell of a step up all by itself."

"Maybe," Travis growled as he arranged his dress uniform tunic carefully at the top of his travelbag. "But if Locatelli's behind this, hell may very well be the relevant neighborhood."

Fornier shook his head. "You're way too young to be this cynical," he said. "Anyway, who says Locatelli's hand is anywhere near this? For all you know it was Castillo who recommended you for *Casey*'s ATO."

"With my sterling performance on the bridge during that drill cementing it?" Travis shook his head. "Not likely."

"Fine," Fornier said, clearly starting to lose his patience. "So

Castillo decided you needed a lesson in humility. Welcome to the human race. But maybe while he was delivering the message he also saw something he liked about you, some potential that hadn't come through before."

"I doubt it," Travis said. "About all I did was regurgitate what was in the manual. Or half of what was in the manual. No, given Heissman's reputation, I think they all just want me out from under Castillo's fatherly care and underneath a genuine hammer for a while."

For a moment Fornier was silent. Travis looked around the cabin, mentally counting out the items he'd already packed and trying to figure out if he'd missed anything.

"There are two ways to approach life, Travis," Fornier said into his thoughts. "One: you can expect that everyone's out to get you, and be alert and ready for trouble at every turn. Or two: you can assume that most people are friendly or at least neutral, and that most of the time things will work out."

"Seems to me option two is an invitation to get walked on."

"Oh, I never said you don't need to be ready for trouble." Fornier grinned suddenly. "Hey, we're Navy officers. It's our *job* to be ready for trouble. I'm just saying that if you're always expecting betrayal, you're never going to be able to trust anyone." He shrugged. "And speaking from my own experience, there are a fair number of people out there who are worth your trust. Not all of them. But enough."

"Maybe," Travis said, sealing his travelbag and picking it up. "I'll take it under advisement." He held out his hand. "It's been great serving and rooming with you, Brad. Keep in touch, okay?"

"Will do," Fornier promised, grasping Travis's hand in a firm grip and shaking it. "Best of luck."

BOOK THREE

1543 PD

CHAPTER SEVENTEEN

THERE WAS A SOFT TONE from the repeater display in Llyn's cabin aboard *Score Settler*. Starting awake from his light doze, he checked the readout.

Finally—finally—a hyper footprint. McConnovitch and *Hosney* had arrived.

Llyn rubbed the sleep out of his eyes, feeling a surge of relief. The bulk of the Volsung task force had been orbiting this uninhabited red-dwarf for the past two weeks, with only one of the battlecruisers still absent, and Gensonne was starting to get twitchy. The fresh data McConnovitch was bringing in from Manticore should allay the admiral's lingering concerns about the particulars of the force he would be facing.

Another ping came from the board, this one marking an incoming transmission.

Llyn rolled his eyes. It wouldn't be McConnovitch—*Hosney* was still a good nine light-minutes out. Undoubtedly Gensonne.

And of course, it was. "Is that finally your man?" the admiral growled.

"Yes, I believe so," Llyn said.

"About time," Gensonne said sourly. "He'd better have something good after all this."

"I'm sure he will," Llyn said, sitting firmly on his patience. McConnovitch was a good man, and one of the best data scavengers in the business. But he tended to play a little loose with plans and timetables. Given the nature of his work, that wasn't unreasonable.

Gensonne, unfortunately, was at the opposite end of the spectrum, treating his precious schedules like they'd been handed to him on stone tablets. McConnovitch hadn't kept to that schedule, and the admiral hadn't been shy about stating his view of such sloppiness on a regular basis.

But the waiting was finally over. Once McConnovitch confirmed the RMN's weakness, Llyn could turn the Volsungs loose and then head off to where his Axelrod superiors waited to hear that the operation was finally underway. By the time Gensonne had Landing and the Manticoran government under control, Axelrod's people would be on their way to take over.

Or rather, the nation Axelrod had now made a deal with to "invade" and "conquer" the Star Kingdom. The handful of Axelrod "advisors" who would also be aboard those ships would be staying very much in the background, guiding the actions only if and when necessary.

And like any good puppet show, if they did their job properly, the hard-eyed critics in Haven and the League would never see the strings.

The minutes ticked down; and precisely on the nine-light-minute timetable, Llyn's com pinged. "I'm getting his transmission now," he told Gensonne. "I'll send it on after I've decrypted it."

Gensonne gave a little grunt.

"Make it fast."

"As fast as I can," Llyn promised. "But he'll be running a semi-manual encryption, which means I'll need to work through it partly by hand."

"You're joking," Gensonne said with another grunt. "You never hear of computer encryption algorithms?"

"Sure," Llyn said. "They're the ones a good hacker can grab and use to open your whole com system to unfriendly eyes and ears. Sometimes the old classics work best."

"If you say so. Just hurry it up."

"I will."

Llyn keyed off and checked the new transmission. It was a data packet, and the origination ID was indeed *Hosney*.

He frowned, feeling a prickling on the back of his neck. No greeting, no identification, just the data packet? That didn't sound like McConnovitch.

The transmission ended, and the report came up on his display. Frowning, Lynn began to read.

And the prickling on his neck turned into a shiver.

Green Force Two, scout unit, call-signed Janus: four ships.

Green Force One, main Manticore/Sphinx defense unit, call-signed Aegis: nine ships, including two battlecruisers. Not one, but two.

Red Force, Gryphon defense unit, call-signed Backstop: four ships, including yet another battlecruiser.

Llyn leaned back in his seat, mouthing a curse. The ten-ship, one-battlecruiser enemy that Gensonne was expecting to meet was in fact seventeen ships and no fewer than *three* battlecruisers. And that didn't even count the two battlecruisers and six other warships that McConnovitch marked as being currently in refit.

Gensonne wasn't going to be happy about this. Not at all. In fact, he might be unhappy enough to take his ball and go home.

And given the unanticipated uptick in the RMN's numbers, the contract Llyn and Gensonne had signed not only allowed the Volsungs to bail, but also required Axelrod to pay them a hefty cancellation fee.

There was no way Llyn was going to let that happen. Not after coming this far.

Taking a cleansing breath, he began combing methodically through the numbers.

Looked at more closely, it wasn't that bad. Not really. Green Forces One and Two were a formidable array, but the fact that they *were* split into two groups meant that Gensonne should be able to take them on one at a time. Even if he couldn't, it was still two RMN battlecruisers against the Volsungs' three.

Even better, Red Force was way the hell over at Manticore-B. Those ships should be out of the picture until long after the battle was over. And of course, all the ships in dock for refit might as well not even be there.

No, Gensonne wasn't going up against anything he couldn't handle. Not with his three battlecruisers, his fourteen other ships, and his massive confidence.

There was certainly no reason to bother the admiral's little head with silly numbers and needless concerns.

He finished his editing, then keyed for transmission to Gensonne's flagship.

"I've decoded the report, Admiral. Sending it to you now."

"Thank you," Gensonne said. "I trust nothing has changed since your last report?"

"Nothing of significance," Llyn assured him. "Nothing at all."

☆   ☆   ☆

Commodore Rudolph Heissman, commander of the light cruiser HMS *Casey* and the other three ships of Green Two, was undoubtedly a very busy man. Nevertheless, from Travis's point of view at the far side of Heissman's desk, it looked like he was taking an extraordinarily long time to read through Travis's transfer orders. Seated beside him, Commander Celia Belokas, Heissman's exec, didn't look to be in any more of a hurry than her boss.

Finally, after a mid-sized eternity, Heissman looked up. "Lieutenant Long," he said, his flat tone not giving anything away. "According to this, you have great potential."

He paused, as if expecting some kind of response. "Thank you, Sir," was all Travis could think to say. The words, which had sounded tolerably reasonable in his head, sounded excruciatingly stupid when he heard them out in the open air.

Heissman apparently thought so, too. "You know what I hear when someone uses the phrase *great potential*, Mr. Long?" he asked, his expression not changing in the slightest. "I hear someone making excuses. I hear someone who hasn't worked to reach the level of his or her ability. I hear someone who doesn't belong in the Royal Manticoran Navy. I hear someone who *absolutely* doesn't belong aboard HMS *Casey*."

"Yes, Sir," Travis said. That response didn't sound any better than the previous one had.

"I don't want to see potential," Heissman continued. "I want to see results." He cocked his head. "Do you know what the assistant tactical officer's job is, Mr. Long?"

"Yes, Sir." The words sounded marginally better this time. "To assist the captain and tactical officer in combat maneuvers and—"

"That's the job description," Heissman interrupted. "What the ATO *does* is find patterns and weaknesses in the enemy, and avoid them in his own ship."

He gazed into Travis's eyes, his expression hardening. "Captain Castillo talks a lot about luck. I don't ever want to hear you use that word aboard my ship. Understood?"

"Yes, Sir," Travis said.

"Good," Heissman said. "As I said, part of your job is to know the weaknesses of your own ship and find ways to minimize them. Step one in that procedure is obviously to know your ship." He nodded to his side. "In light of that, Commander Belokas has graciously agreed to give you a tour. Pay attention and listen to everything she has to say. Afterward, you're going to need a lot of hours with the spec manual before you're anywhere near up to speed."

"Yes, Sir," Travis said. He shifted his eyes to Belokas. "Ma'am."

Heissman's eyebrows rose a fraction of a centimeter. "Unless, of course, you've already spent some time in the manual," he added, as if the thought had only just occurred to him. "Have you?"

"As a matter of fact, Sir, yes, I have," Travis confirmed, trying not to grimace. He'd only spent eighty percent of his waking hours during his two weeks of groundside time poring through everything he could find on *Casey* and her equipment. Which, considering all the bureaucratic hoops he'd had to jump through to even get the manuals, Heissman almost certainly already knew. "Just the surface information, of course—"

"In that case, *you* can give the tour," Heissman said. "You'll tell Commander Belokas everything you know, and she'll start on her list of everything you *don't* know. That sound fair to you?"

"Yes, Sir," Travis said.

"Good," Heissman said. "You have two hours before you're to report to Lieutenant Commander Woodburn, so you'd better get to it." He nodded briskly and lowered his eyes to the report. "Dismissed."

☆   ☆   ☆

"I trust you won't take this wrong, Ensign," Captain Adrian Hagros said stiffly as he floated at the back of HMS *Hercules*'s entryway, "but what the *hell* are you doing aboard my ship?"

Crown Prince Richard Winton—or more accurately, the freshly minted Ensign Richard Winton—suppressed a smile. Not because of the question or the impudence, but because he knew full well the looks the two King's Own bodyguards behind him were giving *Hercules*'s commander right now.

Which merely raised Richard's opinion of Hagros another couple of notches. Awkward situation or not, the man refused to either shrivel or mince words. Now, more than ever, Richard was glad he'd made this decision.

"I'm an officer of the Royal Manticoran Navy, Sir," he reminded Hagros politely. "I'm here because this is where my orders sent me."

"Sure," Hagros said. "And your orders didn't send you to *Invincible* or *Swiftsure* because...?"

"Because small-ship experience is as important as big-ship duty, Sir," Richard said. "Because *Hercules* is where the normal assignment rotation had scheduled me. And because I don't want any special privileges."

A familiar set of expressions flicked across Hagros's face, mirroring the equally familiar thoughts likely going on behind them: first, that a broad range of experience was only necessary for a career officer, which Richard most definitely wasn't; and second, that special privileges were practically a way of life for the Crown Prince, whether he wanted them or not.

Richard knew that was what Hagros was thinking, because it was what everyone else had thought, every frustrating step of the way.

But Richard had made it this far. He'd avoided cushy duty, he'd avoided abnormally prestigious duty, and he'd forced them to put him on a normal ensign's track. He wasn't about to be stopped now just because *Hercules*'s captain didn't think a century-old *Pegasus*-class corvette was worthy of the Crown Prince's presence.

Maybe Hagros saw that in Richard's eyes. Or maybe he just realized that the Crown Prince's presence here meant better people than Hagros had already tried to send him to a more comfortable posting and failed.

"Glad to hear it," he growled. "Because you're not going to get any here. The yeoman outside will show you to your quarters." His eyes flicked over Richard's shoulders. "And your men to theirs," he added. "You're to report to Lieutenant Petrenko in Forward Impellers in one hour. Any questions?"

"No, Sir."

"In that case, welcome aboard, Ensign," Hagros said, a little less severely. "A word of warning: corvettes are old ships, and their crews have to work their tails off. Be prepared to have yours worked off, too."

"I'm looking forward to it, Sir."

Hagros snorted as he gave Richard a sharp nod. And, perhaps, just the faintest hint of a smile. "Dismissed."

And as Richard floated down the passageway behind the

yeoman, he found himself breathing deeper in anticipation. No more arguments with his father, no more persuasion of nervous bureaucrats in BuPers, no more need to define his position and stand firm on it. Finally, *finally*, he had a ship.

He would work his tail off, all right. His current orders had him serving aboard *Hercules* for the next year. He would spend that year becoming the best damn officer *Hercules* and Hagros had ever seen.

☆   ☆   ☆

"Admiral Gensonne?"

His eyes and attention still on Llyn's report, Gensonne reached over and keyed the com. "What is it, Imbar?"

"Hyper footprint, Sir," Captain Sweeney Imbar, *Odin*'s commander, reported. "Looks like *Tyr* has finally arrived."

Gensonne grunted. About fraggy time. They'd been waiting on Blakely to get his butt here for four solid weeks, and the rest of the captains were getting antsy. Now, with the last of Gensonne's three battlecruisers on site, they were finally ready to get this operation underway. "Send Captain Blakely my compliments," he instructed Imbar, "and tell him to haul his sorry carcass in pronto so he can start loading supplies and armaments. We head for Manticore in five days, and if he's not ready he'll be left behind."

"Aye, Admiral," Imbar said, and Gensonne could visualize the other's malicious grin. Imbar loved relaying that kind of order.

Gensonne keyed off the com, and with a scowl returned his attention to Llyn's report.

Seventeen warships. That was what the Volsung Mercenaries were bringing to the battlefield: three battlecruisers, six cruisers, seven destroyers, and one troop carrier. There were also the four fuel and support ships that would remain parked outside the hyper limit, but those didn't really count. The Manticorans, in contrast, had only thirteen warships with which to counter.

Well, seventeen, technically, if you added in the group guarding Gryphon. But they were way the hell over at Manticore-B. If the Volsungs did their job properly, that force could be left out of the equation. Llyn's spies hadn't been able to get a complete reading on the ship types in each of the two Manticore-A groups, but the earlier report had said the larger force had a single battlecruiser, and there was nothing in this latest intel to suggest that number had changed. The additional ships in the new intel had to be small: destroyers or corvettes.

Plus the fact that all the enthusiasm in the galaxy could mount impeller rings and graduate crewmen only so quickly. Even if Llyn's current count was off by a ship or two, the Volsungs should be facing no more than the same number of ships they themselves were bringing to the battle.

Still...

Gensonne murmured a ruminative curse. The wild card in this whole thing, and a wild card that Llyn either hadn't noticed or had deliberately downplayed, was this damn HMS *Casey*. The tables listed it as a standard light cruiser, but it was clear from the specs Llyn's spies had been able to dig out that there wasn't anything standard about it, certainly not for ships out here in the hinterlands. From the profile alone, he could see that the Manticorans had put in a modern grav plate habitation module and a high-efficiency radiator system, and had extended the length of their missile launchers. Possibly a railgun launch system; more likely just an absorption cylinder that would minimize the missiles' launch flares. Nothing really revolutionary, and nothing Gensonne couldn't handle.

Still, it was far more advanced than it should be, and better than most of the Volsungs' own secondhand and surplused ships. The report didn't get into details about armament or defenses, but Gensonne had no doubt that *Casey*'s designers hadn't neglected to pack some serious firepower aboard.

And if King Edward had had the authority, the confidence, and the cash to turn his designers loose on *Casey*, he might well have used that same combination to speed up the de-mothballing of those other ships.

The smart thing would be to put off the operation until Gensonne had time to send his own people to Manticore. Get a real military assessment instead of having to rely on Llyn's paper-pushing guesswork.

But all he had here were military ships, which would raise way more eyebrows than he wanted. The only civilian spy ships he had available were way the hell back in Silesia. Getting word back there, and then getting one of them to fly to Manticore and to report to him here would take over a year.

Gensonne had no interest in putting off the operation that long. Llyn was even more adamant about the timing.

The only other option was to use Llyn's courier ship. But

couriers were generally diplomatic vessels, and one in private hands would raise nearly as many eyebrows as one of Gensonne's military ships.

Besides, if he couldn't trust Llyn's spies to give him accurate data, he sure as hell couldn't trust Llyn himself with the job.

Gensonne scowled. The ongoing mystery underlying this whole thing was what in blazes the Manticorans could possibly have that was worth this much effort. Llyn was paying the Volsungs a huge sum of money to take over three lumps of real estate on the bloody back end of nowhere. Gensonne had tried on numerous occasions to wangle that secret out of the smug little man, and every time Llyn had calmly and artfully dodged the question.

But that was all right. The Volsung Mercenaries weren't without resources of their own... and if Gensonne still didn't know the *why*, he now at least knew the *who*.

Llyn's employer, the shadowy figure quietly funding this whole operation, was one of the top people in the multi-trillion, transstellar business juggernaut known as the Axelrod Corporation.

So the question now became why Axelrod would be interested in Manticore. Was it the treecats? Something else hidden in the forests of Sphinx or the wastes of Gryphon?

"Admiral?" Imbar's voice came from the com speaker.

"Yes?"

"Captain Blakely's compliments, Sir," Imbar said. "He confirms hauling carcass as ordered, and anticipates fourteen hours to zero-zero."

Gensonne checked his chrono. "Tell him that if he doesn't make it in twelve he might as well not bother," he warned.

"He anticipated that request," Imbar said, his voice going a little brittle. "He said to tell you that fourteen should do just fine if you can get the loaders to haul carcass at even half the speed he's doing. If you can't, he'll just have to do it himself." The captain gave a little snort. "He added a *Sir* to that, but I don't think he really meant it."

Gensonne smiled. Blakely was as arrogant and snarky an SOB as they came. But he was also a hell of a scrappy fighter, and Gensonne was willing to put up with the one if he could have the other. "Tell him he'll be losing one percent of his profit cut for every ten minutes after twelve hours he ties up."

"Yes, Sir, that should do it," Imbar said slyly. "I'll let him know."

"Do that," Gensonne said, his attention already back on the upcoming campaign.

Standard military doctrine, of course, said that you went after the biggest ships first, taking them out as soon as you could clear away their screening vessels. But in this case, it might well be smart to seek out *Casey* earlier rather than later and make sure she was out of the fight. If she *was* the Manticorans' modern showcase, her destruction might help convince them to sue for terms more promptly.

Which could be useful. The accepted laws of war dictated that a planet was supposed to surrender once someone else controlled the space around it, a convention designed to avoid the wholesale slaughter of civilians in prolonged combat. Taking out *Casey* would give the Volsungs that control all the faster, and once Gensonne had King Edward's formal surrender document any forces that remained at large would be legally bound to stand down.

Gensonne liked quick surrenders. It saved on men and equipment, and it boosted profits. Especially since any Royal Manticoran ships that survived would become the property of the victors. That would *definitely* be a part of the surrender agreement, and even old ships could be profitably integrated into his existing forces. If eliminating *Casey* quickly helped bring that about, so much the better.

And if *Casey* wasn't, in fact, anything special?

He shrugged. It was most probable the ship would have to be destroyed in the initial attack, anyway. It would have been nice to get his hands on the Manticorans' one really modern vessel, but a man couldn't have everything.

"Admiral, I have a response from Captain Blakely," Imbar once again interrupted. "He sends his compliments, and says he'll see you in hell."

Gensonne smiled. "Tell him it's a date," he said. "I'll be the one wearing white."

☆　　☆　　☆

"Commander Donnelly?" Chief Lydia Ulvestad called from the com station. "Signal from Coxswain Plover. He and the others have left *Aries* and are heading back."

"Thank you, Chief," Lisa said, feeling yet another twinge of annoyance over this whole thing. Granted, she and the rest of *Damocles*'s crew had little enough to do these days. But there was still something fundamentally insulting about the RMN having to send ratings to one of their own former ships simply because the MPARS weenies couldn't figure out how to make their new missiles work.

Especially when Breakwater had already siphoned off some of the Navy's own people to assist them. *They* were the ones who were supposed to be doing this grunt work, not *Damocles*'s people.

"Did Plover say whether or not they got the missiles working?" she asked.

"Sounds like it, Ma'am," Ulvestad said. "From what I heard, it sounded like an electronics problem, and Mallare and Redko are good at fixing those." She hesitated. "I don't know if you knew, Ma'am, but Missile Tech Townsend is aboard *Aries*."

"Yes, I knew that," Lisa said, feeling her throat tighten. Travis had mentioned that over a hurried lunch a couple of weeks ago, during one of the rare times the two of them were in Landing at the same time. He'd seemed to think that he might have had something to do with Townsend's transfer, though he hadn't gone into details.

But except for that brief cloud, the rest of the time they'd spent together had been good. Actually, it had been more than just good. The people who remembered Travis as "Rule-stickler Long," and those who used the strange *travesty* catchword that he'd somehow been saddled with—they all missed the point. Yes, Travis was rigid when it came to rules and procedures aboard his ship; but when he was off-duty, and if he could be persuaded to relax, he was surprisingly pleasant company. He was smart, quick with a quip, considerate, and attentive.

In fact, what had begun as a dog-sitting favor and grown into a friendship was slowly blossoming into—

Lisa shook the thought away. She didn't know where her relationship with Travis was going, and wasn't at all sure she wanted to. She'd tried the romance thing once before, and had gotten herself thoroughly paint-stripped for her efforts. She wasn't in any hurry to rush into that thorn bush again.

Though with Travis it would probably be different. There'd been warning signs with Rolfe, red flags which she'd ignored in the rose-colored haze, but which were painfully obvious in the cold light of day. There were no such flags with Travis.

Of course, that might only mean that there were different signs

230 David Weber, Timothy Zahn & Thomas Pope

there which she was also deliberately avoiding. No one was perfect, after all, and Travis probably had a dozen habits or quirks that would make him hard to live with.

Still, she did enjoy his company.

"Signal from *Aries*, Ma'am," Ulvestad said into her thoughts. "Captain Hardasty's compliments, and her thanks for lending us Mallare and Redko."

At least Hardasty was being polite about it. "My compliments in return," Lisa said. "Did she give any indication that the problem has been fixed?"

"Nothing directly," Ulvestad said. "But Plover did mention he'd heard both *Aries* and *Taurus* would be staying in Manticore orbit for a while to run some tests."

Lisa nodded. A sensible decision—it would be foolish for the two corvettes to head directly to their new Unicorn Belt postings until they were sure their missile systems were up and running. Manticore-B might be MPARS's stronghold, but most of the real weapons expertise still resided here at Manticore.

Unless Hardasty wanted to head in from the Belt later to Gryphon and ask Admiral Jacobson for help. Given that *Aries* had been pulled out of Jacobson's Red Force before being handed over to MPARS, Lisa doubted that such help would be cheerfully given.

"Well, do remind her that we're scheduled to leave in three hours to rendezvous with the rest of Green One," she said. "If she needs assistance after that, she'll have to get it elsewhere."

"Yes, Ma'am."

Lisa checked her chrono. Captain Marcello would be arriving for his watch in about half an hour. Lisa would want to make sure the shuttle was properly squared away and that *Damocles* was ready for her departure to join the rest of Admiral Locatelli's force.

And then it would be a trip to the officers' mess for a quick dinner. Alone, probably. Certainly not with anyone who understood her and could make her laugh.

It really was amazing, she decided, how much she missed Travis.

☆ ☆ ☆

"Well?" Gensonne asked, drumming his fingers impatiently.

"We're ready, Sir," Imbar said. He listened a moment longer, then keyed off the com. "All ships are in position; all synch timers are zeroed. We await your order, Admiral."

Gensonne nodded. Which was as it should be. All ships, all crewmen, all awaiting his order.

All ships, of course, except for Llyn's courier. Gensonne had invited him to come along and watch the show, but he'd made his excuses and taken off, no doubt to report to his Axelrod masters. Perish forbid that someone from such a genteel, dress-suited establishment should soil his hands with something as disagreeable as actual combat.

But that was fine. Gensonne could have found something useful for Llyn and his ship to do, but he hardly needed them. All he needed was Llyn's money, and he had the first portion of that safely in hand.

He would also make sure he had all the rest before he and his ships left Manticore. Maybe he would make a little ritual of handing over the keys to King Edward's palace in exchange for the last set of bank chits. That would probably appeal to the little man's sense of humor.

In the meantime, the Volsung Mercenaries had a job to do.

"Signal all ships," he ordered Imbar. "Translate on my mark."

And they would carry out that job with skill and precision, he promised himself. The skill and precision that Gustav Ander-man had always prized, and which the old lunatic had claimed Gensonne didn't have.

Well, the Volsungs would show him. They would show *everyone*.

And when this was all over, maybe Gensonne would take the new ships and crews he could buy with the money Llyn was paying and go back to Potsdam. And he would show his former chief just how skillful and precise an attack could be.

It was something worth thinking about.

In the meantime...

"Ready all ships," he called. "Ready: *mark*."

CHAPTER EIGHTEEN

THE MIDWATCH WAS TECHNICALLY the first watch of the ship's day, though whether it felt like the earliest or the latest was largely a function of how a given crewmember's biological clock operated. Some of *Casey*'s officers and crew actively hated it, while others were less passionate on the subject but not any happier with the duty.

Travis had no such animosities toward midwatch assignments. On the contrary, he rather enjoyed them. Midwatch was the quietest period of ship's day, with the bulk of the crew asleep back in the hab module, only essential operations running, and minimal routine maintenance scheduled.

It was the best time of day, in short, to just be quiet and think.

He certainly had plenty to think about. For the past six weeks most of his waking hours had been devoted to learning everything he could about *Casey*, her armaments, her capabilities, and her crew. Lieutenant Commander Woodburn, whose personality could best be described as prickly, had ridden him hard, pretty much the entire time. But unlike some of the officers back on *Phoenix*, Woodburn was eminently fair and always seemed more interested in teaching Travis the ropes than in making himself look superior or his student look stupid.

So had everyone else aboard. In fact, as near as Travis could tell, everyone treated him exactly like they did all the other officers. Either *Casey*'s men and women didn't follow politics or they didn't know Travis was related to Baron Winterfall.

Or else they knew and simply didn't care.

Travis hoped it was the latter. If it was one of the other reasons, sooner or later the word would get out, and it would be *Phoenix* all over again.

He sent his gaze slowly around the bridge, at the men and women strapped into their stations, casually alert even in the quiet of absolutely nothing happening. *Casey* wasn't exactly home—Travis wasn't sure if any place would ever truly be home for him—but the ship and her crew had all the little quirks that he'd always imagined would exist in a home. Granted, Woodburn wasn't the only occasionally irritating personality aboard, and Travis had had his share of small clashes with some of them. But for the most part, the crew seemed eminently compatible with each other.

The commissioned complement had even more of that same pseudo-family feeling. On the bridge, Commodore Heissman typically dispensed with the formalities that Captain Castillo had always maintained aboard *Phoenix*, addressing his senior officers by their first names or even nicknames, some of which Travis still hadn't puzzled out. There was an air of easy camaraderie, the kind that Travis had read about in military-themed books and had experienced to some degree back when he was a mere gravitics tech aboard *Guardian*.

At the same time, that familiarity and camaraderie went only so far. Heissman and the other senior officers still addressed Travis formally as *Lieutenant* or *Mr. Long*, and he was of course expected to reciprocate with that same formality. Hopefully, it was just a matter of Travis being on informal probation, and that somewhere along the line he would be accepted as a full-fledged member of *Casey*'s family.

Unless there was some of *Phoenix*'s same political-appointee underpinnings roiling quietly beneath the surface. If so, he might as well get used to being *Casey*'s ugly duckling. Especially once they figured out who his half-brother was.

"XO on the bridge," Lieutenant Rusk called from the tracking station behind him.

Travis swiveled around to see Commander Belokas float onto the bridge. "Ma'am," he greeted her, reflexively reaching for his restraints before he could stop himself. Regulations said that when a senior officer entered the bridge all crew members were to immediately come to full attention, a standing order Captain

Castillo had enforced aboard *Phoenix*. Commodore Heissman and Commander Belokas dispensed with that particular formality, and Travis was still getting used to that difference.

Briefly, he wondered if the officers and crew of the battlecruiser *Invincible* similarly had to float upright in zero-gee every time the great Admiral Carlton Locatelli came into any compartment, not just the bridge. From what he'd seen of Locatelli's nephew's attitude, he suspected they probably did.

"What can we do for you, Ma'am?" he asked as Belokas drifted across the bridge, her gaze moving back and forth between the various monitors.

"I was wondering if there was anything new on that flicker we picked up during Lieutenant Dahl's watch," she said.

"I don't believe so, Ma'am," Travis said, frowning as he pulled up the log. There hadn't been any mention of activity on the watch report he'd read when he'd arrived on duty an hour ago.

No wonder. The flicker Belokas was referring to was the barest bloop, something that would never even have been noticed if the rest of the universe hadn't been so quiet and *Casey*'s crew so bored. Dahl, the Forward Weapons division head, had put it down to a sensor echo; the CIC supervisor, after a thorough examination of the gravitic equipment, had suggested it could also be a hyper ghost, a phenomenon that shipboard instrumentation was unfortunately not well-equipped to pinpoint or identify. For that, a large-scale orbiting sensor array was necessary, and Manticore wasn't likely to be buying one of those monstrosities anytime soon. Furthermore, the bloop had occurred a full sixteen hours ago, with nothing since then, which again argued for an echo or hyper ghost.

But if the frown on Belokas's face was any indication, she wasn't happy with either explanation. An odd reaction, really, given that such ghosts weren't exactly unheard of out here.

Especially not in that particular sector, which was notorious for iffy sensor resolution and rough downward Alpha transitions. Travis had looked into the phenomenon once, and as far as he'd been able to learn no one knew what it was, though it had been tentatively ascribed to an interaction between Manticore's twin suns and some as-yet unmapped set of grav waves.

"There's been nothing new, Ma'am," Travis told her. "Do you want us to run another sensor diagnostic?"

For a few seconds Belokas didn't answer, but merely continued her drift toward Travis's station. He watched her approach, his heartbeat picking up a bit. He was still somewhat new to this whole officer-in-charge thing, and he already knew how bad he was at reading Belokas's expression and body language. Should he have run such a diagnostic already? Was she holding her peace merely because she wanted to be close enough to chew him out quietly, without the rest of the bridge crew listening in?

"More diagnostics won't tell us anything new," she said at last, wrapping her long fingers around his station's handhold and bringing herself to a halt. "Let's try something else. Run me a simulation of what a soft translation about fifteen light-minutes outside the hyper limit would look like."

"Yes, Ma'am," Travis said as he swiveled around to his console. That possibility had already been considered, he'd seen from the report. But between the diagnostics and the hyper ghost hypothesis, that scenario had apparently been dropped. Certainly there was no record of anyone having done a simulation or even a data-curve profile.

Fortunately, it was a fairly simple job, with most of the necessary templates already stored on the ship's computer. A couple of minutes, and he was ready. "Here we go," he said, starting the run. "I set it to cover the full range of thirteen to eighteen light-minutes. If that doesn't work, I can extend it outward—"

"Hyper footprint!" Rusk called from behind him.

For a fraction of a second Travis thought the other was talking about the simulation. Then his brain caught up with him. "Acknowledged," he said, swiveling again and checking the proper display. It was a translation, all right, a big, fat, noisy one.

And it was right on the same vector where the earlier bloop had registered. "We have anything on her?" he asked.

"She's reasonably big," Rusk said. The displays were coming to life as CIC collected and collated the data from *Casey's* various sensors and sent the results to the bridge. "Low-power wedge, low acceleration. Probably a freighter, possibly a passenger liner. There's something funny about her wedge, too—some sort of non-rhythmic fluctuation. Trouble with her nodes, probably."

Travis looked at Belokas, wondering if she would formally relieve him and take command. Ships didn't show up at Manticore every day, and those that did seldom showed signs of serious and imminent trouble.

But the XO was just gazing silently at the displays. Waiting, apparently, for the Officer of the Watch to respond to the situation.

Travis squared his shoulders. Rare or not, the situation was adequately covered by standard regs. "Send a request for identification and status, and inform the rest of Janus that we have a visitor," he ordered. "Then send an alert to System Command." He squinted at the tactical. "What is she, about ten light-minutes out?"

"Yes, Sir, just a shade under," Rusk confirmed. "So about twenty minutes until we get a reply."

"Unless she *is* having problems, in which case she's probably already screaming for help," Belokas said. She tapped her cheek thoughtfully. "Where's Aegis at the moment?"

"The far side of Manticore," Travis said. "About twenty-two light minutes away from us, maybe thirteen or fourteen from the bogey. Shall I send an alert directly to Admiral Locatelli?"

"That would be a good idea," Belokas confirmed. "If the bogey's in trouble, we're definitely closest. But depending on what's going on, the admiral may want to reconfigure his force while we head out there." Her lips compressed briefly. "And while you're doing all that, may I also recommend that you call Commodore Heissman to the bridge."

☆　　☆　　☆

"—and I think the reactor's bottle is also starting to fail," Captain Olver's frantic voice boomed over *Odin*'s com speaker. "My engineer says it could go at any time."

Gensonne listened closely, hoping Olver would remember his instructions to keep his voice pleading but not whiny. People hated whiny, even upstanding naval types willing to risk their lives for those in danger. Making *Naglfar* look stoic and sympathetic would encourage the Manticorans listening to his distress call to charge to the rescue with a minimum of delay and, hopefully, a minimum of prudence.

"Repeating: this is the personnel transport *Leviathan*, heading for the Haven Sector with three thousand passengers," Olver continued. "The same power surge that damaged our forward alpha nodes and the fusion bottle's also compromised our life-support system—we're trying to fix it, but it's not looking good, and I don't know how long before it fails completely. If you have any ships in the area, for the love of God please get them out here.

We're making as many gees as we can, but I don't know how much longer before we'll have to shut down the wedge completely, and we're a hell of a long way from anywhere. Whatever ships you've got—freighters, liners, ore ships—anything we can pack our people into—please send them. For the love of God, please."

The plea broke off as one of Olver's crew came up with his own anxiously delivered and almost off-mike report on the supposed fusion bottle failure, and Gensonne keyed off the speaker. They were still a good distance out from the inner system, but it looked like the nearest Manticoran force was about ten light-minutes away, which meant a twenty-minute turnaround for any conversation.

The Manticorans' response should be interesting. In the meantime, Gensonne had plenty of other matters with which to occupy himself. "What's the status of the main force?" he called across the bridge.

"We've temporarily lost contact, Admiral," Imbar called back. "They're definitely still behind us, but they're hard to spot with their wedge strength this low."

Gensonne grunted, looking across the relevant display screens. Being difficult to spot was the whole idea, of course. But knowing exactly where to look should make the task a lot simpler.

Though perhaps he was being too harsh on Imbar and the sensor team. The fourteen Volsung ships had translated into n-space together sixteen hours ago, coming in softly and quietly about forty light-minutes out from Manticore-A, where they ought to have been well out of range of RMN sensors. The enormous passive arrays typical of more populous star systems would certainly have picked them up, but shipboard gravitics' range was always far more limited. The invaders had sorted themselves into Gensonne's six-ship Advance Force and *Thor*'s eight-ship Main Force, then headed toward the inner system in two waves spaced about an hour apart. Running their acceleration low to build up speed while keeping their wedges hopefully undetectable, they'd headed in toward their targets.

Targets that were gratifyingly right where they were supposed to be. The two destroyers of the Sidewinder Force, *Umbriel* and *Miranda*, had conducted a quiet recon during the past forty-eight hours, doing a soft translation far outside the system, drifting along as they marked the locations and vectors of the two main Naval forces, then translating out again and rejoining the two main

Volsung groups. From their data Gensonne had calculated where the Manticorans should be and adjusted his forces' insertion vector so that they would encounter the smaller Green Two force well before the larger group of Green One ships could move to support them.

Now, after hours of tedium, things were finally about to heat up. Far ahead, *Naglfar* had translated right on the hyper limit—not with the same undetectable entry as the rest of the Volsung ships, but with a big, noisy translation that should have grabbed the attention of every RMN ship in the region. That sloppy entrance, along with Olver's frantic plea for help, should get the Manticoran ships falling all over themselves scrambling to come to his aid.

It would no doubt be highly entertaining to see how a Manticoran boarding party would react to finding out that a shipload of supposedly helpless civilians was actually five battalions of crack Volsung shock troops. Sadly, Gensonne would miss out on that picture. If all went according to plan, the Manticorans' first encounter with those troops wouldn't be in deep space, but at the Royal Palace in Landing City.

By then, of course, the surprise would be long gone. Still, the purpose of this exercise was capture and occupation, not entertainment. And once the RMN had been eliminated, Volsung control of the Manticoran centers of power would be a mere formality.

"Got a bearing on *Naglfar*, Admiral," Imbar called. "We're on a good intercept course. We should pass it in about ninety-seven minutes."

Gensonne checked the tac display. Ninety-seven minutes was shorter than he'd planned, but within acceptable parameters. "Have Olver increase acceleration to ninety-five gees," he instructed Imbar. He could always have *Naglfar* cut back later if he needed to fine-tune the intercept. "Any movement from the Manticorans yet?"

"No, Sir," Imbar said. "But Green Two should just be hearing Olver's distress call now."

"Keep an eye on them," Gensonne ordered. "Once we know their jump-off time and acceleration, I want a quick plot of their zero-zero intercept. We need to make sure we're far enough ahead of *Naglfar* that they won't be able to turn tail and run once they spot us."

Though the Sidewinder force's follow-up mission should help alleviate that problem. If the destroyers had translated on schedule at their own insertion point around the edge of the hyper limit, there was a good chance they could help cut off any retreat the Manticorans might attempt.

"Yes, Sir," Imbar said. "We've got a confirmation on Sidewinder's second group of wedges, now bearing oh-two-one by oh-one-eight. From the signature there seem to be significantly more ships there than in the first group. That confirms they're the main Green One force, with the smaller group also confirmed as Green Two."

"Redesignate accordingly," Gensonne ordered. "Green One's distance?"

"Just under fourteen light-minutes."

Gensonne nodded in satisfaction. The Sidewinder recon data had been a bit fuzzy, given the destroyers' distance from the inner system. But the data and Gensonne's own extrapolations had been right on the nose.

Now, with the defenders' positions confirmed, the plan was officially a lock. Assuming the Manticorans bought into Olver's story, Green Two would rush to *Naglfar*'s rescue and be quickly destroyed by *Odin* and the rest of the advance force. If Green One followed and moved to engage, its ships should arrive just in time for a one-two punch as *Thor* and the rest of the main force moved up close behind Gensonne's advance force.

If Green One opted instead to avoid battle and run for home, the end result would still be the same, just a few hours later. Either way, Manticore was as good as taken.

Llyn would be pleased. More to the point, Llyn's bosses at Axelrod would be paying a nice contractual bonus.

Smiling tightly, Gensonne settled back and waited for the Manticorans to take the bait.

☆   ☆   ☆

"We're making as many gees as we can," the tense voice came from the bridge speaker, "but I don't know how much longer before we'll have to shut down the wedge completely, and we're a hell of a long way from anywhere. Whatever ships you've got— freighters, liners, ore ships—anything we can pack our people into—please send them. For the love of God, please."

Heissman gestured, and Chief Kebiro at Com keyed the volume back down. "XO?" the commodore invited, looking at Belokas. "How many passengers do you think we can take?"

Belokas huffed out a breath. "Between the four of us, I don't think we can take more than five hundred. And *that's* if we pack them to the deckheads. Not exactly luxury travel."

"Still beats suffocating in the cold," Woodburn said with a grunt.

"That it does," Heissman agreed. "All right. Aegis will probably get the distress call directly, but go ahead and send them a copy, just to be sure, along with a request for aid. They're farther out, but they've got a lot more room."

"Assuming *Leviathan* can hold its bottle together long enough for Locatelli to reach them," Belokas warned.

"Nothing we can do about that," Woodburn said.

"So we *are* going to head out there?" Travis asked.

All eyes turned to him. "You have something, Lieutenant?" Heissman asked.

"Something *solid*?" Woodburn added. "Because hunches don't—"

He broke off at a small gesture from Heissman. "Continue," the commodore said.

Travis braced himself. "There's just something about this that feels wrong, Sir," he said, hoping the words didn't sound as lame to the others as they did to him. Especially since Woodburn had already warned him that no one was interested in his hunches. "The timing, the vector—same bearing as the hyper ghost—the fact that they came *here* instead of trying for somewhere else—"

"Their wedge *is* showing signs of stress," Heissman reminded him. "And all indications are that it's a merchant or passenger liner, not a warship."

"Sir, zero-zero intercept course is plotted and ready," the helm reported. "I'm assuming *Leviathan* will be able to maintain her current accel. If her wedge goes down, we'll have to recompute."

"Understood," Heissman said. "Feed to the other ships, and let's make some gravs." He looked at Travis. "And order all crews to Readiness Three," he added. "Just in case."

☆   ☆   ☆

"They're coming," Imbar announced. "Vector . . . too early to tell for sure, but it looks like they're lining up for a zero-zero intercept with *Naglfar*."

"Excellent," Gensonne said with a warm glow of satisfaction. The Manticorans had fallen for it. "Do we have a fix on Sidewinder yet?"

"Not yet," Imbar said. "But we're monitoring the area where they should be. Assuming they made it in all right, they should be lighting off their wedges sometime in the next couple of hours to fine-tune their own intercept with Green Two."

Gensonne nodded. Having *Umbriel* and *Miranda* arrive just in time to catch the Manticorans in a cross-fire would be helpful, but it was hardly vital to his plan. If the two destroyers were too far out to get in on this first skirmish, they'd be able to take on a similar attack role when the Volsungs came up against Green One.

And if they also managed to miss out on that one, they'd still be useful as scouts and gadflies, sweeping the area ahead of the Volsung fleet toward Manticore proper after the two groups of defending forces had been disposed of.

One way or another, Gensonne promised himself, every ship in the Volsung assault force would earn its pay today.

☆   ☆   ☆

Janus was still two hours away from their projected zero-zero with *Leviathan*, and the four ships were making yet another course correction as the damaged liner once again adjusted her own acceleration, when *Gorgon* signaled the news that two more faint wedges had appeared in the distance.

"Shapira says it's pure luck she spotted them in the first place," Belokas said, hovering close beside Heissman's station as they gazed together at the unexpected and, to Travis's mind, unsettling data *Gorgon* had sent across. "Given that our wedges were all turned that direction, and our crews busy with the course change, I tend to agree with her."

"Captain Shapira has a bad habit of ascribing to luck things which properly belong to training and vigilance," Heissman said thoughtfully as he gazed at the tactical. "Make sure we log a commendation for her and her bridge and CIC crews. What do you make of it?"

"They're definitely smaller than *Leviathan*," Belokas said. "Could be small freighters. Definitely not ore ships or anything else that's supposed to be running around out there."

"Or they could be small warships," Woodburn added. "Destroyers or light cruisers. Especially—there! Now, isn't *that* interesting?"

Travis felt his eyes narrow. As suddenly as they'd appeared, the mysterious wedges had vanished. As if the ships had finished with whatever course change they'd come out of hiding for and then dropped back into the covering blackness of interplanetary space.

Woodburn was obviously thinking the same thing. "They're

hiding, all right," he said grimly. "You'll also notice that they saved their maneuvers for a period when we were doing some adjustments of our own and were theoretically at our least attentive. With all due respect, Commodore, this is starting to look less like a rescue mission and more like an invasion."

"Agreed," Heissman said. "I believe we may owe Mr. Long an apology."

"I believe we do, Commodore," Woodburn agreed, giving Travis a small nod. "Looks like you were right about them, Lieutenant. Nicely called."

"Thank you, Sir," Travis said. Prickly, but fair.

"And now that we know what game we're actually playing," Heissman continued, "what's the status on our battle inventory? Mr. Long?"

"Not as good as it should be, Sir," Travis said.

And instantly regretted the words. The fact that Janus wasn't running at full strength was the fault of the politicians in Parliament, not RMN Command. But his thoughtless comment could easily be construed as criticism of that leadership.

Or, worse, as a criticism of his own commander. Neither was acceptable, especially not on that commander's own bridge.

Fortunately, Heissman didn't seem to take it that way. "No argument here, Lieutenant," he said, a bit dryly. "Continue."

"*Without* the editorial comments," Belokas added more severely.

"Yes, Ma'am," Travis said, wincing. Especially since *Casey* was already better armed and equipped than most of the rest of the fleet. "My apologies. We only have eighteen missiles, but both fore and aft lasers are fully functional, as are the broadside energy torpedo launchers. One of our autocannon is a little iffy—cooling problems; the techs are working on it. Loads are at about sixty percent. We also have nineteen countermissiles."

"What about the other ships?" Belokas asked.

"*Gorgon* has eight missiles and *Hercules* and *Gemini* each have four," Travis said. And they were lucky to have that many, he reflected silently. "Their point-defenses are about in the same shape and with the same load percentage as ours."

"How many of the missiles in that list are practice rounds?" Heissman asked.

"None, Sir," Travis said, frowning. "I didn't think I should count those."

"They still *look* like real missiles, even if they can't go bang," Heissman pointed out. "What's the count?"

"We and *Gorgon* each have two; *Hercules* and *Gemini* each have one," Travis said. But if the missiles had no warheads...?

The confusion must have shown on his face, because both Heissman and Woodburn favored him with small smiles. "Never underestimate the power of a bald-faced bluff, Mr. Long," Heissman said. "At worst, a dummy missile can make an enemy waste rounds from their point-defenses. At best, its wedge can shred a hull with the best of them."

The Commodore's smile vanished. "So basically, we're under-armed, undercrewed, and even with Aegis pulling all the gees they can we're a fair ways from any reinforcement. Recommendations?"

"The safe move would be to break off," Woodburn said. "Our limping passenger liner could be anything up to and including a battlecruiser. Maybe even a battleship—it's certainly big enough. The problem is that by the time we have accurate sensor data it'll be too late to get away."

He gestured. "And then we've got those two ships playing hide-and-seek out there. We're lucky to see a couple of visiting ships a month; and now we've suddenly got *three* of them on the same day? *And* three ships which seem to be coordinating movements?"

"So you're recommending we alert Command and break with an eye toward a rendezvous with Aegis?" Heissman asked calmly.

"I said that would be the safe move," Woodburn corrected, just as calmly. "But we're not out here to play safe. We're out here to look for trouble, and when we find that trouble to assess and deal with it."

"So your actual recommendation is that we fly into the mouth of the beast?" Belokas asked.

"Right square into it," Woodburn confirmed. "But I also recommend we have *Gorgon* start drifting a little behind us and the corvettes. Not so fast or far that our friends out there take notice and wonder what we're up to, but far enough for her to run communications between us once we raise our sidewalls." His lips compressed briefly. "Hopefully, she'll also be able to stay clear long enough to send back a full record of whatever's about to happen."

Travis swallowed. The implication was painfully clear. Woodburn didn't expect *Casey* or the two corvettes to survive the approaching encounter.

But that, too, was why Janus was out here.

"XO?" Heissman invited.

"I agree with Commander Woodburn's assessment and proposed action, Sir," Belokas said, her voice formal.

"Do you further agree that the circumstances justify the expenditure of one or more of our missiles?" Heissman asked.

Under the circumstances, Travis reflected, that particular formality sounded incredibly stupid. But none of the three senior officers so much as batted an eye.

"I do," Belokas said.

"As do I," Woodburn said.

"Very good," Heissman said, his tone matching theirs. "Alert all ships as to the situation, and have them stand ready for further orders. Albert, draw up a proposed timeline for detaching *Gorgon* and shifting us into combat formation. XO, go to Readiness Two. If we've got any spare warheads aboard, have the crews start swapping them into the practice missiles."

"Yes, Sir." Woodburn nudged Travis. "Come on, Lieutenant. We have work to do." He pushed off the hand grip and floated toward his station.

Travis followed, long practice enabling him to stay close to his superior without bumping into him. "A question, Sir?" he asked.

"Why *Gorgon* instead of one of the corvettes?"

Travis felt his lip twitch. "Yes, Sir," he admitted. "*Gorgon* has more missiles, more armor, and better sidewalls. If we're heading into a fight, we could use her up here with us."

"She also has aft autocannon," Woodburn reminded him. "If it comes down to the last surviving ship of Janus Force making a run for it, we need to make sure it's the ship with the best chance of making it through a barrage of up-the-kilt missiles."

Travis nodded, an odd and unpleasant thought shivering through him. Woodburn's military logic was solid enough, but there were more than just military considerations here. Ensign Richard Winton, the Star Kingdom's Crown Prince, was currently serving aboard *Hercules*. By all political logic, it seemed like Heissman should have designated *Hercules*, not *Gorgon*, to run Janus's backup and communications.

Yet he hadn't. Clearly, for Heissman, military considerations trumped everything else. Which, Travis supposed, was the way it should be.

But that led to an even less pleasant thought. Like *Gorgon*, *Casey* also had aft autocannon. But she also had an aft laser, which gave her an even better chance of survival against up-the-kilt attacks. If the most critical priority was to gain information on the intruder and then run, Woodburn's military logic should have put *Casey* into Janus's rear position. Depending on what kind of warship was lurking behind the crippled-liner masquerade, having *Casey* in the battle probably wouldn't make that much of a difference in the outcome anyway.

Again, that option didn't seem to have even entered Woodburn's mind. Or Belokas's, or Heissman's.

And again, that was as it should be. They were in command, and they would of course take *Casey* into the thick of whatever was about to happen.

Yet Travis *had* thought of it.

Did that mean he was a coward?

Maybe *Leviathan* really was a damaged liner. Maybe there was a perfectly reasonable explanation for those other two here-then-gone wedges. Maybe this was just a bizarre coincidence that all of them would get together and laugh about over a drink someday.

But if it wasn't, then they were all about to see how the RMN handled a real, non-simulated battle.

Back on *Phoenix*, Travis had wondered whether a taste of warfare would shake up some of the Star Kingdom's complacency. Now, it looked like they were going to find out.

☆   ☆   ☆

"General Quarters, General Quarters," the gravelly voice of Captain Hagros came through *Hercules*'s Forward Impeller Room's intercom speaker. "Set Condition Two throughout the ship. Repeat: set Condition Two throughout the ship."

"Well, diggity damn," Impeller Tech Chief Labatte muttered. He glanced over at the man seated beside him. "Sorry, Sir."

"That's all right, Chief," Ensign Richard Winton said, feeling his collection of stomach butterflies coalescing into a dark, leaden mess. *Readiness Two*. Combat imminent.

Janus Group, HMS *Hercules*, and Ensign Richard Winton were going to war.

To *war*.

It was insane. The Royal Manticoran Navy hadn't engaged in any sort of combat for nearly a hundred years. No one, from Admiral Locatelli on down, had the slightest idea how to prosecute a full-scale, multi-ship battle.

But they'd better learn. They'd better learn damn fast. The survival of the Star Kingdom could well depend on what happened here today.

"Sir?"

"Right with you, Chief," Richard said. He gave his head a quick shake, chasing the fears and doubts to a back corner of his mind. His Navy and his people were depending on him. More importantly, his father the King was depending on him.

And he would *not* let them down.

"Run me another diagnostic on the impellers and sidewalls," he ordered. "Especially that iffy Number Two. Figure out which components are most likely to fail, and move replacement parts close to hand."

"We may not have everything we're likely to need," Labatte warned.

"Oh, I'm sure we don't," Richard said sourly. "We'll just have to make do with what we've got."

"Right." Labatte gave a little snort. "Ironic, isn't it? If Breakwater had taken *Hercules* for his precious little MPARS fleet instead of, say, *Taurus*, we'd be sitting off on the sidelines right now."

Instead of getting ready to die, the thought ran through Richard's mind. "Lucky for us," he said aloud. "We get to fight back against an invasion."

"That we do, Sir," Labatte said. "Okay. Here's the diagnostic, and here's the likely failure list. I'll grab Nathan and start collecting the gear."

"Good," Richard said. "Let me know if you need any help."

CHAPTER NINETEEN

IT WAS TIME.

Gensonne ran his eyes over *Odin*'s bridge displays one final time. He and *Tyr* were in their combat stack, *Odin* a thousand kilometers above the other battlecruiser, where the constraints of wedge and sidewalls gave both ships optimal fields of fire for their missiles and autocannon. The two heavy cruisers, *Copperhead* and *Adder*, were in their own stack a thousand kilometers ahead and slightly above and beneath the two battlecruisers, positioned so that their countermissiles could protect both of the larger warships. Fifteen hundred kilometers ahead of the cruisers and another thousand to starboard, the destroyer *Ganymede* guarded the starboard flank.

Ideally, Gensonne would have liked to have *Phobos* mirror-image *Ganymede* on the formation's portside flank. But with communications through sidewalls tricky at best, it was more important for *Phobos* to hang far back in com-relay position. In the heat of battle a communications blackout, even a brief one, could spell disaster. The only way to assure that didn't happen was to dedicate one of his ships to bounce signals back and forth through the unobstructed gaps at the other ships' kilts.

Besides, his full force was hardly necessary to complete the task at hand. In a pinch, *Odin* and one of Gensonne's cruisers could easily take out the four undersized ships on which the Volsungs were closing. Probably without even scratching their paint.

Just the same, Gensonne would indeed throw the full weight of his force against the Manticorans. After all, the only thing better than a painless victory was a *fast* painless victory. And a fast *crushing* painless victory should have a salutary effect on the ships in Green One, as well.

He keyed the com. "Admiral to all ships," he called into the microphone. "Stand by battle stations. Relay status data now."

For a moment nothing happened. Then, in proper order, the status board indicators began to wink on. *Odin* showed green; *Tyr* showed green; *Copperhead*—

Gensonne felt his eyes narrow. Floating in the sea of soothing green were a pair of red lights. "Captain Imbar?"

"It's her ventral autocannon," Imbar called from the com station. "Starboard sensor miscalibration. They're working on it."

Gensonne mouthed a curse as he looked back at the status board, where more green was filling in around *Copperhead*'s red lights. Should he give *Copperhead* a few more minutes? The Manticoran force was in deceleration mode, their kilts to the incoming Volsungs as they aimed for a zero-zero at the distant *Naglfar* that was now well behind the advance force. If Gensonne signaled *Naglfar* to raise her acceleration a bit, the Manticorans would presumably respond by increasing their deceleration rate, which would postpone the rapidly approaching moment when the enemy's sensors would finally pick up the warships coasting stealthily toward them.

Gensonne straightened up, feeling the uniform collar peeking out from above his vac suit's helmet ring pull briefly against his neck. Ridiculous. Even if every one of *Copperhead*'s lights went red he still had overwhelming superiority.

Besides, the far larger Green One force was also burning its way toward them across the Manticoran system. Postponing the Green Two skirmish would mean less time to reorganize and rearm before Green One showed up.

Green Two was nearly in range.

Time for them to die.

"Tell *Copperhead* to keep working until they get it right," he growled to Imbar. Keying his mike again, he straightened a little more. "All ships: stand by to light up wedges."

☆   ☆   ☆

Heissman had sent Belokas and Woodburn off the bridge for a short break, and Travis was strapped into the Tactical Officer station when the moment everyone aboard *Casey* had been waiting for finally came.

Only it wasn't the single ship they were expecting. It was far, far worse.

"New contact!" Rusk snapped from Tracking, the words cutting across the low-level conversation murmuring across the bridge. "I make it six ships on intercept vector at two hundred fifteen gees. Missile range, approximately sixteen minutes."

"All ships, increase acceleration to two KPS squared and go to Readiness One," Heissman called into his mike, the calm of his voice in sharp contrast to the sudden pounding of Travis's heart. "Mr. Long?" he added.

Surreptitiously, Travis touched the helmet of his vac suit, fastened securely beside his station. Knowing it was there made him feel marginally safer. Marginally. "Six ships confirmed for Bogey Three," he said, his eyes flicking back and forth between the displays and CIC's running analysis of the incoming data. One of the many things Woodburn had beaten into him over the past few weeks was that you never simply took a computer's word for anything when you could do your own assessment and analysis. "From wedge strength I'm guessing two battlecruisers, two heavy cruisers, and two light cruisers or destroyers. One of the latter is hanging back in com position."

"Which pretty much confirms they're a war fleet," Woodburn's voice came over Travis's shoulder.

Travis looked up to see the TO float up behind him, the other's hard gaze flicking coolly across the displays. "Yes, Sir," Travis agreed, reaching for his restraints.

To his surprise, Woodburn waved him to stay where he was.

"Any read on origination or class?" Heissman asked. "I know they're not running transponders."

"Too far away for anything definitive," Woodburn said. "But the over/under configuration matches Solarian military doctrine."

"Which doesn't tell us much," Belokas pointed out as she floated rapidly across the bridge toward her station. "A lot of militaries run Solarian doctrine."

"Maybe they'll be kind enough to tell us who they are," Heissman said. "Everyone watch and listen." Reaching over, he keyed the com. "Unidentified ships, this is Commodore Rudolph Heissman, Royal Manticoran Navy. Kindly identify yourselves and state your business in Manticoran space."

There was a pause, a little longer than the lag time necessary for the signal to make the round trip. Clearly, the other commander had been expecting the call and already knew what he was going to say. "Greetings, Commodore Heissman," a deep voice boomed from the bridge speakers.

Travis looked at the com display. The face now filling the screen was light-skinned, the color of a man who seldom ventured out into the sun, with blue eyes and a mouth with a sardonic twist. From the shape and angles of its creases, Travis guessed that *sardonic* was the mouth's most common mode. Above the face was a slightly balding carpet of pure blond hair cut in short military style. Below the face, a couple of centimeters of high-collared tunic could be seen above his vac suit.

"Black collar line, blue-gray knitted collar," Woodburn murmured. Travis nodded, already keying the parameters into the computer for an archive search.

"My name and origin are unimportant," the man continued, "but for convenience you may address me as Admiral Tamerlane. My business is, I regret to say, the destruction of you and your task force. I am, however, willing to discuss terms of surrender."

He tilted his head slightly, and as he did so one of the muted insignia on his collar came into better view. A curved comet with a star at its inner edge, Travis decided, and added it to the search criteria. "This is, naturally, a limited time offer," Tamerlane continued. "I read you as coming into missile range in just under eighteen minutes; somewhat less, of course, if you break off your pointless attempt to escape and turn to offer battle. I'll await your answer." He reached off-screen and his image vanished.

"Confident SOB," Heissman commented. "Anyone recognize him or his accent?"

The bridge remained silent, and as Travis glanced around him he saw shaking heads. "Mr. Long?" Heissman asked.

"The uniform could be Solarian," Travis affirmed, scanning the search results. "But a lot of Core World navies wear something similar. What we could see of the insignia looked more like something the Tahzeeb Navy uses."

"Similar, but not exact," Belokas said. "Though that may indicate they've worked with them. Best guess is that they're mercenaries."

"Probably," Woodburn agreed. "Not sure what calling himself Tamerlane means. The original was an Old Earth conqueror who ran roughshod over a good chunk of the planet a little over two thousand years ago."

"Tamerlane was also considered a military genius," Heissman said. "I wonder which of those two aspects he's trying to reference."

"Either way, definitely the megalomaniac type," Belokas said. "Confident, but probably not so confident that we can goad him into telling us what he has planned for Manticore after he runs us over."

"Certainly not until he's sure we can't send anything useful back to System Command or Aegis," Heissman agreed. "Speaking of Aegis, what's their current ETA?"

"They're still nearly two hours away," Belokas said. "We could postpone the battle a bit by pushing our compensators right up to the red line, but it wouldn't be enough for them to get here before we have to fight."

"What about Bogey Two?" Heissman asked.

"Nothing since their last course adjustment," Woodburn said. "Depending on where in the plot cone they are, they'll probably reach sensor range within the next ten to twenty minutes."

"So no allies, but probably more enemies," Heissman said. "In that case, I see no point in delaying the inevitable." He keyed his com. "All ships, this is the Commodore. We've been challenged to a fight, and I intend to give them the biggest damn fight they've ever been in. *Gorgon*, maintain current course and acceleration—your job is to record what's about to happen and get the data back to Manticore. *Hercules* and *Gemini*, stand by for a coordinated one-eighty pitch turn on my mark."

Travis frowned. "A *pitch* turn?" he asked quietly. Most turns he'd seen had been of the yaw variety, where the ship rotated around her vertical axis, instead of a pitch flip that sent the ship head over heels and briefly put the stronger but completely sensor-opaque stress bands between the ship and the incoming threat.

"A pitch turn," Woodburn confirmed, an edge of grim humor to his voice. "We can launch a salvo of missiles just before our wedge drops far enough to clear their line of sight, which will keep them from spotting the booster flares. By the time we've turned all the way over the missiles will be clear and ready to light off their wedges once Commodore Heissman decides which target he wants to go after first."

Travis nodded. *Casey* herself had electromagnetic launchers that didn't betray themselves with such telltales, but both *Hercules* and *Gemini* had the standard boosters on their missiles, vital for getting the weapons far enough from the ship to safely light up their wedges. If the Janus ships could launch without Tamerlane spotting the missiles it would give the Manticorans at least a momentary advantage.

"Pitch turn: *mark*," Heissman called. "Stand by two missiles from each corvette and four from us, again on my mark."

Travis looked at the tac display. *Casey* and the two corvettes were turning in unison, their loss of acceleration sending *Gorgon* toward the edge of the field even as the invading formation seemed to leap forward.

And the enemy would unfortunately have plenty of time to work on closing the remaining distance. Pitch turn or yaw turn, either type of one-eighty took a good two minutes to complete.

"Missiles on my mark," Heissman said softly, his eyes on the tac.

"Missiles ready," Belokas confirmed. "Target?"

Heissman watched the tac another moment, then turned to Woodburn. "Suggestions, Alfred?"

"I'd go with all eight on one of the cruisers," Woodburn said. "The way they're deployed strongly suggests the battlecruisers have opted for extra missiles instead of carrying their own counter-missile loads, which would mean they're relying on the cruisers to screen for them. If we can kill one of them right out of the box, we may have a shot at doing some damage to one of the big boys."

"I'm sure Admiral Locatelli would appreciate us softening them up a bit for him," Belokas said dryly. "I'll go with Alfred on this one."

Heissman looked at Travis. "Mr. Long?"

Travis looked at the tac display. Three small ships against six..... "I'd throw four at each cruiser, Sir."

"Reason?"

"We still don't know exactly what specific classes their ships are," Travis said. "Watching their defenses might give us some clues as to what they are and how to more effectively attack them. By attacking two at once, we'll get that data a bit faster."

"Alfred?" Heissman invited.

"We'd still do better to saturate one of them," Woodburn said. "Frankly, Sir, we're not going to get off a lot of shots in the time we have. We should concentrate on doing as much damage as possible."

"You may be right," Heissman agreed. "But Mr. Long is also right. Information is what we need most, both for ourselves and for Admiral Locatelli. I think it's worth the risk." He keyed his com. "*Hercules* and *Gemini*: one missile from each of you at each of the leading cruisers. We'll throw an additional two at each one."

He favored Travis with a small smile. "Let's see how well Admiral Tamerlane can dance."

☆   ☆   ☆

Invincible's bridge was already buzzing with tense activity when Metzger arrived, interrupted sleep still tugging at her eyelids. She scanned the displays as she maneuvered her way through the maze of people, stations, and monitors, looking for a clue as to why Commander McBride had sounded Readiness One.

And then, she spotted it.

Six contacts, bearing straight toward Manticore.

Six.

With only the four ships of Green Force Two standing in their way.

"Report," she ordered quietly as she glided past Locatelli and braked to a halt beside the CO's station.

"That bogie Janus reported a few hours ago has just turned into six bogies," McBride said grimly as he unstrapped and floated free. "No IDs yet—Janus is still too far out for any fresh transmissions to have reached us and we can't read any fine details from here. But the wedge strength alone implies they're warships." He gestured to the display. "The admiral has declared a Code Zulu."

Code Zulu. Metzger turned the words over in her mind as she strapped into the command station. *Code Zulu.* The absolute worst-case scenario in Locatelli's personal set of contingency plans. The contingency code Metzger had never, ever expected to hear.

Invasion.

God help us. "We've increased acceleration to one point nine KPS squared," McBride continued. "But we're still a solid hour from whatever's about to happen."

"Understood," Metzger said, wincing. One point nine KPS squared was almost ninety-four percent of *Invincible*'s top acceleration, a full nine percent past the standard safe line for her compensator. But it would certainly get them to the combat arena sooner.

Whether the time gained by that kind of red-lining would be useful was another question. One school of tactical thought was that two forces rushing at each other should make no attempt to decelerate, but should simply fire their missiles in a single massive assault before blowing past each other's formation, with the hope that enough would remain of their own side to collect the survivors after the dust settled.

But that strategy wasn't an option here. Whatever happened to Green Two, Green One had to stay between the invading force and Manticore as long as it could. That meant that, however fast Locatelli forced his ships to travel on the way to the battle, he would have to bleed off that extra closing velocity as the enemy approached, forcing the two sides into as close to a face-to-face standing slugfest as possible.

And in the meantime, Green Two would be facing the invaders alone. Four ships against six, with the biggest one on the Manticoran side a light cruiser. *Casey.* Where Travis Long was currently serving.

Where Metzger had worked long and hard to put him.

There was a time for feelings of guilt. There was a time for feelings of fear.

This wasn't either of those times.

McBride had disappeared, heading across to his battle station in CIC. But the Tactical Officer, Lieutenant Commander Perrow, had now arrived and was heading for her station directly in front of Metzger's. "TO, I want a current status check of all targeting systems," Metzger ordered as Perrow shot past. "And run me your list of Aegis's weapons and their readiness states. Whatever we've got—more importantly, whatever we're missing—I want to know about it."

☆   ☆   ☆

The three nearer Manticoran ships finished their turn—a pitch turn, interestingly enough—and with that, their throats were open to attack. "Stand by missiles," Gensonne called. The first salvo would go to *Casey*, he decided. *Odin*'s telemetry could control six missiles at once, and while he normally would have added in a few missiles from his entire squadron in order to hit the cruiser with an overwhelming salvo, at this point it would be more useful to see what kind of defenses the Manticorans could bring against a slightly less overwhelming attack. "Fire salvo: one through six, targeting—"

"Missiles!" Imbar snapped.

Of course missiles, was Gensonne's first reflexive thought. He'd already said to stand by missiles.

And then he realized what Imbar was actually saying, and jerked his head around to the tac display.

There were missiles out there, all right: eight of them, creeping toward him with wedges down and only the relative velocities between them and the Volsungs providing them any movement at all. He opened his mouth to demand that Imbar tell him where they'd come from and why they weren't running under power—

And then, abruptly, all eight missiles lit up their wedges and leaped forward toward the Volsung force.

"Where the *hell* did they come from?" Imbar snarled.

"It was that damn pitch turn," Gensonne said as he finally got it, throwing a glance at the countdown timer. One hundred and three seconds until impact. "They fired while our view of their booster flares was blocked."

Imbar grunted. "Cute."

"Very," Gensonne said darkly. "But don't worry about it. We can play cute, too."

Only for the next hundred seconds or so, he couldn't. Forty seconds from now, sixty seconds before the incoming missiles' projected impact, *Copperhead* and *Adder* would launch a salvo of countermissiles into the path of the incoming weapons. Forty-five seconds after that, all six Volsung ships would open up with their autocannon in an effort to stop any missiles that made it through the countermissile gauntlet.

The frustrating hell of it was that for most of the missiles' run it would be impossible to tell which ship or ships they were targeting. Still, if Heissman had any brains he would be aiming this first salvo at one or both of the cruisers. A properly competent flag officer should have deduced from the Volsungs' configuration that the cruisers were the ones carrying the countermissiles, and were therefore the ones that needed to be taken out before the Manticorans could have a reasonable shot at *Odin* or *Tyr*.

Well, let them try. The cruisers were carrying full point-defense loads, and if Heissman wanted to waste his missiles battering against them he was more than welcome to do so.

Except...

With a curse, he spun around to the status board. There, still glowing red amid the field of green, were the lights marking *Copperhead*'s troubled ventral autocannon.

And if one of the Manticoran missiles happened to come in from the side with the bad tracking sensor...

"All ships: cease acceleration on my mark," he snarled, turning back to the tac. The two standard responses to a situation like this would be for *Copperhead* to either yaw to starboard, turning her port side towards the attack and her faulty starboard sensors away from it, or else pitch up or down to interpose its wedge between the ship and the incoming missiles.

Unfortunately, if the rest of the force was under acceleration at the time, both countermoves would instantly break the Volsungs' formation. The only way to maintain their relative positions would be for all six ships to kill acceleration and coast.

Of course, that would also give the Green Two ships a breather from the doom arrowing in on them. Still, it was hard to imagine what they could do with those extra few minutes. The rear ship, the one Heissman was clearly hoping would get clear with data from the battle would gain a little distance, but it was already too little too late.

As for the other three ships, they would have to do another turnover if they hoped to do any more running themselves. Any such move would be relatively slow and instantly telegraphed.

No, Heissman's force wasn't going anywhere. Gensonne could afford the time to do this right. "All ships, cease acceleration: *mark*. Imbar?"

"All ships coasting," Imbar reported. "Formation maintained."

Gensonne nodded, peering at the tac display. *Copperhead* was already taking advantage of the lull and was starting her starboard yaw.

Hell with that. If they were going to be forced to coast anyway, there was no reason for *Copperhead* to waste any of her point-defense weaponry. "Von Belling, belay your yaw," he ordered into his mike. "Pitch wedge to the incoming fire."

"I can handle it," von Belling's voice came from the speaker.

"I said *pitch wedge*," Gensonne snapped.

"Aye, aye, *Sir*," von Belling said with thinly disguised disgust. "Pitching wedge."

On the tactical, *Copperhead* changed from her yaw turn to a vertical pitch, dropping her bow to present her roof to the incoming missiles. Gensonne watched, splitting his attention between the cruiser and the incoming missiles. If von Belling's momentary bitching had left the maneuver too late, the admiral promised himself darkly, he'd better hope the Manticoran missiles got to him before Gensonne did.

Fortunately, it wasn't going to come to that. *Copperhead* turned in plenty of time, and as *Odin's* autocannon roared into action Gensonne watched the incoming salvo split into two groups, one set of four targeting each of the cruisers. The ones aimed at *Copperhead* disintegrated harmlessly against her roof, while *Adder's* countermissiles and autocannon made equally quick work of the other group. "Stand by for acceleration," Gensonne ordered. *Copperhead* was starting her reverse pivot, and as soon as she was back in position the Volsungs could resume their full-acceleration pursuit of the Manticorans.

Meanwhile, there was no reason Gensonne had to wait for acceleration before he took the battle back to Heissman. "Missiles ready?" he called.

"Missiles ready," Imbar confirmed.

"Six at the light cruiser," Gensonne said. "Fire."

CHAPTER TWENTY

WINTERFALL'S FIRST HINT THAT something was seriously wrong was when he arrived at the House of Lords to find that the usual pair of ceremonial guards at the entrance had been replaced by a quartet of Marines.

Armed Marines.

Breakwater's brief summons had made the unspecified crisis sound serious. Apparently, it was more serious than Winterfall had realized.

There were a few other Peers visible in the vast entryway foyer, which was usually a place for conversational greetings and small talk. But no one was lingering this morning. Everyone Winterfall saw was on the move, hurrying toward their offices or the offices of friends and political allies.

No. Not everyone. At the entrances to the two office wings were another pair of armed Marines.

What in the world was going on? Some kind of insurrection? Civil unrest?

A coup?

Yvonne Rowlandson, Baroness Tweenriver, was already waiting in Breakwater's office when Winterfall arrived. "Come in, Gavin, come in," Breakwater said, beckoning him toward the conversation circle. His movements were nervous and jerky, Winterfall noted mechanically, the movements of someone who'd been shaken badly off balance. "I've just received word from Defense Minister Dapplelake that the Star Kingdom has been invaded."

261

Winterfall felt his eyes widen, fighting suddenly for balance as his foot caught on the carpet. *"Invaded?"*

"Six warship-strength contacts have been spotted approaching Manticore," Tweenriver said, her voice quavering a little.

"I see," Winterfall said, hearing some of the same tremor in his own voice.

"There'll be an official announcement from the Palace sometime in the next half hour," Breakwater said. "By that time, all of Parliament should have been informed, and Burgundy will have convened an emergency session."

"Understood," Winterfall said. Breakwater was trying to keep his voice under control, but Winterfall could see the same fear he and Tweenriver were feeling in the Chancellor's eyes.

Only in Breakwater's case, it wouldn't be just the possibility that the Star Kingdom might be facing the end of its existence. Piled on top of that fear would be the bitter knowledge of how tirelessly Breakwater and his allies—including Tweenriver and Winterfall—had worked to strip the Navy of its strength, weapons, and manpower. To undermine the very Navy that was now all that stood in the way of their own destruction.

And with that additional bitterness was the certainty that even if the invaders were somehow miraculously driven off, Breakwater's own career was over.

As was Winterfall's, probably. Of all of Breakwater's allies, he'd been the most vocal and the most visible.

"The reason I asked you here ahead of the official convening," Breakwater continued, his voice almost an intrusion into Winterfall's swirling thoughts, "is that I've been informed that the first group of ships in the invaders' path is Green Task Force Two, the so-called Janus force. Leading that force is the light cruiser *Casey.*" He paused. "I don't know if you've kept up . . . but that's your brother Travis Long's ship."

Winterfall stared, his stomach suddenly churning. *God*—in all his petty political angst he'd completely forgotten about his brother. "You're sure that's where he is?" he asked, silently cursing himself for not knowing. Breakwater was right—he *hadn't* kept tabs on his brother's career.

And now Travis was facing an invading force immensely larger than his own.

Which meant he was about to die.

A dozen images flashed across Winterfall's vision. Their mother, and how Winterfall was going to tell her of her son's death, and whether she would really care. His own last meeting with Travis, nearly three T-years ago—or was it four?—a brief chat over a hurried lunch, hurried because Winterfall had to get back to Parliament to vote on some damn bill he couldn't even remember and that clearly hadn't made a scrap of difference to the Star Kingdom. The half dozen times since then when Travis had been available on Manticore, and Winterfall had thought about screening him, and somehow never gotten around to it.

But then, why should he have? There was no rush. He and Travis were both young and healthy, and a job in the Navy was as safe as a career in Parliament. There was plenty of time.

Only now, that time was gone. Gone forever.

"All MPARS forces have been alerted, of course." That was Breakwater again, his voice sounding distant and irrelevant. "But Cazenestro has ordered them to stand down. The crews aren't really set up for this sort of thing, and none of them is close enough to reach the battle region in time anyway. Of course, if Gryphon comes under attack as well, the MPARS ships there may be able to assist."

"Yes," Winterfall murmured.

"Right now the reports are fairly sketchy," Breakwater continued. "But I have a direct line to the Central War Room, and I should get any news as soon as it comes in. If you'd like, you can wait here until Burgundy calls us to order."

"Thank you," Winterfall managed through the tightness in his throat. "I think I will."

☆   ☆   ☆

"All missiles destroyed," Lieutenant Rusk reported from the tracking station. "No hits."

"Acknowledged," Heissman said. "Alfred? What have we learned?"

"Their point-defense seems comparable to ours," Woodburn said, peering closely at CIC's running analysis. "Countermissiles on the cruisers, autocannon on everyone else. Looks like a pretty high quality of both. Their ECM is also good—they got a soft kill on at least one of our missiles, possibly two. They also don't seem shy about spending ammo."

"Missile trace, two," Rusk called. "Thirty-five hundred gees, estimated impact time one hundred fifty-three seconds. Correction:

four missiles, same impact projection...correction: *six* missiles. Missile trace, six, impact one hundred forty-eight seconds."

"Not stingy with their missiles, either," Woodburn amended tightly.

Travis winced. Six missiles, with all four of the Manticoran ships at only sixty percent of point-defense capacity.

Woodburn was clearly thinking along the same lines. "Commodore, I don't think we're ready to take on that many birds."

"Agreed," Heissman said. "But we also need to pull more data on their capabilities."

"So we're going to take them on?" Belokas asked.

"We're going to split the difference," Heissman corrected. "Start a portside yaw turn—not a big or fast one, just a few degrees. I want to cut the starboard sidewall across the missile formation, letting just one or two of them past the leading edge and trusting the countermissiles to take those out. That way we get a closer look at the missiles and their yield without risking having too many coming in to block."

Travis stole a glance at Woodburn, waiting for the TO to point out the obvious risk: that if the incoming missiles' sidewall penetrators functioned like they were supposed to, taking four or five on *Casey*'s sidewalls could be a quick path to disaster. Most of the time that kind of maneuver was a decent enough gamble, given the notorious unreliability of such weapons. But any time there were that many threats things could get tricky.

Especially if Tamerlane's ships were carrying more advanced sidewall penetrators that *weren't* so finicky.

But Woodburn remained silent. As Travis had known he would. The commodore had already agreed that *Casey*'s mission was to gather information that would be crucial in helping Locatelli defeat this invasion.

The missiles crept closer. Travis watched the tac display as Belokas fine-tuned *Casey*'s position, a vague idea starting to form at the back of his mind. If he'd seen what he thought he'd seen during the first Janus salvo...

He swiveled around to his plotter and ran the numbers and geometry. It would work, he decided. It would be tricky and require some fancy timing, but it might just work.

There was a throbbing hum from the launchers' capacitors as *Casey* sent a salvo of countermissiles blazing out into space...and it occurred to him that if Heissman's trick didn't work, there was a good chance he would never know it. At the speed the missiles were traveling, they would reach the edge of the countermissiles' range barely two tenths of a second before reaching *Casey* herself. If the defenses failed to stop the attack, or the sidewall was breached—

There was a muted double flash on the tac as two of the missiles slammed into the countermissiles and were destroyed. Travis's eyes and brain had just registered that fact when the deck abruptly jerked beneath him and the tense silence of the bridge was ripped apart by the wailing of emergency alarms.

He spun to the status board. None of the four missiles that had slammed into the starboard sidewall had penetrated, but two of them had detonated a microsecond before impact, and the resulting blast had overloaded and possibly destroyed the forward generator.

"Sidewall Two is down!" Belokas shouted her own confirmation across the wailing alarm. "Sidewall Four undamaged, taking up the slack."

"Casualties," Chief Kebiro added tensely from Coms. "Seven down, condition unknown. Corpsmen on the way; crews assessing damage."

Travis mouthed a useless curse. Each of the two generators on each side of the ship was designed to be able to maintain the entire sidewall. But as the old saying went, two could live as cheaply as one, but only for half as long. *Casey*'s starboard sidewall was still up, but it was running now at half power. Another double tap like that one, and it could go completely.

And the cruisers and battlecruisers out there were showing no signs of running out of missiles to tap them with.

The alarm cut off. "Alfred?" Heissman asked, as calm as ever.

"Their missiles seem comparable to ours," Woodburn said, his own voice more strained. "Slightly better ECM, I think, but our countermissiles handled them just fine."

"Which again suggests mercenaries rather than some system's official fleet," Heissman said. "Certainly not any fleet connected with the Solarian League. They wouldn't be using second- or third-generation equipment."

"That's the good news," Woodburn said. His voice was subtly louder, Travis noted distantly, as he if was leaning over Travis's shoulder. "The bad news is that their missiles are as good as ours and they probably have a hell of a lot more of them."

"I wonder what they're waiting for," Heissman mused. "This is the perfect time to launch a second wave."

"Probably taking a moment to analyze their data," Belokas said. "I imagine they're as eager to assess our strengths and weaknesses as we are to find theirs, and trying not to spend any more missiles than they have to. They'll certainly want to know everything they can about us before they tackle Aegis."

"And since we can't stop them from doing that," Heissman said calmly, "it looks like our best-hope scenario is still to slow them down long enough for *Gorgon* to collect and transmit as much data as we can collect, while we inflict the maximum damage possible."

"Between us and the corvettes we still have eighteen missiles, plus four practice ones," Belokas said. "If we throw everything we've got, we should at least be able to take down one of those cruisers."

"We can't control nearly that many at once," Woodburn reminded her.

"As long as Tamerlane's ships aren't evading, that may not matter," Belokas pointed out. "They'll still have to defend, and even if all we can accomplish is to drain their point defenses it'll be worth it."

"Or we might be able to do a bit better," Woodburn said. "Mr. Long has an idea."

Travis twisted his head to look up at the other. "Sir?"

Woodburn pointed at the simulation Travis had been running. "Tell them," he ordered.

Travis felt his throat tighten. Suddenly, he was back on *Phoenix*'s bridge, offering half-baked advice to Captain Castillo.

But Heissman wasn't Castillo. And if the trick worked...

"I think the upper cruiser's ventral autocannon is having trouble," he said. "If it is, then—"

"How could you possibly know that?" Belokas interrupted, frowning at him. "They never even fired them."

"Because he was starting to turn to starboard when he shifted to rolling wedge instead," Travis said. "That looked to me like he was getting ready to favor that side when he changed his mind." He felt his lip twitch. "I had some experience with balky autocannon back on *Phoenix*. That definitely looked like a sensor miscalibration problem."

"Alfred?" Heissman asked.

"He could be right," Woodburn said. "I just checked, and that aborted yaw is definitely there."

"Assume you're right," Heissman said. "Then what?"

"We start by assuming Tamerlane's as smart as he thinks he is," Travis said. "If so, he'll have seen his cruiser's brief yaw and guess that we also saw it and came to the correct conclusion. If we did, he'll expect us to try to take advantage of the weakness by throwing a salvo of missiles at it."

"At which point he'll again have to either use an iffy point-defense system or else roll wedge," Woodburn said, reaching over Travis's shoulder to key the simulation over to the commodore's station. "If he does the latter, we may be able to catch him by surprise."

For a couple of heartbeats Heissman gazed at the display. Then, his lip twitched in a small smile. "Yes, I see. It's definitely a long shot. But long shots are where you go when you've got no other bets."

He gave a brisk nod. "Set up the shot."

☆   ☆   ☆

"Analysis complete, Admiral," Imbar announced as he hovered over Tactical Officer Clymes's shoulder. "Similar countermissiles as ours, with about a thirteen-hundred-klick range, and similar autocannon loads."

Gensonne scowled. So the Manticorans' countermissiles had a shade less range than the equipment aboard *Copperhead* and *Adder*.

And *Casey* was supposedly the most advanced ship of the Manticoran fleet. If Llyn had been right about that, then the weaponry aboard the larger Green One ships burning space toward him would be even more subpar.

Yes, it could have been worse. But it could also have been a whole lot better. He'd tried like the fires of hell to talk Llyn into providing him with more cutting-edge equipment, but the damn little clerk had turned down every request. The Volsungs didn't need anything better, he'd insisted soothingly, and furthermore the Solarian League would rain down on all of them if they ever got wind of it.

Which was a bald-faced lie. The Axelrod Corporation was way too powerful to worry about offending whatever bureaucrats were in charge of enforcing such regulations. Llyn simply didn't want a bunch of free-lance mercenaries running around with really advanced equipment.

But that would change. When Llyn saw how quickly and efficiently Gensonne delivered Manticore, Axelrod would surely want the Volsungs on board for whatever project was next on their list.

And Llyn could bet his rear that the subject of advanced weaponry *would* come up again.

"Salvo ready, Sir," Imbar said.

"Acknowledged," Gensonne said. The question now was whether they'd wrung out every bit of data Heissman and *Casey* could provide. If so, it was time to end the charade and finish them off. If not, a little additional restraint might still be called for.

"Missiles incoming," Clymes called into his musings. "Looks like two from each of the corvettes."

Gensonne swiveled toward the sensor display. Sure enough, both of the smaller ships were showing the unmistakable signs of booster flares. A waste of time; but then, what else did they have to do? "Six missiles at the cruiser," he ordered. "Fire when ready." On the display, the missiles cleared the corvettes' wedges and lit up their own.

Two missiles from each corvette... but from *Casey*, nothing.

He frowned. Could the damage his attack had inflicted on the cruiser's sidewall have bled over into its launchers or control systems? Llyn had said that *Casey* was Manticoran-designed. Had the builders unintentionally incorporated a fatal flaw into its architecture?

"More flares," Clymes called. "One more from each corvette."

"Still nothing from *Casey*?"

"No, Sir."

Which made no sense, unless the cruiser had genuinely lost the ability to launch its missiles. Definitely a tidbit worth knowing, especially if similar flaws had been incorporated into the Manticorans' other ship designs.

And really, it didn't matter which of the Manticorans were shooting and which ones weren't. What mattered was that they were trying the same saturation attack they'd tried before, and it was pretty obvious where that attack was aimed. Heissman was apparently the observant type, and von Belling's partially completed yaw turn earlier had tipped off the Manticorans as to where *Copperhead*'s weakness lay.

Which, again, was hardly a problem. His task force was still coasting, which meant *Copperhead* could repeat its earlier maneuver without breaking formation. "Order *Copperhead* to pitch wedge," he instructed Imbar. "*Adder* will prepare countermissiles; all other ships, stand by autocannon."

He listened as the acknowledgments came in, his eyes on the six wedges cutting through space toward his force at thirty-five hundred gees acceleration. A minute fifteen out, with probably forty seconds before they would either tighten their angle toward *Copperhead*, or widen it to target both *Copperhead* and *Adder*. At that point, Heissman would show whether he'd truly observed *Copperhead*'s weakness or was a one-trick pony who was throwing missiles at his opponent simply because that was all he knew how to do.

Which would be pathetic, but hardly unexpected. Manticore had been at peace a long time. Far longer than was healthy for them. War was what kept men strong and smart. Peace turned them into useless drones, where the species-cleansing consequences of survival of the fittest no longer operated.

Could that be why Llyn had chosen Manticore as his target? Could it be that Axelrod was looking for undeveloped real estate and figured no one would notice or care if a couple of fat, lazy backwater planets underwent a sudden regime change?

It sounded like a colossal waste of money. Still, Axelrod had money to burn. If they wanted to spend some of their spare cash to set up their own little kingdom, more power to them.

Copperhead had finished her pitch, her roof once again presenting its impenetrable barrier to the incoming missiles. The missiles were still holding formation, with no indication as to where they were heading. Whatever Heissman's plan, though, he must surely have accepted the inevitability of his own destruction. Best guess was that his goal was to simply keep throwing missiles in hopes of draining the Volsungs of as many resources as he could...

Gensonne looked at the gravitics display, feeling his eyes narrow. The Manticorans had launched six missiles—Clymes had confirmed that. And six missile wedges were indeed showing on all of the displays.

But according to the sensors, all six missiles were running a little hot.

Why were they running hot?

On the tactical, a spray of countermissiles erupted from *Adder*'s throat, blossoming into a cone of protection that would shield both itself and the battlecruisers riding a thousand kilometers behind it. Gensonne watched as the cone stretched out toward the incoming missiles—

And felt a sudden jolt of horrified adrenaline flood through him. *One* cone. Not the two cones this configuration was supposed to provide to shield the battlecruisers. Not with *Copperhead* turned roof-forward protecting itself from those Manticoran missiles.

Still nothing new from the sensors. Still nothing new on the missiles' track. But Gensonne was a warrior, with the instincts a warrior needed to survive. And his gut was screaming at him now with a certainty that all the ambiguous data in the universe couldn't counter.

Copperhead wasn't Heissman's target. *Odin* was.

"Full autocannon!" he snapped, his eyes darting to the tactical, wanting to order an emergency turn and knowing full well that it was too late. Six missiles showing... only his gut was telling him that wasn't the full number bearing down on them. Somehow, *Casey* had managed to launch its own contribution to the salvo, slipping them in behind and among the corvettes' missiles with just the right timing and geometry to keep them hidden until they could light off their wedges.

Odin's four autocannon were hammering out their furious roar, filling the space in front of the ship with shards of metal. Gensonne watched in helpless fury as the incoming missiles swung wide of *Copperhead*'s wedge, passed safely through the very edge of *Adder*'s countermissile defensive zone, and dove straight through *Odin*'s open throat—

And with a thundering roar the ship exploded into a chaos of screaming alarms.

☆   ☆   ☆

"Got him!" Rusk shouted, his voice hovering midway between triumph and disbelief. "One of them made it through."

"Damage?" Heissman asked.

"Assessing now," Woodburn said. "Lots of debris, but with something the size of a battlecruiser that could be mostly superficial."

"Missile trace," Belokas called. "Six on the way."

"Countermissiles and autocannon standing by," Woodburn confirmed.

"Assessment's coming a little cleaner," Rusk said. "Looks like they took damage to their bow, probably enough to knock out their telemetry system. If we're lucky, it'll have neutralized at least one of their launchers and maybe their forward laser."

"Excellent," Heissman said. "Fire four more missiles—let's see if we can get in before the upper cruiser realizes what happened and turns back to defense position."

"Aye, Sir," Travis said, checking the tracks of Tamerlane's incoming missiles and feeling a flicker of grim satisfaction. They were still almost certainly going to die, but at least they'd managed to bloody Tamerlane's nose.

The vibration of the autocannon rumbled through the bridge. "All missiles destroyed," Woodburn announced. "Four hard kills, two soft. Our missiles are still on target."

Travis was gazing at the enemy formation, trying to anticipate what Tamerlane would do next, when two new wedges flared into view at the edge of the display.

Bogey Two, the pair of mysterious ships that they'd spotted earlier, had arrived.

CHAPTER TWENTY-ONE

CAPTAIN HARDASTY—WHOSE NAME, in Chomps's opinion, said it all—had yelled at *Aries*'s reactor crew for being slow. Then she'd yelled at the impeller crew for being slower.

Now, it was Chomps's turn.

"Missiles?" Hardasty's grating voice rasping over the intercom. "Come on, Missiles, wake up. What's your status?"

"Working on getting the tracking system up, Ma'am," Chomps called toward the mike, resisting the urge to say something nasty under his breath. Ensign Kyell, who was nominally in charge of *Aries*'s weapons, was elsewhere; but Spacer Second Class Ghanem wasn't, and she didn't like him much. Or any of the other Navy personnel, for that matter. And in many cases, the feeling was mutual.

He'd hoped that some of the animosity he'd first noted aboard *Aries* would fade with time. So far, though, that wasn't happening.

Still, Chomps suspected that even Ghanem would be on his side on this one. What in the world *Aries* needed her missiles prepped for on yet another mindless MPARS drill he couldn't imagine.

"Well, work harder," Hardasty gritted out. "Everyone—attention; everyone—listen up. We just got an update from HQ, and this is *not* just another stupid drill. We've got six incoming wedges—" she broke off as someone at her end of the intercom said something inaudible "—damn it; make that *eight* incoming wedges," she corrected. "Looks like warships, and they're—oh, damn. We've got missile traces, people. *Lots* of missile traces.

"They're taking on Janus Force."

Chomps looked at Ghanem, saw her eyes go wide. "Oh, my God," she whispered.

"We can't get there in time to help," Hardasty continued, her voice grim. "But if they make it past Janus, and then Aegis, we're about all that'll be left between them and Manticore.

"So let's get it together, people. Let's get it together *now*."

The intercom clicked off. "Oh, my God," Ghanem said, a little louder this time. "Chomps—what do we do?"

What are you asking me *for*? But he left the words unsaid. Of course Ghanem would look to him for advice. She was only MPARS. He was Royal Manticoran Navy. Of *course* he would know what to do in a situation like this.

Only he didn't. No one knew.

"Like the captain said, we get it together," he told her. "Here— you finish running the tracking check. I'm going to make sure the missiles' plasma feeds are ready to go."

☆   ☆   ☆

"Telemetry transmitters out," a strained voice came from *Odin*'s bridge speaker, barely audible above a cacophony of shouts and curses. "Number one laser's offline, number two's iffy, and One and Three autocannon are fried."

"Record indicates there were ten missiles in that salvo," Imbar snarled over the noise. "How the *hell* were there *ten* damn missiles?"

"Because *Casey*'s got a railgun launcher, that's how," Gensonne snarled back, a red haze of fury clouding his vision as he skimmed over the sensor summary of what had just happened.

There had been no way to know until the last fraction of a second where any of the individual missiles had been aimed, of course—by the time they reached the formation they were already going way too fast for that. The standard counter-move—the only counter-move possible—was for all ships to have already opened fire with autocannon and countermissiles, creating a hopefully impenetrable wall of metal.

Only in this case, *Copperhead*'s defensive wedge pitch had left the standard defensive zone with a fatal gap. The missiles had exploited that flaw, bypassing both cruisers and continuing on straight at *Odin*.

That should have been the end of it. With *Odin*'s own autocannon the only thing blocking their path, ten missiles should have been able to overwhelm the defenses and turn the battlecruiser into a ball of superheated plasma.

But *Odin* had been lucky. Incredibly lucky. In order to hide those four extra missiles, Heissman had been forced to run his salvo in an unusually tight formation. The result was that while *Odin*'s autocannon had only taken out four of the six leaders, the debris chain reaction from their destruction had taken out three of the trailing group. Of the surviving leaders, one had failed to detonate completely and the other had been knocked off track by *Odin*'s ECM. Not entirely off track, unfortunately, and its detonation had been close enough to blind the battlecruiser's portside sensors and take out a few other pieces of minor electronics.

Only the final missile, one of the four from *Casey*, had managed to get through. And even that one had detonated just high enough off-center to fail as a kill shot.

But it had been close enough. It had been hell-and-gone close enough.

All of *Odin*'s topside and forward telemetry arrays and sensors were gone. Both forward autocannon were gone, AC1 destroyed, AC2 marginally functional but useless without any active sensors. The dorsal missile launch-cell hatches had been slagged, and the dorsal radiator vanes were wrecked.

And that didn't even begin to list the secondary damage that had been done internally. The crews were still assessing and reporting on that.

Still, *Odin* was a functioning warship, and that was what mattered. Heissman had rolled his dice and failed, and he wouldn't get a second roll. Gensonne would make sure of that.

"So that's how they launched an extra four missiles without our seeing them." Imbar swore viciously. "And that's why the ones we saw looked too hot."

"You think?" Gensonne bit out.

"Four more missiles on the way," Clymes warned. "*Copperhead* is turning back ... *Copperhead*'s on it."

"About time," Gensonne muttered under his breath. He ran his eyes over the lengthening damage report, trying to think. The reactor should survive all right—there was plenty of redundancy in the radiator system. The missile crews might be able to release and jettison the damaged missile hatches, though that would take time. The ventral sensors were mostly functional, though there could be scrambled-software issues from the near-miss.

"Enemy salvo destroyed," Imbar reported. "*Copperhead*'s countermissiles made a clean sweep."

Gensonne gave a grunt of acknowledgment, his mind still focused on his ship. Beam weapons were probably gone, or at least not safe to fire. And with only two autocannon still functional *Odin* was at severe risk from any future saturation attacks.

"New contacts!"

Gensonne snapped his attention back to the tactical. If the Manticorans had somehow sneaked more ships into play—

They hadn't. The two new wedges had appeared right at the edge of the combat zone, leaping forward as they drove in from the left flank toward the Janus formation.

The Sidewinder force, *Umbriel* and *Miranda*, had finally arrived.

"Admiral?" Imbar called.

"I see them," Gensonne told him, his lips curling back in a snarling smile. About damn time. "Order them to fire missiles. Hell, order *all* ships to fire."

He straightened his shoulders. They had enough data. They had more than enough data.

Time for Heissman and his ships to die.

"Target the ship at the rear first," Gensonne said. "Then destroy the rest."

☆　　☆　　☆

And in that single, awful microsecond, everything changed.

"Missile trace!" Rusk called out grimly. "Four from Bogey Two—look to be targeting *Gorgon*. Bogey Three ships are also firing with . . . missile trace ten on the way."

"He's learned everything he can and decided it's time to end it," Heissman commented. "Time for us to do the same."

He hit his com key. "*Hercules*, *Gemini*: split tail. Repeat, split tail. Good luck."

Travis winced. The split tail was the officially designated last-ditch maneuver for this kind of situation. The two corvettes were to pitch wedges toward Tamerlane's main force and accelerate away in opposite directions, with each ship's resulting vector taking it above or beneath the enemy force, hopefully before any of the opposing ships could rotate fast enough and far enough to fire a last shot up the escapee's kilt.

It was a risky tactic at best, given the range of modern missiles and lasers. But with a second threat now on Janus's flank, it was even worse. The geometry made it impossible for the ships to position their wedges in such a way as to block against missiles coming from both directions at once.

Worse, for *Casey* at least, the sidewall facing Bogey Two was the one already running on a single generator. Another solid hit there and the barrier could go completely, leaving that entire flank open to attack.

On the tactical, *Hercules* and *Gemini* were pitching in opposite directions, the first corvette aiming to go positive over Tamerlane's force, the second aiming to go negative. Far to their rear, Travis saw that *Gorgon* was rolling her wedge toward the two ships of Bogey Two, her kilt still open to Tamerlane's main force.

Leaving *Casey* to face the enemy alone.

"Commodore?" Belokas prompted tautly.

"Hold vector," Heissman said, his eyes shifting back and forth between the two sets of missiles converging on his force. "I want to fire off one last salvo of countermissiles, see if we can clear a couple of Bogey Three's missiles off *Gorgon*'s tail."

"We've also got two missiles coming in on our starboard flank," Woodburn warned. "If we cut things too fine, we could lose it all."

"Understood," Heissman said. "Stand by countermissiles...fire. Pitch ninety degrees negative and kill acceleration."

Out of the corner of his eye Travis saw all heads turn. "Pitch ninety degrees negative and kill acceleration, aye," the helmsman said. "Pitching ninety degrees negative; acceleration at zero."

"Kill acceleration, Sir?" Belokas asked quietly.

"Kill acceleration," Heissman confirmed. "We're going to go straight through the center of their formation." His lip twitched. "The distraction may give the corvettes a better chance of escape."

There was a moment of silence, and Travis heard Woodburn murmur something under his breath. "Understood, Sir," Belokas said briskly.

"Starboard missiles coming in hot," Rusk warned. "Not sure the sidewall can take them."

"So let's try something crazy," Heissman said. "As soon as the missiles reach energy torpedo range, flicker the sidewall and fire two bursts along the missiles' vectors, then raise the sidewall again. Maybe we can take out at least one of them before it hits."

Travis felt his throat tighten. Energy torpedoes, bursts of contained plasma bled straight off the reactor, were devastating at short ranges. But they hadn't exactly been designed as missile killers.

Woodburn was clearly thinking the same thing. "It's a long shot," he warned. "Especially since we might not get the sidewall back up in time. We could miss completely and end up with both missiles coming right in on us."

"Granted," Heissman agreed. "But the other option is to trust a half-power sidewall to keep them out on its own." He smiled faintly. "And so far, our long shots have been paying out pretty well."

"True," Woodburn said, returning the commodore's smile. "Very good, Sir. Energy torpedoes standing by."

On the tactical, the image that was *Gorgon* suddenly flared and vanished. "*Gorgon*'s gone, Sir," Rusk said grimly.

Travis felt a sudden swirling of nausea in the pit of his stomach. An entire ship, all those men and women, suddenly gone in a split-second flare of nuclear fire.

But he couldn't let himself think about that. Not now. He was an officer of the Royal Manticoran Navy, and his full focus had to remain on his own ship and her people.

"Lower enemy cruiser swiveling to target *Gemini*," Rusk continued.

"Computer standing ready to flicker sidewall and fire energy torpedoes," Woodburn added.

"Acknowledged," Heissman said. "Hand off to computer."

"Hand off to computer, aye," Woodburn confirmed. "Here we go..."

Travis felt the slight vibration of distant heavy relays as *Casey* blasted a barrage of torpedoes into space. They were amazingly fast weapons, nearly as fast as the beams from shipboard X-ray lasers. There was a second vibration as the second salvo followed the first—

"Sidewall back up," Woodburn called. Travis held his breath...

The hope and crossed fingers were in vain. An instant later, *Casey* gave a violent and all-too-well-remembered jerk and a fresh alarm screamed.

The missiles had been stopped. But the second starboard sidewall generator had been overloaded and destroyed.

"Damage?" Heissman called as the alarms once again blared across the bridge.

"Generator gone," Belokas reported. "Secondary damage to that area. Casualties reported; no details yet."

Travis felt a tightening in his chest. Starboard sidewall gone, only a third of their missiles left, and heading on a ballistic trajectory straight into the center of an enemy formation.

Worse, at the distances they would be passing the other ships, they would be well within beam range. Knife-fight range . . . and with *Casey*'s throat, kilt, and starboard flank open, Tamerlane's only decision would be which of his ships would get the honor of finishing her off.

He frowned at the tactical, his fingers keying his board. Tamerlane had already shown he was smart and reasonably cautious. He would assume *Casey* had lasers fore and aft, and would therefore most likely choose to send his attack in from starboard, where there were no defenses except the energy torpedoes and a much bigger cross-section of ship to target.

Casey was down to six real missiles, but they still had two practice missiles. And with the electromagnetic launch system instead of solid boosters they ought to be able to just goose one of those missiles from a launch tube without instantly sending it blasting away.

And if they could . . .

He cleared his throat. "Commodore Heissman? I have an idea."

☆   ☆   ☆

A small shudder rippled through *Hercules*'s hull as her ventral box launcher spat out its final missile. "There it goes, Sir," Labatte murmured. "That should be the last of them."

Richard nodded. And with that, *Hercules* was no longer a warship. She was nothing more than a floating assembly of parts and people, powerless to do anything against the invaders sweeping toward Manticore.

Powerless to do anything except possibly escape. If that was even still possible.

"I suppose we can still help protect *Casey*, though," Labatte continued. "Assuming we haven't completely drained the autocannon, that is. I wonder what—holy *crap*!"

"What?" Richard demanded, jerking around to look at the status boards. The impellers and sidewalls were still holding firm, or at least as firm as they ever were on this ship.

"New contacts, Sir," Labatte said tautly, jabbing a finger at the gravitic repeater display. "Two of them. *Damn* it all."

Richard bit back a curse. In the stress of the battle, with his mind focused on keeping *Hercules*'s balky impellers running, he'd completely forgotten the two off-again, on-again wedges that *Gorgon* had spotted several hours ago.

Those ghost ships had now arrived. And the IDs that CIC had marked on them—

"Hell in a basket," Labatte muttered. "Destroyers. We're in it now, all right, Sir. Up to our necks."

The image on the gravitic shifted. "We're pitching," Richard said, frowning. Pitching a *lot*, actually.

And why pitching at all? The captain should be rolling the ship if he wanted to block missiles from the incoming destroyers.

"Looks like we're doing a split tail," Labatte said. "Hell. Here they come."

Richard looked at the gravitic. Here they came, all right: a double barrage of missiles, one group from the two destroyers, the other from the main invasion force.

Unfortunately, there was no way to tell how many of them were heading for *Hercules* and how many were targeting the other Janus ships. But there were more than enough to go around.

"There we go, Sir," Labatte said, nodding toward the display. "Looks like the captain's rolling to interpose wedge on the missiles."

"Yes," Richard murmured. Unfortunately, the salvos were coming close enough together that it would be impossible to block both sets. It looked like Captain Hagros had opted to block the destroyers' attack with *Hercules*'s roof and hope that the sidewalls could handle whatever came in from the main invasion force.

He looked at the main status board. "Alpha Four is going twitchy again," he warned. "Might need a fine-tune."

"Could be," Labatte said, unstrapping. "I'll take a look, Sir. Keep an eye on Six, too, if you would—it's got some weird synch going with Four, and the last thing we want is to lose both of them."

"Right," Richard said. "Make it fast."

"You got it, Sir," Labatte said, shoving himself toward the hatchway. "If we're going to die, we should at least make them work for it."

☆　☆　☆

The flurry of activity and noise was over, and the Central War Room deep beneath the Palace had gone quiet.

Too quiet.

I should say something, King Edward thought as he sat on the command platform between Defense Minister Dapplelake and First Lord of the Admiralty Cazenestro, his hands gripping the ends of his armrests. *Something inspiring, or soothing, or heroic.*

But the words eluded him.

Besides, words were of no more use. Not from here. All the orders anyone could think of had been given; all the ideas anyone could come up with had been implemented; all the straws anyone could grasp at had been grasped.

Lord Dapplelake and Admiral Cazenestro had done everything they could. The crisis was out of their hands now, and in the hands of the men and women in that small collection of ships out there.

They can do it, Edward told himself firmly. They were brave and well trained, and they were the sons and daughters of the Star Kingdom. Whatever they could do to hold back this senseless assault, they would do it. And they would win.

Or die in the attempt.

"Your Majesty; My Lords?" the young petty officer at the monitor station called hesitantly. "It looks—" his voice broke. "*Gorgon* is gone."

Edward gripped the chair arms a little harder as he looked at the gravitics display. Sure enough, *Gorgon*'s wedge had flickered out.

"They may still be alive, Your Majesty," Dapplelake murmured hesitantly. "Her impellers could have failed without taking out the rest of the ship."

"Perhaps," Edward said.

But it was a fool's hope, and they all knew it. In his mind's eye he could see the likely and inevitable sequence of events: Commodore Heissman sending *Gorgon* to the rear to act as com relay... the invaders first probing Janus's capabilities with missile attacks, deciding they had enough data, and launching a full-on attack... *Casey* perhaps throwing countermissiles, perhaps choosing instead to continue with a barrage of ship-killers... she and the other ships firing their autocannon... one or more enemy missiles still managing to slip through the defensive field of shrapnel...

And one of those missiles sending *Gorgon* and her crew into eternity.

He took a deep breath. *Gorgon* was the first to die today. But she wouldn't be the last.

"Any news from *Vanguard* and *Nike*?"

"Let me check," Cazenestro said, swiveling one of his displays a little closer and punching for the proper status report. "*Vanguard* has her forward reactor on-line and is starting to bring up her impellers. *Nike*'s reactor is stable, and they're starting her impellers."

"Looks like the last of the crews are on their way up," Dapplelake added, looking at his own display.

Edward nodded, feeling his heart ache. The crews, such as they were. The battlecruisers, such as *they* were. Paper tigers, the whole lot of them: minimal training, minimal weapons, and no chance against even a competently managed corvette, let alone a full invasion force. Both battlecruisers had been in dry dock for the past two months, undergoing refit and repair, and while both were minimally spaceworthy, neither was even remotely battleworthy.

But they were all that Manticore had left. If the invasion tore through Janus and then Aegis—and there was every indication that it would—then *Vanguard* and *Nike* could at least make a show of moving into their path and challenging them.

Another fool's hope. But fool's hopes were about all they had left.

Fool's hopes, and prayers for some kind of miracle.

☆   ☆   ☆

"Because I've got the shot and you don't," Captain Blakely said with his usual irritating air of pedantic superiority. "You want Heissman and *Casey* shredded, fine. But you're the one in charge of this little operation, and you can't just go running off formation whenever you feel like it. Not with Green One about to come barreling down our throats. You need to be standing right out front where you can be the admiral." He paused, a slight smirk flicking across his face. "And where you can be ready to take that first shot."

Gensonne glared at the com display, wanting with all his soul to slap the other down.

But unfortunately, he was right. *Casey* was on a flat trajectory that would take her across the Volsung array, as fat and easy a target as anyone could ever hope for. But *Tyr* was in position to chase her down and deliver that death blow. *Odin* wasn't.

Equally important, *Tyr* still had her full armament in good working condition. *Odin* didn't.

"Fine," he growled. "Just watch yourself. You're going to be well within range of Heissman's energy torpedoes, and you'd look even stupider than you do now as a glowing ball of hot gas."

"You want to come over here and hold my hand?" Blakely countered. "I know how to stick a pig. Besides, there's no way he can beat my shot—a laser's charge, acquire, and fire sequence will always beat an energy torpedo's acquire, charge, and fire. I'll have him by at least a quarter-second, maybe even half a one."

"Thank you, Professor," Gensonne bit out. "I *do* know how weapons systems work."

"Glad to hear it," Blakely said. "And *that* assumes he's even got target locks left after what we did to his sidewall." He gestured impatiently. "You concentrate on taking out Green One and making sure Llyn pays on time when we're done. I'll take care of Heissman and the Manticorans' precious *Casey*."

"Fine," Gensonne growled again. "Just make it fast. I want you back in the stack before Green One arrives."

"I'll be back before you know it," Blakely said soothingly. "If you get bored, have Imbar bring you a book."

Cursing under his breath, Gensonne keyed off the display. For another moment he scowled at the empty screen, then turned back to the tactical. Again, Blakely was right—the firing sequence for energy torpedo systems was by its very nature slower than that of a spinal laser. Heissman would probably try to move his ship within the wedge to throw off *Tyr*'s targeting, but provided Blakely fired within a half second of the instant the cruiser came into view, he should have no problem gutting the Manticoran ship before they could fire back.

So Blakely wanted to rub Gensonne's nose in the fact that he'd taken out the punk-sized ship that had slapped *Odin* across the head? Fine. Gensonne was bigger than that. He could see the full picture. That was why he was an admiral, and Blakely was just a captain.

And if Blakely had ambitions that direction?

Gensonne smiled tightly. For his sake, he'd better not.

☆ ☆ ☆

Three quarters of a second.

Travis had run the numbers. So had Woodburn, and Heissman, and probably everyone else on the bridge and in CIC. And those cold numbers led to the equally cold conclusion that *Casey* was doomed.

The enemy battlecruiser had finished her rotation, her forward spinal laser lined up on the spot where *Casey* would be passing through the formation ninety seconds from now. She would be at point-blank distance, barely a thousand kilometers away, an insanely short range in these days of long-range missiles and high-powered X-ray lasers.

The captain of that ship would certainly recognize the risks. But he'd undoubtedly run the numbers, too. The instant his bow cleared the edge of *Casey*'s wedge, his targeting sensors would pinpoint *Casey*'s location, send the data to the ship's spinal laser, and fire. It would all be automated, with no human hand required, and if the battlecruiser was running modern electronics the whole operation would take between a quarter and a half-second.

It would be the battlecruiser's single shot, given the laser's recharge time. But with a nearly two-second window of opportunity, that half second would be all she needed.

Casey's return fire had also been keyed in and automated, and would also fire at the best speed possible. But the reality of energy torpedo response times meant that her counterattack would take nearly half a second longer than the battlecruiser's.

A half second longer, in other words, than *Casey* had to live.

Three quarters of a second.

Travis knew what an X-ray laser could do to a ship. If the battlecruiser's beam hit *Casey* it would slice straight through the hull and interior compartments, gutting the cruiser like a fish. If it happened to hit the fusion bottle, the end would come for everyone aboard in a single massive fireball. If it didn't, the crew would die marginally more slowly: some as the air was sucked out of broken work zones into space, others as they floated helplessly into eternity wrapped in their vac suits.

And all that stood between them and that fate was Travis's crazy idea. Travis's idea, and Heissman's willingness to try it.

Three quarters of a second.

"Ten seconds," Woodburn announced.

Travis took one final look at his displays, automatically starting his own mental countdown. Ten kilometers to *Casey*'s aft, held loosely in place twenty kilometers out from her starboard side by a tractor beam, was one of the practice missiles, waiting for the automated order that would light up its wedge and send it leaping through space. With the enemy battlecruiser a thousand kilometers away, Travis's mind automatically calculated, it would take the missile seven and a half seconds to reach it. Under the present circumstances, an unreachable eternity.

Fortunately, that wasn't where the missile needed to go.

Travis looked back at the tactical, marveling at how he was even able to calculate timings with his adrenaline-pumped time sense racing like a missile on sprint mode. His mental countdown ran to zero—

On the tactical, the battlecruiser appeared around the edge of *Casey*'s roof, free and open to fire. A quarter second, Travis had estimated before her spinal laser tore through the helpless cruiser.

And off *Casey*'s starboard flank, the practice missile lit up its wedge and leaped forward.

Not heading away from the cruiser or toward the battlecruiser, but tracing out a path alongside and parallel to *Casey*'s hull.

Missiles had just two preset acceleration rates: a long-range mode of thirty-five-hundred gravities, and a sprint mode of ten thousand. Those settings couldn't be changed, at least not by any equipment *Casey* had aboard, and even at the slower acceleration the missile wouldn't be pacing *Casey* for long.

But it didn't have to. With a wedge size of ten kilometers, and with *Casey* herself just under three hundred seventy meters long, the missile's wedge could block the enemy laser from the moment its leading edge passed *Casey*'s bow to the moment when its trailing edge traveled beyond the cruiser's stern.

For a crucial three-quarters of a second.

Sometime in that heartbeat the battlecruiser undoubtedly took its single shot. Travis never knew for sure—the missile's wedge completely blocked *Casey*'s view of what was happening on the other side. Then the missile was past, and momentum had carried the battlecruiser halfway through the open area between *Casey*'s stress bands.

And with a final, massive barrage of energy torpedoes, *Casey* went for the kill.

☆   ☆   ☆

Gensonne stared at his displays, his mouth hanging open, his brain fighting to disbelieve what he was seeing. It was impossible. The numbers had proved that. *Tyr* couldn't possibly have missed its shot, and *Casey* couldn't possibly have fired first.

But the numbers had lied. Somehow, they'd lied.

And as Gensonne watched in utter horror, *Tyr* disintegrated.

The bowcap went first, the hull metal peeling away like so much scrap paper as the first globe of superheated plasma tore through it. Even as that blast burned itself out the second slammed into the battlecruiser, tearing deeper into the hull. The forward impeller ring went with that one, and *Tyr*'s wedge vanished in a tangle of dissipating gravitational forces.

It was too savage, too quick for any human eye to sort out, or for any human mind to grasp before it was all over. *Tyr*'s only hope was that the twin reactors, clustered in her aft section for protection against attack from exactly this angle, were protected enough to somehow survive....

They weren't. The final torpedo slashed through the shattered ship—

And *Tyr* became an expanding ball of fire, torn metal, and broken bodies.

For a long moment no one on *Odin*'s bridge spoke. Gensonne shifted his eyes toward *Casey*, still coasting her way through the formation.

Or rather, what was left of the formation.

"Admiral?" Imbar spoke up, his voice hushed. "*Casey*'s coming up on *Phobos*. Do you want her to take a shot?"

Yes, Gensonne wanted to scream. *Yes, take the shot. Kill them all.*

But he couldn't give that order. Whatever black magic Heissman had used against *Tyr*, there was no reason he couldn't use it against *Phobos*, too. Gensonne didn't dare risk a second ship when he didn't have the faintest idea how *Casey* had killed the first. "No," he said, the word a strangled lump of useless fury in his throat. "Order *Phobos* to roll wedge, and let them go."

He stretched his neck against his tunic. Besides, his main fleet was still back there, right in the direction *Casey* was heading, ready to light up their wedges and move in to support what remained of the advance force. They would deal with *Casey*, and then they would all deal with Green One.

He looked back at the expanding dust cloud that had been *Tyr*. "See you in hell," he murmured. "I'll be the one wearing white."

☆   ☆   ☆

It all happened too fast for Travis to see the details. But bare seconds after *Casey*'s floor cut off their view, the gravitics confirmed the battlecruiser's wedge was gone. Seconds after that, the radar and lidar spotted the edge of a violently expanding debris cloud.

The tactic had worked. The battlecruiser had been destroyed.

But that didn't mean *Casey* was out of the woods yet. Travis felt himself tensing as they sped toward the com ship at the far rear of the Bogey Three formation, wondering if *Casey* still had one battle yet to face.

But the loss of his battlecruiser had apparently left Tamerlane shaken. *Casey* sped past the aft ship, catching only a glimpse of her rolled wedge.

It would be too much to say that there was a collective sigh of relief. But Travis could feel a definite lowering of tension.

Belokas broke the silence first. "What now, Sir?" she asked.

"I don't know," Heissman said thoughtfully. "The manual has a surprising dearth of information on what to do when you're intact and behind an enemy formation. Probably because it doesn't happen very often."

"I suppose we'll have to improvise," Woodburn said.

"I suppose we will," Heissman agreed in that same thoughtful tone. "Let's get a little more distance to make sure we're out of aft laser range, then see what we can come up with."

☆　　☆　　☆

"Bloody hell," Dapplelake said, his voice hushed and disbelieving. "Did that battlecruiser just—?"

"It's gone," Cazenestro confirmed, sounding just as disbelieving as the Defense Minister. "Or at least, its wedge is down. How in God's name did Heissman pull that off?"

"We were hoping you could tell us that," Edward said, a small part of the pressure on his chest easing as he gazed at the gravitics display. One of the invaders' two most powerful warships; and *Casey* had just destroyed it.

"I wish I knew, Your Majesty," Cazenestro said. "*Casey*'s a good ship, but I would never in a hundred years have bet her against a battlecruiser. She must have gotten in close enough for an energy torpedo launch, but God only knows how she managed that without being gutted herself in the process."

"At least now we've got a much fairer fight on our hands," Dapplelake said. "Locatelli has two battlecruisers, and they've only got one."

"Except that Green One's battlecruisers are only partly manned and armed," Cazenestro said grimly.

"I was taking that into account," Dapplelake said. "Just be glad he's got as much as he does." He inclined his head to Edward. "Thanks to you, Your Majesty."

Edward nodded silently. And thanks to Prime Minister Burgundy and all the favors he'd burned in order to make the Navy's rearming happen. Favors that had cost him friendships. Favors that had earned him the enhanced animosity of people like Breakwater and his faction. Favors that had in many ways made him an embarrassment or pariah even among his own supporters.

Now, finally, that sacrifice was going to be vindicated.

And then, even as Edward began rehearsing what he was going to say to Parliament and the Star Kingdom's citizens, the gravitic display again changed.

Only this time it wasn't the welcome disappearance of an enemy wedge. This time it was a new group of contacts suddenly appearing in the distance.

Eight of them. Coming in along the same vector as the first wave, clearly part of the same invasion force.

Heading toward Manticore.

Eight of them.

"Oh, my God," Dapplelake murmured. "What the hell do we do now?"

Edward had no answer.

CHAPTER TWENTY-TWO

IMBAR WAS STILL SWEARING VICIOUSLY under his breath. The rest of *Odin*'s bridge had gone deathly silent.

It was a strange silence, Gensonne noted distantly: one part disbelief, one part anger, one part determination.

At least, one part had damned well better be determination. Because this battle was far from over. *Far* from over.

"What the *hell*?" Clymes spoke up suddenly. "Admiral, the main force just lit up their wedges."

"What?" Gensonne snarled. *What the hell* was right—De la Roza wasn't supposed to fire up until Gensonne gave the order. "Get me *Thor*. You hear me, Captain?"

"I hear you, Admiral," Imbar growled, his tone barely on the right side of courteous. "Working on it."

Biting furiously against the words that wanted to come out, but which there was no point in saying—yet—Gensonne let the time-lag seconds play themselves out.

And then—

"De la Roza," the bridge speaker boomed abruptly with the voice of *Thor*'s captain. "What the hell just happened there?"

"What the hell just happened *there*?" Gensonne shot back. "You were supposed to wait for my signal. Now Green One is going to have time to adjust their timing and strategy."

There was another pause as the signal bounced to *Thor* and back—

"Excuse *me*, Admiral," De la Roza said in Captain Imbar's same barely polite tone. "I saw one of your battlecruisers go ashcan, and after the damage you took earlier I figured it was probably you. That left *me* in overall command, and I decided that what was left of your formation might like some extra support sooner rather than later."

"Well, *I'm* not dead, and *you're* not in command," Gensonne snarled. "That was Blakely, not me. Next time, you damn well find out the lay of the land before you take action. Understood?"

Another delay— "Understood, Admiral," De la Roza said. "What are your orders, Sir?"

Gensonne ground his teeth. He would let this slide for now, but only because they had bigger fish to fillet.

But it wasn't over, not by a long shot. He would be having a *very* long discussion on proper procedure with De la Roza somewhere in the near future. And Imbar could probably use an attitude refresher, as well.

"As long as you've announced your presence, you might as well join the party," he told De la Roza. "Stay on vector and keep formation."

"Acknowledged, Sir," De la Roza said. "You want to decrease acceleration and let us catch up to you?"

Gensonne glared at the tactical. With one of his battlecruisers gone, that was indeed the logical thing to do. It would let the two groups combine forces and bring a much more powerful formation to bear on the incoming Manticorans. It would certainly be the cautious thing to do.

But Gensonne hadn't gotten where he was by playing it safe. Besides, bringing the two Volsung forces together in a single battle stack would run the risk of letting some of the Manticoran ships slip through their fire zone, and he had no wish to have even a marginally functional enemy force at his rear when he was trying to talk a planetary government into surrendering.

"Just stick with the plan," he told De la Roza. "If I decide to make any changes, I'll let you know. And watch out for that cruiser, *Casey*. You see her?"

"Yeah, we see her. What the *hell* did she do to *Tyr*, anyway?"

"God only knows," Gensonne growled. "Just watch her. Whatever trick she's got up her sleeve, I don't want to lose anyone else to it."

"Oh, we'll watch her," De la Roza promised darkly. "We'll watch her *real* close."

☆　　☆　　☆

"CIC reads eight contacts in Group Two," Tactical Officer Perrow said, half turning in her station to look at Metzger. "XO is pretty sure at least one is a battlecruiser. *Damn* it—sorry, Ma'am. Looks like they just got *Gemini*."

Metzger nodded, eyeing the empty spot on the gravitic display where the corvette's wedge had been. The split-tail maneuver was considered a last-ditch effort precisely because it left a ship wide open to attack as the attacker passed above or below it. One of the invading ships had taken out *Gemini*, and *Hercules*'s death was probably not far away.

Casey, against all reasonable odds, had made it completely through the enemy formation intact. Metzger would bet heavily that Tamerlane's reluctance to engage her was largely due to the loss of Group One's second battlecruiser at *Casey*'s hands.

She would also bet heavily that however that trick had been pulled off, Travis Long had been involved.

Meanwhile, Aegis had their own problems. And those problems had just doubled.

"What's ETA on Group Two?" she asked, keeping her voice steady. "Specifically, vis-à-vis Group One?"

"They're currently about fifty minutes apart," Perrow said. "But Group Two is coming up fast. Assuming neither group changes their acceleration, they'll probably be no more than thirty minutes apart by the time we're in combat range of Group One."

"Possibly closer than that," Locatelli said. The calmness in his voice, to Metzger's admiration and secret resentment, didn't sound forced at all. "Sometime in the next ten minutes we're going to do a one-eighty and decelerate."

Metzger felt her throat tighten. Standard military doctrine when facing two separate enemy waves was to plow through the first group, doing as much damage as possible while minimizing damage to your own forces, and then continue on to the second, with the goal of preventing the enemy from consolidating his forces. It boiled down to concentration of firepower, a strategy that dated all the way back to Old Earth's gunpowder era.

But Aegis couldn't do that. Locatelli was responsible for the defense of Manticore and Sphinx, and if he blew past the invaders he would leave both worlds completely open to attack with nothing to stop them but the token missile base on Thorson, Manticore's single moon.

And so Aegis would turn and decelerate, trying to better match the invaders' own speed, making sure to stay in their path as long as possible so as to inflict as much damage as they could.

Unfortunately, Aegis having more time to throw missiles at the enemy also meant the enemy would have that same extra time to throw missiles back. And Metzger had little doubt that even after Tamerlane's encounter with Janus the enemy still had more armament left than Aegis could muster.

Locatelli was apparently thinking along the same lines. "CIC, what's current data on Janus's duel with Group One?" he called.

"It's a little spotty, Sir," McBride's voice came from the bridge speaker. "The clean relay we had with them went down when they took out *Gorgon*, and with *Casey* and *Hercules* wedge-on to us we're obviously not getting any fresh data from either of them. But we're tentatively reading Janus as having thrown twenty-two missiles during the engagement. Casey may have lost another to a misfire—it was a little hard to tell."

"Enemy damage?"

"Obviously, the battlecruiser that *Casey* took out," McBride said. "I'm pretty sure the other battlecruiser also took some damage, but we can't tell how much. The other four ships seem intact."

"But they've obviously spent a lot of missiles of their own," Metzger pointed out. "Not to mention Janus drained some of their point defenses."

"Correct," McBride confirmed. "But since we don't know how many missiles or countermissiles they started out with, there's no way of knowing how many they have left."

And *Invincible* wasn't exactly flush on missiles at the moment, either, Metzger reminded herself silently. Of the twenty-four she could theoretically carry, she had only eighteen.

There should have been two practice missiles, as well, which could at least have been used to further drain the invaders' autocannon and countermissiles. But Locatelli had spent both of those in his exercise with *Phoenix* and they'd never been replaced. Distantly, she wondered if the admiral was regretting that action now.

"What about those two?" Locatelli asked, gesturing to the screen. "Janus's designated Bogey Two. They're destroyers?"

"Yes, Sir," McBride said. "Probably *Luna*-class. Same design as our old *Protector*-class."

"And presumably of similar vintage," Locatelli rumbled. "No idea how well-armed they still are, either."

"Probably well enough to create some havoc, though, Sir," Metzger pointed out. "We could detach *Phoenix* and *Damocles* to try to intercept them."

"Yes, we could," Locatelli agreed. "The problem is..." He nodded toward the tactical.

Metzger felt a lump form in her throat. The problem, of course, was the rest of the invasion force coming toward them. After Heissman's split-tail, Janus was essentially out of the fight, and Aegis was woefully understrength. Detaching two destroyers to chase after Bogey Two would make the numbers even more lopsided.

But Locatelli couldn't just let the enemy run unchallenged through the system. No matter what happened with the main invasion fleet, a pair of destroyers who reached Manticore orbit might still be enough of a threat to force King Edward and Parliament to surrender. *Someone* had to go after them—to harass, harry, and delay if nothing else—and Locatelli's ships were the only ones in position to do that.

And with a sudden premonition, Metzger knew what the admiral was going to do.

He couldn't afford to send two ships. He couldn't afford to send zero ships.

And so, he was going to send one.

It was, on the face of it, insane. Standard battle logic was to *never* send one ship after two. Not just because of the disparity in missile numbers, but also because two ships could often maneuver a singleton into a position where she couldn't defend against both at the same time.

But it was the insanity of desperation. One ship would be detached—a suicide mission, in all but name, but one that was necessary to keep the enemy away from Manticore.

The only question remaining was which ship it would be.

Damocles had the higher missile load. Military logic suggested she could harass Bogey Two longer, as well as better draining the enemies' defenses.

Phoenix, on the other hand, was current home to Locatelli's nephew. *Family* logic might suggest sending him as far from the main battle as possible.

Maybe Locatelli had already followed both logic pathways. Maybe he knew that others would follow them, too.

Or maybe he was as good and as objective a commander as his reputation implied.

"Com, signal *Damocles*," he ordered. "Captain Marcello is ordered to break off and pursue Bogey Two, hereafter designated as Group Three. Primary mission is to keep them away from Manticore. If Marcello can engage and destroy, so much the better."

"Aye, aye," Com replied.

"What about *Phoenix*?" Perrow asked.

"What about her?" Locatelli countered.

"I wondered if you wanted her to stay on forward point alone, or to move back in the formation," Perrow said. "Possibly between *Sphinx* and *Bellerophon*."

Where, Metzger noted, *Phoenix* and Ensign Locatelli would be inside the heavy cruisers' countermissile screen. Once again, an opportunity for Locatelli to show a little quiet favoritism.

Once again, he passed on the offer. "*Phoenix* will stay where she is," he said. "XO, have you worked out our optimum turn-over time?"

"Yes, Sir," McBride said. On Metzger's tac display, the XO's proposed maneuver came up. "Of course, that assumes they don't tweak their own formation."

"If they do, I'm sure you and the TO will find the right counter to it," Locatelli said. "Captain Metzger, keep an eye on *Casey*. If and when she turns enough for us to send a signal, instruct Commodore Heissman that he's to do whatever he can to harass Group Two."

"Yes, Sir," Metzger said. Did that include Heissman losing his ship, she wondered briefly, if it came to that?

Of course it did. That was the RMN's job: to die for the lives and freedom of the Star Kingdom's citizens.

Besides, most of Janus had already been lost. Most of Aegis would probably be following soon. What would the loss of one more ship really matter?

"I suppose we should officially identify ourselves," Locatelli continued. "Com, get a laser on the battlecruiser. And then, Captain, once the conversation is over—and it's likely to be short—prepare all ships to come around in a one-eighty. Deceleration will be set at one point eight KPS squared."

"One point eight KPS squared, aye," Metzger said, feeling a cold lump settle into her throat. This was it.

Janus had had their shot at the invaders. Time for Aegis to set up for theirs.

☆　☆　☆

In modern warfare, it was usually only those on the bridge or CIC who knew what was going on beyond the hull. Most of the officers and crew, their full attention focused on their own duties, never even knew about the missile that killed them.

Crown Prince Richard Winton certainly never did.

☆　☆　☆

The War Room had gone suddenly silent. King Edward barely noticed. The walls and displays and monitors had gone faint and blurry, their lines and edges wavering as if in a summer afternoon's heat haze. Edward barely noticed that, either.

Because there was one monitor that still remained in sharp focus. One monitor that was still connected to reality, to the core of the King's being. It was the monitor that showed the remnants of the Janus task force.

The monitor where *Hercules* had just winked out of existence.

Where his son had just died.

Slowly, dimly, he became aware that quiet voices had begun again around him. Hushed voices, whispering updates and status reports.

And then, with a sense like the wrenching of a dislocated shoulder, he remembered that other fathers across the Star Kingdom had also lost sons and daughters this day. That wives had lost husbands, husbands had lost wives, children had lost parents. Most of them didn't yet know about those losses, but that didn't make the horror any less terrible or permanent.

And Edward remembered that he wasn't just a father. He was also the King.

The King of everyone.

The time for full mourning would come later. Right now, his job was to do whatever he could to keep as many of his subjects alive as possible.

He took a deep breath, the expansion of his lungs feeling like it was driving shards of glass into his heart. "So that leaves *Casey* as the only remaining Janus ship," he said, forcing his voice to remain calm. Even in a crisis, the King's voice should remain calm. "What do we have on Aegis's combat readiness, My Lord Cazenestro?"

He heard the First Lord's answer. He even tried to listen to the answer. But for the next few minutes, even the realities of war could only penetrate so deeply into his heart.

His son was dead.

☆   ☆   ☆

"New contact!" Commander Shiflett's voice came sharply over *Damocles*'s bridge speaker. "Two contacts bearing two-four-oh by two-seven. Range, approximately eight point six million kilometers."

Lisa's first, horrifying thought was that more of the invaders had somehow gotten in behind them without anyone noticing. But an instant later she realized that was impossible. In which case—

"Got an ID," Shiflett continued. "HMS *Aries* and *Taurus*."

Lisa's reflexive dismay was replaced by an equally reflexive hope. Two more RMN ships, unexpectedly in position to aid in *Damocles*'s mission of harassing the two invading Group Three destroyers.

And then, once again, reality abruptly reached across the universe and slapped her across the back of the head. Of course the two corvettes weren't Navy. Not anymore.

MacNiven, at the helm, got there first. "*MPARS?*" he said, the word halfway between a question and a curse. "I thought they were ordered to stand down."

"They were," Captain Marcello growled. "Apparently *Aries* and *Taurus* didn't get the memo."

"Or ignored it," Lisa murmured.

"Or ignored it," Marcello agreed. "Well, beggars can't be choosers. Com, get a laser on them—our compliments, and see if Captains Hardasty and Kostava can bring anything to this party."

"Aye, aye, Sir."

She relayed the message, and Lisa started her usual mental countdown. At the MPARS ships' distance, a round-trip message would take almost a minute.

In the meantime, she'd ordered an additional check of the weapons systems' battle-readiness, and those reports were starting to come in.

She was halfway through the stack when the com speaker came to life. "Captain Hardasty; *Aries*," a woman's brisk voice came. "Sorry to be late to the festivities, Captain Marcello. Actually, you're lucky we're here at all. We were supposed to be halfway to Manticore-B by now, but we had some trouble with our reactor, and *Taurus* needed to retune one of her nodes—"

"Yes, yes, fine," Marcello cut in.

Or rather tried to. At half a light-minute away, the woman could prattle on forever before she even heard Marcello's interruption.

Luckily, she didn't. The reactor trouble, the node trouble, crews who didn't necessarily know which end of a missile was which— "But we're finally locked and loaded and ready to go," she concluded. "What do you need us to do?"

"We've got two enemy destroyers coming in," Marcello said. "Group Three. Our orders are to keep them away from Manticore, and if possible to take them out. It looks like you're in position to come at them from an angle."

The slow minute ticked by. Lisa finished reading through the reports, confirming that all was in order.

Which wasn't to say all was exactly well. *Damocles*'s missile count sat at seven, and her autocannon loads were about sixty percent of what they could carry in their magazines. That was probably a shade better than typical for RMN ordnance levels these days, but not exactly optimal for actual battle.

Of course, *Aries* and *Taurus* had another six missiles between them. But that would mean zipper if the two captains couldn't bring their ships properly into play.

"And box them in?" Hardasty came back. "Good idea—let's do it. Unfortunately, our TO, Ensign Badakar, is a little . . . inexperienced . . . so we're a bit unprepared for this kind of thing."

"Understood," Marcello said. "What *are* you prepared to do?"

The time lag started. "Ensign Badakar, TO?" Marcello asked.

"One moment, Sir," Lisa said, punching up the Navy personnel records. "Ensign Rol Badakar, class of 1541, first assignment *Damocles* . . . looks like he was kept aboard after the transfer to MPARS, basically an extended snotty cruise. Average scores down the line."

"*And* inexperienced," Marcello said sourly. "I suppose we shouldn't be surprised."

Lisa nodded. The reactivation of the battlecruisers had made the supply of suitable TOs and ATOs even thinner on the ground than usual, and Cazenestro certainly wouldn't have given the Navy's best to MPARS.

An attitude and policy which now threatened to turn around and bite them all on the butts. Hardasty and Kostava's blatant disregard for their orders had unexpectedly added two more ships to the Star Kingdom's defense. But without proper tactical expertise, they would be next to useless.

"Whatever we can," Hardasty's response came back. Her voice, Lisa noted, was tense but firm. "Just tell us what you want us to do."

Lisa felt a stirring of somewhat grudging admiration. Going into battle with full personnel and training was risky enough. Going in with one hand tied behind your back and your feet hobbled was three steps above courageous. One final surprise from the universe in a day that had already seen more than its share of them.

"No problem," Marcello said. "My TO, Lieutenant Commander Donnelly, will handle liaison with you." Lisa felt a rustling in the air behind her as he gestured. "Commander?"

"Yes, Sir," Lisa said, glad that the positioning of her bridge station put her with her face away from Marcello. It was the logical decision, and the two MPARS ships certainly needed her.

But the liaison job would mean that she wouldn't be able to focus her full attention on her own ship, which was her primary job as *Damocles*'s TO. Fleetingly, she wondered what Cazenestro and the Admiralty would say about *that*.

And realized suddenly that she didn't care. Hardasty and Kostava had ignored orders. If Marcello and Lisa had to ignore protocol, that was what they had to do. Desperate times, and all that; and these times were about as desperate as they got.

"Working up coordinated intercept courses for them now."

"Excellent," Marcello said. "Captain Hardasty, Lieutenant Donnelly is working up intercept courses for you and *Taurus* to coordinate with our plans. Be ready to receive and implement."

Once again, the long delay began. "As soon as you send the course, TO, you and the XO will swap positions," Marcello told Lisa. "You can coordinate their movements as well from CIC as here, and you'll get any changes in Group Three's activity a shade faster there."

"Understood, Sir," Lisa said.

"And cheer up, everyone," Marcello said, raising his voice to include the rest of the bridge and CIC. "We started out one ship against two. Now, we're three against two."

Lisa made a face. Right. Three ships rushing to the defense of the Star Kingdom. Two of those ships MPARS.

God help them all.

☆   ☆   ☆

"Well," Captain Heissman commented coolly. "That changes things a bit."

"It does indeed," Woodburn agreed, just as coolly. "Possibly more than just a bit."

Travis stared at the gravitics display, a chill running through him. Thirty seconds ago, the plan had been for *Casey* to wait until she was out of the invading force's missile range, then roll wedge back over and chase after them, with the goal of catching up and attacking their rear. If they were lucky, Admiral Locatelli and Aegis would arrive into attack position from in front at about the same time, allowing them to catch the enemy in a pincer.

But that tactical high ground was gone now. With the dramatic and totally unexpected appearance of the eight new ships of Tamerlane's second wave, it was *Casey* herself who was about to be caught in the pincer.

"Suggestions?" Heissman invited. "Celia; Alfred?"

"I don't see a lot of options to choose from," Woodburn said. "Even if we push the compensator to the limit, we can't finish decelerating and then accelerate back toward Manticore fast enough to stay out of their missile range."

"We could roll wedge and get out of here," Belokas suggested hesitantly. "Plenty of time for that. But that would take us out of the battle. I don't like the thought of that."

"Not when we still have six missiles we can throw at them," Heissman agreed. "So let's split the difference. We'll hold our attitude and head positive until we're clear of their missile range. Then, we'll pitch ninety degrees and head back across the top of their formation, continuing our deceleration. Assuming they don't detach a ship to take us out, we should be able to curve around behind them and become the same up-the-kilt nuisance we were planning to be for Tamerlane's first wave."

"Sounds good, Sir," Belokas said.

"Best we're going to get, anyway," Woodburn said. "There's the whole question of whether we'll be able to catch up with them in time to do any good, but it's better than nothing. And they have to start decelerating *sometime*."

"Unless they intend to slam full-speed into Manticore," Heissman said grimly.

Which along with being suicidal was utterly forbidden by the Solarian League's Eridani Edict. But Tamerlane seemed to be one of the shadier types of mercenary, and Travis wasn't willing to trust that he would play by any of the established rules of warfare. He doubted Captain Heissman had any such trust, either.

The worst part of such a scenario was that if such an attack did indeed happen—if Tamerlane flew one of his ships into Manticore or fired a missile at the planet—System Command would see it coming but not have the slightest hope of doing anything about it. The speeds would be too great, the response time too short, the fixed defenses on Thorson too inadequate.

The response time too short...

"Which we will fervently hope they don't," Woodburn said. "I've got a course plotted, Sir. But I'm thinking that Mr. Long has that look in his eye again."

"Does he, now," Heissman said. "Mr. Long? You have a thought?"

The words had almost an air of bantering about them, Travis noted distantly. But beneath the joke, he could sense some genuine respect.

His last idea had worked. Maybe he could make it two for two.

"I was thinking, sir," he said. "Our floor is currently toward the second wave, so they can't see anything we do in here. I was thinking we could just hold position and let them get closer—"

"*Closer?*" Belokas asked.

"Yes, Ma'am," Travis said. "But while their line of sight was blocked, we would ease the rest of our missiles out of the tubes and tractor them into place off our flank, pointed back toward the second wave. We let the wave get to close range, then accelerate positive, as you've already suggested, Sir. As soon as our wedge is clear, we activate the missiles and fire them."

"Clever," Heissman said thoughtfully. "If they're not paying attention they may not notice the threat until the missiles light up their wedges. And even if they do, they won't have nearly as much time to react as they would if we fired at usual missile range."

"At the very least, they would spend some of their point defenses destroying them," Travis said, a small warmth growing inside him. *Two for two...*

"Very clever, indeed," Heissman said. "Unfortunately, not practical." He gestured. "Helm, initiate the TO's course."

"TO's course, aye," the helmsman replied.

"And you might want to close your mouth, Mr. Long," Heissman added, a small smile on his face. "That look ill becomes a proper bridge officer."

Travis hadn't realized his mouth was open. "I don't understand, Sir," he managed, the warm glow turned to ashes and the familiar twisting pain of embarrassment.

"Oh, it would work," Heissman said. "At least, after a fashion. The problem is that once the missiles were away we'd have no way to control them. Telemetry is iffy enough through a sidewall; it doesn't work at all through a wedge."

"I know that, Sir," Travis said. "I was thinking the missiles would use their own internal guidance systems."

"And if those systems were more sophisticated, I'd be tempted to give it a try," Woodburn said. "Unfortunately, they aren't. You saw the kind of ECM Tamerlane's ships have. They'd have the missiles off course before they even got within countermissile range."

Travis grimaced. He'd hoped that knowing the basic parameters of the attackers' ECM would allow the missile techs to do a quick reprograming of the internal guidance systems. Apparently, it wouldn't. "Yes, Sir. I see."

"I don't think you do, Lieutenant," Woodburn said, not unkindly. "At least, not completely."

"Under other circumstances it might still be worth a try," Heissman said. "But in this case, sitting here coasting for that long would mean that once we started our loop we wouldn't have a hope of catching up with them once we were behind them. You heard what Alfred said: whether we can manage it is questionable as it is. But that's our only chance of staying in the battle, and we'd be giving it up for a very small chance of success."

"Yes, Sir," Travis said again. This time, he meant it.

"Good," Heissman said. "Bottom line: don't stop coming up with ideas, and *never* stop pitching them. You've already saved *Casey* once today. You may have another chance before this day is over."

CHAPTER TWENTY-THREE

"GREEN ONE HAS REACHED extreme missile range, Admiral," Imbar announced.

And with their kilts still flapping open to the breeze. Gensonne smiled tightly, his simmering fury over *Tyr*'s destruction self-focusing into something razor sharp and bitterly cold.

The loss of his second battlecruiser had forced a change in his original plan. Fortunately, he had a backup already drawn up. Time to implement that new plan.

And to end both the battle and the Star Kingdom of Manticore.

"Admiral?" Imbar prompted.

"Hold your fire," Gensonne said. "Locatelli was trying to match our speed as best he could, but he isn't going to sit kilt-first to us much longer. No point in firing when the missiles will be just in time to shred themselves against their wedges. We'll wait until they're almost facing us with their throats wide open."

"Yes, Sir," Imbar said. "I just hope..." He trailed off.

"You hope what, Captain?"

"Nothing, Sir."

"I said you hope *what*, Captain?" Gensonne repeated.

Imbar's shoulders hunched. "I was just wondering if the Manticorans might have a few more surprises in store," he said reluctantly.

"Like what?" Gensonne growled. "Throwing a party for us, maybe?"

"I mean surprises like *Casey*," Imbar growled back. "Or surprises like having two battlecruisers instead of the one that little worm Llyn told us they had."

"Aspect change, Admiral," Clymes announced. "Green One has ceased deceleration and is turning."

"Pitch or yaw turn?" Gensonne asked.

"Yaw, Sir."

"Sidewalls up?"

"Not yet."

"There—you see?" Gensonne said, gesturing in the direction of the distant enemy. "Standard yaw with sidewalls down so that he can keep us in sight the whole time he's turning. Locatelli is either nervous or unimaginative, and either way he's not in Captain Heissman's class. *That's* the kind of backwater navy we expected, Captain, and that's the kind we're getting. *Casey* was a fluke."

Imbar didn't answer.

But then, he didn't have to. Gensonne was well aware of his thoughts: that fluke had cost them a battlecruiser.

Speaking of *Casey* . . .

He looked at the aft tactical display. *Casey* was heading positive at a brisk pace, her floor still toward the Volsung main force, apparently intent on getting clear before De la Roza's ships ran over her.

Or else Heissman was planning to do an up-and-over and come in behind them. In which case, he could still cause trouble.

Gensonne should probably warn them. He opened his mouth—

"Green One has finished their turn," Clymes announced. "Sidewalls up; they're ready for battle."

"Let's not disappoint them," Gensonne said, turning away from the aft display. The hell with more warnings. If De la Roza couldn't figure out what to do about a light cruiser on his tail, he didn't deserve to be commanding a scow, let alone a battlecruiser. "Missile salvo. Target the lead ship—that destroyer—and the portside heavy cruiser."

"Not the battlecruisers?" Imbar asked.

"Like you said: surprises," Gensonne said. "Green One is my party gift for De la Roza." He smiled tightly. "We're just going to unwrap it a little."

"Yes, Sir," Imbar said. "TO?"

"Destroyer and heavy cruiser targeted," Clymes confirmed.

Gensonne nodded. "Your privilege, Captain. Fire when ready."

☆   ☆   ☆

Osterman was at her post in *Phoenix*'s Forward Weapons, monitoring the systems and wondering why anyone would attack the Star Kingdom, when everything went to hell.

Literal, violent, cacophonous, bloody, deadly hell.

She awoke in stages, first feeling the agony in her ribs, then the slightly less demanding pain in her left forearm, then the stink of burning fluids and insulation, then finally the hot sticky wetness on the left side of her head. A stern warning from the manual flashed into her mind—*when seriously injured, refrain from moving until medical personnel have arrived and assessed your condition*—and carefully opened her eyes.

The hell hadn't been a dream or a nightmare. All around her the compartment was all twisted metal and half-melted plastic, the whole thing encased in a smoky darkness that was relieved only by red indicators and the sporadic glow of occasional emergency lights. Through the half-open hatchway she could see that the passageway outside was in the same state of chaos.

For a long moment she just stared at the devastation, one small, detached section of her mind cataloging her injuries, another slightly larger section trying to deduce what she could about *Phoenix*'s overall condition. She herself appeared to have some cracked ribs, with the breath-synchronized tweaks of extra pain that suggested that one or more of those jagged edges might be dangerously near a lung. Her left forearm was also broken, though her fingers were working more or less correctly. The warmth on the left side of her face seemed to be blood streaming from a gash in her scalp just above her temple.

She was a mess. But at least she was still alive.

Phoenix, for all intents and purposes, wasn't.

Osterman hadn't had time to get her helmet on, but she was still breathing. That meant that whatever the enemy missile had done to the ship, at least her section had remained airtight. The size of that bubble of mercy, of course, was impossible to guess.

There was power, too, at least enough to run the indicators and some of the electronics. Even as she pondered whether that meant the reactor was still functional or whether they were living on battery power she caught a hint of reflection from down the passageway that was a bit whiter than the emergency lights. That would be one of the regular lights, which didn't feed off anything but main reactor power.

So the reactor hadn't scrammed or been blown clear of the ship. They had air and power. A near-miss, then, with the missile detonating far enough from its target for a mission kill but not complete vaporization. Under normal circumstances, that would mean rescue was at least a possibility.

Only these circumstances were hardly normal. The level of damage strongly implied that some of the nodes had been damaged, which meant no wedge, which meant no motive power. The last time she'd checked, *Phoenix*'s net movement had still been away from Manticore, which meant that right now the wrecked ship was coasting farther and farther from any chance of help.

Worse, no wedge meant no defenses. *Phoenix* was laid bare, as helpless as it was possible for a ship to be. The first enemy that felt like throwing another missile at her would reduce her to component atoms.

Phoenix was dead. Osterman would soon follow.

But there was nothing to be gained by floating uselessly and waiting to meet her God. At the very least, she should poke around a bit and see if anyone in this section was still alive.

Pushing off the edge of the control board with one foot, she managed to snag a handhold with her right hand. She maneuvered her way out into the passageway, clamping her teeth against the pain, and began her search.

☆   ☆   ☆

The wave of missiles from Group One had spent their fury, and inflicted their damage.

Their devastating, crushing damage.

Metzger wanted to turn her head. To look away from the displays and their neutral, antiseptic numbers and figures. To look at Admiral Locatelli, and offer whatever condolences and sympathy she could.

But she didn't. She couldn't. Her job was to maintain *Invincible*'s combat readiness, and that job required one hundred percent of her focus.

Besides, the admiral had just lost his nephew. He deserved whatever brief moment of privacy she could give him.

The private moment lasted approximately five seconds. "Damage assessment, Admiral," McBride reported from CIC. His voice, Metzger noted, seemed unusually subdued for a man who often claimed to have no emotions. Perhaps it was her imagination. "*Sphinx* is gone completely—looks like her reactor containment failed. *Phoenix*—" This time, Metzger definitely wasn't imagining the catch in the XO's voice. "*Phoenix* is down," he continued stolidly. "Her wedge is gone, along with most of her starboard side. Her reactor's still functioning, but just barely. No way to know how long it'll survive. If it goes, it's unlikely the automatics will be able to eject it. Not with that much damage."

"Understood," Locatelli said. "What about her personnel?"

"No way to tell, Sir," McBride said. "The bow...I'm sorry, sir. There's just no way to tell if anyone survived."

"I didn't ask about the bow, XO," Locatelli said tartly. "I'm interested in the status of *all* of her crew."

"Yes, Sir," McBride said. "Bridge and CIC have gone silent. No way to know if that's transmitter failure or...lack of anyone there to talk to."

"Keep trying," Locatelli said. "Captain, what's status on the rest of Aegis?"

Metzger skimmed down the latest report summary. "*Swiftsure* reports her ventral launcher and Number Three autocannon are out," she said. "*Bellerophon*—"

"Was *Swiftsure* hit?" Perrow interrupted, frowning. "I thought the only missiles that got through were on *Sphinx* and *Phoenix*."

"*Swiftsure*'s troubles are mechanical," Metzger said. "Ditto for *Bellerophon*, whose starboard sidewall is down. *Pegasus*, *Aquila* and *Libra* report fully functional and combat-ready." Or at least as functional as mere corvettes could be, which wasn't very.

"We do with what we have," Locatelli said. "Signal *Bellerophon* to move a thousand klicks negative so she can cover both us and *Swiftsure*."

"What about her lost sidewall?" Perrow asked. "She may not be able to hide that."

"I'm sure she can't," Locatelli agreed. "Given that, we may be able to use her as bait somewhere down the line to draw in one or more of Tamerlane's ships."

"Yes, Sir," Perrow said. She didn't sound happy with that idea, but they were in a battle for their lives and the TO was too good a tactician not to realize that Locatelli had to use every trick and tool he could get his hands on. "I'll note that if our data is correct, *Casey* also lost a sidewall just before she took out Tamerlane's other battlecruiser. He might be a little leery of moving in on a ship with the same supposed problem."

"Even better," Locatelli said. "Pulling them in or driving them back—whatever *Bellerophon* can do to break their formation could be useful. XO, keep a close eye on them. See which way they're jumping."

"Yes, Sir," McBride's voice came from the CIC speaker. "So far, nothing—missile trace!" he interrupted himself. "Missile trace, four, thirty-five hundred gees, estimated impact one hundred thirty-two seconds."

"Got 'em," Perrow confirmed. "Standing by countermissiles and autocannon."

Metzger looked at the tactical. Six missiles incoming, all right.

She frowned. Group One had just fired nearly twice that many missiles in its last salvo, an attack that had taken out two of the defenders' ships. The standard follow-up to such a devastating attack was to send out a second equally massive salvo while the enemy was still reeling.

But Tamerlane had only fired six missiles. That wasn't even close to massive.

Could he be running short of ordnance? Maybe trying to conserve his missiles?

But that made no sense. Aegis was the only force standing between the attackers and Manticore. Tamerlane had nothing to gain by saving his missiles instead of spending them right here and now.

The man was up to something. The question was, what?

Perrow had spotted it, too. "Pretty small follow-up," she commented uneasily.

Locatelli didn't reply. Metzger watched as the missile traces crawled their ever-increasingly quick way toward Aegis. "Admiral?" she prompted.

"He's goading us," Locatelli said abruptly. "Trying to make us return fire."

Metzger frowned. Okay, that *could* be what he was doing. A massive salvo would overwhelm *Invincible*'s telemetry and control systems, forcing her to choose between controlling her countermissiles or sending out a salvo of missiles of her own. By sending only six missiles, maybe Tamerlane was offering Aegis the chance to fire back.

But to what end? Tamerlane had already traded missiles, countermissiles, and autocannon rounds with the RMN ships. What else was he hoping to learn?

"And since he probably already knows everything about our armament that he needs to," Locatelli continued, "it follows that he's simply trying to get us to waste some missiles. TO, what was the final count on our practice missiles again?"

"Four, Sir," Perrow said.

"Launch them," Locatelli ordered. "All four, and target the battlecruiser." He gave a little snort. "He wants us to take a shot at him. Let's not keep the man waiting."

☆　　☆　　☆

"Missile trace," Clymes called out. "Missile trace four; ETA one hundred twenty seconds."

Gensonne smiled. Green One's commander had taken the bait. He'd fired back at the invaders; and in so doing, he'd just wasted four precious missiles.

"All ships: cease acceleration on my mark," he called toward his microphone. "*Mark*. Roll and yaw ninety-ninety on my mark. *Mark*."

He shifted his attention to the tactical. The five ships of his advance force were moving precisely as ordered, in perfect synch with each other. Now, when Green One's missiles arrived, they would find nothing to expend their energy on but a set of five impenetrable wedges. A standard enough tactic, as far as such things went.

Only Gensonne wasn't going to play it the standard way. As soon as his ships' turn was finished, leaving them pointed cross-wise to their current vector, they would run their impellers to full acceleration, moving out of the Manticorans' attack envelope.

And with that, he would force Locatelli into an impossible choice. He could turn aside in an attempt to chase down Gensonne, thus leaving Manticore open to Captain De la Roza's force. Or he could hold course and face De la Roza directly, thus leaving Gensonne free to create as much havoc as he chose. Or he could split his forces and try to do both.

Gensonne rather hoped he would choose the third option. It would make the enemy so much easier to destroy.

But whatever Locatelli did, it didn't matter. He'd already lost. He just didn't know it yet.

☆　　☆　　☆

Phoenix's bubble of mercy turned out to be larger than Oster-man had feared, extending across most of the portside bow and continuing aft almost to the bridge and CIC. It was also wider, extending all the way out to Axial Three in places.

But none of it was in better shape than Forward Weapons. Most of it was much worse.

And then there were the bodies. They were everywhere: floating twisted and limp, some with clothing matted with blood, others burned instantly by burst plasma conduits, others with no visible marks at all. It wasn't until she reached Beam Weapon Control that she finally found another living human being.

And even then, the universe had one last joke to play on her.

"About time," Ensign Locatelli rasped as Osterman eased herself through the hatchway into the compartment. "I was starting to think the whole crew had deserted their posts."

Despite the deadly seriousness of the situation, Osterman had to fight to keep from rolling her eyes. The kid was trying for the same kind of gallows levity his uncle was reported to have shown in the Gryphon Snarlery crisis thirty years ago. Only, as usual, he didn't have the history or the basic chops to pull it off.

"Not unless you consider being called to a higher court or getting caught on the wrong side of a blast door as desertion, Sir," she said. "Are you hurt?"

"I'll live," Locatelli said. "On second thought, probably not. How bad is it?"

"Bad enough," Osterman said, moved by some obscure impulse to cushion her customary bluntness. "As far as I can tell, this is the only section of the ship that's still intact. Every internal com I've tried is down, and, I haven't been able to raise anyone on my uni-link."

"Maybe that's because your uni-link isn't working," Locatelli said. "I've been trying, too, and you obviously didn't hear me."

Osterman scowled. It said a lot for the foggy state of her mind that that possibility had never occurred to her. The indicator light said her uni-link was working, so it must be working. She really should have known better.

"We've got a couple of compartments aft that are still holding pressure," the ensign continued, jabbing a thumb at the damage control schematic. "I haven't been able to get through to anyone in any of them, either, but there could be damage control parties headed this way right now."

"Maybe," she said, unwilling to spot him the point. "Bottom

line: they aren't here now, and even if they show up we're still defenseless and toothless. If Tamerlane decides we're worth another missile, we're done."

"Maybe," Locatelli said. "Maybe not."

"Maybe not *what*?" Osterman gritted. She hated it when people went all coy and clever. "Not done?"

"Not toothless." Locatelli pointed a finger at the status display to his left. "According to this, *Phoenix*'s laser is still functional."

Osterman caught her breath, hardly noticing the extra-sharp twinge in her side. The laser was still *functional*? That couldn't be right.

But the status display begged to differ. The lights and numbers did indeed show that the laser could still be fired.

If they could get it some power. *If* they could repair the control and firing circuits. *If* they could find some sensors and maneuvering jets to aim it.

And *if* they could find a target worth all that effort.

The first three were by no means guaranteed. But as for the fourth . . .

"Did you happen to notice how far away the second wave was from us when we got hit?" she asked. "I was busy monitoring the autocannon."

"As of a couple of minutes before we were hit, they were thirty-six minutes out," Locatelli said.

"So they're probably around twenty-five minutes away," Osterman said. "Looks like the capacitors have grounded, so we're going to have to kluge some cascade relays directly into the plasma stream. Can you go get them? My left arm's not good for much."

"Sure," Locatelli said. Popping his straps, he pushed himself out of the monitor station.

And as he floated up into the middle of the compartment, Osterman felt a shiver run through her. From the knee down, Locatelli's right leg was gone, the cut end of his vac suit flapping gently as he moved.

"I figured the medics were busy, so I bandaged it myself," the kid said. "The cascade relays are in Number Six?"

"Should be, yes," Osterman said mechanically, trying without success to tear her eyes from Locatelli's torn leg. "I'll head up to the line control crawlspace and see what it'll take to get the targeting running. Meet me there. Sir."

"Right."

The ensign floated out of the compartment and disappeared down the passageway. Osterman shook her head sharply, the resulting jolt of pain clearing her frozen mind, and headed for the hatchway.

She'd seen accidents where men and women had lost body parts. She'd seldom seen anyone handle the situation this well. Maybe Locatelli had inherited more of his uncle's personality, drive, and toughness than anyone had given him credit for.

More than *she* had given him credit for.

She headed down the passage, a surprising thread of optimism appearing through the darkness of the situation. She'd started this project as little more than a make-work job, something to keep her mind and hands busy while she waited to die. Now, suddenly, it had become something more.

Maybe—just maybe—*Phoenix* wasn't yet out of the fight.

☆   ☆   ☆

"Aspect change, Captain," Commander Jenz reported from *Thor*'s CIC. "*Casey* is definitely rolling above us."

"And angling negative to kill her positive momentum," Obregad, the TO, added. "Plus she's still working on killing her forward vector. Looks like she's planning to come up on our rear, all right."

"Of course she's planning to come up on our rear," De la Roza growled, glaring at the tactical. When *Casey* had first headed positive, he'd hoped Heissman was being smart and bugging out.

But no. He was clearly the kind of noble idiot who didn't know a losing battle when he was in one. Either that, or the Manticorans had the death penalty for desertion under fire. De la Roza had worked in systems where that was the case.

Because at this point, further resistance was completely and utterly useless. The Volsungs would win, the Manticoran government would surrender, and that would be that. There wouldn't be any wholescale nuking of the planet; no rape and pillage and looting; no cries of children, no wholescale arson, no economic collapse. The King would surrender, and life would pretty much return to usual.

Heissman wasn't protecting friends and family anymore. All he was protecting was Manticore's government. De la Roza had seen plenty of governments come and go, often with the average citizen barely noticing.

But the *Casey*'s commander was clearly determined to be stubborn. And that stubbornness was going to cost him.

Unfortunately, it was going to cost the Volsungs, too. CIC's current projection was that *Casey* would be able to kill her current vector—forward for *Casey*, backward for the Volsung force Heissman was trying to catch—and get nearly to missile range before *Thor* and the rest of his force reached engagement distance with the approaching Green One ships. Unless De la Roza wanted a gadfly at his rear, he was going to have to detach one of his ships to deal with her.

Only it wasn't quite that simple. CIC was sifting through the data Gensonne had sent, but they still didn't know how the damn light cruiser had taken out *Tyr*. If *Casey* tried it again against whoever De la Roza sent, it might be smart to make sure there was a second ship close enough to see what the hell the Manticorans' secret weapon was. The problem was that detaching two ships would drop his force down to six. Worse, one of the logical ships to detach to block *Casey* was the destroyer *Fox*, which was currently trailing behind the main force in com-relay position. Without someone back there, De la Roza would have to risk the miscommunication that often happened to ships trying to lase messages and data through their sidewalls.

But it was a risk he would have to take. There was no way in hell he was going to take *three* of his ships out of the combat stack.

Still, the Volsungs continued to hold the high ground here, both in absolute number of ships and sheer capability. Unexpected losses or no, they were still on track to win this thing.

"Signal *Fox* and *Selene*," he ordered. "They're to fall back and dog *Casey*'s vector: engage and destroy. And tell them to be quick about it."

☆   ☆   ☆

"All ships have rolled wedges, Admiral," Imbar reported.

"Good," Gensonne said, studying the gravitics display. A nicely executed maneuver. Whatever slippage might have occurred earlier, all of his captains and crews were back to their top game. "Signal all ships to hold vector until the incoming missiles have been destroyed. On my mark, we'll move out on our current heading at one-sixty-five gees. Once we do, *Adder* and *Ganymede* will move to forward positions and *Phobos* will fall back into com-relay position."

"Yes, Sir," Imbar said. "Anything else?"

Gensonne pursed his lips, studying the tactical. De la Roza's main force was still nearly half an hour behind him, and of course Gensonne's group was about to diverge from them anyway. The loss of his second battlecruiser couldn't be made up, but it might be wise to at least bolster his numbers a bit. *Umbriel* and *Miranda* were still angling away from him, but the geometry was such that they could rejoin him without too much trouble.

"Signal Sidewinder Force," he told the captain. "Have them alter course to match our vector and stay with us. Warn them to stay on their toes—we may shift our vector as the need arises."

"Yes, Sir," Imbar said again. "Ah...I assume you've noted that changing course to rendezvous with us will take them within missile range of the two Manticoran forces currently hunting them?"

"Then they'll be close enough to destroy them, won't they?" Gensonne countered.

"I meant...yes, Sir," Imbar said, changing his mind.

As well he should. Two Volsung destroyers against a destroyer and a couple of corvettes?

Especially when the two corvettes weren't even regular Navy, but Manticoran Patrol and Rescue Service. Llyn's intel report had included a full rundown on the so-called MPARS, and it was about as pitiful a collection of military wannabes as Gensonne could imagine. If Captains Patterson and Hawkin couldn't figure out how to take out that kind of challenge they deserved to be blown out of the sky.

He felt his throat tighten. Ironically, he could remember thinking the exact same thing about *Tyr*'s Captain Blakely on occasion, too. *That* hadn't ended very well.

"Fine," he growled. "Emphasize to Captains Patterson and Hawkin that they're to watch themselves and not get cocky. The Manticorans aren't quite the pushovers we were promised."

"Yes, Sir," Imbar said, sounding marginally happier that he would now be giving the Sidewinder force an extra head's-up.

Gensonne snorted again. The Volsungs still had the advantage. They were still going to win.

And whatever ships and men Locatelli cost him, Llyn and his bosses at Axelrod would replace them. Gensonne would make sure of that.

CHAPTER TWENTY-FOUR

BY THE TIME ENSIGN LOCATELLI RETURNED with the cascade relays, Osterman had most of the wiring fixed, rerouted, or half-assed kluged.

Which had sounded a lot easier up front than it had turned out to be. Several of the plasma conduits had been ruptured in the attack, and though the plasma itself had long since dissipated it had left behind jagged tangles of superheated metal and plastic. Osterman sported a half dozen new burns of varying degrees, plus a couple of new cuts along her cheek and side.

She'd thrown bandages on the worst of them. More pain medication would have been nice, but she couldn't take the risk. Throbbing agony was a distraction, but she could work through it. Numbness and mental fog she absolutely couldn't afford.

She'd skipped the usual disinfectant protocols, of course. No point to any of that.

"What the hell took you so long?" she growled as he maneuvered the package through the hatchway. That wasn't how petty officers were supposed to talk to officers, but her arm was aching fiercely in counterpoint to her new burns and cuts, and she was in no mood to play a game that was in its last few minutes anyway.

"I had to go right to the edge of CIC to collect enough of the relays," he said, his face screwed up with quiet agony. He'd collected a few fresh burns of his own, Osterman noted with a twinge of guilt, and it was a good bet that he'd gone as light on the pain meds as she had. "From what I could see through the hatch vision port, it looked like CIC was breached and depressurized before they could get their helmets on."

Osterman nodded heavily. She'd held out the secret hope that either the bridge or CIC had survived, and simply hadn't responded for some reason to Locatelli's uni-link calls. Clearly, they hadn't.

"But it looked like at least some of the gear is still functional," Locatelli continued. "Most importantly, the com repeater system."

"Really," Osterman said, a small flicker of hope twisting through the knot in her stomach. If they could contact *Invincible* or *Swiftsure*, their range of options would suddenly open up.

The brief hope evaporated. To get into CIC would require her to set up a micro airlock, and there was no way she could do that with only one useable arm.

"I can't go in there," Locatelli continued, gesturing toward the tear in his vac suit where his leg had been. "But *you* can."

"Except—"

"I've already got the micro lock set up for you," he said. "I figure that between you and *Invincible* you can come up with a plan."

"Yes, Sir," Osterman said, her grudging new respect for the kid rising yet another grudging notch. "Can you get those relays installed by yourself?"

"I'm an officer, Chief," Locatelli said, giving her the pain-colored ghost of a smile. "We can do anything. Says so in the manual. Get going—if I finish before you get back, I'll be forward with the tracking sensors."

☆　　☆　　☆

In perfect unison, the five ships of Group One pitch/yawed wedge.

Just in time for Aegis's missile salvo to be obliterated by the invaders' wedges.

Metzger smiled tightly. The admiral had called it, all right. Tamerlane had been playing it cute.

Little did he know he'd pulled out only half a victory.

"Practice missiles impacted on the battlecruiser's stress band," Perrow confirmed.

And now, having goaded Aegis into wasting what he assumed were real missiles, Tamerlane would come back around to face his opponents.

Only the invaders weren't rolling. Instead—

"Acceleration!" Perrow snapped. "Group One is heading— Admiral, they're *running*."

Metzger stared at the tactical in disbelief. They were running, all right, their new course taking them away from Aegis's vector at a sharp angle.

"Hardly," Locatelli said grimly. "Tamerlane's simply splitting his forces."

"But that doesn't make sense," Metzger protested. "The two groups together have an overwhelming force. Splitting them up leaves each one on a par with us."

"On paper, maybe," Perrow muttered. "Probably not in reality."

"You're missing the big picture, Captain," Locatelli said. "Tamerlane understands his chess. He's not out to destroy pawns, per se, but to checkmate the king. In this case, quite literally."

Metzger felt her stomach tighten. Of course. If Tamerlane could get past Aegis and reach Manticore, he could sit in orbit and deliver an ultimatum straight to Landing and King Edward.

And Eridani Edict or no, the king couldn't trust the invaders not to do something horrendously devastating. He would either have to surrender or else risk the destruction of his world and his people.

"Which leaves us only one option," Locatelli continued. "TO, plot me a course to come up behind Group One. Once you have it, send it to all ships, and inform them that on my mark Aegis will be doing a yaw turn to pursue Group One and engage."

"Leaving Group Two unopposed, Sir?" Metzger asked quietly.

"Group Two is twenty minutes away," Locatelli reminded him. "Group One has a clear opening all the way to Manticore. For better or for worse, that's the one we have to deal with first."

Metzger sighed. "Understood."

"Course computed, Admiral," Perrow reported.

Her proposed course joined the rest of the ship vectors on Metzger's tac display. She studied it, the knots in her stomach tightening another few turns. This was a bad idea—she could feel it in her bones. Getting Aegis to chase his ships was exactly what Tamerlane wanted them to do, and Locatelli was going to walk right into whatever trap their enemies were planning.

But Locatelli was right. Manticore was under two separate threats, and Green One was all that stood in the Star Kingdom's defense. The threats had to be dealt with in order.

Admiral Locatelli, the overall System Commander, had made his decision. It was Metzger's job to follow the orders she'd been given, and hope that the missile base on Thorson would somehow be up to the task of holding off Group Two until Aegis could deal with Group One and return.

Assuming Aegis was up to *that* task.

"All ships standing by, Admiral," McBride reported.

"Thank you, XO," Locatelli said. "On my mark..."

"Sir!" Chief Warren called suddenly from the com station, half turning to look wide-eyed at Locatelli. "We're getting a signal. It's weak and the focus is a little erratic—" His throat worked. "Sir...it's from *Phoenix*."

☆　　☆　　☆

"Watch it, Captain," Lisa called into the microphone. "They're changing course."

The seconds of the time-delay counted down—a shorter delay, now, than it had been at the beginning of the pursuit. Lisa took advantage of the lull to run the numbers on Group Three's latest maneuver. They were doing a yaw turn to starboard, and had thrown a few more gees into their deceleration. Added up, it looked like they'd given up on their original thrust toward Manticore. Was it possible they'd decided to abort and run?

She snorted under her breath. No, of course not. A more careful look at the newly-altered vector of Tamerlane's force made it clear that the destroyers were simply heading back to hook up with Group One.

"I see them, Commander," Hardasty's voice came back. "Adjusting our course to maintain intercept vector. I see Group One is on the move, too. Think they're trying to hook up together?"

"Looks that way," Lisa confirmed. The destroyers were still fine-tuning their maneuver, and she made sure to fine-tune her own readings and analysis accordingly.

"Good," Hardasty said with satisfaction.

Lisa felt her throat tighten. Hardasty could call it good if she wanted. After all, the two MPARS ships were still a fair ways out, and by the time they reached missile range her projection was that the enemy destroyers would probably be flank-on to them, with no way to launch any sort of attack in their direction.

Damocles, unfortunately, was in a much less sanguine position. The destroyers' new course wouldn't *quite* put them nose-to-nose with her, but there would be enough of an opening through the edge of their widened throats to make missile exchanges possible.

And *Damocles* only had seven missiles to spend in that exchange. With two opponents with an unknown number of missiles in their own arsenals, that wasn't a happy balance.

"TO?" Marcello's voice came over the CIC speaker.

"I've got a revised course, Sir," Lisa called back. "Sending it to you now."

"Are missiles and crews ready?"

Lisa checked the reports again. "Both launchers signal ready, Captain," she confirmed. "Lieutenant Nikkelsen claims his crews will be able to reload the launchers in thirty-five seconds."

"Tell him they'll have twenty-five," Marcello said. "Better—tell him that I'll be treating the fastest crew to dinner and an open bar in Landing when this is over."

Lisa smiled despite the tension dragging at her face. A nice, generous, morale-boosting offer.

Too bad there wouldn't be anyone left alive to collect.

"I'll pass that on, Sir," she said.

"Good," Marcello said. "Helm, initiate the new course. These bastards are running for mama. Let's see if we can nail them before they get there."

☆　☆　☆

Gensonne's first, incredulous thought was that his little Thu'ban Sidestep maneuver had caught Locatelli by surprise.

Because it certainly looked like it had. Off on his port flank now, Green One was just sitting there, still pointed at the spot where Gensonne's force had been a few seconds ago.

But as the seconds turned into a minute, and still no movement, he realized that the Manticoran hadn't simply been surprised by *Odin*'s departure. He'd seen it, all right, assessed the situation, and decided to wait for De la Roza and *Thor* instead.

Gensonne shook his head. There were really no good decisions here, but letting the advance force go in favor of taking on De la Roza was the worst of the lot.

Because the battle Locatelli had now committed himself to would never happen. At least, not in the way he thought it would. As soon as the advance force was far enough away that Green One could no longer catch it, Gensonne would order De la Roza to break off and run transverse to his current vector, drawing Locatelli even farther out of position and leaving Gensonne plenty of time to reach Manticore, destroy the lunar defenses, and deliver his ultimatum.

And once the King surrendered, it wouldn't matter how many ships or missiles the Royal Manticoran Navy had left. With the nation's capitulation, the RMN would be legally required to stand down.

"Aspect change," Clymes reported. "Green One battlecruiser turning toward us."

Again, Gensonne shook his head. Making the wrong decision was bad enough. But making the wrong decision, then changing his mind and trying a different one, was even worse. All Locatelli had accomplished was to waste some time and throw his force into confusion—

"Missile trace," Clymes added. "Missile trace four—tight cluster. Acceleration thirty-five hundred gees; impact time ninety-two seconds."

Gensonne frowned as he studied the tactical. All right, so Locatelli *wasn't* a complete idiot. He'd simply been waiting to turn and fire until the Volsungs' new angled vector had opened the aft end of their sidewalls to attack.

It wasn't a classic up-the-kilt shot, of course, and it would take some very fancy telemetry control to make it work. But if those missiles could be made to pass the edge of the Volsungs' sidewalls and explode before they impacted on the far sidewall or the wedge they could still do serious damage.

Worse, because it wasn't a straight up-the-kilt shot, *Odin's* ECM would be trying to operate through her own sidewall and therefore be effectively useless. The missile would have a free ride right up until the point where it cleared the sidewall.

Could that be the Manticorans' secret weapon? Not a weapon at all, but merely a breakthrough advance in missile control?

Possibly. Certainly that kind of back-room R&D wasn't like fancy hardware that Llyn's spies and information grabs might have missed.

It was very unlikely, he knew. Llyn's people couldn't be *that* incompetent.

Still . . .

"Signal all ships," he ordered. "Cease acceleration on my mark, then pitch thirty degrees negative on my mark."

"Thirty degrees, Sir?" Imbar asked, a frown in his voice.

"Did I say thirty degrees, Captain?" Gensonne shot back. "Then make it thirty degrees."

Which was really a shade more than they needed, he knew. But after *Tyr*, Gensonne was inclined to err on the side of caution. A thirty-degree shift in their course would put their sidewalls directly across the battlecruiser's line of fire, eliminating that angled back door. "They're going to fire some missiles," he continued. Imbar didn't deserve an explanation, but there was no reason not to give him one.

"Will we then be returning to our present course?" Imbar persisted. "Or will we stay on that new one?"

There was some implied criticism in the question, Gensonne noted. More than Gensonne deserved. Definitely more than Imbar was entitled to deliver. Maybe he thought the Old Man was losing his nerve.

Maybe someone else would be promoted to *Odin*'s captain after all this was over.

"We'll keep with that course," Gensonne told him, making it clear that the discussion was over. "It'll take us where we need to go. Maybe not as quickly or as directly. But it'll take us there."

"Yes, Sir," Imbar said, the same undercurrent of reservation in his voice.

Gensonne turned back to the tactical. The hell with him. The hell with all of them. Let them think whatever they wanted. All he cared about was getting this over with without losing any more of his ships.

"Cease acceleration: *mark*," he said, watching the monitors. *Odin*'s acceleration dropped to zero as the impellers eased their pressure on the stress bands. He looked at the missiles, checked the tactical's projected impact... "Pitch: *mark*."

"Pitching," Clymes confirmed. "Sidewalls in blocking position. Missile impacts in twenty seconds."

Gensonne watched the tactical. The Manticorans weren't as helpless as he'd first thought. He'd learned that the hard way.

But as long as he was able to anticipate their movements, all their grand strategy and clever tactics amounted to little more than useless flailing.

Because there was still no way they could win. No way at all.

☆　　☆　　☆

"Loop complete, Captain," Woodburn announced from *Casey*'s tactical station. "Looks like they left us a reception committee."

"It does, doesn't it?" Heissman agreed. "Celia, what do you make of them?"

"They're both destroyers," Belokas's voice came from CIC. "One is *Hyperion* class; the other isn't coming up on our ID list."

"Something new?" Heissman asked.

"More likely something obscure and obsolete," Belokas said. "All their stuff seems to be surplused or secondhand."

Heissman grunted. "Be grateful for small favors."

Travis studied the tactical. The two enemy destroyers had formed a stack in front of them, moving backwards at presumably the speed the rest of the group had been traveling when they detached and turned to face *Casey*'s projected vector.

They weren't accelerating toward *Casey*, as if preparing to engage. That was something. But the fact that the rest of the invasion force was still accelerating toward Manticore meant the two ships still blocked any advance *Casey* might try to make.

"So how do you want to play this, Alfred?" Heissman asked.

"That depends on what we're going for," Woodburn said. "If we just want to pin them here, then we should keep accelerating until we match their speed, then hold position, looking mean and growling a lot. If we want to try for a kill—and not get killed ourselves—we need to find an opening. As things stand, unless they're out of autocannon rounds, throwing missiles at them is probably not going to accomplish much. Especially since they can always pitch wedge against our salvo without losing their formation."

"Celia?"

"I'm leaning toward Alfred's first option," Belokas said. "We can't realistically take them out, not with only six missiles left and two-to-one odds."

"Agreed," Heissman said. He cocked an eyebrow. "Unless Lieutenant Long has any suggestions?"

Travis looked at the tactical again, trying hard to think. They couldn't just sit back here, not with the Star Kingdom in deadly danger and the rest of the Navy engaged.

But he had nothing. "No, Sir," he admitted. "The stalking-horse gambit might work, but only if they pitch wedge for the first missile and then pitch back in time for the second. If they use autocannon, they'd probably take out both missiles."

"And they're unlikely to be considerate enough to pitch wedge for us," Woodburn said. "Though we'll keep that in reserve if it looks like either is turning back to the battle. At that point we might as well drain some of their point defenses."

"Of course, if one or both turn back, we'll have clear shots up their kilts," Heissman pointed out. "And we're likely fast enough to catch up to missile range before they can rejoin the rest of their group. Very well. Helm, match their velocity. Once we're there, add enough so that we're drifting toward them—not too fast, just enough to make them think we're angling to get into missile range."

"Accelerating, aye, Commodore."

"And what was the rest, Alfred?" Heissman asked.

"Look mean and growl a lot?"

"Right," Heissman said. "Let's figure out exactly how we do that."

☆   ☆   ☆

"Uh-oh," Ensign Kyell said tightly from the other side of *Aries*'s secondary tracking system. "They're changing course again."

"Which way this time?" Chomps asked, grunting out the last word as the bolt he'd been fighting with finally gave up and came loose.

"Not ours," Kyell corrected. "Not Group Three, I mean, at least not yet. I mean the first-wave force—Group One—Tamerlane's ships. They've angled...looks like a little to port."

"Is Aegis correcting to match?" Chomps asked, peering into the guts of the tracking console and resisting the urge to curse whoever had done the incredibly sloppy job of rewiring the thing. Husovski, probably—the woman didn't have the brains God gave celery, and believed herself well-enough connected that she didn't need them.

But at least the problem was obvious. That loose wire floating along the edge needed to be resoldered to the hex connector right *there*. Easing two fingers and the soldering iron into the gap, he tacked the wire back in place.

"Not so far—wait a second," Kyell interrupted himself. "Yeah, there they go."

"Aegis?"

"No, Group Three."

Once again, Chomps sat firmly on his temper. "Where exactly are they going?"

"They're adjusting," Kyell said. "I'm guessing they're back on an intercept course with Group One's new vector. Not really sure."

Chomps poked his head over the top of the console and peered at the display. *Aries*'s tracking software was about as lame as it could get, and the ship didn't have any tactical computing capability worth beans.

But as near as his own untrained eye could tell, Kyell was right. The two destroyers of Group Three were still trying to make a rendezvous with Tamerlane's Group One.

"Looks like it," he told Kyell. "Wish I could tell whether that was going to bring them closer to us or to *Damocles*."

Kyell hissed between his teeth. "*I* wish I knew which one I was hoping for," he muttered. "God, I feel like I'm going to throw up. Is going into battle always like this?"

Chomps stifled a sigh. Like he would know *that*.

But he didn't say it. Kyell was scared—probably everyone aboard was scared.

Chomps couldn't really blame them. At least he'd started life in the RMN, where everyone had at least had some basic training in battle technique, even if they never expected to use it. These poor dumb MPARS weenies didn't even have that.

They were scared. But they were still doing their jobs.

And they were doing those jobs well. Damn well. Better than he would ever have guessed them capable of. Despite MPARS being basically fed off the Navy's scraps—and with his new first-hand knowledge, he knew exactly the quality of scraps they were getting, Breakwater's efforts notwithstanding—*Aries* was still flying, and her officers and crew still preparing to fight and probably die for the Star Kingdom.

And in perhaps the final irony, *Aries*'s people had shoved aside all the years' worth of rivalry and defensive animosity and were looking to Chomps and the handful of other RMN people aboard for leadership and encouragement. After months of being looked down on by those same weenies, and admittedly looking down on them in turn, it felt like a rush of fresh air.

Now all he had to do was live long enough for all this new-found respect and camaraderie to pay out some dividends.

That was going to be the tricky part. Chomps wasn't exactly privy to bridge chatter up here in Weapons, but as near as he could figure from the displays *Damocles* and the two MPARS ships were going to get into missile range of the enemy destroyers at approximately the same time. If anything, in fact, *Aries* and *Taurus* would probably get there a little sooner.

Which was theoretically just fine. Despite the chronic weapons shortages everywhere in the Star Kingdom, Chancellor Break-water had managed to scare up three missiles each for his two new corvettes. Not a huge number; but then, typical destroyer defenses weren't exactly generous to begin with and the bandits must have used at least some of their autocannon rounds in their brief encounter with *Casey* and the Janus force. Once the fighting started, the six missiles that *Aries* and *Taurus* had between them should make a good accounting for themselves.

The problem was that throwing those missiles was about *all* the corvettes could do, because if the destroyers fired back they would be up the devil's own favorite fishing creek. Breakwater hadn't been nearly as vigilant about the corvettes' defenses as he had about their missiles, and *Aries*, at least, was running barely quarter-loads on her two autocannon. One good salvo from the enemy would drain them, and then it would be roll wedge or else get the hell out of Dodge, both of which would take *Aries* out of the fight.

And to Chomps's mild surprise, he could sense that the officers and crew of his new ship weren't going to do that. They might be MPARS weenies, but they were also citizens of the Star King-dom. They would do whatever they could to protect their worlds.

Which, again, didn't mean that they couldn't use a little reas-surance. "Every battle's different," he told Kyell, quoting from the boot-camp list of sage military platitudes. "You just need to be as prepared as you can be..."

He trailed off. The lines on the display were changing...

"What?" Kyell asked anxiously, turning his head toward the monitor. "What is it?"

For a moment Chomps continued to gaze at the monitor. If he was reading the thing right—and there was half a chance he wasn't—

Pressing his wrench onto the tac strip, he gave himself a shove across the compartment to the intercom. "Bridge; Forward Mis-siles," he called. "Is the—?"

"What's wrong?" the XO interrupted. "Trouble with the missiles?"

"No, Sir, no trouble," Chomps assured him. "I need to know if the ship vectors we're getting are true or projections."

"They're true, Townsend," Captain Hardasty voice cut in. "Why?"

"Because it looks to me like Group Three have themselves in a pickle," Chomps said. "When we reach missile range—which is, what, about ten minutes from now?"

"Twelve and a half," Hardasty said. "And *Damocles* will get there about five minutes behind us. What's your point?"

"My point, Ma'am, is that in the position they're in, they can put their wedge or sidewalls against us and *Taurus*, or they can block against *Damocles*, but they can't block all of us at the same time."

There was a pause. "All right, yes, I see that," Hardasty said slowly. "So what does that mean?"

"It means, Ma'am," Chomps said, feeling a smile creasing his cheeks, "that we may just have an unexpected edge here. Here's my thought..."

☆ ☆ ☆

"She's definitely altering course, Admiral," Clymes said, his tone halfway between disbelief and excitement. "She's...yes. She's leaving the Green One formation and coming after us."

Gensonne shook his head. Unbelievable. Yet another mistake for The Grand Poo-Bah Admiral Locatelli.

And this one was huge. Fatally huge. The whole point of splitting the Volsung forces had been to tempt the Manticoran commander into splitting his. Now, as *Odin* and her escorts veered away, the Manticoran had finally taken that bait.

Only he'd done it in the worst possible way. Instead of dividing his remaining seven ships into more or less equal groups, he was sending his second battlecruiser, alone and unsupported, to chase after Gensonne's force.

Granted she would be coming up behind him, with *Odin*'s kilt hanging invitingly open. But it was still a foolish and desperate move.

Maybe that was all the Manticorans had left. Foolish and desperate moves.

Unfortunately for Locatelli, in this case it wasn't just desperation. It was suicide.

Because he'd apparently forgotten that De la Roza's ships were nearing missile range. And that they, too, could change course.

"Signal *Thor*," he ordered. "Tell De la Roza that I have a barreled fish for him."

"Aye, aye, Admiral."

"You really want him to divert for this?" Imbar asked quietly. "Maybe that's what Locatelli's going for."

"To what end?" Gensonne scoffed. "Diverting De la Roza's advance? Not even worth the effort."

"I meant moving *Thor* off her vector," Imbar persisted.

"Again, why?" Gensonne countered. "Besides, De la Roza won't *be* changing his vector. All he needs to do is kill his acceleration, yaw about twenty degrees, and fire a couple of missiles up the battlecruiser's kilt. Yaw back, and he's maybe two minutes behind his current schedule. Two minutes won't make or break anything."

"I suppose," Imbar said reluctantly. "The move just seems so ... stupid."

"They're out of ideas," Gensonne said. "This way, at least, they go out fighting instead of surrendering."

"There is that," Imbar agreed, still sounding doubtful.

"Captain De la Roza acknowledges, Admiral," the Com rating called. "He says to enjoy the show."

"We will," Gensonne said, smiling. Three minutes from now, four at the most, and he would once again have a two-to-one battlecruiser superiority over the Manticorans.

Nothing would make up for *Tyr*'s loss. But this would help.

And yes, he would indeed enjoy the show. Very much.

☆   ☆   ☆

"Your Majesty; My Lord?" the petty officer called from the monitor station. "*Vanguard* and *Nike* report ready to sail."

Edward felt his throat tighten. Ready to sail. Not ready to fight, or to defend themselves, or even to seriously threaten. Just ready to sail.

But that was all the Star Kingdom had.

"Your Majesty?" Cazenestro murmured from his side.

Edward braced himself. When crumbs were all you had, crumbs were what you ate. "Signal Admiral Locatelli that we're sending them out," he said. Technically, he knew, Locatelli should be the one making this decision, not the King and the First Lord. But Locatelli was light-minutes away, and fighting for his task force's survival. He already had enough human lives resting in his hands. "Then give the order."

Cazenestro nodded. "Send them out," he called to the petty officer.

He looked at Edward. "And may God have mercy on their souls," he added quietly.

Edward nodded soberly. "And on ours."

CHAPTER TWENTY-FIVE

TO CHOMPS'S SURPRISE, HARDASTY AGREED.

Not that agreement necessarily meant enthusiasm.

"You'd better be right about this," she warned, three separate times. "We're sticking our butts out on this, big time."

"Yes, Ma'am," Chomps said. "It'll work, Ma'am."

Hardasty's grunt was clearly audible over the speaker.

"It had better," she said, for the fourth time. "And you're sure Commander Donnelly will also get it?"

"Yes, Ma'am," Chomps said, for the fourth time.

At least he sure as hell hoped she did. *Damocles* was too close to the enemy destroyers for them to risk even an encrypted laser signal to clue Captain Marcello in on the plan.

But Lisa Donnelly was aboard, and Chomps knew from the Cascan incident that she was more than capable of picking up on this sort of thing.

He hoped she was paying really good attention.

"Okay," Hardasty said. "Here we go."

Chomps looked across the compartment at Kyell, found the other gazing back at him. Giving the ensign a smile and a thumb's-up, he turned back to his console.

It certainly *should* work, he knew. That pirated freighter—*Izbica*—had been the last unusual or unfamiliar ship in Manticoran space, certainly the last such visitor preceding this invasion. Logically, it was likely the source of the most up-to-date intel Tamerlane could have received before his attack.

Chomps knew what Tamerlane was likely to know. The only question was how clever Tamerlane and his captains were.

And just as importantly, how clever they *thought* they were.

"Unidentified warships, this is Captain Ellen Hardasty of the Manticoran Patrol and Rescue Service ship *Aries*," Hardasty's authoritative voice came over the speaker. "You are hereby ordered—"

☆   ☆   ☆

"—to strike your wedges and surrender," Captain Hardasty's harsh voice came over *Damocles*'s CIC speakers. "If you fail to do so, we *will* open fire."

"What the *hell*?" Shiflett's voice muttered beneath the words coming from the com relay.

"We have a full complement of Zulu Kickback missiles," Hardasty continued, "and full authorization to use them. I say again: strike your wedges or be destroyed."

Lisa caught her breath. *Zulu Kickback . . .*

Townsend?

"Someone pull up a crew listing for *Aries*," she ordered. "See if Missile Tech Charles Townsend is still aboard."

"You've got something, TO?" Marcello's voice came.

"Maybe, Sir," Lisa said. "Remember Townsend on Casca?"

"A pain in the butt who almost got himself killed," Shiflett put in sourly.

"But who knew how to use bluffs and play to people's perceptions," Lisa reminded her. Her brain was spinning, sifting through Hardasty's words and trying to figure out what Townsend's angle was here. Was Zulu Kickback a reference to the Case Zulu live-ammo tests at Casey Rosewood, like it had been on Casca? Or was it simply there to let Lisa and Marcello know that he was playing something?

"Here it is, Ma'am," the lieutenant at the tracking station spoke up. "Yes, Townsend is still aboard *Aries*."

And, suddenly, Lisa got it. "Captain, we need to fire a missile at the destroyers," she said. "Right away."

"We're barely within range, TO," Marcello pointed out. "We'd do better to wait another few minutes."

"No, Sir, we need to fire now," Lisa said. "*Aries* is running a bluff. Rather, she's running a double bluff. We're both in missile range of the bandits, and they can't block both of us. That's why

Hardasty called out her threat. She wants to make them open their kilt to her."

"Why would they do that?" Shiflett objected. "*Aries* is closer to them than we are."

"Right," Lisa said, punching up a quick missile tracking vector. "But the destroyers know now that *Aries* and *Taurus* are MPARS ships.

"*And they know MPARS ships aren't armed.*"

For a long second the speaker went silent. Lisa held her breath, running the logic through her mind again. If that wasn't what Townsend was going for...

"Cute," Marcello murmured. "Let's see if it works. Give me a launch vector."

"Plotted and to you," Lisa said, keying the transfer.

"Got it," Marcello said. "Forward missiles, here are your vectors: one missile per target. Launch on my mark."

Lisa ran an eye over the status board. Everything looked normal.

But there was something lurking in the back of her mind. Something important.

Then, in a sudden rush, there it was. The last maintenance report on the dorsal launcher— "Wait—"

"*Fire!*"

With a thundering blast of sound, the whole ship bucked like a terrified horse, throwing Lisa against her restraints. There was a second roiling explosion, like the hull above her was being shattered.

And the universe went black.

☆   ☆   ☆

"*Damocles* has launched," Hardasty announced. "Targets..."

Chomps held his breath. Now if the invaders would just be clever enough to see through a poor, stupid Manticoran bluff...

"Targets are rolling wedge," Hardasty said. "Rolling to block *Damocles*...damn and a half. They're doing it. They're actually turning their kilts straight toward us."

Chomps smiled tightly. And if those were indeed Luna-class destroyers, they had no aft defenses. Which meant that if Hardasty was ready to put it all on the line—

"Signal *Taurus* to launch missiles," she ordered. "All three, targeted on the lower bandit—control as best they can, just get them moving. We'll take the upper one. Kyell?"

"We're ready, Ma'am," Kyell called toward the intercom, his voice trembling with excitement or fear or both. "Vectors set; missiles primed and charged."

"On my mark," Hardasty said. "Ready...*fire.*"

☆   ☆   ☆

"I can't tell a thing from this," Ensign Locatelli complained, his voice drifting back from the depths of the crawlspace that ran alongside the laser emitter. "Are you sure we've got the target?"

"Pretty sure, Sir, yes," Osterman said, peering at the uni-link she'd wired into the firing system.

Though in truth she wasn't nearly as certain as she would like to be. While *Phoenix*'s laser firing equipment was still functional, the software had been seriously corrupted in the destroyer's death throes.

Fortunately, she'd found an intact memory module in one of CIC's systems that had enough space for what they needed. *Invincible* had downloaded replacement software, and then Osterman had removed the module, brought it back to the fire-control system, and wired it in. The system display had been cooked along with the software, but she'd managed to solve that problem by wiring in a uni-link to act as a repeater and let her keep track of what she was doing.

She couldn't use her own uni-link, of course. She already knew it was damaged, and she wasn't about to risk using it for something this vital. She'd used Commander Sladek's instead, taking it off the XO's body.

Some people might have considered that ghoulish, Osterman reflected, stripping equipment from a dead officer's body. She preferred to think of it as Commander Sladek being a part of this last-ditch effort to strike a blow for King and kingdom. As if the XO's ghostly finger would now be alongside hers and Locatelli's on the firing switch.

The XO, a junior officer, and a senior petty officer. A nice yin/yang balance, really. If this story was ever told, Osterman suspected with a touch of grim humor, people would probably say that part was made up.

"Well, if they're going to take the bait, I wish they'd get to it," Locatelli muttered. "These things are getting hot."

Osterman frowned. "What things?"

"These relays," Locatelli said. "Yeah, I know they're supposed to be wired to the heat sinks. But the couplings were shot, and most of the brackets were too warped to work. It's okay—I've got them."

"Except—" Osterman clamped down hard on the protest. Except that the whole system was about to surge with an incredible burst of energy, and if there were any gaps in the containment sheath there was a good chance Locatelli would be vaporized.

A fact that was, at this point, completely irrelevant. The instant that laser fired, *something* was going to fail in this jury-rigged system she and the ensign had thrown together. Whether it was the current couplings, the plasma conduits or the damn reactor itself, they were both dead.

But that was okay. That was the risk she and Locatelli had both agreed to when they signed up.

Most of the rest of their shipmates had already paid that price. Time for them to do likewise.

Only please, God, she prayed silently, *first let us get off this one, last shot.*

"Chief, I've got movement," Locatelli snapped into her thoughts. "Can you confirm?"

Osterman focused on the uni-link's display. It was hard to see, but—

Yes. There was movement, all right. The second group of enemy ships had halted their acceleration and were coasting.

And as she clenched the uni-link tightly, she saw that the battlecruiser was doing a combined yaw/pitch, swiveling her bow toward the distant *Swiftsure* as the RMN ship chased after Tamerlane and the other battlecruiser.

Presenting her kilt to Group Two as the biggest, fattest bait around.

There was a distant hiss of attitude jets as the data from Locatelli's tracking system and *Invincible*'s downloaded programming combined to line up *Phoenix*'s dying hulk with the distant battlecruiser. "Almost there," she called to Locatelli.

"Fire as soon as we're on target," Locatelli ordered. "I don't want to trust this kluge any longer than we have to." He hesitated. "And let me say, Chief, that it's been an honor to serve with you. I hope I wasn't *too* much of a pain in the butt."

Osterman smiled. "No, Sir, not at all. No more than any other ensign."

"Thanks, Chief. See you on the other side."

The uni-link signaled target acquisition. Bracing herself, Osterman pressed the firing key.

She had just enough time to see the distant battlecruiser begin to disintegrate when *Phoenix*'s last remaining plasma line ruptured.

☆　　☆　　☆

"No!" someone screamed. "*No!*"

A full, rich, scream, Gensonne thought distantly as he stared at the tactical. The kind of scream that a woman would make, or a terrified child, or a coward.

It took him a full two seconds to realize that the scream had come from his own lips.

Someone on *Odin*'s bridge was swearing, long complicated, vicious curses. It might be Gensonne himself—he couldn't spare the mental energy to track it down. Every fiber of his being, every fraction of his brain was focused on the tactical display.

It wasn't possible. *It wasn't possible.*

But it had happened.

Thor was gone.

Disintegrated in the fury of laser fire.

But that was impossible. None of the Manticoran ships was even close to beam range. How in God's name could they have done it?

"There," a voice intruded into Gensonne's spinning mind. A dark voice, trembling with rage and hatred and accusation. Imbar's voice. "That cloud of debris—right there. That's where the shot came from."

With a supreme effort, Gensonne turned to follow the captain's pointing finger. The debris cloud, his numbed brain registered, was what was left of the Manticoran destroyer he'd already killed.

Only apparently he *hadn't* killed it. He'd only wounded it.

And in his casual arrogance he hadn't thought it worth wasting a missile to finish it off.

"*Damn* it!" Clymes snarled suddenly. "Admiral—they got *Umbriel*."

Gensonne swiveled around, his heart thudding, a second wave of disbelief flowing through the growing detachment. This was happening too fast. Way too fast. There shouldn't be this many shocks happening one right after the other. Modern warfare was slow, deliberate, with time to think—

"Admiral—"

"*Shut up!*" Gensonne snarled, twisting around to see who the damn fool was who had dared to interrupt his thoughts this time.

But no one was looking at him. Their eyes were on their consoles and displays, their faces studiously turned away from their admiral's wrath.

"Admiral!" the voice came again.

And this time, Gensonne belatedly recognized it: the ATO calling from CIC. "Yes, I know," he thundered. "*Thor*'s gone—*Umbriel*'s gone—"

"The hell with that," the ATO snarled back. "We've got two more battlecruisers coming up from Manticore orbit."

Gensonne felt his eyes widen. "Say again?"

"There are two damn battlecruisers coming from Manticore," the other said tensely. "God's sake, Admiral—what the hell do we *do*?"

With an effort, Gensonne found the right display. Two more wedges had indeed appeared, coming around the edge of Manticore's moon, heading out to join the battle.

"Admiral?" That was Imbar, his earlier fury replaced with apprehension.

It was a trick, of course. It had to be. There was no way the Manticorans had two more major warships to throw at him.

But it didn't matter. Even without them, the enemy now held the high ground. Gensonne was outmatched, and without a great deal of luck he couldn't expect to win.

And if those incoming battlecruisers *weren't* a trick...

"Signal all ships," he said quietly. Quietly, because there was no longer anything to be gained by shouting. "Break off and retreat. I say again, break off and retreat."

"Aye, aye, Admiral," Imbar said, and Gensonne thought he could hear a hint of relief in the captain's voice.

Small wonder. No matter how much armament and training a military force might have, without a modicum of luck there could be no expectation of victory.

And today, the Lady had been firmly on the Manticorans' side.

But if there was one thing Gensonne knew, it was that the Lady was notoriously fickle. She was with Manticore today, yes.

But she wouldn't be with them forever.

Someday, when she had deserted this place, he would be back.

"All ships acknowledging," Imbar reported. "Breaking off now."

"Set course for the hyper limit," Gensonne ordered. "As fast as we can get there without coming into enemy attack range."

"Yes, Sir."

Gensonne turned back to the tactical and inclined his head in mocking salute. "Don't worry, Captain," he added. "This defeat isn't permanent. We'll be back."

He glowered at the display. "We will *absolutely* be back."

☆   ☆   ☆

"My *God*," Kyell breathed, his eyes wide as he stared at the display. "Did you see that, Townsend? Did you *see* that?"

"I saw it," Chomps assured him. And what a lovely sight it had been.

And still was, for that matter. The expanding cloud of dust and debris wasn't visible to the naked eye, or at this distance even the enhanced eye. But *Aries's* lidar and radar systems were on the job, and the picture they painted was a very satisfying one indeed.

One enemy destroyer: gone. The other enemy destroyer...

Not gone. Not completely, anyway. Its wedge was still up, which meant its impellers and reactor were still intact.

But at least one of *Taurus's* missiles had made it inside the protective blanket of stress bands and sidewalls. Surely it had caused *some* damage when it went bang.

"Wait a second," Kyell said, floating a little closer to the monitor. "Are we still moving *toward* them?"

"Looks like it," Chomps said. "Why?"

"*Why*? We're out of missiles, man. We've already thrown everything we've got."

"So?" Chomps countered. "They don't know that. It's still all about giving them a choice between us and *Damocles*. They jumped the wrong way the last time. Let's see if we can make them do it again."

"I don't think she's going to jump at all," Kyell said. "Not sure, but I think she's leaving."

Chomps frowned, studying the shifting vector projection on the display as the destroyer went into a combination pitch and roll. It definitely seemed to have given up on rendezvousing with Group One.

And then the vector darkened as the destroyer cranked up its acceleration. The trace shifted again as its new vector was added to its original speed and direction...

Kyell was right. The destroyer was making a run for the hyper limit. And she was running about as fast as a destroyer of that class could reasonably be expected to travel.

"Sure is," he said. He pointed to another part of the display. "So are the others. All of them."

"I'll be damned," Kyell murmured. "So it's over. Right? It's over?"

Chomps swallowed. "It's over," he confirmed.

Only it wasn't.

The Star Kingdom had repulsed this attack, certainly. But someone had put a lot of time, money, and effort into this invasion. That someone wasn't likely to give up after just one try.

The Battle of Manticore—he assumed the history books would call it that—was over. But whatever else was going on was still going on. Whoever their attacker was, he was still out there.

The Star Kingdom had better figure out who he was, and where he was, and *why* he was. And they'd better do it fast.

☆   ☆   ☆

And with that, suddenly it was over.

Winterfall stared at the big display in the Lords' chamber, a prickly feeling on the back of his neck. The surviving invaders were running, driving toward the hyper limit as fast as their ships could go.

It was strangely surreal, those vectors now pointing away from Manticore instead of toward it. Like something out of an old saga, or the random scribblings of a minimalist artist.

But there was nothing surreal or imaginary about the bellow of victory that erupted spontaneously from the floor, or the roar of applause that suddenly filled the chamber.

The invasion had been repulsed.

The Star Kingdom was safe.

For now.

A hand plucked at his sleeve. "Come on," Breakwater said, standing up and all but pulling Winterfall up beside him. "Come *on*," he added, striding toward the nearest exit.

"What's the matter?" Winterfall asked as he hurried to catch up. Breakwater pushed through the door and into the deserted corridor beyond, Winterfall right behind him. "My Lord, what's the problem?"

"There's no problem, Gavin," Breakwater said as he picked up his pace. "Merely an opportunity." He glanced back over his shoulder at Winterfall. "One that I have no intention of squandering."

Winterfall frowned. An opportunity? "My Lord—"

"Hush," Breakwater said. He'd pulled out his tablet and was punching commands into it. "*Casey, Casey*—hmm. No official word, but she was apparently still alive and functioning as of an hour ago. Hopefully, she's still with us."

"*Casey?*" Winterfall echoed, completely lost now. "What does *Casey* have to do with this?"

"Because that's the ship your brother is on," Breakwater said. "Preliminary reports said *Casey* acquitted herself well in the early part of the battle. Though on second thought, even if she was destroyed we can probably still use your brother's presence—"

"Wait a moment," Winterfall said. "What does my brother have to do with this?"

"*Casey* acquitted herself well, and you're the brother of one of her officers," Breakwater said impatiently. "Surely you can connect the political dots."

"Yes," Winterfall murmured, a belated shock wave of memory hitting him. Travis was on *Casey* . . . only before that he'd been aboard *Phoenix*.

A ship which he and the rest of the Lords had just watched being destroyed.

A shiver ran straight through him. His brother had nearly been killed.

Might still have been killed, in fact. As Breakwater said, there was no official final word on most of the ships that had been in the battle.

People died in wars. On a distant, intellectual level Winterfall had always known that.

But suddenly it seemed a whole lot closer and more personal.

Never mind that he'd lost contact with Travis over the years. Never mind that they'd never been remotely close to begin with. Travis was still his brother.

"Ah," Breakwater said with clear satisfaction. "Excellent. The reports are starting to come in and it looks like MPARS's two newly-armed corvettes played a major part. If we can put those two together, we'll be looking to gain some serious points in the Lords and the general populace."

"Yes," Winterfall murmured again. The visceral shock was fading, his brain already shifting from his brother to the political realities and possibilities.

Travis was alive, or he was dead. Either way, there was nothing Winterfall could do to affect things. What was important right now was that he and Breakwater make sure they rode atop the wave of this thing.

Because if the past few hours had proven anything, it was that the doomsayers had been right. There were deadly dangers and threats out there, and the Star Kingdom was not immune from those threats. Before the dust had even settled, Dapplelake and Cazenestro would be demanding more money and manpower for their Navy, and unless Winterfall and Breakwater did something quickly the King and Parliament would fall all over themselves granting those demands.

And that would be folly, because the RMN that Dapplelake envisioned was still the wrong way to go. Big ships were impressive, but what the Star Kingdom needed was a fleet of smaller, more agile ships that could swarm an invasion force and destroy it. The two MPARS corvettes—and *Casey* herself, for that matter—had clearly demonstrated that the military doctrine of bigger and better battlecruisers was a dead end.

Manticore didn't need more battlecruisers. What it needed was more and better system defense craft.

What it needed was a larger and more powerful MPARS.

"You coming?"

With a start, Winterfall realized that during his ruminations he'd fallen behind. "Yes, My Lord," he said, hurrying to catch up. Cazenestro, he suspected, would be on the net within minutes, pushing the RMN's agenda.

He and Breakwater needed to get there first.

☆　☆　☆

And suddenly, it was over.

Metzger gazed at the tactical, afraid to believe it. Surely Tamerlane was just repositioning his ships in the wake of his second battlecruiser's destruction. He was heading out to regroup somewhere near Sphinx, or maybe with an eye toward crossing over to Manticore-B and harassing Gryphon and the completely underequipped Red Force guarding it.

But the invaders' behavior didn't fit either scenario. In fact, as the enemy ships poured on gravs and their individual vectors stabilized it was clear that all of them were heading for the hyper limit as fast as they could get there. By the time they reached it they would be spread over a good hundred fifty degrees of sky.

They weren't regrouping. They were running.

She swiveled in her station to look at Locatelli. The admiral was also studying the tactical, his eyes flicking between the displays and the incoming status reports from the rest of the Manticoran forces.

He seemed to sense her eyes on him and looked up, and for a moment their eyes met. Unconsciously, Metzger braced herself, waiting for the order to do whatever *Invincible* could to adjust her own vector to pursue...

"Open com to all ships," he ordered. "Send the following: This is Admiral Locatelli. All ships are to break off any attacks that cannot be launched within the next ten minutes and make for Manticore orbit. Repeat: all ships are to break off any non-pending action and return to Manticore."

Metzger glanced around the bridge. Judging from the bridge crews' expressions, they were about evenly split between those who were relieved it was over and those who weren't quite yet ready to give up.

Locatelli must have sensed that, too. "While I believe we have repulsed this invasion of our kingdom," he continued, "it's conceivable that our attackers have more ships at their immediate disposal, in which case this apparent retreat may be a ruse to lure us out of position to defend our homeworld. In addition, we have many injured aboard our vessels, some of whom require more extensive treatment than we can currently give them."

Metzger looked around again. The fire was slowly fading from the faces of the eager-beaver contingent as they saw the logic behind Locatelli's decision.

A logic which he had no need to lay out for them, she knew. He was Admiral Carlton Locatelli, System Commander of the Royal Manticoran Navy, one step below First Lord Cazenestro, two steps below Defense Minister Dapplelake, three steps below King Edward himself. Locatelli ordered; his men and women obeyed. That was all there was to it.

But he hadn't simply given the order. He'd taken the time to bring his people into his confidence and to show them the reasons behind his decision.

There were instances, Metzger reflected, when there was no

time to offer explanations. By taking the time here, Locatelli had now planted the seeds of confidence that his officers and spacers would carry when those other instances arose.

One of the marks of a good commander, and Metzger carefully tucked it away for future reference.

"And as you secure from battle," Locatelli went on, "I want you to know that I am immensely proud of each and every one of you. Today, the Royal Manticoran Navy was given far more than it could chew." He smiled tightly. "And we chewed it. Congratulations to you all."

He gestured. "Transmission sent, Admiral," Warren confirmed from the com station.

"All defenders have broken off, Sir," McBride reported from CIC. "Though a couple of them seem to be taking their time about heading to Manticore."

"I see them," Locatelli said. "Our two MPARS ships. Probably waiting for orders from their own chain of command."

"Or else they're concerned about that last enemy destroyer," Metzger offered. "I note that *Damocles* is also still on station."

"Yes, I see," Locatelli said. "Given the remaining Group Three bandit's squishy exit vector, Captain Marcello may be waiting to make sure she's actually leaving." He snorted gently. "Or else he's making sure the MPARS ships aren't left alone."

"So that he can protect them?" Metzger asked.

"Or to make sure they aren't involved in any heroics on their own," Locatelli said. "As I said, *Aries* and *Taurus* may still be waiting for orders, and Breakwater may be looking for an opportunity."

Metzger felt her lips compress. Politics. Coming off a desperate battle, with the survival of the entire Star Kingdom hanging by a thread, and all Locatelli could think about was the whole Navy/MPARS political feud?

Of course he could. And he probably should. *Someone* had to keep Breakwater under control.

"Chief Warren, get me a signal to Manticore," Locatelli said into Metzger's thoughts.

"Yes, Sir. Ready, Admiral."

"This is Admiral Locatelli, commander of the Green One and Green Two Home Defense forces," Locatelli called. His voice was subtly different, Metzger noted. Richer, deeper, more commanding.

A voice for Parliament and the people. A voice for the ages. "We have met the enemy. He is vanquished. We have spilled our blood upon the field of combat. The field remains ours. We have faced doubts about our strengths and resolve. Those doubts are ended. A long life to the King, and may the Star Kingdom endure forever."

He gestured, and Warren again cut off the com. "Very stirring, Sir," McBride said, sounding a little bemused. "A bit short, though, wasn't it?"

"Shorter is always better, Commander," Locatelli assured him. "The time for long speeches will come. Chief Warren, signal *Damocles*. Tell Marcello he's authorized to remain on scene until he's sure the threat in that area has ended."

"Yes, Sir, I've been trying to raise Captain Marcello," Warren said uncertainly. "I'm not getting anything."

"What do you mean?" Metzger asked, shifting her eyes to the proper display. *Damocles*'s wedge was there on the gravitic, which meant reactor and impellers were still functioning.

"I'm not getting any response to my transmissions," Warren said. "Something must have happened. Something bad."

"I see," Locatelli said. "Signal *Swiftsure* to head over there and assess the situation."

"Yes, Sir."

"Thank you," Locatelli said. "Captain Metzger?"

"Sir?"

The admiral took a deep breath . . . and as he did so, some new age lines seemed to settle in across his face.

It was an illusion, Metzger knew. A person's face couldn't really age that quickly or that visibly. But the sense nevertheless remained.

The admiral let out the breath in a long sigh. "Take us home, Allegra," he ordered quietly.

Metzger nodded. And wondered distantly if she perhaps had a few new age lines of her own. "Yes, Sir. Heading home."

CHAPTER TWENTY-SIX

ADMIRAL LOCATELLI FINISHED HIS STATEMENT, and for a moment the palace conference room was silent. Surreptitiously, Winterfall studied the other faces gathered around the table, trying to read their reactions to the report.

The analysis wasn't hard. Nor was it in the least bit surprising.

Prime Minister Burgundy, Defense Minister Dapplelake, and First Lord of the Admiralty Cazenestro were solidly behind Locatelli. Chancellor Breakwater, Secretary of Industry Baron Harwich, and former Defense Minister Lady Calvingdell weren't convinced. The rest of the Cabinet members were more or less neutral.

As for King Edward...

The King was sitting aloof at the head of the table, his expression and body language suggesting that he was trying to stay above the politics roiling across the table beneath him.

As, really, he should be. He was the monarch, and his job was to somehow weld all the disparate elements and points of view into a functioning whole.

Or perhaps his distance was more personal. He had mourned the death of his son, as had all of Manticore, as he had mourned the other losses of that terrible day. But the scars would remain, as would the pain, for a long time.

Still, as Winterfall studied the King, he had a sense that there was something more going on behind those dark eyes. Something that wasn't just the concern and anxiety that everyone around the table was feeling.

Something he was waiting for, and expecting.

Edward let the silence go on another second. Then, he nodded gravely toward Locatelli. "Thank you, Admiral," he said. "The Star Kingdom is immensely grateful for your courage and commitment, and for the courage and commitment of the rest of the Navy—and MPARS—" he added, nodding in turn toward Breakwater, "—in repulsing this unexpected attack. I know that everyone around this table has questions, and we'll endeavor to give all of you a chance to raise them in the time we have left before Parliament convenes."

"Of course, Your Majesty," Locatelli said. "Before we move on, there's one other matter I'd like to bring up."

And there it was. The words, the tone, and the body language all made it clear. Whatever Locatelli was about to say, it was something he and the King had already set up.

Winterfall shot a look at Breakwater. The Chancellor's eyes were narrowed, his torso a few centimeters forward from the back of his chair. Winterfall hadn't been given advance notice of this; clearly, neither had Breakwater.

And that had been a mistake. A serious one. In the current confused fog swirling through the Star Kingdom, it wasn't a good idea to cut out one of the major political players. Throwing something at Breakwater without giving him a chance to consider it first was an invitation for immediate opposition.

"I note that Defense Minister Dapplelake and First Lord of the Admiralty Cazenestro have recommended several RMN officers and enlisted for the Manticore Cross and the Cross of Military Valor," Locatelli said, his tone going subtly more formal. "As most of you already know—" he glanced around the table, his eyes lingering a bit on the least militarily astute among the group "—these awards are the highest honors that can be bestowed on military personnel who have shown exceptional valor in the face of an enemy. The Manticore Cross is awarded to officers, while the Cross of Military Valor is reserved for enlisted."

All of which Winterfall knew, though up to now the award protocol had been mostly a matter of historical interest. Only one MC had ever been awarded, to Captain Franklin Casey, and that had been over a hundred years ago. As far as Winterfall knew, no one had ever received the Cross of Military Valor.

"What I'm proposing," Locatelli continued, "is a change in

designation to something more personal and, as future generations look back, something more relevant to the Star Kingdom's history."

And then Winterfall got it.

The Manticore Cross, one of which was already slated to be posthumously awarded to Locatelli's nephew, was going to be renamed the Locatelli Cross.

Winterfall looked at the King, his mind churning with a mixture of chagrin at the manipulation and grudging admiration at the subtlety. With Admiral Locatelli standing as the undisputed hero of the battle, as well as being the public face of the Navy, the Cabinet could hardly deny him that small bit of glory. Certainly not with the nation still riding the emotional rush of Manticore's victory.

The subtlety came in the way that glory would feed straight back into the admiral's own prestige. Having his name attached to the nation's highest military honor would give him a small but significant bit of extra psychological leverage as Parliament settled down to make the hard decisions about the future of the Star Kingdom's defense strategy. And as Winterfall had seen time and again, major decisions often hinged on the tiniest of margins.

The real genius of it was that there was nothing Breakwater could do to stop him. Rejecting Locatelli's request would come across as the most petty and vindictive of political actions, a mud ball that would bounce straight back at the Chancellor. There wasn't even the option of compromise—either the Manticore Cross became the Locatelli Cross, or it didn't, with no middle ground.

The fact that the King was clearly backing Locatelli's play made it all the more pointless to oppose it.

But that didn't mean Breakwater wouldn't try. Winterfall knew the man, and knew that he would stand by his convictions and fight to hold onto his territory no matter what the cost.

"Accordingly," Locatelli continued, "and keeping in mind the tremendous heroism and skill involved in the reactivation of HMS *Phoenix*'s laser and the subsequent destruction of an enemy battlecruiser—"

Breakwater leaned forward a little more in his seat, and Winterfall sensed him bracing himself for combat—

"—I propose that the Cross of Military Valor be renamed the Osterman Cross."

Winterfall stared at Locatelli, feeling the profound sense of having all the wind sucked straight out of his sails. The *Oster-man Cross*?

And an instant later felt a flush of shame. Of course the King hadn't been playing politics with this. Not the Battle of Manticore, where for a few hours the very existence of the Star Kingdom had hung in the balance. What the public needed now was the trust in their leaders, and the confidence that their defenders were up to their role.

They needed heroes. And Locatelli and the King were giving them one.

Winterfall looked at Locatelli, another small rush of shame rolling through him. He'd never really liked the admiral. But today, at least for a little while, he could respect him.

"An excellent suggestion, Admiral," King Edward said, nodding. "There's an official procedure to go through, but I have no doubt that the name change will be approved." He looked around the table, as if daring anyone to object.

And for once, even Breakwater was silent.

"Then let's move on to questions," the King continued. "My Lord Burgundy, perhaps you would care to start."

☆   ☆   ☆

"I wanted you to know," Heissman said, gazing up from his desk with an unreadable expression on his face, "that I put in for a Conspicuous Gallantry Medal for you."

"Thank you, Sir," Travis said, feeling an odd warming inside him.

Though like every other emotion that he'd felt over the two weeks since the battle, the warmth was stained with darkness.

He was relieved he'd survived, of course, and equally relieved that so many others had done likewise.

But too many hadn't. Far too many. Five ships had been destroyed completely, including every other ship in Janus Force. Many other ships, like *Casey* herself, had come away with serious damage and loss of life, either from enemy fire or catastrophic failure of their own run-down systems.

Given all that, even talking about awards felt painfully premature, if not flat-out obscenely morbid. But Admiral Locatelli was already well on his way to grabbing the lion's share of the credit for the victory, both in Parliament and with the media. It was only right that the rest of the heroes—the *true* heroes, in Travis's opinion—got some of the recognition before Locatelli made off with all of it.

"Don't get too excited," Heissman said sourly. "The request was denied."

The warm feeling vanished. "Sir?" Travis asked in confusion.

"Certain persons in authority," Heissman said, pushing through the words as if he were trudging through a set of snow banks, "are of the opinion that your ideas were mostly luck, and that their success relied on both that luck and on the overall competency of *Casey*'s officers and crew."

"Yes, Sir," Travis said. "I mean...well, of course it was a ship-wide effort. Ideas aren't worth anything without teamwork and—"

"And teamwork alone isn't enough when you're facing impossible odds," Heissman cut him off brusquely. "Which I attempted to make clear. You'll still get the same Royal Unit Citation medal as everyone else aboard—they can't deny you that—but career-wise, I'm afraid you're going to be lost in the general shuffle." He stared hard at Travis's face. "I get the feeling you have an enemy or two in high places, Lieutenant."

Travis winced. What was he supposed to say to that? "I haven't deliberately invited any animosity, Sir," he said, choosing his words carefully.

"Deliberately or not, you've apparently succeeded," Heissman said. "I'm guessing the latest batch is coming from your time aboard *Phoenix*."

Travis felt his lip twitch. Yes; the late Ensign Fenton Locatelli, nephew of the now famous and highly acclaimed hero of Manticore. Even before the battle Admiral Locatelli probably had had enough clout to prevent Travis from getting any awards. Now, it was a foregone conclusion.

But there was nothing Travis could do about it. And even if there was, he wouldn't have bothered to try. Compared to the sacrifice so many men and women had made to protect their worlds, his own modest contributions seemed pretty small. "I do appreciate your efforts, though, Sir," he said. "If that's all—"

"Not quite," Heissman rumbled. "Let me start with the obvious. I know this sort of thing is a kick in the shin, but I wouldn't spend too much time worrying about it. There are plenty of political animals in the Fleet. But kilo for kilo, there are a lot more of the rest of us."

The rest of us meaning those who wanted to do their jobs to the best of their ability? Or was Heissman also including the drifters who really didn't care where they were as long as they pulled a steady pay voucher?

Because there were certainly plenty of those, too. Distantly, he wondered if they would now be making a concerted effort to get out of the Service. "Yes, Sir," he said aloud.

"And I'm not including the loafers you're always writing up," Heissman continued. "That really bothers you, doesn't it? People who don't follow proper procedure?"

"Procedures are there for a purpose, Sir."

"Even when you can't see that purpose?"

"There's always a purpose, Sir," Travis said, a little stiffly. "Even if it isn't obvious."

"I appreciate your optimism in such things," Heissman said. "But I have to say it makes you something of an anomaly. Typically, someone as solid as you are on following procedure is mentally rigid in all other aspects of life. You, on the other hand, not only can think outside the lines, but sometimes draw your own."

"Thank you, Sir," Travis said, wondering if that boiled down to a compliment or an indictment. "But I really didn't do anything all that extraordinary."

"People with a talent for something never think it's a big deal," Heissman said dryly. "The point I was going to make was that both of those characteristics are going to make you unpopular in certain circles. But you *will* be noticed, and appreciated, by the people who matter. For whatever that's worth."

"Thank you, Sir," Travis said. "Please understand in turn that I didn't join the Navy for glory or recognition. I joined to help protect the Star Kingdom." He hesitated. "And if necessary, to die for it."

"I know," Heissman said, his voice going a little darker. "Unfortunately, *that's* going to make you unpopular in certain quarters, too. Genuine, unashamed patriots are an embarrassment to the cynical and manipulative."

Some of the lines in his face smoothed out. "Which leads me to my final question. This whole *travesty of this, travesty of that* sarcastic catchphrase that seems to follow you around. What's all that about, anyway?"

Travis sighed. "It started back in high school," he said reluctantly. "One of the teachers fancied himself a scholar and a wit, and liked to give his students nicknames. I was Travis Uriah Long, or Travis U. Long, which he thought sounded like Travis Oolong, and oolong was a type of Old Earth tea. Hence, Travis Tea."

"Travesty," Heissman said with a nod, a small smile playing across his face. "And with your penchant for enforcing even minor regulations, the sarcastic direction was probably inevitable."

"Yes, Sir." Travis braced himself. "I'd appreciate it, Sir, if you didn't...pass it around too much."

"Not a problem," Heissman said. "Well. I've just been informed that *Casey*'s going to be another month in dock, so everyone's leave's been extended. But you may be called up for more testimony at any time, so don't stray too far from Landing City."

And then, to Travis's surprise, he rose to his feet. "Well done, Travis," the commodore said as they exchanged salutes. "I look forward to returning to *Casey* with you. *And* as soon as possible."

His eyes went a little distant. "Because I have a feeling Manticore's about to lose the nice, peaceful backwater status we've enjoyed for so long. I don't know how or why. I don't think anyone does. But I can guarantee this much: as of two weeks ago the RMN is no longer a joke and a political football. Someone out there has us in their sights."

His expression tightened. "You said you were willing to die for the Star Kingdom. You may very well get that chance."

☆   ☆   ☆

"Well, *damn* it all," Breakwater growled, peering at his tablet. "They've denied him."

Winterfall frowned up at him. "Who's denied what to whom?"

"The Navy has denied your brother a Conspicuous Gallantry Medal," Breakwater said. "I suppose you'll have to drop that part from your speech now."

"That's all right," Winterfall said, scrolling back to the relevant section of his upcoming speech. It would have been nice to include that tribute to his brother, a tribute which, as Breakwater had pointed out earlier, would also have subtly raised Winterfall's own prestige.

But he could get by without it. Besides, the heroism and accomplishments of the two MPARS corvettes were more important to his side of the argument, and that wasn't something Locatelli and the Navy could take away.

He was deleting the reference to his brother when an odd thought abruptly hit him.

Could it be that the Navy was refusing Travis a medal because of *him*?

Even worse, it suddenly occurred to him that the first thing he'd focused on when he'd heard the news was how it would affect his own political advances.

Was that right? Because it sure didn't *seem* right.

He looked up again at Breakwater. The Chancellor was talking quietly with Baroness Tweenriver and Earl Chillon about the upcoming debate on additional MPARS funding, the minor tweak of Lieutenant Travis Uriah Long's medal or lack of it clearly already forgotten.

What the hell was Winterfall doing, anyway?

He looked down at his tablet. What he was doing was protecting the lives, freedom, and security of the Star Kingdom of Manticore, in the best way he knew how. The freshly-awarded Manticore Cross gleaming on Admiral Locatelli's chest was driving public acclaim and momentum, and Winterfall knew full well that Dapplelake and Cazenestro would be hurrying to parley that acclaim into more money and manpower.

But that would be a mistake. Dapplelake's dream Navy, bigger and stronger than ever, wouldn't make the Star Kingdom more secure. On the contrary, it would make Manticore look more and more to their neighbors like a threat.

And that was absolutely the wrong path for the Star Kingdom to take. Haven and the distant Solarian League were the big dogs on the street, and they would not look with favor on a star nation that was building up its collection of force-projection ships.

Maybe Dapplelake hadn't read the history of Gustav Anderman. But Winterfall had. After conquering Kuan Yin and reorganizing it as Potsdam, Anderman had proceeded to take over five other systems, at least three of them merely because he deemed them to be a threat to his new empire.

Manticore was a long way from Potsdam, and Anderman was getting on in years. But the self-styled Emperor was also at least half crazy. Who knew what he might deem to be a threat?

And it was painfully clear that if Anderman came calling any time soon, the RMN wouldn't have a hope in hell of stopping him.

Dapplelake might not be able to add up all of those numbers. King Edward, as former Navy himself, might not be able to see the bigger picture. That task fell to Breakwater and his allies.

Including Winterfall.

It was an incredibly petty move to punish Travis for the activities of his half-brother. But Winterfall couldn't allow guilt or outrange to dissuade or distract him. He was a member of the House of Lords, and his responsibility was to the entire Star Kingdom.

He'd taken an oath to defend his nation. So had Travis. Both of them had to serve now as they saw fit.

Scrolling to the bottom of the page, Winterfall got back to work on his speech.

CHAPTER TWENTY-SEVEN

"I WAS STARTING TO THINK they weren't going to let you go at all," Lisa said as she waved Travis in through her open door.

"They almost didn't," Travis said, taking in her smile and her grace with the hunger of a starving man. After two solid days of testimony before Parliamentary committees, he'd had more than his fill of dour faces and half-hidden verbal knives. A nice smile and no ulterior motivations were a welcome change of pace. "I hope I'm not *too* late."

"No problem—spaghetti sauce is very forgiving," Lisa assured him. "Let me take your coat."

Travis's first impulse was to say no, that he could hang up his dress jacket himself. "Thanks," he said instead, taking it off and handing it to her. She was trying to do him a favor, and he needed to make himself let her.

"They only had *me* on the stand for about three hours," she commented over her shoulder as she crossed to a small closet and carefully slipped the jacket onto a hanger. For a moment, as she hung it on the rod, Travis thought he saw her eyeing the paltry single new ribbon, his Royal Unit Citation, on the upper right chest.

But if she was wondering at the lack of anything more prestigious, she made no comment. "And that was more than enough," she added, heading toward an archway leading from the foyer. "I can't imagine what you had to go through. Come on—we can talk while I put the pasta on. I'll let you do the French bread, if you don't mind."

"French bread is one of my specialties," Travis assured her, determined to keep the mood light. Along with the dour expressions over the past two days, he'd also had his fill of weightiness. "You want something cut in half, put on a tray, and tossed into an oven, I'm your man."

"Glad to hear it," Lisa said. "My skill set only extends to dumping spoonfuls of Italian spices into a saucepan. In here."

"How are you and *Damocles* doing?" Travis asked, looking around curiously as he walked under the archway into the kitchen. It was the first time he'd been in her apartment, and he was struck by the fact that the décor exuded the same sense as he'd gotten in his brief visit to her quarters back on *Vanguard*. Lisa Donnelly was a comfortable mix of strength and softness, a woman who knew her abilities and neither downplayed nor flaunted them.

As *Damocles*'s tactical officer, she'd proven those abilities three weeks ago in what was now officially designated the Battle of Manticore. It was only a matter of time, he knew, before she would be given her own ship and the coveted gold star of a starship commander. The only real questions were when, and which ship.

Travis hoped it was a battlecruiser. Lisa would be awesome with a battlecruiser.

"There's the bread," she said pointing. "I'm doing fine—a few bruises, but nothing serious. *Damocles*, not so much. What exactly have you heard?"

"Not much," he said. "There was some vague statement about her being towed back to Manticore, but I wasn't able to get any details."

"That's because no one wanted to give them out," Lisa said dryly. "When we tried firing a missile from our dorsal launcher, the end exploded and nearly took a chunk of our hull along with it."

Travis whistled softly. He'd heard rumors that *Damocles*'s problem had been severe, but he'd had no idea it was *that* bad. "What happened?"

"Officially, it failed because of undetected structural fatigue," Lisa said. "Unofficially—and this is why no one's talking about it—one of the techs accidentally left an entire hydraulic repressurizing rig attached to the inside."

"Ouch," Travis said, wincing. "And when the missile tried to get out...?"

"It was slowed down just enough that the booster fired too close to the tube," Lisa confirmed. "The shockwave knocked out the whole amidships electrical system, including the bridge and CIC. We were basically helpless for the next half hour, until the techs could get the backups up and running."

"You're lucky the whole ship wasn't wrecked," Travis said.

"Don't we know it," Lisa said soberly. "The most embarrassing part is that I'd seen the report that one of the hydraulic rigs had gone AWOL, but didn't put it together with the work that had been done a week earlier until it was too late."

"Not exactly your problem."

"Technically, no. But I'm the TO. I should be on top of everything that has to do with the ship's weapons."

"Mm," Travis said, not agreeing but recognizing that it wasn't something he wanted to argue with her about. "I presume a court-martial is in the works for whoever left it there?"

"I doubt it," Lisa said. She held out a piece of uncooked spaghetti to Travis and raised her eyebrows in silent question. He shook his head; taking it back, she bit off a piece with a crunch that set Travis's teeth on edge. "It's the usual story: the petty officer who screwed up is related to one of the Cabinet ministers. Someone both sides of the RMN debate are courting, moreover, which means no one wants to see him embarrassed."

Travis made a face, his frustrations with Ensign Locatelli flooding back.

But he wouldn't voice them. *Speak no ill of the dead* and all that aside, the report on what the ensign and Chief Osterman had accomplished had clearly shown that there had been more to the young man than Travis had realized.

Or maybe just more than he'd been willing to acknowledge.

"We were just lucky that *Aries* was able to get one of the bandits," Lisa went on, taking another bite of the raw pasta. "Then the battle ended, and we could take our time and bring our systems back up carefully."

"Lucky, yes," Travis murmured. He'd heard all about the ploy that had cost the invaders that destroyer, and how it had come about.

Especially the small but important role played by one Missile Tech First Charles "Chomps" Townsend.

Who had been aboard the MPARS corvette *Aries* because he, Travis, had filed the report that had gotten him kicked out of the RMN and sent there.

Of course, he didn't know for sure that Chomps's demotion was his fault. Such things weren't mentioned in the public portion of Navy records. But he knew that Chomps had been disciplined for hacking into *Phoenix*'s computer files, and he also knew that no one would ever have caught him if Travis hadn't insisted on following the rules.

On the other hand, Travis's action and its consequences had put Chomps into a position where he'd helped win the battle. Did that make it all right?

Or was that just more rationalization?

"Did you know that former RMN Missile Tech Charles Townsend came up with a nice little tweak on that?" Lisa asked, her back to Travis as she loaded pasta into a cooker. "He was one of your classmates at Casey-Rosewood, wasn't he?"

Travis took a deep breath. *Keep it light*, he reminded himself. And that included not tearing scabs off old wounds in front of others. "Yes, he was," he confirmed. "We had many long and healthful twenty-five-klick hikes together."

"Ah, yes—the good old days," Lisa said. "It's good to have memories." She smiled briefly at him over her shoulder. "Better to have friends. When you finish the bread, can you pull out the salad? It's already mixed."

"Sure," Travis said, opening the oven and sliding the bread pan onto the rack. Yes, friends were what was important. Not medals. Not public recognition. Not rank. Friends.

The trouble was that Travis was showing an ominous talent for losing those friends. Friends, and everyone he'd learned to care for.

His old drill instructor, Jonny Funk: dead. His former *Phoenix* cabinmate and friend, Brad Fornier: dead. His shipmates aboard *Vanguard*: dispersed and effectively lost track of. His brother, Baron Winterfall: never much more than a stranger to begin with. His mother: same thing.

And now Chomps Townsend, who would probably never speak to him again.

In fact, now that he thought about it, the only real friend he truly had left was Lisa Donnelly.

How long, he wondered, before he somehow drove her away, too?

Probably not long. Probably not long at all.

☆　　☆　　☆

One of the great truisms of modern life, Chomps had long since learned, was that it was the task of the small fish to hurry up and wait for the big fish. He'd experienced it with the RMN brass, with the MPARS brass, and most of all with the Lords.

It was a shock, then, when he was barely inside the door of Countess Calvingdell's outer office when the receptionist waved him through.

The first time Chomps had been in Calvingdell's office her desk had been a hodgepodge of military items, mementos or reminders of her then-status as Defense Minister. The second time he'd been here, after the Cascan incident, most of those items had been sent away as she was transitioned out of the cabinet and Dapplelake transitioned back in.

Now, the third time, the desk was almost bare.

But at least it was neat. Chomps didn't know a lot about Calvingdell, but he *did* know that she liked having things neat.

Which was ironic, really, given her current situation.

"Townsend," she greeted him briefly as he walked toward the desk, her eyes still on her tablet. "How was your stint in MPARS?"

"It was different, My Lady," Chomps said, choosing the most diplomatic of all the possible answers.

"Different how?"

Well, she'd asked for it. "Less disciplined," he said. "Not as well equipped. Fewer gaps in the organizational structure. Less training for the officers and crews. More arrogance and animosity to the regular Navy people." He felt a smile tug at his lips. "But very comparable fighting spirit."

At that last one, she finally looked up. "Comparable?"

"Certainly in my experience," Chomps said. "So am I going back? Or am I being reinstated in the RMN?"

Calvingdell favored him with a smile. It was a thin, cynical smile, one that left everything above her lips wooden and unreadable. "Neither," she said softly. "Not you."

She turned her tablet around so that he could see it. "But before we get into that," she continued, tapping the tablet's edge for emphasis, "I have a question. Tell me everything you know about this man.

"Tell me about Travis Uriah Long."

DISCARD